The Virgo Club

Suzanne Power lives in Wexford with her partner and two boys.

Also by the Author

Fiction
The Lost Souls' Reunion

Non-Fiction
Being You

THE VIRGO CLUB

Suzanne Power

Hodder
LIR

Copyright © 2004 Suzanne Power

First published in 2004 by Hodder Headline Ireland
A division of Hodder Headline

The right of Suzanne Power to be identified as the Author of the
Work has been asserted by him in accordance with the Copyright,
Designs and Patents Act 1988.

A Hodder/LIR paperback

3 5 7 9 10 8 6 4 2

A CIP catalogue record for this title is available from
the British Library.

ISBN 0340 835656

Typeset in Plantin Light by Hodder Headline Ireland
Printed and bound in Great Britain by Clays Ltd, St Ives plc.

Hodder Headline Ireland
8 Castlecourt Centre
Castleknock
Dublin 15
Ireland
A division of Hodder Headline
338 Euston Road
London NW1 3BH

For Finn and Rory

AUGUST

1

A hot afternoon – 1 August – we are looking at pavements crowded with sweaty, irate bodies too lethargic to move at the usual breakneck London pace.

There are three of us sitting at lunchtime in the window table at Angelo's. Angelo is busy being rude to his other customers and we are drinking his Sicilian wine, at only four pounds a bottle. We know his rudeness hides too much heart. As we've been coming here for fifteen years; he couldn't hide it that long. In return we reveal to h im everything there is to know about us, on the first and third Tuesday of each month.

A fourth is missing. We've already eaten. The other two continually ask questions about what might have happened. None of us misses a meeting of the Virgo Club unless we've a life-threatening excuse. I'm not asking where she is.

The wine is burning a path to my stomach. I'll have indigestion soon. Treachery does this. If she doesn't show I'll give all my money to charity. I make a mental pact with God in return for not having to handle this today. But she will walk through the door. She won't be her usual self.

Helen. Those who don't know her would be mistaken in thinking she's a cold fish. They couldn't be more wrong. She works as a doctor in A and E at one of the worst-equipped hospitals in the country. Helen will never take private work. It would make her as sick as I'm feeling now. Besides, she loves the cutting edge of A and E.

Helen is my oldest friend. She's always been the most private of us. I wonder if it will be the same today. Does she know everything? The queasiness has a lot to do with how much I've drunk. I couldn't really eat Angelo's food and now he's treating me like I've broken his heart. My glass tips and falls over the saucer of olives, whose staining juice is black on red cheesecloth. Where is she? The others are talking about calling a taxi to leave. I've already allowed them to go through the pointless process of ringing her answering machine.

'If she was on call she'd have got a message to us,' they figure.

Our twice-monthly lunches began when all we could afford was Angelo's place and now that we can afford more we wouldn't go anywhere else.

How they started is a story in itself. The four of us have Virgo birthdays. Catriona, 23 August; Rorie (Yes, the boy's name. No, not with a *y*. If she had a penny for every time she said it, she'd never have to buy a lottery ticket again.), 29 August; Helen, 2 September; Dette, 19 September. Don't ask who the oldest is, she'll clock you. The youngest doesn't worry about her age – well, she doesn't have to as much, does she? Even Helen, the horoscope cynic, thinks the star sign is an amazing coincidence, and it's been enough to knit us together over the years.

Angelo's was where we celebrated the first meeting of the Virgo Club. And once a year, on the first Saturday of September, we take over the whole restaurant. Angelo does a fabulous set menu in return for knowing exactly what it's like to be in a ladies' changing room or in a labour ward. Not that he needs the information. He's the world's nicest gay man, and I think the nicest men in the world are gay. If I could persuade him to marry me I would. He could be Will, I could be Grace. I wouldn't give a damn if I never had sex again. I'd have good food, interesting conversation and great companionship. The whole of my life would be an orgasm.

On the first Saturday Angelo's a guest of honour at our table, the fifth member of the Virgo Club, even though he's a Capricorn. On Tuesdays he always joins us for dessert and a little pontificating. If he was still in Italy he'd be running the Vatican. A part of Angelo is conservative enough to be pope, very traditional, the décor of his place hasn't changed since it opened. When something breaks, wears out or tears, he gets an exact replica to replace it. We eat and drink from the original menu. 'I don't believe in specials. Everything on my menu is special.'

He's gorgeous in that proud Italian way – straight nose, full lips and high brow. Why would God create such perfection and not allow woman to enjoy it? For years women have come here, tongues lolling, hearts cracking. And he's blown a fit if they ask for parmesan on the *friutti di mare*, 'Why don't you bring petrol and pour it over? It will taste better.'

And other niceties. They tend to lose their crush on him and want to run him over. It's for their own good, he tells us. 'Women in love with me – very boring. For me, for them, for their husbands.'

Helen will deny this, but I'm the one who discovered this place. She claims it was both of us together, but I came for lunch on my own and was still here at dinnertime. I was thinking of falling in love with Angelo, because my boyfriend was giving me a hard time – then Angelo told me his boyfriend was giving him a hard time. We're still having the same conversation.

Angelo's lunches have been a constant in lives that have run very different courses. How the hell the four of us ever got to be such good friends is beyond me. We might have very different lives but we have the Virgo thing. Dette's prize possession is a Prada handbag, though that's likely to change by next week. Helen's is a photograph of her with Nelson Mandela. Catriona and Rorie exist somewhere between the two. They have social consciences and lipstick.

No, I haven't told you who I am. I'm trying to figure out where I fit into the situation that has developed. This lunch happened four and a half months ago, and it happens again every day in my mind. I want to replay it now, at Angelo's, with Angelo. What went on with me in the past few months is more than has occurred in the previous ten years. The same for the others. Tuesday, 1 August, was one of those all-change days for Virgos. Our collective horoscope in *Vogue* – so it must be true and if not true at least stylish – read:

The planetary alignments at present are truly unique. Events will unfold that will, if you let them, change your life. But the choice is always yours.

They tend to stick that in, don't they? The disclaimer. Just in case you ditch your job and follow a stranger you met on a plane round the world to the address he gave you. Only to find that his wife and three kids are delighted to meet you as well, and you have to stay to dinner and sings songs round the piano with them afterwards. It's never their fault, is it? It's never anyone's fault but your own.

Normally we each bring along a paper or magazine and reveal what is supposed to happen to us that day, week or month. Except Helen. She reads the *Guardian*. Catriona and Rorie sort of believe in their stars. Dette pretends not to, but she's addicted to omens in a way the rest of the four aren't.

'Don't cross your forks. Bad luck.' Her mother coming out in her. 'Never put shoes on a table,' she says when she's drunk, testing fate with her stilettos. Dette without stilettos is a pigeon who can't figure out where home is. Lost.

On Tuesday, 1 August, we've not read our horoscopes yet. We've been waiting for Helen to arrive so she can tell us all what eejits we are. Dette diverts us with something she found in a second-hand shop – a book, *Sex and Your Star Sign*. 'It's full of stuff. I'll lend it to Helen later for her to pretend not to read. Apparently Virgos are crap in bed.'

'What?' Even Capricorn Angelo raises an eyebrow.

'Yes, page seventy-nine: "Virgo is a head sign. This means passion does not always take precedence. A Virgoan will find it hard to relinquish control and let ecstasy take them where it will." Which is why we're the

Virgin sign,' Dette says drily. She's had more sex than all of Man United.

'I might be Bernadette but I ain't no saint.' She thinks Dette sounds French and her Irish-Catholic mother, who refuses to call her anything else but her full name, takes great pleasure in reminding her that the saint was too.

'Yes, but she didn't shop in Chanel.'

'I wonder what it means by relinquishing control through the star-wheel position? Anyone, except Dette, ever tried it?' Catriona's holding the book at a forty-five-degree angle to try to make sense of the illustration. Angelo grabs it from her, sighs dramatically, turns it upside-down and hands it back.

'Ah.'

'I hate upside-down sex,' Rorie winces. 'Unless I'm in Australia. Otherwise it's too much trouble for too little.'

'Speak for yourself,' Dette grins.

'I will, and don't bother speaking for yourself. You're vulgar, very, very vulgar,' Rorie chides.

'Now, what about something better than sex?' Catriona's pointing. Angelo's waiter is bringing tiramisu. Chocolate, cream, alcohol and cake – the only thing missing is a fag.

'If I'm reincarnated, and I'm bound to be, bring me back as the sponge. A life between cream, booze and chocolate. Then let me be eaten by Ralph Fiennes.' Catriona's playing to us, her only audience, these days. But we're appreciative, so she continues. 'Knowing me, I'd end up in Danny DeVito's lower intestine. He'll be having lunch with Ralph that day, and they'll share dessert.'

Catriona was born on the cusp of Virgo, so she has to

make sure she behaves true to our sign's form or she might be thought a Leo. Dette, slap in the middle, is the least virginal, Rorie the least analytical. Virgos are supposed to navel-gaze. Helen's the only one who has all the traits, but for the habitual tidiness, and doesn't give a snot about the stars. But she's there, analytical, practical, perfectionist, nit-picking, workaholic and painstaking. We have smatterings, she's been pebble-dashed.

We met through school, college and first jobs. Two of us grew up together, the other two the same. By the age of twenty we were all friends. That's about to change.

The door opens at five minutes to four. A dusty old clock is directly above it. The bell jangles irritatingly for the millionth time. Angelo likes it because it's a continental thing. Hair all over the place, blouse unironed, frowning, Helen sits in the same place she has sat for years. So that's the four of us in situ as always. But it's not as always. The only indication that something is wrong is that her eyes are red, but dry.

We know not to speak. She'll talk when she's ready. One of the others gives her a glass of water. 'No, thanks, I'd rather the wine.' Her first words, calm, soft Irish accent. I watch her raise the glass to her lips and gulp rather than sip. I'm afraid now.

From then on everything happens in slow motion. I watch her lips open and form words – I can even see the tip of her tongue. I concentrate on that, to avoid hearing what she has to say: 'He's been having an affair. In my bed. While I'm at work.'

She doesn't wait for the others to register it. She tells it like she's telling us about a day at work, though not everyone gets to save one life, lose another and remove strange things from strange places in the course of it – Helen treats it like its accountancy. In a way that is what Accident and Emergency is. A balancing act, lives lost and won. Why would she treat the crises of her own life any differently?

'He wanted to be caught. He knows I won't have the cleaner do two things – our bed and our toilet. I do them, or no one does. I haven't done them for ages. I found something.' She doesn't want to be specific.

'Come on, Helen. Euan's not as thick as most men. I'd credit him with a lot more intelligence than leaving evidence in his own bed and bathroom.' Dette pushes a fag and her pronouncement into the ashtray crowded mostly with her butts, though Rorie has contributed one or two. Catriona does not smoke. She gives out to Dette, who has a cough like an unserviced engine. Dette points to the packet's ultra-mild label and says, 'I have given up.'

This conversation is a ritual – we have a lot of those.

We four have stuck together over many years, throughout many differences. It's been a longer marriage than Dette had, a more satisfying relationship than Rorie and Catriona ever had. Helen had it all – Euan, friends, job, kids, looks, brains. Helen loves me. I've betrayed her.

Angelo puts tiramisu in front of her without asking. 'For bad news you need dessert.'

'What did you find?' Catriona asks, in a voice barely above a whisper. The colour has drained from her face. She has the look of someone who was once beautiful and forgot. It's not the extra weight – she's so tall and has clothes-hanger shoulders, she can carry extra stones which Rorie and Dette, both vying to reach five-foot three and failing, complain about, since they can't put on a pound without looking barrel shaped and the barrel shape, Dette advises, is never in. Even Rubens likes a waist, she says. Catriona has a waist, a shape, no matter what size she is, but she has lost the grace she was named for. Her mother always knew she was going to be a lady. She got to be. And found she didn't want it. She still has the peaches-and-cream skin, the dark rust-red hair of women who feature in sepia photographs of 'famous beauties of the day' – a perfect advert for Pears soap, or lavender water, or Crabtree and Evelyn. She decided to go for dowdy. It's safer. Catriona, who had it easier than all of us growing up and suffered from it, needs safety.

She was always jealous of Helen's fearlessness and her desire to reach for it all. But she wouldn't have wished this for a lot of reasons.

Then there's Rorie, gripping the wine glass in a manner Dette would say was like a builder hanging on to his enamel tea mug. There are tears in her eyes. Her honest, wide, cat-grey eyes, and she's rubbing at them now with that stripy jumper she's been wearing since the dawn of time, along with those once-black, now-grey jeans. If Rorie could have been a boy she would have been. Her ma, who we all love, was fully expecting her to be one, hence the name. She was amazed when she was handed a girl. 'I don't know. She still looks like a Rory to me. I'll stick an *ie* on the end instead of a *y*. They're sure to do that in America, so it'll do for Dublin.'

Of course, Mrs Marks was right. Rorie's the right name. She wears a dress about as often as Hailey's comet visits Earth. And she'll die in her Doc Martens. Her hair, dark blonde, wavy, down her back, is only long because she never cut it. She doesn't think about it. It's just there, on her head. School-uniform hair. You have to have it so why bother doing anything with it? Especially when wearing it short brings out your resemblance to your crap dad.

Rorie's cumbersome home cut has brought Dette close to tears on more than one occasion. As close as Dette gets, which is not close at all. She's not crying now. She's puffing away, looking anywhere but at Helen, whispering, 'Shame.' Helen and Euan falling apart is bound to surgically remove the last microscopic traces of faith that Dette might have had in relationships. She's sitting there, all made-up, not wanting to witness this because the make-up might fall apart.

Euan and Helen are the most solid couple we know. Love has been the most unreliable thing for all of us, except Helen. To outside eyes, Euan isn't the remarkable one in their partnership. Helen has everything, though she does nothing to draw attention to it. Euan teaches chemistry at the local comp for a pittance. His pupils love him the way his kids love him, and his kids love him bigtime – even Beatrice, Helen's eighteen-year-old daughter. Every closet has a skeleton.

Euan is handsome, in a distracted sort of way. Together his and Helen's distraction made for a focus the rest of us envied. They did a lot of living for each other, them against huge odds, in the early days. But they were always laughing. I hadn't heard much of that in recent years. Maybe the odds wore them down.

I don't know when it changed, but for some time I've been afraid for them, the silences between them. I wonder in doing what I did, if I was afraid of never finding what they had for myself. I know what you're thinking. There is more to this, and you'll have to put aside your ideas about what friends can do to each other with each other's husbands. You'll have to understand more.

Helen talks to Catriona, who won't stop asking questions. She's slipping like a duck on ice. 'Look. I found a condom in the toilet. Partly flushed. We both meant to have the plumbing looked at. We were too busy. We're always too busy.'

'How do you know it wasn't yours?'

'I have a coil.'

'How do you know it was a condom?' Catriona persists.

'Because it looked like one.'

'Did you fish it out?'

'No. But when I saw it I did the jealous-wife ransacking. I found a packet of three under the bed. One missing.'

'What did you do then?' Angelo wants to know.

'I tidied up again. The place was a mess. I can't afford to let it get messy on Tuesdays – by the end of the week it's out of control.'

'You didn't think to call Euan?'

'No. I waited for him to come home at lunchtime. He always comes home. The house is empty. I thought he might bring her with him. It's the most obvious time.'

Dette whistles out like she's been punched in the stomach. She slips *Sex and Your Star Sign* into her Prada.

Rorie asks what we all want to know. 'How did he explain?'

'It wasn't his.'

'That's what they all say at first,' Dette snips.

Catriona puts a finger to her lips. 'What are you going to do now?'

'I've asked him to tell me the truth when he's the

stomach for it. If he does I'll give him another chance, of course. I phoned a relationship counsellor on the way here, so he can talk to her.' Helen says it like she's signed for a new appliance.

Typical of her to set up the shrink as soon as the worms are out of the can. Typical of her not to wait until the hurt sinks in, not to reel, but to cope – too well. That's Helen for you.

'I thought you said you'd never go to a therapist,' Rorie says, quietly.

'I did. I'm going for him. He's the one with the problem.'

'Helen…' Catriona starts to say till, this time, Dette puts a finger to her lips.

Soon we will take out mobiles and cancel all arrangements, so that we can stay. We'll drink and eat and talk, and she won't cry. Tuesday, 1 August, will be a long day.

2

'Why do commentators have to shout?' Catriona tries to change the subject from Helen's problems. The problem is, she wants to change it to only one thing: George, her husband, a great package with a disappointing present inside. 'We're not in the stadium. We're at home, watching telly, with men. Who like football.' She says it like it's serial murder.

'Atmosphere,' Rorie supports Celtic loyally. 'Atmosphere.'

'I'd rather lock myself in the fridge than watch it,' Dette sighs. 'Now, footballers, there's a different story. You can lock me in a fridge with a footballer and a magnum.' Dette never eats, fridges are for chilled juice and champagne. 'Once—'

'Please,' Catriona says, 'not another conquest story. I haven't had sex for four weeks.'

'Please,' Dette responds, 'not another no-sex-with-George story.'

'What's the problem with sex for you?' Rorie probes.

'I have to have it with George.'

'No, you don't,' Helen swallows half a glass and gasps before the rest of the sentence. 'You can have it with anyone you like. Ask Euan.'

'The problem with George is that his name is George,' Catriona ignores her, out of embarrassment. 'Solid. Rock solid.'

'That's what drew you to him,' Helen points out.

'George can't think outside the M25. He thinks the Home Counties are called that because everyone wants to live there.'

Helen follows me to the ladies' as soon as I get up from the table. I had wanted a few minutes on my own to catch my breath. Four months later I'm still waiting.

'The worst thing about it,' she slumps onto the floor, 'is the surprise. I hate surprises. No good at them.' Her eyes droop. We should all have been home by then.

'And why didn't you tell them?' She is getting to her feet as if they aren't hers.

'I thought it was your business.' I can't look at her reflection in the mirror.

'Come on,' Helen snorts. 'You're avoiding something.'

'What do you mean?'

'You don't think it's big enough news?'

'Helen, don't. It's the worst I've heard for years.'

'You didn't even offer to come to the house and see me. I'm thinking, she hasn't said she'll come over, but she will. She knows how much I need her now. I don't have to say it. I'm no good at saying it. She knows that'

'I was shocked, Helen. I didn't know how to react.'

'Oh, my God,' she stares at me. 'The last time you

had that look was when you were trying to keep my twenty-first a secret. And we all know how well that went. What do you know?'

That was when I started to cry. 'I've been feeling sick all day.'

'You feel sick. How do you think I feel?' Helen opens a handbag that has seen better days, the zip only closed halfway. She pulls out a tube of supermarket-bought, fragrance-free moisturiser and rubs it into her paper-white skin. She whispers, 'It can't be you. You would never do it to me. You would never…' She turns to leave. 'Now I've to wait on two people to tell me the truth.'

When we were younger and drunker even than we are today, Helen told me, 'I know you fancy Euan.'

After denying it for a good five minutes I relented. I've never been dishonest with her. 'Aren't you angry at me?'

She smiled a huge smile, 'Nah. He's not the right one for you. Not organised. Your man will be someone who organises you to do all the things you should be doing now.'

Having a friend like Helen is like having a mammy. She's almost exactly the same age, but I always feel she knows more – she's better than me in some way. I think it's her personal defence system and her having Beatrice so young. And me not knowing what the hell I'm at, at thirty-nearly-six. Helen's lived ten lives for my one.

Back at the table the others have pulled out the papers and magazines.

'Look at this,' Catriona laughs. 'A new *you* will be revealed by the next full moon, which is a Virgo moon by the way. So I did learn something from that workshop, apart from the fact it's easy to part me from my money.'

Her last course was Raising the Moon. She tried to get Dette to go along, said it was to explore the lost sense of femininity, robbed from us by twenty-first-century living.

'No, thanks,' Dette's lips curls. 'Now, if they run one on Raising the Bosom, I'll have that. Thirty-five next month and my tits are already reaching my toes. Which is more than the rest of me can manage.'

Everyone raises an eyebrow. Dette's been lying about her age so long she thinks she's telling the truth.

'It also says: "Something unexpected will happen when you least expect it." Not a cliché in sight there.' Helen has taken the paper from Catriona, to join in, to belong, but as usual her earnestness gets in the way of it. And her situation. Everything seems to refer to it.

Rorie finds a snippet in a glossy. 'Listen to this. They're trying to make it sound scientific: "A recent lack of clarity caused by a meteor storm around the planet Venus", our home planet, "has only just cleared and brought revelation with it…"' Her voice trails away.

'Let's have a spot of Hailey von Hewson. You can rely on Hailey, despite her deplorable choice in pen names.' Dette pulls out her column – Catriona and Rorie seem to have lost the power of speech at the look on Helen's face. She scans it and bites off some of her trademark lipstick. Dette wears lipstick to bed. Really. In case burglars break in. 'What if one of them's good-looking?'

'Nope, you won't want to hear this one either.'

'Oh, go on!' Helen smiles a worn-out smile. 'It's all made up anyway.'

'Not Hailey, I'd swear by Hailey,' Catriona insists. Dette is ready to punch her.

'Dette!' Helen has on her this-is-an-order voice.

'"As I wrote in my start-of-the-year forecast, this is a challenging year for Virgos, with many preconceived ideas losing face. If you have the man you think you have, you're wrong; the job you think you have, you're wrong; the life you thought you wanted, you're—"'

'OK. You can stop.'

Dette reaches for the Chianti; she has made us switch to something more expensive than the Sicilian. 'If we drink it all day, we die tomorrow.'

Helen fingers the foil from Dette's fresh pack of cigarettes. Rorie and Catriona look at each other for want of looking anywhere else.

'Things are bad enough without you taking years off our lives,' Helen says to Dette. 'Give me one.'

Two hours later we are all puffing and talking about anything but the future – even organic-gardener Catriona is smoking.

'Why don't you grow something useful, like pot?' Dette is slagging her.

'No, thank you, not with a chief inspector over the fence.'

'Fair dos,' Helen claps loud enough to get four tables looking at us. 'Organic's the only way to go.'

Rorie and Dette raise eyes and sympathise with each other – they're not organised enough to save the environment. But they have very tidy flats in the same building. Unlike the other two, who could live in a sewer and find it cleaner than their previous addresses. It's funny, because Catriona and Helen live in swanky houses. Rorie and Dette make do with housing trust. When Dette's marriage failed and she had nothing left but her knickers, Rorie told her of the cheap rents. They've since managed to convert them to mortgages, and the fact they're buying their own places, by themselves for themselves, is a huge source of pride. In the beginning Dette wasn't so enamoured at the prospect: 'Hardly a Chelsea penthouse.'

She moved in two weeks later and that night Rorie opened her door after a loud single knock to find a bag of free make-up sitting on the landing, without a thank-you card. Dette has trouble with goodbyes, thank-yous and sorrys. But she'd give you her bra, and that's not just any old bra. Dette's every last penny goes on designer clothes.

'How can you spend a week's salary on a push-up?' Helen is mystified.

'I'm a *now* person,' Dette insists, 'not a *later*. When I go, dump me in a rubbish truck, but make sure I'm wearing Karan black.' When tenants were offered the chance to purchase their housing-trust flats, Rorie jumped, and persuaded Dette to do the same. 'Why do I need to own it?' she'd asked, like it was a waste of money. 'I could buy a Versace with the down payment.'

'Because you don't want to have to be sixty down the disco in a boob tube looking for a way to pay the rent,' Rorie said smartly. And was Dette ever grateful. Her home had been her little palace for five years.

Six o'clock in the evening, the dusty clock chime is as knackered as we are.

'Maybe some dinner?' Angelo suggests. 'Or do you want to go home?'

The others look at Helen.

'Dinner.'

The others look at each other, say nothing.

Helen sighs. 'Only eight hours old and I'm finding the betrayed-woman bit a bore.'

'Good. So you've decided to leave him,' Dette says grimly.

'Come on,' Rorie intervenes. 'Helen has to make up her own mind about this.'

'I said I'd give him a chance.'

'That's fair play, Helen, for you,' Dette shrugs. 'If you don't ditch him, he'll only do it again.'

'That,' Rorie insists, 'is a matter of opinion. Just because your husband did doesn't mean Euan has to.'

'Right,' Catriona agrees. 'You have to remember there are children involved here.'

'Oh, I see. Those with children feel more pain in separation than those without?'

'No need to talk about that now. You have something more important to discuss,' Angelo comes in. 'Helen, you have a man and the question is if you want to keep him. I think you have had him for a long time and I would take a long time to decide. Now, when there is hurt, is not the right time. Wait.'

'Fool,' Dette sighs.

'She's not a fool,' Catriona speaks loudly. 'Not every marriage has to end badly.'

'You seem to forget Euan has had an affair here. Not everything can end up sweet, though I know you'd like to think so.'

'Enough, Dette.' Rorie turns on her stage-manager voice.

'Sorry. Pissed.'

Catriona nods stiffly.

Helen rubs her temples. 'I'll tell you one thing. I wouldn't wish this shock on any of you.' She looks at me. 'Even you.'

'At least I know George'll never do it to me. He might be dull, but he's there. I think I'll give him a call. See how everyone is at home. They'll be wondering...' Catriona wanders off.

'The great thing about going out with Martin is I *know* he won't be faithful forever. It takes all the uncertainty out of it,' Dette lights a fresh cigarette from her last one, before stubbing the old one out and sighing.

'And what does it leave you with?' Rorie eyes her.

'Great sex, good company, for as long as it lasts. That's all I'm looking for. That's all I'll ever be looking for.'

'I don't think you're telling the truth. I think you fancy the pants off Martin and you might like it to be more. But he's too young, so you don't have to think about risking more involvement.' Dette's don't-mess-with-me tone has caught at Rorie, making her speak more out of turn than she would normally.

'Excuse me, Lady Madonna, but are you not the one living with the man who has never committed to her for more than four nights a week?'

'I don't pretend it's anything other than it is.'

'Well, neither do I!'

'Yes, you do. You think you're keeping men where you want them. But you never go out with anyone older than my hamster. And he only lived to be sixteen, in hamster years. You never go out with men.'

'That's not true. Younger blokes are attracted to me.'

'So are older men,' Helen interrupts. 'Your husband was older.'

'Wrong there,' Dette points her fag. 'He was the original Peter Pan. And I was a right Wendy.'

They are still laughing when Catriona comes back.

'Magda answered.' She sits down and frowns. 'Everything's under control. As usual.'

Magda is Catriona's au pair. The four of us have come up with plan after plan for relieving Catriona of her. At one stage, Helen was even going to take her on and then do what Catriona hadn't the stomach for – sack her. For being too good.

'Is she still wearing your clothes when you go out?' Dette tilts her head.

'I told you, that was just a suspicion. I have nothing to base it on. Besides, nothing of mine fits her now that I'm a fat woman and she's a Geri Halliwell.'

'That's the bloody problem with her,' Rorie says. 'She's blameless. Never trust anyone that perfect.'

'The kids love her.'

'Kids are puppies. They'll fall in love with the next one if she's nice to them,' Helen says.

'George likes her too. She makes him proper dinners and he never goes to work looking crumpled since Magda. She told me he was in the shower and couldn't come to the phone.'

'How does she know he's in the shower? It's an en-suite. She'd have to have been in your...?' Dette's eyebrows rise.

'Stop it, Dette. George would never do anything like that to me.'

'This time yesterday,' Helen is looking at the last of the commuters, the committed workforce sacrificing a summer evening to stay past eight in the office, 'I'd have said the same thing.'

'What's that supposed to mean?'

'What it says. The most reliable men can't be trusted,' Dette interrupts.

'Why?' Rorie snaps impatiently. Things were bad enough for Helen without this.

'Because they're men,' Helen and Dette say in unison.

'Don't you ever wonder about John?' Catriona asks.

'Doesn't everyone?' Helen says.

'Shut up, Helen. No one slags off my boyfriend unless I start the proceedings.' Rorie holds up her hands. 'I suppose there was a time when I wondered about him. Now I'm not even worried that I no longer wonder. It's like I know he's never going to be completely mine. And once I accepted that, I started letting him go. To tell you the truth, I'd probably be happy if he went altogether. I just don't know how to take that step, after all this time with him. Fifteen years. We're like old socks.'

'No, he has a wife to mend those.' Dette does wry better than anyone else. Catriona and Helen nod.

'I'm glad you're thinking of letting him go,' Catriona whispers. But everyone is listening. 'He's never been particularly good for you.'

'Try rephrasing that. Try he's been bad for you.' Dette pushes it, as she always does.

'You only get away with that because your husband was worse,' Rorie says.

'At least he was my husband.'

Rorie looks like she is going to cry.

'Dette, leave it,' Helen comes in. Umpire, as always.

After the *antipasto* it started up again. Affairs, how they start, why they happen, why they never work out.

'How many of us here have been unfaithful, even once?' Rorie asks the question.

Helen is the only one who doesn't raise her hand.

'That's because you married Euan so young. And you were too boring to want boyfriends. The rest of us are normal.'

'Thanks, Dette.'

'Are you saying,' Catriona interrupts, speaking to Dette, 'that fidelity is no longer the norm? Because if you are I don't believe you.'

'No, I'm not saying that. I'm saying fidelity doesn't exist any more. It's a vanishing art. Did you see that survey in my magazine last month? Seventy-five per cent of respondents had had affairs. And they were the ones willing to admit it.'

'And we all know how reliable magazine surveys are,' Helen raises her eyes to heaven.

'Listen here, Mrs Doctor-person-everything-has-to-be-proved-scientifically, that survey set the mag back thirty grand in research-agency fees. Put that in your iron lung and smoke it.'

'Sorry, Dette, didn't mean to be disparaging of a publication with the words "It's official – James Nesbitt has Britain's best bum" on its cover.' Helen holds up *Madame* magazine.

'And did you look at the particular arse in question, Helen Larkin?'

'I did indeed. And I concur with the findings of a few sad individuals who thought it worthwhile voting on the subject. And don't tell me there were thousands of votes, dear. I know from past conversations you're lucky to get four.'

'True, but that's only Editorial. In Beauty we're inundated. Even when all I'm giving away is pads for lost pee-pee when the pelvic floor collapses.' Dette is beauty editor of *Madame* and does giveaways every month. 'Which reminds me.' She hands over our goody-bags. We get them once a month if we have been good girls – if we haven't, we have to beg. Helen takes them for her nursing staff and patients, which annoys Beatrice – Dette has to give her things separately because Helen insists she is too spoilt already. Rorie keeps whatever she got and promised to start using it some day – as soon as Rimmel gives up making her tinted moisturiser and clear lip gloss. It's all she has and all she wants in the way of make-up. Only Catriona tries the stuff religiously and insists on reporting back on their performance in writing. 'At least it gives me a reason to feel useful.'

Since the arrival of Magda, Catriona has been written out of her own life as being labour intensive and inefficient. Magda runs things in a more streamlined fashion. In short, they work.

'Anyway, this was a proper fuck-off survey.' Dette brings us back to the subject. 'It found serial monogamy was the closest to fidelity the modern lover will ever come. Five years max, and it's time to move on to the next pasture. Euan's done well to be faithful for as long as he has. By today's standards he deserves an Olympic medal.'

'He deserves a kick in the goolies. I mean, sorry Helen, drunk here, but he's supposed to be the lovely one. The one we all hoped to find some day.' Rorie's head is reaching for the table. As a stage manager she works long nights, and on Tuesdays she is normally tucked up in bed by ten.

'And what about George? Why does none of you want to find a man like George?' Catriona is querulous. Catriona only ever gets querulous when she has close to two bottles of wine inside her. Things are bad.

'Because you're never done slagging him off, Catriona. It's hardly a sales pitch, is it?' Helen smiles. 'Mind you, right now I'd swap Euan for him.'

'Would you? Would you really?' Catriona seems delighted at the compliment.

'Yes, I would. He's handsome and he's there and he's aware of what it means to work hard. Euan thinks me working hard is a fault, or something. As if I have control over when people have accidents in their lives. I can't walk out at five if Mr Rogers of Laburnum Avenue has a heart attack at five to five.'

'No, you can't,' Rorie agrees. 'You do a great job, Helen. If it wasn't for A and E my mother would be dead now.'

'And Danny Mendelson's mickey would still be stuck in a Coke bottle,' Dette smiles. Though she still insists she didn't put it there.

Catriona winces. 'Seriously, Helen, do you think George is worth fancying?' Drunken repetition. A sure sign that the evening should be over.

'Well, if she doesn't, Magda does,' Rorie nods.

'Yeah, and the Audrey Hepburn lookalike I saw him lunching with in Tokyo the other day,' Dette pipes up.

'George!' Catriona's exclamation. 'In an Asian restaurant?'

'I think you're missing the point here, Mrs Morehampton. Mr Morehampton was spotted with a beautiful woman.'

'Oh, that'll have been a client. George has lots of those.'

'This client had her hand on his arm and was offering him some of her sushi,' Dette elaborates.

'Sushi! Why didn't you tell me before? I can't believe he ate sushi.'

'He didn't. But he was willing to try and I didn't tell you because, like you say, it was George. Extramarital's not in the rule book.'

'But I don't know if I think any man is trustworthy, not after today.' Helen reminds us of her original point.

'He wouldn't do that to me,' Catriona is still going on at us a half-hour later. 'He wouldn't eat sushi after all the times he's refused it with me. It's not fair! He never does anything exciting with me. Ever, ever—'

'Well, be glad you don't think he's doing anything exciting with Magda,' Rorie tells her.

'Hate Magda, hate her, hate her. Sorry, that's racist.'

'No,' Dette is dry even when she's at her drunkest. 'It's realistic.'

'George is afraid of sex,' Catriona pronounces.

'He's got four kids. He can't be that afraid of it.' Rorie feels obliged to defend the absent.

'Don't be silly, he's not afraid of it with me. He just doesn't think he's any good at it. And he's right, you know. Neither am I. I'm too tired to star wheel. My kids keep me up half the night. Magda's offered to go to them, but I won't let her. I'm afraid she's a vampire.'

'They're Transylvanian, not Polish,' Rorie offers reassurance.

'What's "star wheel"?' Helen wants to know.

'Never mind. We'll explain later,' Dette seems keen to move on. 'Tell you what, Rorie, you could always line one of us up to snog John and for you to catch us. Throw a fit of outrage, weep at the betrayal. That'd put him outside the door with his bags.'

'Not a bad idea,' Rorie tries to focus, on what she isn't sure. She feels warm, very warm, and ready to sleep on a pin. 'In fact, that's one way you could all avoid it.'

'Avoid what?'

'Betrayal. We could try to seduce each other's partners.'

'Ridiculous,' Helen shakes her head.

'No way,' Catriona bleats.

'Brilliant,' Dette muses. 'Why not?'

'I wasn't being serious. Just a wild thought.'

But it is the only thing we talk about, through dinner, then through the night that becomes the next day. The four of us discuss it again and again. Before we leave Angelo's, late, very drunk and very full, we make a promise to each other that leaves all our lives changed.

Angelo did tell us. 'This is a terrible thing to do.'

'No, it's not, we're Virgos,' Helen – the one who believes in astrology least – pronounces. 'You want something done? Ask a Virgo. We're the do sign of the zodiac. We motivate. We organise. We proceed.'

We proceed like sheep behind Helen and write the names of our lovers on slips of paper, provided by Angelo. Then each of us draws out the name of another woman's lover and takes it away with us. In the morning we have the name in our purse. And we think, That was a stupid idea, and we still carry out the task. Why? I can only think it's because we live under the sign of carrying out anything to the bitter end.

I wish we'd listened to Angelo. 'What you do, it's Russian roulette.'

'What's that?'

'A game where each one playing fires a gun with only one loaded chamber at their temple,' Helen explains to Catriona. 'Have you never seen *The Deer Hunter*?'

'I have not. *Bambi*'s too violent for me. I'm not interested in it, or this suggestion.'

'Well, I am, because all I know is I woke up this morning and I thought I was living in one world but I'm not. And I might as well have the upper hand in this new one. Euan says he won't do it again. We'll soon find out. And I'd rather have one of my own friends test him than for him to sneak off with someone else, probably one of his sixth-form students. I know it'll save me a lot of agony. I've got to go before I fall down.'

I'm sure the speech is what persuaded us all. A dinner was organised. The game began.

Four months later, I sit alone at the table where we got drunk, hatched our plans and dissipated into a summer night. It's December. Our Christmas lunch should be in full swing. The summer heat has gone and so has the Virgo Club, I think.

Angelo has brought me a *grappa* to warm me up. 'You wait,' he smiles. 'They will come.'

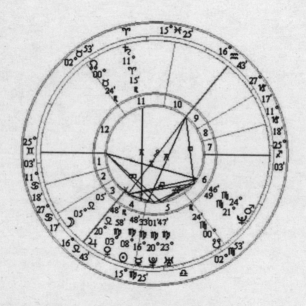

*Helen Larkin, female, Saturday 2 September 1967 at
12.00 a.m.; Baldoyle, Dublin, Ireland
(53N24'00 6W08'00)*

3

HELEN

Scorpio on the Sixth

You tend to become obsessed with your work. You then drop everything else and totally immerse yourself in what you are doing. The more challenging (and dangerous) it is, the better you seem to like it. You work with an intensity that makes your co-workers and co-dwellers uneasy. You can be trusted – once you have given your loyalty, it can be forever. Your major health difficulties are caused by not dealing with stressful situations as they occur – when you postpone them, they have a tendency to burst out of you in an uncontrollable fashion. You hope to control rather than understand. But your approach has the opposite effect. Deal with your emotions or deal with the consequences.

******

He was asleep at the kitchen table when she walked in at ten to two. Already the morning after a terrible night before. It was a kitchen full of life and she felt a stab of pain because she realised that, somehow, she had not been a part of it for a long time. Like she'd said at lunch – you can't make people live and die between nine and five, they have a habit of doing so after office hours.

There was clutter. Helen and Euan had never been ones to throw things out. She hadn't cooked a meal in six months. But there was always the intention. As long as she had that, she might change. Find the stop button, learn to relax more.

Helen looked now at the crown of Euan's head. The hair was as thick as it had been when she first met him, sixteen years ago, ginger biscuit with flecks of gold. The layers were long because he didn't bother to get it cut regularly, and she loved nothing better than holding on to them when they made love and feeling grateful that still, after all this time, she found him as attractive as she had when they met. In fact, her feelings had grown stronger as his skin had found a few comfortable crags to settle into. What was most desirable was the way Euan ignored his good looks. He never considered them, and the lack of vanity, the sincerity in his eyes had given her the harbour she had never thought she would have. Her father and mother had had a loveless life, which had made Helen want to get away to a better one.

When she had moved to London to study medicine, she had been eighteen and was awarded an international scholarship as if it was a bus pass. But Helen was always the swan, graceful above water and pedalling like mad below the surface.

Then Beatrice.

A man for one of her first nights in London, a night when she was afraid. A bed and a baby that she didn't want. He, like the cliché, didn't want either of them.

Most would have gone back home, to Ireland – to disapproving parents who would do their best for her and the child and make them both suffer for of it. Not Helen. She went to the course director, explained the situation coolly, in the manner that would make her a great doctor. She asked for a year out and a fresh start.

'How can you afford this?' the director wanted to know.

'If I still have the scholarship I can do it.'

'OK, Helen. I'll write to them and ask that it be held for a year, due to family circumstances. We won't go into any details. They might not think you're up to resuming such a workload. I know different.'

She worked full-time as a care assistant in the same hospital in which one day she would be a consultant. She did weekends at a canteen. Beatrice was born healthy after six hours of straightforward, efficient labour. Helen went back to work almost straightaway as a cleaner of private houses, with Beatrice strapped to her in a sling. By the following September Beatrice was almost one, weaned, had never seen her Irish family and was ready to be left with Helen's one friend in London, me, as a minder. It worked. Beatrice never knew how much her mother suffered for her, studying at night so she could have some time with her during the day. Helen didn't want her to know that. It might have made things easier between them. Beatrice was born a Virgo – just – 22 September at a minute to midnight. It's a fact she denies, not wanting to be part of her mother's club. She insists she's a Libra. Not a bit of it.

A Virgo mother and daughter are a match of similarities, but not of synchronicity. From the time Bea was two they fought like cats, neither used to losing. Over the years neither did, so they lost each other. If Helen saw Bea as a problem child, then Helen was a problem mother.

It was Euan who kept the peace.

Helen saw him on her first day back at medical school. He was one of the new arrivals and he already had a flock of other swans around him. They were beautiful and they bit. Helen Larkin knew she had to try. All year she knew she had to try.

By the following summer term she hadn't even spoken to him. It became clear, thanks to her lack of social skills and her responsibilities at home, that to meet him she'd have to do something she had never done in her life, something she considered almost as vile as murder. Helen Larkin had to take up sport.

Hill walking.

She saw his name on the list for a long weekend in the Lake District.

Well, she thought as she put her name down, at least I won't have to wear shorts and hit something. How hard can hill walking be? A hill, you walk up it. Easy.

Beatrice was left in London for a weekend. She was almost two and outraged.

'It's for your own good,' Helen whispered into her reddened ear. 'You might get a daddy out of this.'

'Mammy, you're always going away.'

On the side of Scafell in May, in supposed early summer but in driving wind and rain, Helen wondered when the helicopter was going to land to evacuate her, or at least give oxygen. For God's sake, the others were medical students too. Did they not realise her life was in danger?

They did, but only because they were threatening to lynch her. She was holding the rest of them from the summit and the pub.

At the rest point the others had already waited half an hour for her. Helen squelched up in soggy trainers, soaked jeans and donkey jacket that now weighed as much as she did. The rest all sat around in wind-resistant, rainproof splendour sharing tea and soup from their Thermoses, which she hadn't thought to bring. No one rushed to offer her a cup.

'You clearly aren't enjoying this. And what the hell are you doing here without rain gear?' The group organiser – a woman with a severely pointed chin and manner, the kind who would be jogging marathons at ninety – wanted to know.

'I thought it would be good to get some fresh air,' Helen mumbled. Her face contorted with the need not to hit Pointy on her chin. Anyway, she was too tired.

'Go to the park next time. Now we're going to have to find someone to stay with you while the rest of us carry on doing what we came here to do.'

'I will,' Euan stepped out. He handed Helen a cup of something warm. 'Here, you look perished, drink this.'

It was Oxo. She hated Oxo – her mother used to pour it on her potato and pretend it was gravy. Now she drank it and discovered that it still wasn't gravy, it was much better and very warm. She still gave Euan an Oxo cube each year on his birthday.

Pointy's irritation turned to dismay. Euan had been striding out with her in the leading group; she'd visions of them climbing mountains, running marathons together into old age. 'I thought you wanted to press on, Euan.'

'No. It'd be nice to take things easy. What's the point in belting through? We'll be back in London soon enough.'

Scottish. Helen hadn't heard his accent before. Beautiful, like the rest of him. Jaysus. Sean Connery's love child, hello.

Pointy was not giving up. 'We were setting the pace.'

'I wasn't aware it was a race,' Euan said, in the quiet way that Helen would come to recognise when there was no arguing with him.

It had not been how she thought she'd first approach him – muck-splattered, reddened, numbed, soaked. She looked like a half-sucked, hairy boiled sweet.

'I'm sorry. I thought there'd be a path, or something. Labour wasn't as hard as this.' He had to know about Beatrice from the beginning, if this was going to work.

'How is your little girl?' He already knew about her then. Who was she kidding? Everyone knew she was the eighteen-year-old mammy who'd had to drop out and plop back in again, with bags under her eyes you could hold a purse in.

'She's great, and I should be with her,' Helen wheezed. 'Not here, anywhere but here.'

He laughed, which brought the feeling back into her extremities. He was taking off his jacket to give to her and she refused it point-blank. Eventually they reached a compromise. She hid under the wing and he put his arm round her. By the time they got back to the hostel she didn't think hill walking was all that bad, now it was over. Everyone had gone to the pub.

Euan had whiskey, and with boiling water and sugar from the kitchen they made their own toddies.

She told him everything about herself. She never told anyone anything about herself. Working class, parents hate each other, grew up too quickly. She was determined to be something.

'Well,' he smiled again – she was beginning to wish he wouldn't, because it made her feel so different and she couldn't bear to lose that already, 'you *are* something. The whole year is in awe of you. You make it look so easy.'

'But it's not.' She frowned in the way that made her freckles knit. 'I just put the work in.'

'I know.' He separated them out with his thumb pad – eventually he'd wear a smooth part in his skin from doing that. 'I've seen you in the library. Not that I'm in there often, but every time I am you're there.'

'I'm surprised you noticed,' Helen said. 'I thought you were oblivious to the common people, with all the beautiful ones twittering around you.'

'Ah.' She could feel his smile in the dark. 'There's nothing common about you, girl. I'm the common one. I'm not going to be anything special, especially a doctor.'

'Nonsense, your patients will love you.'

'But will they get better? I won't have a clue what's wrong with them. No. I like people OK, but I don't love medicine. You'll be a brilliant doctor and I'll be proud of you. This is the future.'

She didn't flinch, since it was the one she wanted.

'My friend,' she smiled. 'She's a Virgo too. She says we

always get what we want in the end because we never forget we want it. I'm not one for fabricating realities, Euan.
I've a young child and a good thirteen years of slog ahead
of me to make consultant.'

'So serious, Helen. Already.' Then he saw she was too
fragile for joking. She needed to know. He was scared of
that, but he still told her, 'I look forward to being there
when it happens. Now, do you hate all sports?'

'No,' she shook her head. 'I love lying-down ones. The
trouble is, there's only one of those.'

'We only need to play one.'

Now he was waking up, to the reality of what they had
become.

'This,' Helen whispered to herself, wiping away her
private tears – she had not shared them with anyone still,
not even Euan, 'is what you get when you want too
much. You end up with more than you bargained for.'

The first time he met Beatrice was on the Monday,
straight after they got back from the Lake District. He
came empty-handed, but brought his smile. They had
cake.

'They're sugar-free, the ones I make,' Helen hastened
to tell him. 'I'm making sure she eats a healthy diet.'

And he could see Helen did all the things for Bea a
mother should do, and none of the things that were the
reward. It was the first time he learned not to say too
much in front of the woman who would be his wife.
'Really?' he said. 'No wonder they taste so vile. I'll be
chef.'

By Friday they were a family.

Euan would catch hold of Helen's hand and pull her on to the floor to play with Bea and him. She thought all the time of the books waiting for her on the table, of the lack of time between now and the exam. He did not study. 'I'm going to fail anyway. Let me mind Bea.'

Needless to say, his own parents were not happy with him moving in with a woman, a toddler and no money or qualifications between them.

Then they met Helen and they saw what Euan saw – a purposeful, honourable woman with a written future. Even if she did make them sign a petition against hospital cutbacks before they'd shaken hands.

'If she's any more earnest, she'll fall over,' Euan's dad shook his head. Helen had to go in for a pathology lesson, had offered them the opportunity to sit in the gallery and watch the dissection of a human heart. 'But she's good, son, she's good.'

His mother saw Euan's hurt. 'She'll always do the right thing.'

'What about the wee girl?' his dad asked, practical and to the point.

'I'm adopting her.'

'Well, son, you always do the right thing too.'

They had attended the marriage ceremony in a poky registry office conducted by a woman who needed to go to lunch and was already late. Helen's parents were not available. Euan had written to them when she wouldn't. He got no reply. He knew it hurt her. She knew it didn't matter since she had her own family now.

'What they don't know they don't want to know,' she said to him.

She had helped him break it gently to his father that

he had failed his exams and was going to become a teacher instead.

When Euan's dad got cancer six years ago, Helen and Euan flew up to Glasgow every fortnight and Helen spoke to consultants to get him the best care. After the funeral Euan's mother went to live with his sister in Aberdeen.

Bea cried at her grandfather's graveside, and so did Euan. Helen held both of them and wished she could pay the same kind of tribute in grief to a man who had given his son his sense of humour and his love of life, which had been Euan's chief inheritance.

At home, having been appointed senior registrar, she gave Euan what he wanted more than anything. Helen was not sure she wanted more children. She was only sure she wanted Euan. 'I know what you're doing for me,' Euan said, when she conceived almost immediately.

She took three months off for Kelly and the same for Joyce. Euan took a year's career break each time. For her the first day back at work was hell – she missed her girls so much. But the buzz of work, of life at its edges, took over quickly. Euan was a natural father. Bea was twelve when Kelly was born, turned out to be a natural sister. The girls loved her. She loved them.

And Helen got left out somewhere, between shifts. She knew she wasn't doing as well by the family as Euan. She'd treated being a wife to Euan the same way she treated anything she approached – it was a thing to do well or not at all. With the girls it was different – they had needed so much of her she felt she was drowning. Her life as she had known it had been so hard to put together, not something she could let go of easily. It wasn't that she didn't want to give in the same way to her children. When she held each of her newborn babies for the first time, she felt something inside her reach out that was more powerful than anything she had ever felt, including her feelings for Euan. The fact it was so powerful was what threatened her, she had to get free of it. It was a territory too unknown for her, too far for her to go. So she retreated. And had the perfect excuse to – work. There was always work.

The problem with never forgetting you want something is that you have to make sacrifices and she was called to make them, every day. Euan understood this because he understood her. He rarely criticised. Now, looking back, if he had been more demanding they might not be in this situation.

Some part of unreachable Helen loved Euan for having seen how easily she could break. He chose to cushion her from all that happened outside her working life. The arrangement worked well. But when they had dark moments Euan would say, 'You treat me like a task.'

He didn't say it often because he knew his approval meant more to her than anything. His joy each time she climbed a rung of the ladder was more than her own. She didn't understand sometimes why she did what she did, but she knew she could never do anything else.

Lately Euan had been saying she treated all of the family like a task, because she was trying to be a dutiful mother and her diary was blocked off with 'B' or 'K' or 'J' in the same way as her working hours were marked. It was not fair of him, being organised was the only way to do things. Today, when she'd flicked through it she saw there wasn't a single 'E' marked.

*****

Euan lifted his head and caught sight of her at once. 'Helen,' his voice was hoarse with sleep.

This was the place where she was happy. Now what would happen to that? She saw the faces of her children in the photographs and their shining eyes were not for their mother holding them but for their father, holding the camera. She knew they were not as easy with her as they were with him. That was inevitable since he spent more time with them. But she had only just realised how uneasy they were with her. She did not know how to get down on the floor and be with them. She couldn't throw herself around the room to music with abandon, she couldn't make up stories. She just hadn't been brought up that way. She knew she had a poker up her bum but, even with her surgical training, she didn't know how to extract it.

But she loved, every bit as much as he loved. When they were rowing once about it she had said to him, 'You should have told them, Euan, the girls!'

'You should have told them yourself! Or, better still, shown them.'

'They hate me.'

'They don't hate you, they just don't know you as well as they might.'

'It's not as if I'm out enjoying myself. I'm working to keep this family.'

'And what is that supposed to mean, Helen?'

'Nothing.'

'With you, Helen, it always means something. Do you think I'm not keeping this family just because I work less and earn less than you?'

'I never said that.'

'You didn't have to. All I can tell you is that we don't have to live in a five-bedroom house in Ealing. We could live in a three-bedroom and we could go for camping trips instead of foreign holidays and shop at Kwik Save instead of Waitrose. It's not as if either of us was brought up to live in splendour.'

'I've earned these things, Euan. I've earned this comfort.'

'And you're losing by it.'

'I want our kids to have what I never had.'

Euan had gone silent at this.

'Come on, say it.'

'I don't want to. It'll only hurt you.'

'Say it.'

'Anyone can give a child money, but children don't give a curse about it. They need love. You never had it and you're making the same mistake with your own children. That's what sad about it.' He spoke in the quiet voice.

'Helen! Thank God.' He stood up and swayed a little, or maybe it was her. 'Did you go on and see them at Angelo's?'

She nodded.

'You left too quick. I didn't get a chance to explain everything.'

'No, just to deny.'

'I didn't deny. I told you it didn't happen recently.'

She rubbed her eyes and pushed the glasses she wasn't wearing out of the way. 'Euan.'

'I don't know how it got there,' he pleaded, for the second time that day, except it was now the next. She felt depressed for all the times she was going to hear this excuse in the future. 'I honestly don't. Look, if I wasn't telling the truth I wouldn't have told you anything. I'd stick it out with the lying, wouldn't I? The point is, I didn't lie to you. I told you something had gone on. I could have just stuck to my guns.'

'Euan,' Helen said wearily, 'when did it happen?'

'Six months or so ago, maybe more.'

'That means you've lied to me for that long.'

'I know,' he agreed. 'But I'm sorry. I forgot it even happened myself. The thing was over before it even began. There didn't seem to be a right time. I didn't want to put anything else on to you. And, like I said, I never actually had sex so—'

'So you thought it was OK not to mention that you'd been about to?'

'No, no. I just knew how upset you'd get and I knew it would never happen again. I wanted to save you.'

'You wanted to deceive me.'

'I would never deceive you – well, not apart from that time when I did. God, I sound pathetic.'

'We both do.'

'Don't be so reasonable, Helen. That's how you always avoid things.'

'I'm reasonable because I spend large chunks of each day dealing with the unreasonable. I'm reasonable because I know to be otherwise will make things a lot worse.' Helen raised her hands, 'Let's leave it until the morning, can we? I have to be sober by seven.'

'OK,' Euan looked relieved. 'Let's go up.'

'No,' Helen pulled off her coat and headed towards the sitting room, 'I'll take the sofa.'

'Men are supposed to take the sofa,' Euan said, after the silence filled with all the things too-late-at-night is filled with.

'Most men aren't married to A and E doctors who can sleep anywhere.'

'Helen, don't be so kind to me.'

'I don't know how to be anything else.'

4

'Sorry to call so early. I just thought I'd ring to make something clear.' Rorie had caught Helen before she went out the door to work. Seven a.m. Late. 'I was very drunk. I think we should stop this before we even begin it. It'll lead to all sorts of problems.'

'Why?' Helen was rubbing her temples again. The heaviness must lift soon or she'd have to drink another cup of coffee. She already had four in her system. People didn't realise how unhealthy doctors had to be. Long hours and high stress, everything they didn't recommend. 'You said yourself that you needed to get rid of John.'

'I didn't put it like that.'

'Well, you said maybe it would be better if you and he weren't together. But you can't do it on your own. John's your Magda, isn't he?'

'I think I loved him a lot more than Catriona's ever loved her au pair. In fact, I still love him, Helen, which is why I'm still with him.'

'Ah, come on, Rorie.'

'I'm not *in* love with him. But I have a lot of good memories.'

'Name one.'

'The holiday to Tuscany.'

'Rorie, that was eight years ago.'

'The dinner he gave me for my birthday.'

'That was a good while ago too.'

'Five years,' Rorie said.

'Rorie, I've got to go to work. And you've got to go through with this.'

'Because I haven't the courage to let him go properly?'

'Because you know he's not right.'

'Why don't any of you like him?'

Helen didn't want to say that he'd tried to drop the hand more than once with Catriona, a couple of times with Dette and even once with her. Men who dropped the hand with Helen risked being stitched up by her afterwards. She could be colder than a sperm bank.

'We don't like that he's never been able to give you full commitment. I have to hang up now, but that doesn't mean I'm not thinking about you.'

'I know, give me one more minute. Please. It's important. If I run my chief reservation by you, you'll analyse it in that computer brain of yours.'

'OK, but hurry.'

For one minute after she'd woken on the couch Helen had thought it a normal day. The hangover that came crashing in on her had seen to that. She had to hang up on Rorie because she wanted to get out of the house before the kids and Bea – now about to turn eighteen, fly the nest quicker than Concorde and even more removed from her – woke up and saw her in this state.

'I think it'll lead to us telling lies to each other,' Rorie said.

'The whole point of this is we can be honest with one another, which will help us to be honest with ourselves.'

'So why are we lying to each other already?

'How so?'

'By not saying who we drew out.'

'If we knew the woman who was going to try to seduce our man we'd be watching her every move. She needs anonymity.'

'I suppose so. I spoke to Dette on the way home in the taxi and she's keen. The way only Dette can be. Catriona…I don't know about Catriona.'

'Catriona's afraid of her own shadow. Don't worry. This is for our own good. If we learn he's to be trusted we're happy. If we learn he's not then we're better off.'

'I just feel uneasy.'

'You always feel uneasy.'

'True.'

'Rorie, are you still there?'

'Yeah.'

'Is there anything else?'

'No.'

'I have to go then.'

Helen reached for the coffee pot and the bottle of paracetamol and codeine. She pulled the slip of paper out of her purse. George. Interesting George, as Dette called him. Catriona's money-spinning husband. It would be difficult to seduce a man she'd nothing in common with. She didn't know the first thing about flirting.

Especially with George. The man starched his upper lip.

The noise of footsteps behind her told her she'd lost her opportunity for a quick exit. Euan was still wearing the clothes he'd had on last night. He held a sleepy Joyce in his arms. 'She heard the phone,' Euan whispered. 'I think she'll go off for another half-hour now. Normally I don't wake her until quarter to.'

That was why Helen rarely got to see her younger daughters in the morning. They both slept well and didn't wake until their father stirred them. On the rare occasions their mother did, she was just back off night duty and too tired to play with them. Recently Kelly had pointed out to her, when Joyce was throwing a fit at the breakfast table, 'You didn't make the noise.'

'What noise?'

'The one Daddy makes when he pours the milk.'

Euan had come in and snapped, crackled and popped. Later on, as she dressed them, Kelly kicked up a fuss, crossing her arms, screeching, 'I wear this one!'

'No, Kelly, it's not clean.'

'Daddy says yes.'

'Daddy's not here to say yes. Now, do as I say.'

Soon she had regretted standing up to a four-year-old girl. When she tried to hug Kelly, her daughter went stiff.

'I don't like you.'

'Oh, Kelly, why not? Because I made you angry?'

Kelly could have been Helen's father when she said, 'You don't like me, or Joyce, or Daddy. Or Bea. You always shout at Bea.'

The only time she saw Bea was when Bea chose to see her. Bea only chose to see her on practical matters. 'When can I have a car? When are you going to let me go to Creamfields? Why have I no rights at seventeen when I'm legally allowed to marry and have children? Why do you have to make me as miserable as you? Wait until September twenty-second – I'm gone.' It was interesting that she wasn't claiming 23 September as her birthday this year, as she had on every other one since she turned thirteen and realised the full implications of being a Virgo.

It made for pleasant viewing, their rows – both red-haired, both fighting what they knew was in them. They'd been poured from the same mould and neither liked to be reminded of it.

Bea's beauty made Helen want to cry, so perfect Helen couldn't show her appreciation of it. Where Helen had rejected her own looks and body, Bea seemed obsessed with labels, make-up and magazines that showed her she was too fat, even at size ten. Even her A levels were not a subject for discussion. She'd sat them in art and English because that was the only way Helen would agree to pay her an allowance. She was not allowed to do nothing. 'It's all rubbish. All I really want to do is be in front of the camera. Why can't you let me do what I want?'

'You can, as soon as you're eighteen. You can throw your life away and develop osteoporosis, just like Dette. But now you'll make some stab at qualifications.'

'I don't want qualifications. I don't have to be like you.' Until her move to secondary school, Bea had been the brightest kid in her class. Then she'd swallowed a bitter pill and started to eye Helen as if she was a hit man.

'It's not about being like me. It's about having something to fall back on. How many times do I have to tell you?' Helen opted for patience.

'I wish Dette or Rorie was my mother. Dette would let me smoke. Rorie would let me eat additives.'

Bea loved Dette, who popped stories of celebrities, models and prima donnas into Bea's mouth like sugar cubes. Helen had a sense that if she had been more fashion conscious, Bea might have been less so. But she could not change now. It was who she was. This was where she was. In a kitchen full of recyclable materials waiting to be brought for recycling. In limbo.

On the day Kelly had told her she didn't love her, following in her big sister's footsteps, Helen told Euan what had happened.

'Helen, Kelly's four. She'll love you tomorrow.'

'No, she won't. Why do you allow her to wear dirty clothes? Why do I have to be the villain of the piece because I establish a bit of order?'

'Because she doesn't want to wear dirty clothes very often and she's not a robot. She doesn't have to do exactly what we tell her all the time. You have to give on the unimportant things to have leverage on the important ones. You're always in a hurry when you're dealing with them. Children hate hurry. You've got to act like you've all the time in the world.'

'All the time in the world? I don't have a spare second.'

'It's your choice. No one's asking you to do this.'

Now Euan was standing in front of her with the daughter they had made in his arms and she thought, He's right. I always take the shortest route to things. Then another voice said, But I haven't slept with someone else. For Helen, nothing was as bad. She couldn't stop herself seeing another woman's hands on his body. Finger-printed skin. 'Please, who was it?' she asked.

'I can't say.'

'So it is someone I know.'

'I won't confirm or deny.'

'If I find out it's her,' Helen would not say the name in front of Joyce, 'I will never get over it.'

'It's not going to happen again,' Euan said.

'We'll soon see about that.'

'What do you mean?'

'You'll show by your actions.'

'I'm telling you now, it won't be an issue again. If you can forgive me this time. But that's the trouble. You've never forgiven anyone anything since you grew up in that house and left it.'

He was talking about Ireland again. A place she hadn't visited in over eighteen years. He was always talking about Ireland. She never thought about it.

The rush-hour traffic was terrible and she sat in it for an hour. She stopped crying only when she pulled into the hospital car park. When she'd dried her face she put on some moisturiser and dialled a number from her car phone as she waited for her eyes to return to normal.

'First Investment, can I help you?'

'Can I speak to George Morehampton, please?'

Helen had thought to wait until Saturday, but for some reason she felt that the earlier she began the better it would be. It was a diversion.

'Hello, George Morehampton.'

'George, Helen Larkin here.'

'Helen, I thought your second name was Clarke.'

'No, I didn't change my name after I married Euan.' Unlike your wife, who was made to. The man made Thatcher look left wing.

'I need some confidential advice. By that I mean very confidential. I don't even want Catriona to know about it.'

The silence that followed was long enough to make Helen cringe for fear that she had been too obvious and short enough to make sure there was no trace of impropriety on the part of George Morehampton. He took his manners seriously.

'Come into the office. What time suits you?'

'Lunchtime?'

Another brief silence before George had recovered enough to say yes. Helen smiled for the first time in two days. She could hear George's consternation and Catriona complaining about it.

'He goes to the loo twice a day, morning and evening, same time. He won't ever hear of me coming to lunch because he goes out with the other senior management to the same place. The only person he will cancel for is a customer. When he makes love to me I know how long it will take, and he does exactly the same things in exactly the same order. He gets his hair cut every second Wednesday. He likes to go for a week to Scotland and two weeks to Cornwall. He hates abroad. George cannot accept that the world is not square and if he finds out it is he will get a mallet and hammer.'

'Lunchtime,' George returned. 'I think that will be fine. After all, you're a customer.'

'I know you'll keep this secret, George.' Helen was attempting to smile. How did someone so good-looking ever get to be so unimpressive? He was much more classically handsome than Euan. Tall and dark with piercing blue eyes. His frame was that of a sportsman – rugby in winter and cricket in summer. A perfect Englishman, except he was not charming. He was as awkward as she was. The tea his secretary had brought in had grown as cold and grey as the room they were sitting in. Helen had thought he'd at least offer to take her out for a sandwich, but the fact that it was lunchtime had passed George by.

'Fine, Helen. We can look at some options that will perform well for you but don't represent too much of a risk. Although I must point out all investment is risky.'

So why are you in it, George? You've never risked a pair of pants. 'That's fine, George, whatever you say. I must thank you for the advice. I'm lost when it comes to numbers.' That, at least, was the truth.

George's suit was expensive and unfashionable. Catriona must have let him shop for it on his own. He'd probably been to the same tailor for years.

'Aren't you hungry?' She made a last-ditch attempt to get him out of the office.

'I'm afraid it's past two and I never leave the office after two. In case someone calls. I've asked Tracey to bring me back a sandwich.' George said it like he'd threatened to run nude through the building.

'Fine. See you on Saturday, then, for dinner. All of us.'

Back in the car she thought through the meeting. He hadn't risen to any of her attempts to get friendlier. She might as well have been a new client rather than a friend of over a decade's standing. She'd never forget the day when Catriona, who once had, if not a glittering career, then one that was about to sparkle, bounced into the bed-sit she and Euan shared, like a stray sunray, and said she had fallen in lust with a member of the local Conservative Club who'd invited her to his end-of-season rugby bash.

They'd laughed until they realised it was going to end up as a marriage.

'Why?' Helen had not even bothered to hide her disbelief when Catriona had told them of her intention to accept George's proposal at Angelo's, eight years ago.

'Because he's everything I should want. And I can live with the things I don't like. He's as safe as houses. And he's got a big one. Very, very big.'

And they'd all watched her give up the stage for something none of them thought she was suited to. But they were wrong, Catriona embraced her new role with a vigour Helen could only admire. She was much better with her kids than Helen was with hers, much freer. And she was a good wife to George, if chaotic.

'He's made me promise not to wear kohl to the management dinners,' Catriona once sighed. 'Or jangly jewellery. He says it's nice, but not right for our life.'

Helen looked at her own bare face and puffy eyes – no sleep, too much booze and a broken heart would not be recommended at any skin-care counter, though Dette would say it was the diet of the average model.

What had she been thinking of? To seduce you needed to look seductive. She looked disposable. Only one person could help with this. She phoned Dette. 'Can you come shopping for clothes with me? I'm the back of a bus.'

'Of course. Always happy to help other people spend their money. Especially now I have none of my own.'

'Why not?'

'I'm unemployed.'

'Oh.' Helen didn't know what else to say. 'How did that happen?'

'My boss sacked me, but don't worry, Helen, I know you worry about everyone. This is the best thing that's happened to me in a long time. Really.'

Helen could hear the element of persuasion, the bewilderment. Dette loved that magazine and her pots of goo. It had been her life since the end of a marriage that had never begun.

'I might even get a haircut,' Helen offered. Dette had been threatening to attack Helen in the night with scissors for as long as they'd known each other, and they'd known each other too long.

'Oh, please,' Dette laughed, 'I may see you at your job if you keep this up.'

An ambulance siren drowned their conversation.

'You see? I'm already there.'

Helen went through the automatic doors just ahead of the paramedics carrying two builders who had fallen when a faulty scaffold collapsed. Half an hour later, as she fought to save one of their lives, she'd forgotten that by Saturday she would be seen as she had never been seen before.

5

A Soho coffee bar at five to eleven. Dette was on her third cigarette and Helen was complaining of nausea.

'Listen,' Dette said. 'I'm nauseous at having to get up before midday on a Saturday. Do you think you could lay off me about a couple of fags?'

Helen was not eating her croissant because she was nervous. Dette was not eating hers because she never ate. They were fighting over Helen's rash offer to cut off all her hair. Dette was holding her to it.

'I read somewhere you should never have your hair cut in a crisis.'

Dette raised her eyebrows and upper lip in a way only Dette could. 'Never get your hair cut on your own in a crisis. You have me with you. You can't do this to me. I practically had to give Jude a blow-job, which is what his salon is called, by the way, to get you an appointment. I don't want you being rude to him.'

'He's gay, isn't he?'

'He could've closed his eyes and pretended. And he

would've if he hadn't had one cancellation in a fortnight and that happened to be on a Saturday, and he put you in at the top of his waiting list.'

'OK, OK, but please don't make me too stylish,' Helen begged. 'I don't think I could stand it. Everyone will ask me what happened and why now. The first thing any betrayed wife seems to do is go out and get a new image.'

'If you keep this up,' Dette warned, 'I'll have to abandon you and go and do something selfish.'

'I've never gone out for a day's shopping with anyone. Even my wedding dress was a Monday-morning raid on John Lewis. I just never understood looking at more than one thing when the first thing fits you.' A growing sea of fabric, which Dette was pouring into her arms, submerged Helen. And they were only in the first shop. Full of snobbish assistants showing their nostrils. Full of things that seemed to cost more than a car, and the less of it there was, the more it cost.

'Do you ever do anything but work?' Dette looked at her.

'Now, don't give out to me. You were just the same until this week. You lived for that job, Dette.'

'I did, because I did nothing but enjoy myself and chase new perfumes. Inserting catheters? Mouth-to-mouth with the dying? I'd rather die myself. You live on a different planet.'

'This is a different planet,' Helen waved at the waxed floor, the mirrored walls. Clothes seemed to be a low priority in all this architectural splendour. It looked like it had been robbed. But it was *doing* that, with the prices it charged. 'And I'm the alien.' She surveyed her scuffed shoes – her lightweight trousers and blouse would have been rejected by a charity shop.

'My God, Helen, be careful there. You might just make a joke.' Dette threw a chiffon, viscose, bellicose skirt thing at her. 'We'll start with that.'

'Can I help you?' An assistant marched over, antlers bristling at the careless handling.

'You can. Dette Morgan, *Madame*. Doing a makeover. Need some coffee and accessories. Now, if you can manage it, later if you want us to go somewhere else and credit them.'

'Dette Morgan? I read you every month. Your piece on skin-tone blenders changed my life! My nose was always red before you. I never go anywhere now without your number one. And it's half the price of my old brand. You're a sensation.' The pawing stag had turned obsequious fawn.

'Thanks,' Dette wobbled, or maybe it was the subtle lighting, which no doubt added a hundred quid to the cost of each item. 'It's nice to be appreciated.' Helen hoped Dette wasn't going to lose it and say she'd just been sacked. 'Actually, I must tell you – they've found a cure for the Big C.'

'Cancer?' Helen raised her head.

'No,' Dette and her new best friend hissed. 'Cellulite.'

And they had a fevered discussion for a full five minutes, which resulted in one assistant dashing out to buy two pots of new goo before the rush started on it. The other led Helen and Dette to the changing area, like she was guiding royalty. 'You're so brave,' she gushed at Dette. 'You write the truth about beauty. We know we can trust you.'

'And it's cost me.' Helen watched as Dette took on the St Joan mantle, ermine trimmed of course. No politically correct fake-fur nonsense. 'But I'm willing to pay the price, so you don't get ripped off.

'Now this woman,' Dette pointed at Helen, 'is going to be part of a makeover called Five Easy Pieces. How to transform a lifeless, dowdy appearance with five items, which interweave, mix and match to make up two or three different looks. Can you do it? And can you give it to us for the price of four?'

Outside the shop, laden with what she had to admit was a whole new identity in dinky carrier bags, Helen said, 'You're not going to make me do a magazine shoot, are you?'

'Well, now that I think of it, I am, or they'll be sending me a bill for the free clobber. And I have to make money somewhere. "Frumpy Doc to A and E Siren" is good copy. The best, in fact. You'll be my first freelance venture.'

'I'm not sure about this, Dette – my reputation.'

'And what about mine? Are we not helping each other out?' Dette had a fag in her hand, even though the one in her mouth was still burning.

'Who's going to take the Before shots?' Helen resigned herself to what had already happened – to smelling like a chimney.

'Me. With a disposable camera I'm going to have to buy right now before we go to Jude's.'

'Who exactly is Jude, and why is he the God of Hairdressers?' Helen asked in the newsagent's.

'Believe me,' Dette snickered, 'you'd rather not know. Now, stand against the wall, say, "Cheese", and make sure we see those shoes. Ecco, or something similarly awful, are they? Give me corns over them any day.'

'You need comfort when you're on your feet all day. I can't help it if comfort's frumpy,' Helen sighed.

'You're a frump with the potential to make any man want you. Your height, your skin, your arse, it's all perfect and it all belongs to you. What a waste. If I had it I'd have earned ten thousand for getting out of bed each day. To-night the lads, whichever one you're after, will be eating out of your hand.'

They'd arranged to meet for dinner at Angelo's with their partners to get the ball rolling on the seduction.

'And what about whichever one you're after?' Helen teased. 'Does he stand a chance?'

'Only if he's sitting down,' Dette grinned. 'Or he'll be bowled over. I'm dusting off the Scarlett O'Hara.' Dette Morgan's plunging red neckline never failed for her.

'If we see anything that would suit Bea, will you tell me?'

'Everything we see will suit Bea. She's stunning and she knows what to do with it. I reckon she'll be one of the greats, you know.' Dette's eyes were shining. 'The catwalk, the covers are all waiting for her. For her birthday I'm fixing her up with a booking at Assets, the modelling agency. She'll be signed, no problem.'

Helen reserved that kind of awe, of prediction, for Nobel Prize winners. Dette saw the dismissal without even looking at her.

'The only problem,' her fag was pointing again, emphatically, 'is her mother. Who won't see that not everyone has to be a world-saver, and sometimes the beautiful do a lot more good than do-gooders. Give her a break, Helen.'

Helen didn't answer. So much was happening at once

that she couldn't risk it. Those tears again, threatening to flood. She was beginning to feel she was no good at anything but saving people's lives. That is, the lives of everyone except those she loved.

'Now get your chequebook out. You're about to spend two hundred and thirty quid on a haircut and highlights.'

'I never understood hairdressers.'

'Well, I haven't washed or dried my own hair for fifteen years. And next week, if my bank balance is correct, I'm going to have to.'

Jude the Coiffeur, owner and head stylist of Blow Job, put a hand on his leather-clad hips and pouted. 'She won't let me do nothing, Dette.'

'I told you you had a style virgin on your hands.' Dette put out her fag slowly, to give Jude time to calm down, and herself time to think before she faced Helen.

'Who cuts her hair normally? Someone at the bingo? I mean, it's just hair – it doesn't say anything about her.'

'Her husband, with the kitchen scissors,' Dette shrugged. 'Every six months.'

She expected Jude to have a fit, but instead he lost the offhand manner that he knew the posh gits who paid through the nose loved him to use – it made them feel even more exclusive. He ran a hand over his own number four – five pounds at a barber's, fifty at his place.

'That's why she's so upset.' Dette saw the chink in his armour, 'It's the end of an era, and a very expensive one at that. You can get someone murdered for cheaper than a haircut in here.'

'Why isn't he doing her hair any more?' Jude wanted to know.

'Because he had an affair.'

'Oh.'

'Give me a moment alone with her, will you?'

Dette had slipped out for a fag while Helen had her consultation with the man who'd been London's most sought-after stylist since he took a half-inch off Julia Roberts and gave Kate Winslet a crop that got her six major motion-picture offers.

Helen was thinking of picking up what was now lying on the floor and seeing if someone would stick it back on with some hair glue.

'This thing that I am sitting in,' Helen hissed tearfully at Dette in the mirror, 'is an antique dentist's chair. I am paying two hundred and thirty quid to sit in a dentist's chair. I'm letting a man who thinks calling a place Blow Job and using a phallic hairdryer logo – and *don't* tell me tacky is the new tasteful – decide what my hair is going to look like. Now it's gone, and what's left of it is going to be pink. Pink! I keep thinking of all the people who were tortured in this chair and now it's my turn!'

'Relax, Helen,' Dette urged. 'The dye is pink. The finished result won't be. And the antique chairs go with the antique look of the place. Old is the new modern. And when he's done you'll be able to see how much better it looks. Don't judge it now, please, honey.'

Helen's shoulders slumped and she started to weep.

'Helen.' Dette wasn't sure what to do next. One of the reasons she and Helen liked each other so much was they never had to be huggy and kissy with each other, which most friendships in this new century seemed to require. They never had to disclose, chum up, let go. 'Stop it. Please. I might have to hug you or something. I can't, Helen, please don't make me.'

Helen was beyond listening. Of all the times to lose it, it had to be over her hair, not her husband, her alienated daughters, the six people who'd been put in coffins this week. She had to break down in a place with mirrored walls. Everyone, *everyone*, was watching.

'Dette, please, clear my area,' Jude had returned and without warning he slipped his arm round Helen. Squeezed her like she was a juicy orange. She seized. 'My own hubby got his marching orders last year. We got married in Vegas and everything. Cost me a fortune. I had us in matching everything. We were supposed to be made in heaven, see? He didn't even leave behind the cufflinks when he went off with his new toyboy.'

Dette shut her eyes, hid behind the mirror wall around the dais where Jude the coiffeur paid court to the locks of the rich, famous, beautiful and Helen Larkin. Helen would now erupt with anger at personal-space invasion. She would leave and Dette would have to take her to a public toilet to rinse out the pink stuff. Never do a friend a favour.

But Helen didn't. She just sniffed, reached for a tissue and her eyes found Jude's in the mirror.

Dette sighed and remembered what she swore by. Good hairdressers were better than any shrink and cheaper because they did two jobs at once. Made you feel better about yourself without all that serious analysis, then sent you off looking fabulous.

Jude was now easing off one of the foil strips like he was taking the bandage off an injured cat. 'Sorry about being so rude, love, earlier. Dette should have said you was going through a bad patch. I'm only rude because the customers like to think they've got an appointment because I turned away Kate Moss. And I could have told you, love – never get your hair done in a crisis.'

'That's what I told her,' Helen pointed at Dette.

'I'll explain what I'm doing, shall I?' Jude picked at some strands to see if the colour was right. 'I don't normally explain. I'm making you a strawberry blonde with copper undertones and I cut off half your hair to make you twice what you are now and younger an' all. I'm gonna go classic cos I don't think I'm ever gonna see you again. At least it'll last a long time and no cheap scissors can mess it up too bad. And I'm doing the whole lot half price, cos I like you. And no smoking in the salon, Dette.'

Dette nearly dropped her cigarette. But she ignored him and kept it lit. Jude the Coiffeur, or Jude Mackenzie, son of Mrs Mackenzie of Mile End, a famous pawn-broker who ran a business from her living room, never offered anyone a discount for anything. 'What about me?' she complained. 'I've got a broken marriage, too, you know. Any time I could afford it I came here and paid you full whack.'

'Yes,' Jude agreed. 'And you get enough muck for nothing.'

Dette couldn't say, 'Not any more.' Her sacking was still a secret from her business contacts. If word got out she was over, she really would be over.

Two hours and a packet of cigarettes for Dette later, Helen Larkin walked out with a feathered fringe and a sleek bob that came to her shoulders. The lightened shade was still warm enough to make her pale skin glow and the brightness brought a smile to her face. She kept sneaking glances in shop windows.

'I can't bear to touch it. It's so beautiful. But all the pulling and dragging and drying's given me a headache.'

'Beauty hurts, Helen. Let's keep moving.' Dette was still smarting.

'Aren't we going to have something to eat? It's lunch-time and I'm starving,' Helen said firmly. 'And you're too skinny.' She eyed Dette's figure, clad in habitual black. 'Let me teach you something about enjoying yourself. We're having a nice healthy meal in that vegetarian place I spotted round the corner and then we'll hit more bou-tiques.'

'Boutiques!' Bernadette raised her eyes to heaven. 'That went out with Joan Collins, Linda Evans, pink eye-shadow and the shoulder pad.'

'And eating, by the looks of you.'

After the healthiest meal Dette had eaten in years, she smiled at Helen. 'I must say, for barefoot food, it's bloody gorgeous.' Dette smacked her lips after a healthy portion of Shepherdess Pie. 'Almost as good as the real thing. Though I like a bit of lamb-kill under my spud.'

The children were eating dinner and fighting to get Euan's attention to tell him what they'd been doing that day. They didn't hear Helen come in and she didn't dis-turb them. She slipped up the stairs, hung up her new wardrobe and winced at some of the monstrosities that peered out from the old. When she came into the kitchen she was in a tracksuit, her feet bare to let the blisters breathe.

'What did you do to your hair?' Euan asked, and the children stared. Bea put down her coffee and looked like she'd seen a ghost.

'It's beautiful,' Euan said. 'A bit better than one of my hatchet jobs. Don't suppose you'll be wanting one of them any more.'

She registered the pain on his face and felt it with him. It was all changing, after too long when nothing changed.

'You look like an angel,' Kelly said, with reverence. She had a big thing for angels at present.

Joyce was looking at Helen's toes, manicured and painted moonstone blue. Dette's treat. It had cost twenty-three pounds fifty and Helen had treated Dette back, that way they didn't feel guilty. Not that Dette had much to feel guilty about – a dress for sixty-five pounds. Helen, in contrast, had a credit-card bill on its way to the two thousand-pound mark. Joyce ran her chubby fingers over her toes and Helen scooped her up and showed her the same on her fingernails. 'Do you like it?'

Joyce nodded shyly.

Bea and Euan watched each other. Helen didn't try to include Bea – too much too soon. For all of them.

'I have a bottle in my bag. Would you like me to put some on you?'

Joyce nodded again, too overcome to speak. Helen left the kitchen with her, and Kelly shouted, 'Me too.'

Upstairs, in the bedroom she had shared with Euan for ten years without ever thinking of a time when she wouldn't, she took out two bags and handed them to her children.

'I bought something for you two.'

Inside the girls found soft, cool dresses with embroidered trim. The price tags were outrageous, but Helen had not winced when she paid for them.

'You look like fairies!' she said as the girls slipped

them over their heads and danced around the room. 'Me too. I've got a fairy dress.'

And she put on a powder blue cotton shift that fell from her shoulders in a bias cut.

'My three beauties.' Euan stood in the doorway.

But the eyes with which she wouldn't look at him said he only had two.

Bea's curiosity got the better of her. She glanced on tiptoe over Euan's shoulder. Helen saw that her hair was plaited, like she hadn't been bothered to wash it. Not like Bea. She looked skinnier, paler, if that were possible. Next stop anorexia. It was coming, and Helen didn't want to think about it. But it was coming. Bea wasn't wearing make-up. Not like her. There was a lack of energy there.

When Helen was small she had watched her mother dress then put on a face to go out to a pub with her father and sit, making no conversation. It was partly why Helen hated make-up, like it put a gloss on things that shouldn't be glossed over. When she looked at Bea she looked at her mother. There was a resemblance that made Helen hurt inside. This was the granddaughter her parents had never made an attempt to see. Also, with war paint, Bea looked so much older, and Helen already felt like she had made another of her. Bea had had to grow up too quickly because of what she hadn't been given.

Now, with her hair plaited and her fresh face, however pale, planted on Euan's shoulder, she looked her age. Helen wanted to rush up to her and kiss her. Instead she picked up a bag and held it out, afraid to go any nearer. 'I bought you something, too.'

'From Monde? For me? Wow,' Bea almost smiled, but her eyes held it back.

'I got one for all of us,' Helen explained. 'I thought we could wear them out together some time.'

'Go easy on the bonding, Helen.' Helen hated the way Bea had taken to calling her by her first name.

'Do you want to see it or not?' She couldn't help snapping.

Euan was putting on his Zen face, his implacable about-to-sort-out-another-scrap face. The little girls were twisting the fabric of their dresses, waiting for it too.

'OK,' Bea surprised them. She sidled into the room, snatched the bag and pulled out the turquoise and gold shift. Her eyes widened. 'My God, it's gorgeous. Where did you get the hair?' She said it like anyone could get hair like Helen's.

'Jude at Blow Job, the place off Neal Street. Where some stars go.' Dette had given her their names and made her say them ten times over, but already they'd disappeared.

'Kate Winslet and Julia Roberts,' Bea said, as if it were ABC and Helen was illiterate.

'Why don't you try it on – the dress?' Helen swallowed the annoyance, made it go somewhere else.

'OK.'

'Yes!' The little girls were excited, twirling and swooping. 'We can be princesses.'

Bea disappeared into the en-suite. The last time Helen had seen her naked was months ago and she'd expressed concern for her daughter's skinniness – she could see every rib.

'Well, I don't have your eat-all-I-want gene. If we knew who my father was we might have known that.'

Helen had never tried to find him because she hadn't known how to. He had left the grubby hotel where people went to do such things before she did. Now she resisted the urge to say that Bea's arms looked like sticks.

'It fits, and it's lovely. Perfect size.'

'Yes, I'm amazed you knew it. You were shopping with Dette, weren't you? She'd know it.'

Helen nodded. Bea was leaving and the girls were trooping after her to see themselves in the only full-length mirror in the house, in Bea's room.

Helen whispered – Euan heard – 'Dette didn't have to tell me.'

6

'Why do you want me to come?' Euan was driving them to Angelo's for dinner.

'Because everyone else has their partner, and I don't want them to think anything is out of place. Why do you not want to come? You always like seeing the girls. It wasn't one of them, was it? You'd tell me if it was one of them?'

'Please, Helen, stop this. Have you said anything to them?'

'No.'

It was the first lie she could remember having told him outright. Though she had kept things from him.

'No one will recognise you.' Euan glanced at her. 'You're so beautiful now.'

'God, the tact of that.'

'Sorry, you know what I mean. I'm not good at dressing things up, Helen, and you've always liked the truth.'

There was a mile of semi-stagnant traffic to sit in before they made another attempt at conversation.

'Am I more beautiful like this?' she couldn't help asking.

'No. The first time I saw you you were the most beautiful woman I'd ever seen.'

'In a donkey jacket on a wet hillside?'

'Yes. And when I saw you hold our newborns. You were beyond beautiful then.'

She didn't want to talk about that.

'There will only ever be one woman for me,' Euan was not looking at her any more, just studying the road. 'I can't imagine being with anyone else, Helen.'

'You've already tried.'

The rest of the journey passed in silence. They were the last to arrive at Angelo's. They were always late when they went out together. This hadn't changed.

The noises of surprise and appreciation made her do something she hadn't done since she was a teenager – she blushed.

'Give us a twirl,' Rorie's partner John asked.

'Give us a kiss,' Martin, Dette's boyfriend, rocked his chair back on two legs and pouted.

Helen, looking directly at Dette, was the only one who saw the brief spasm of something before it twisted into a smile that said, 'Men!'

'You look amazing,' Rorie was staring at her like she'd never seen her before. 'I wish I'd known you were going shopping. I'd have gone with you.'

'You!' Helen laughed. 'I'd have to do the op on your jeans first. You're even worse than me when it comes to fashion.'

'What? I'm wearing a dress tonight. I'd have liked to come with you. I wouldn't mind a few more frocks.'

'You weren't invited,' Dette said pointedly. 'It's bad enough having one frump to transform. Two might have finished me off.'

'You think Helena Christiensen is frumpy.' Catriona chided.

'So she is.' Dette put another cigarette in her mouth, much to the consternation of George, who was seated beside her. 'What she and those other overpaid wagons wear when they're not walking the catwalk is an outrage.'

'Enough,' Helen ordered.

'Where do you want us to sit?' Euan was hanging back.

'Well, we're going to do a little partner-swapping this evening,' Rorie blushed as she said it. 'A different partner at every course, beginning with aperitifs, ending with dessert.'

'I don't know why,' George grumbled. 'We'll have to change the place settings and everything.'

'Don't be silly, darling. We just use the clean cutlery at each one.' The edge in Catriona's voice was unmistakable.

'But that's unhygienic.'

'George, should you be struck down with a mysterious cutlery illness I will save you.' Helen's remark made everyone else smile, but George looked at her gratefully. He was already picking up his starter fork and cleaning it studiously with a napkin.

'We ordered for you,' Dette explained. 'It was past the hour and George likes to eat exactly on it, don't you, George, love?'

'Nothing wrong with regularity,' he defended himself.

'Nothing wrong at all, George,' Helen agreed. They, the responsible ones, knew that.

'OK. Start off with your old familiars and move on to something new next course. Helen, you take a place with Euan beside John and then, after drinks, we get down to business. Those who get on well can put their keys in the middle of the table. And that's a joke, George,' Rorie said.

'It's easy to see why she's such a successful stage manager.' John put an arm around her. 'Everyone has to do what they're told around Rorie.'

'Oh, really, John? Then why haven't you left your wife?' Helen said as she sat next to him.

The others pretended they hadn't heard.

Everyone else was well oiled and chatting like talking was banned from tomorrow. John had turned his back on her after her dig at him. He was picking at a Caesar salad and she could see the hairs on the back of his squatty neck. It wasn't a pleasant view, but it was either look at that or stare at Euan. They had attempted to speak to each other, but wherever they went the shadow was waiting. She was used to awkward silences with people she didn't know. There were only three places where she felt comfortable – with patients, with Euan and with these friends. Now she'd lost one of the comfort zones.

The rest of the table was bright and busy, but the women all listened with their second ears to the silence between Helen and Euan and counted the minutes to when they could release her from it. Rorie gave Angelo the nudge to hurry the next course up. He came to the table to announce its arrival.

'Hello, George.' He patted his shoulder.

Gorgeous George was a gay man's dream and Angelo was happy to point this out to him at every available opportunity. Especially since he knew how uncomfortable it made George. Over the years George tried to play along with Angelo, but never as well as he did on a rugby field.

'How am I looking?' he asked.

'Terrible, as usual,' Angelo sighed.

George had a uniform for out-of-office hours as much as the in-office ones: Ralph Lauren polo shirts – long-sleeved in winter, short in summer (it didn't matter if it was a freezing summer day or a warm winter one, the short sleeves came out on 1 May and the long on 30 September) – chinos, loafers and casual sports jacket. Catriona never went shopping with him because he liked to set off on a Saturday morning early and have breakfast before hitting Bond Street on the button of nine. He went to the same people who sold him the same clothes and he came home to Campden Hill Road, off Kensington High Street, happy, at half-past twelve, in time to take the kids for their Saturday swimming.

'First course over, swiiitch!' Rorie yodelled.

He seemed happy now, for George. Helen slid into the seat beside him and immediately stabbed him in the foot with her chair leg.

'Sorry.'

'Don't mention it.' He was purple with pain.

Relief of getting away from Euan made Helen smile warmly at her target. To her surprise, she didn't have to start the talking. 'You look very nice, Helen.'

From George this was high praise indeed. The man never said anything he didn't mean and found any conversation outside investments and sport painful. 'He has one weakness. Women,' Catriona had complained to her once.

'George has a glad eye?'

'No! If you put him in a room with a squash racket and one hundred naked girls he'd fiddle with the strings of the squash racket and ask them if anyone had a ball. His weakness is he can't speak to us. He doesn't know what to say.'

'So how did you come to be with him?'

'We were both drunk. Come to think of it, we both got drunk every time we met for the first six months of our relationship and, as you know, we got married in the seventh month and conceived in it too. I only found out he was no good with women-type things when I was in labour for the first time,' Catriona sighed. 'He kept patting my hand and saying "Good girl", and looking like he was the one who was going to die.'

Euan had been there from start to finish. He had practically pushed Kelly out.

Poor George, Helen thought. And poor me. I'm his female equivalent.

And that was how it hit her that she didn't have to flirt with him. He was unfamiliar with nuance, much as she was. What she had to do was empathise with him about their mutual lackings.

'Hey, George.' She tapped his arm. He was busy trying to separate the fat from his Parma ham. The whole point of Parma ham was the fat, the flavour.

'We're the only two serious people at this table,' she said. George looked puzzled. 'What I mean is, too serious. We have serious jobs, serious lives. Even our hobbies are serious.'

'I play cricket. That's not serious, it's laughable.'

'You play to win.'

'We never do.'

'But you'd like to.' Helen was finding it hard work empathising with George. He took things too literally, just as she did.

'True,' he admitted. 'And I do play rugby in winter. That's serious.'

'You see?' Helen almost laughed. 'I go on anti-globalisation marches. Before that I went on anti-apartheid marches and before that I went on St Patrick's Day marches because my mother made me be a majorette.'

'A majorette?' Even George was intrigued.

'A majorette?' Euan echoed, from the other end of the table.

'Yes, a majorette. But even that was serious. I was so scared of dropping the baton in front of the thousands watching that I almost cried. And I was cold. St Patrick's Day marches are always conducted in sub-zero conditions down O'Connell Street in Dublin. The coldest street in the world. But that's not the point,' she interrupted herself. 'The point is, George, you and I are a couple of killjoys. We have to try to learn how to have fun.'

There was a sudden silence, the kind that tells you everyone has wind chill. Jaysus, Helen Larkin, you're supposed to empathise with him, not insult him. Euan went back tactfully to his conversation with Rorie.

George looked as if his world was falling apart after Helen's battering with a bulldozer in first gear. The point was, everyone knew George was boring and said he was boring, but no one mentioned it to him, except Catriona.

'Sorry,' she tried to retract. 'I didn't mean that the way it sounded.'

'Don't be,' he said, after a pause. 'I know I'm not the most exciting man. In fact, I'd go so far as to say I'm even less charming than you.' Now Helen knew how he'd felt.

'I'm Irish,' she said. 'I'm supposed to have loads of it.'

'I'm English. I'm supposed to be the perfect gentleman.'

'I never remember jokes,' Helen revealed.

'Oh, I do, but I never tell them.' George sighed.

'Why not?'

'Because the funniest joke in the world sounds unfunny when I tell it. But when I was eight I won the Best Joke award in the school magazine. So I must have been funny at one time.'

'What did you win?'

'A whoopee cushion.'

'What happened to it?'

'My father found it, pronounced it a disgusting item and stuck a pin in it, then threw it in the dustbin.'

'How did he find it?'

'He sat on it. I left it on his office chair.'

Helen laughed, too loud, too long.

'Steady on, Helen. It wasn't that funny.'

She knew it wasn't. But it was the first time she had

ever found George amusing and this caught at her tightened stomach and released all the tension. 'I can't imagine you as a cheeky little kid.'

'Well, what do you see me as?'

'A boy in a business suit.'

'I never wanted to be a businessman.'

'Oh, really?' Helen was wondering if George was going to surprise her even more. 'What were you going to be?'

'A rugby player.'

'Oh, really,' Helen repeated, flat.

Catriona, watching them from across the table, interrupted, 'You're just about to get George's I-could-have-been-a-contender speech.'

Helen had always thought Catriona to be a mouse, but she had a sharp and nasty nibble once in a while and always at George.

'Sorry,' George whispered.

'Don't be,' Helen offered. 'Tell me.'

And she heard a tale that had a lot of sporting references, which went over her head, but a lot of stuff she could relate to. A young man gets a trial for the county youth squad, but his overbearing father forbids him to attend. The boy tries to go secretly, but the father locks him in his room, to get him to study. He also orders him not to attend training for the school team and calls the house from work to make sure his son is at home. If he is not he will be asked to leave, at sixteen, to fend for himself. This is not a threat. It has already happened to George's older sister.

'Why did you give in to that?' Helen was horrified. She'd thought George to have had a problem-free existence – privileged background, good looks, brains. If she was honest she'd always been a bit jealous.

'I had nowhere to go if he threw me out.' George had stopped picking at his Parma ham and had even forgotten his precisely buttered bread roll. 'That's how the English differ from the Irish – no extended family. I was alone in the world but for my sister and mother, and they had the same problems with Dad as I did. He was just a sergeant major without a platoon.'

'What happened to you? Could you not play when you left home and went to university?'

'I ended up with three grade-A A levels and the job I'm in today.'

'George, I'm sorry.'

'Don't be. I earn a six-figure sum. I have four children, one wife and a nice car. I play rugby or cricket most Sundays for the thirds and the seconds. Life is OK. My dad might have been right. It was too great a risk.'

Angelo's waiter came along to whisk away plates – George looked after his bread roll longingly but was too polite to ask for it back. It was time to move places. Helen took George's story with her and found her eyes drawn to him from time to time. He looked as boring as before. But behind the dullness she saw the loss, and it made her want to talk to him again.

Now that she was back in the loop, with no conquest plan, she watched Euan laughing and joking with Dette and Catriona, who were his partners for the next two courses. The way they were lapping it up you'd have sworn they didn't know. But then, she had asked them to behave like that, hadn't she?

Had one of them pulled his name out of the hat? It was impossible to tell. She shifted uncomfortably. 'Please,' she whispered to herself, 'don't let him give in.'

She looked at her three friends and it was like she hadn't known them before now. Before, she would have noted their every move and known what it was about. What had changed? Later on, she realised it was trust.

It hadn't vanished, but it was ebbing away, like a night tide.

At the end of the meal no one seemed ready to leave. Angelo brought more wine and sat down.

'Ah,' he said to Helen. 'Saturday. Why does everyone want to eat out on Saturday? They get better food when a restaurant is not busy.'

'The problem is, during the week they're…' She was preoccupied, watching Euan sit, head inclined, towards Rorie, his final partner for the evening. They'd sat together twice, as it worked out. Was that a sign of anything?

'So,' Angelo whispered, 'how is your little game going?'

'Nothing little about it, Angelo.'

'You are right about this – and you are wrong to play it.'

'Ah, come on. I'm drunk for the second time this week in your restaurant. This idea is making you a fortune,' Helen smiled.

'Who did you pick?'

'Forget it, nosey. If you want gossip you've got the wrong girl.'

'I don't think so,' Angelo laughed. 'I think you are the right one.'

'What do you mean?'

'I mean you are the one with George.'

'I'm not answering that.'

'You don't have to. You just have to tell me that you would like me to do this dirty work for you.'

'Angelo!'

'What? I am the one who should pursue George because he is gay.'

'He has four children.'

'Many gay men have had more.' Angelo lit a cigar and sat back.

Together they looked at George, who was trying to get a tomato stain out of his creaseless beige chinos. Catriona and he looked like they didn't even know each other. She was tousle-haired and wearing linen, crushed by lack of ironing, not design.

'You're not to go near him,' Helen ordered. 'He'd have a heart attack. What is it about gay men that they always think they know when someone else is?'

'They don't think they know. They know.'

'Well, whether he is or not, you stay away. This is going to be hard enough without you interfering.'

'So,' Angelo raised his eyebrow, 'you are his pursuer.'

'I'm not saying and you're not getting involved in this.'

Then George was at Helen's elbow, on his way to the gents'. 'Why did the chicken cross the road?'

'Dunno,' Helen shrugged. 'I panic at punchlines.'

'Well, I won't bore you with the answer, but I will say that I enjoyed talking to you. Thanks.'

He was so genuine Helen wanted to cry – for all the times she had dismissed him and, in doing so, herself.

She was as leaden as he was. 'Everything,' she whispered to Angelo, 'is topsy-bloody-turvy.'

'Helen,' Euan had just extricated himself from a just-out-of-the-door conversation with Catriona, who was drunk. Dette had stood at his other elbow, all red satin and push-up. Both women's cleavages seemed to be vying for Euan's attention, Helen – who was 34A – thought ruefully. 'I want to go home if that's OK.'

'Sure, but we'll leave the car here.'

She was grateful Euan hadn't wanted to stay. Whoever had thrown him bait, he hadn't risen to it.

7

Dette was sitting in the same seat at the kitchen table that Euan had been sleeping at, while waiting for her, only a week before. 'Tell me,' she was urging Helen, 'did you pick Martin?'

'I wish everyone would feck off asking each other who they got. Can't anyone keep secrets?'

'Well, you have the Hippocratic oath to keep you in check. The rest of us can be as fickle as we like. Like I said, if Martin goes as far as the bedroom, you can have him.'

'If it's me who's chasing him.'

Dette went quiet. 'Oh, I think it is – and if it isn't, I think he'll be chasing you shortly anyway.'

Helen laughed because she didn't know how else to hide her embarrassment. 'What makes you say that?'

'Since he saw you yesterday he's said at least five times how amazing you looked. I'm not stupid.'

'That level of paranoia could have you committed.'

'Come on, Helen, he's twenty-five and he's an artist.

To him settling down is sitting still for five minutes.'

'Well, Dette, your choice. Why do you pick them so young?'

'So I can corrupt them.'

'Get out of it.'

'As a matter of fact,' Dette glanced at her watch. 'I have to. I'm meeting Rorie now. She wants advice on how to handle Catriona, who's been on at her to help her break back into the business. Rorie's afraid of what happened last time. And John's writing again.' They both raised their eyes to heaven. John writing meant Rorie would be ignored until he typed 'The End'. 'Where are Euan and the kids?'

'Gone swimming.'

'Would've thought you'd have gone with them.'

'No. It's a Sunday tradition.'

What Helen did not say was that she would've loved to go with them, but she hadn't been asked and didn't know to invite herself. Sundays had always been the day when she caught up on her sleep and put ready-made meals in the oven for when the kids came back with Euan. She'd been glad when Dette had shown up unannounced, although she had felt suspicious. 'I'll have to get on with dinner, even though they won't eat it.'

'Then don't make it. Look, another reason I called over was because I wanted to set eyes on Bea. Can you tell her I've arranged test shots for a couple of weeks' time with Martin's friend Drew? He's the fashion photographer who'll be shooting next month's *Madame* cover. 'I was supposed to be styling that,' Dette sounded wistful. 'I even got Drew the gig. He's doing the shots for Bea as a favour. For someone he thinks is still a mover and shaker, instead of dead slow and stop. That's showbiz. You're in, you're out. Anyway. It's a coup for Bea. Tell her to call me.'

'I will. As long as you tell her to eat something.'

'Don't start on me, Helen. This is her choice.'

'I know, but I'm not that happy about how she's looking.'

'She looked great, last time I saw her. Got to go.'

Helen was just about to start peeling plastic off food when she looked out at the mature garden, now horribly overgrown since Euan hadn't time to sort it out. When he had wondered why she didn't do it, she had told him the Irish didn't garden, they farmed. There was an apple tree groaning with the weight of its crop, half of it fallen to the ground already. 'I'm not making any fecking dinner. I'm making apple tarts.'

A good apple tart was one thing Helen knew how to make, having won a prize for hers in home economics at school. If it was an academic exercise Helen had always been able to rise to the occasion. The recipe had stayed with her, like everything else did. Helen had trouble forgetting anything. Half an hour later every kitchen surface was covered. She turned up the classic hits station on the radio and laughed at herself and what they would say when they got home. The other reason she didn't go swimming, ever, was that she hated the water. Euan said it was because she hated to lose control, but she'd never had an opportunity to learn these things. She hadn't learned to drive until she was in her twenties and had only done so because it was a necessity for work. Euan had taught her, then sworn he'd never do it again.

'You won't have to,' she'd laughed. 'I passed my test.'

'This time. What about when they take the licence back off you?'

Helen's driving was something that everyone said would put her in her own A and E department one day.

Her kids and husband returned to find her floured up to her nose. 'Have you eaten?' she asked.

'Yes,' a guilty chorus came back at her. 'We had burgers at the pool.'

'Good, because it's apple tart and ice-cream for dessert.'

'I can't stay,' Euan said. 'I promised Rorie I'd call over and catch the second half of the Celtic game.'

Don't act like you're suspicious. Do something gracious, Helen admonished herself. 'Oh, fine, bring an apple tart with you. Tell her I was asking for her.'

They watched Celtic together all the time. It didn't mean Rorie was seducing him.

'Helen?' Euan called up to her later that evening. She was in the bathroom, washing the chlorine out of Kelly and Joyce's hair. 'Catriona's on the phone.'

'Tell her to call back later. I'm very busy.' Work was an hour and a half away and she wasn't even going to think about it until she got into her car.

'I think you should come and talk to her.'

'Why?'

'She's upset.' He was outside the door now, with the phone. 'I'll finish off the girls.'

There was no protest at him taking over. They accepted her slipping away as something that happened at least once a day.

*****

'We're married twelve years today and that bastard has played cricket all afternoon. I want to shove the willow up his arse.' Catriona was in full swing.

'You must be gutted,' Helen sympathised. But she resented Catriona's demand to be listened to immediately, however inconvenient. Helen had been bathing her kids, that was more important than listening to this old and tired argument with a new spin.

'He says it's because I told him to ignore it.'

'And did you?'

'Yes, but he's not supposed to.'

'I don't understand.'

'He's supposed to surprise me.'

'Catriona, George's brain does not run to surprises.'

'I thought just this once.'

'You thought wrong – he needs everything spelled out for him. Stop giving him opportunities to fail.'

'I might have known you'd say that.'

'What's that supposed to mean?'

'You know.'

'I don't.'

'I wouldn't be surprised if you'd picked him.'

Helen adopted the calm voice she used in such circumstances. 'Catriona, what's going on with you?'

'It's your new hair,' Catriona was instantly apologetic. 'George has been going on about how lovely you are. I'm glad someone's testing him. Maybe he's been having an affair – or affairs. Maybe he's been seeing an Audrey Hepburn lookalike. Maybe it was Magda with a wig—'

'Stop it, drama queen. I hear you're getting back into the business.'

'In a small way. My arse is so big now that small parts are all I'll get. My leading-lady days were over before they began. It's a part Rorie's got me. I'll hear about it tomorrow when I meet her and the director. I'm scared, Helen – what if George decides to set up home with Audrey or Magda? I've no skills.'

'Will you behave yourself!'

'I can't help it.'

'You can. Stop seeing him for what he's not and start seeing yourself for what you are. You're beautiful, Catriona, even if you have gone loony.'

'Well, thank you. It's what comes of an unoccupied mind. I'm a bit lost at the moment, Helen, something's slipping. And I've got to seduce a man who'll never have any interest in me. Who'd you get? It wasn't George? If it was you're doing a good job of winning him over.'

'I think I know what's up with you. Mad-cow disease. Next time I see you I'm going to give you a nice big injection.'

'Great! Put some confidence in it. You know, this week I saw a woman on telly, Dawn—'

'Catriona, haven't time now. Have to see the kids for a second before I start a seventy-hour week.'

Helen put the phone down. *Femme fatale*. It made a change from Dette having the job.

Rorie didn't phone later to fish and work out if Helen had picked John. She phoned the next day, at seven a.m. again.

'Oh, for God's sake. What is it with you? Are you making a new living as an alarm call?

'No, for God's sake. For curiosity and logic's. Dette and Catriona seem pretty sure you haven't got their men, so you must have mine. Don't be horrible to him, Helen. I know he's a prat, but he's not been all bad to me.'

'Why are you telling me this?'

Suzanne Power

'Because I'm telling everyone. I feel guilty setting John up like this. Especially when I know none of you like him. What chance has he got? One wrong move and you'll eat him alive. And I'm all upset. If you hate him so much, what must you think of me?'

'Are you still ironing for him?'

'Yes. But I like ironing. It relaxes me.'

'Does it relax you to pay your mortgage by yourself?'

'He has a family to support.'

'Listen, Rorie,' Helen had heard the break in her friend's voice. 'I know it's hard for you. It's hard for me to think the man I love so much has been with someone else. But I think it's better to have the truth.'

'I agree.'

'And I'll tell you the truth about one thing. When you were first with John I was a tiny bit envious. He was so exciting. A real writer. And you looked perfect together.'

'Really?'

'Really.' Helen didn't add that it had all changed when she realised he was married.

'So did you get him? In the draw?'

'It makes no sense this, all of you wanting to know. I haven't made one query in this direction and I'm not going to.'

'But we haven't told each other anything! We're waiting until you give in! That's you – disciplined. You never blow your cool. I can't help it if I'm more emotional than you.'

'You aren't this emotional at work, Rorie, or the show would never go on. And you haven't been emotional with John all these years. You've played the game well with him.'

'Only because to play it any other way I would have lost him.'

'Well, maybe you should start throwing wobblies. Now I have to go to something called work. I was on all last night, and I'm in again now, just came home to change clothes.' Twenty-four-hour shifts were common in the job. She did at least two a fortnight.

'Give us a few more minutes. Please. I asked Dette if she'd help me too, to look as good as you. So did Catriona. Dette's pissed off. She says you do one nice thing for someone and look what happens.'

'You know very well Dette's devotion to shopping. She'll have orgasms getting the two of you to spend money. It's not a chore to her.'

'You're right there. She wants to photograph us, put us in a magazine.'

Rorie sounded excited, which was not like her. She was the background person, the woman born wearing jeans and jumpers. Catriona was champing at the bit too. Helen, it seemed, was the only one dreading the transformation feature.

'She might even do Bea, make it a Virgo thing.'

'She bloody won't. Dette's had enough influence there. Bea's too far gone on all this modelling business.'

'Helen, it's what she wants to do.'

And there Bea was, suddenly, pointing at the clock to tell Helen the hospital was waiting, pointing at the apple tart on the counter, mouthing, 'Can I have some?'

'I have to go, Rorie. My daughter is going to eat something.'

'Kelly or Joyce?'

'Bea.' The one no one remembers to call my daughter.

Rorie rang off, abruptly, she still hadn't learned how to finish a conversation. Helen never knew how to start them, so between the two of them they made strangled phone calls.

'There's cream,' Helen pointed to the bowl on the table.

'No, thanks. Like this is fine.' Bea was blowing on it, having overheated it in the microwave.

'It's good to see you eating.'

'I eat all the time, Helen. I stuff my face. You're just never around to see it.'

Helen was about to leave the house when her mobile rang again. 'Yes,' she answered, 'which one of you is it now?'

'Helen?' A male voice.

'Who is this?'

'George.'

'George?'

'Can you meet me for lunch?'

8

'Lamb cutlets, please.'

It had taken George ten minutes to choose from the menu. He hadn't sat still from the moment he had arrived at the restaurant Helen had chosen because it was only ten minutes' walk from the hospital.

'I don't usually have lunch out and I never order lamb when Catriona's about. She makes me feel like I've killed it myself. Thanks for coming, Helen. I expect you want to know why I asked to meet you.'

'I thought it would have something to do with my financial arrangements.' Helen, hoping it was, prayed she hadn't given him so much hope that he'd make a pass at her.

'No, but of course we can talk about those,' George gabbled. 'We can talk about those, of course. No, it's Catriona. I heard her on the phone to you, complaining about me. Came home early from cricket. Heard it all. Terrible, really. It's not that my wife doesn't understand me – I don't understand her and she hates me for it. I'm at the stage where I have to do something about it. On

Saturday, Helen, we had a good talk, didn't we? Steam, Helen, we need to let off steam. It'd be good for both of us.'

'Oh.' Helen watched her salad wilt. The bread in her mouth tasted like cardboard.

'I need a woman who won't get all emotional.'

Helen saw the green exit sign above the door and thought, I can leave. I can leave now before he tries to lay a finger on me. 'I don't know what you mean George,' she said coldly.

His face fell. 'I thought you did. I thought you said we were too serious. We needed to break out a bit.'

'I didn't mean what I think you mean.'

'But I haven't said…Though I suppose you know… and I really shouldn't have thought, but it was just because on Saturday you said…and I thought about it all night and the next day and then you seemed so, I don't know, nice, and I never saw you like that before. Normally you're so…I mean, sorry, you're nice, but you don't let anyone know it. Sorry, I didn't mean that either,' George was purple.

'I think, George, that I'd better go.'

'Fine, yes, fine,' George muttered, and picked up his paper to pretend to read it so that he would have something to do that made him look normal before he left as soon as he could after her.

As Helen stood she saw the advertisement circled in pen.

Ballroom Dancing. Beginners to advanced. All welcome. Madeleina Conti School. Walk in, dance out. Bring loose clothing, plimsolls and a smile.

'George?'

'Hmm?' He was embarrassed now beyond words.

'What exactly were you going to ask me to do?'

'Dancing,' he whispered. 'I want to do dancing. I know this place. It's meant to be good for beginners. So I thought I'd ask you.'

Helen sat again. 'And you can't ask Catriona?'

'No! She'd be far too good and get impatient with me and everything. Anyway, it's for her, to make up for our anniversary. She told me not to remember it, but I always forget that isn't what she means. I need a beginner, someone as bad as me.' He would win no prizes for flattery. 'Her birthday. I thought if I learned a few steps by her birthday I could take her out to dance a little at Angelo's. A surprise.'

'George, what a wonderful idea. But I'm afraid I'm not the sporty type.'

'This isn't sport.' He smiled hesitantly. 'It's a chance to unwind. Express ourselves. I think you'd enjoy it, Helen, I really do.'

'The last time I danced was with Euan at your wedding and I nearly had to treat him afterwards for shock and bruising. I don't do dancy things,' Helen argued.

'You *didn't* do dancy things,' George suddenly got firm. 'I don't want you to think I'm overstepping the mark, but you did say we needed to change a bit, enjoy life more.'

Helen picked up a fork to tackle her tagliatelle. Now that she knew George was not looking to get into her knickers, her appetite had returned. And her enthusiasm to be different from the way she was.

'Which night?'

'Tuesdays,' he could barely get the word out. 'And I know you have to do shifts sometimes, but even if we just got to one or two, it would make a difference.'

'I'll make as many as I can,' Helen promised. 'Why haven't you tried it before, George?'

'I did, years ago, and then I found rugby. Rugby players,' he smiled, 'don't dance. Neither do cricketers or bankers. And I'm all three. It's just a bit girly. I'd hate anyone to find out. And you won't tell Catriona either?' he pleaded.

Remembering what Catriona had said only yesterday, Helen said, 'Your secret's safe with me.'

9

The Madeleina Conti School was less of a school and more of a front room, a big one, boarded and mirrored, the students all sitting in chairs around the edge, trying not catch sight of themselves in the mirror. The average age was ninety, which included Helen and George's to bring it down.

'I thought it was a trendy thing to do now, ballroom dancing.' Helen was lacing up her plimsolls, shocking pink, the only ones to be had in size eight. But she'd rather have died than come without them. Helen had always followed instructions on clothing since the Lake District disaster.

'If you're ninety anything's trendy.' George examined his hands closely. He'd barely looked at Helen since they'd arrived.

'I look like a flamingo.' She surveyed her white track-suit, the only one left in Marks in the long-leg range. Dette hadn't been on hand to help her with this ensemble.

'No, you'd have to stand on one leg.'

'Right now is not the best time to discover your inner comedian, George.'

He seemed nervous, fidgety, but he always seemed that way and, let's face it, she was hardly relaxed herself. If this was what the beginning of an affair felt like, she'd rather have a nice big dinner. She'd missed hers to get to this. The lady beside her whispered to her dancing partner, another lady. They were dressed in matching gold lamé and had the kind of lipstick that made flamingo pink look dull.

'Lovely couple, the new couple.'

'Lovely. Wait till Madeleina sees them. Lovely they are.'

Helen sneaked a look at George. He was in black velour and plimsolls, brand new, just like hers. Another instruction-follower. Very James Bond on him. Anyone else would have looked a prat. No doubt about it, the man made Pierce Brosnan look like a rough diamond. A nice thing about him was his lack of confidence. He could have been a right bighead. Lucky Catriona – if she could only see and draw it out of him, instead of feeling slighted, or irritated, or whatever it was she felt. If she'd any interest in extracting George's poker the way Euan worked on hers, they would have made a nice pair. He was a faithful dog. Like Euan used to be.

The music struck up and the octogenarians, being kind to them, rose to their feet and turned to face each other. Madeleina Conti glided into the centre of the floor, having appeared from behind the curtained area of the room where the music came from. Helen had imagined a wizened old dear done up like Miss Havisham, reliving dreams of past glory. This woman was young, forty or so. Or maybe she was older and knew how to hide it. Dressed in black, dark hair scraped back in a disciplined bun and topped with a black-velvet Alice band. Kohl eyes, red lips, no breasts and big feet. George stopped fidgeting and was staring like he'd never seen a woman in his life. Madeleina Conti was beautiful, in that elegant, skinny dancer, Audrey Hepburn way. Audrey Hepburn. Sure. What was happening to everyone? What was happening to marriage? Why had it survived so long as an institution if all it took for a faithful dog to switch owners was a funeral-clad skinny one with a white cane, pounding out a beat for a bunch of pensioners?

Helen wished she wasn't a doctor; she'd probably have to revive one of this lot after the first tango.

'La dah dah dah dah dah!'

The old dears, mostly women, a few men, were moving to the unmistakable rhythm of South American sexual mystique in violin form. Not surprisingly, the cheer had gone up at the first beat. Most of these people would have been young when the tango was invented. Helen couldn't help being scathing, she wanted to go home. She didn't want to be the hobbled donkey in this fleet of what could only be described as smooth, if aged, racehorses. They were not beginners. They were Madeleina Conti conscripts.

'George!' The teacher was beside them, her eyes shining.

'Madeleina,' he nodded politely.

Helen could read the note in his voice – distance. It was the one she used to keep all uncomfortable situations at bay. If he was interested he certainly wasn't showing it.

And she certainly was. Madeleina moved away from them quickly, evidently hurt by his coldness.

'A customer, is she?' Helen enquired.

'A customer. Shall we?' George took Helen's arm, and removed his eyes from the teacher as if it required effort. He was sweating. Helen watched the pearls on his brow. Then he swung her, and she knew he was a born dancer. And she wasn't. But then, she tried to remind herself as he grinned politely on her third toe crunch, you can't be good at everything. *You* can't be good at anything that isn't work, Helen. You don't try. This was exactly why she was in this position. Dancing, badly, with her friend's husband in South Sheen.

George was humming to the music, whispering encouragement to her. 'Good, Helen, well done, getting better all the time.'

She wanted to deck him, patronising, ballroom-dancing fart.

Madeleina was at George's shoulder. George was refusing to look at her. She smiled at Helen, 'Lovely to see some new faces. Lovely.'

A word that would be found dead in this room from overuse.

'Well, we're trying,' Helen was forced to do the small-talking, the footwork and the steering. Of course it went wrong. Of course she crashed and burned and fell on her bum. And George sprawled on top of her.

'Sorry,' Madeleina offered her hand to them. 'My fault for distracting you.'

George turned to face Madeleina, since he had no option. The colour he went! Was that what public school did to the male psyche? Kept it pubescent into its early forties?

Which was when Helen saw Madeleina's look. Exactly the same as George's. Please, no. Not when she was the one who would have to tell his wife. Some bit of her was sad too. She was supposed to be the one doing the seducing. And here she was, a deranged dyslexic flamingo, while the black swan was doing all the graceful winning.

'George,' Madeleina said it like it was the only name in the world. A name she'd said many times, to herself, waiting to see him again. 'I'm so pleased that you want to dance. It's so good for the soul – loosens it. His soul needs loosening, no?' Madeleina asked Helen.

'This is Helen. She's a friend,' George extended an arm to include Helen in their circle, which was filled not just with attraction but tension, as if they were both hiding something.

'I'm also a friend of George's wife, Catriona. Have you met her?' Helen said it before she could stop herself. The spark between George and Madeleina was threatening to blind her.

'No,' Madeleina's Italian accent was fused with an English intonation. You couldn't tell which she was more of. 'I haven't seen George in over twenty years. Now I see him twice in one month. Lovely.'

'Twenty-two,' George whispered.

'Now, would you like to take your positions?' Madeleina moved away from them as if they hadn't spoken, her mind on her group and instructing them. The part of her that was English was George: cool, professional. 'We'll start again with the waltz, move through it, and the tempo will change and we'll try a cha-cha. Remember, it's fun. Forget your feet, find your partner's eyes. Fall into their rhythm, let them fall into yours.'

'So, you didn't just pick any dance class,' she whispered. Why hadn't he had the guts to come along by himself? No wonder his wife complained about him at every opportunity. Anything outside his routine made him a gutless wonder.

'We'll talk presently. Let's follow what's going on.' George, controlling the control freak. Now she had to cha-cha with him. If robots could cha-cha, they'd look like her.

George, on the other hand, was what George Morehampton should never have been. A natural.

Helen pulled back from him, snapped, 'I thought you said you'd never done this?'

'I haven't, for twenty-two years. The last time was with Madeleina.'

They moved over to their chairs. At this point, Helen liked chairs more than any other object on Earth.

'You said you'd two left feet,' she said, but George was following Madeleina's exit behind the curtain.

'I did. Madeleina uncrossed them for me. I thought they would have got mixed up again. But it's like riding a bike.' He was smiling so broadly she thought he would burst through the walls. He was so obviously in his element. No trace of guilt. Helen found herself wondering if all the passion she'd sensed in him was about the dancing. He just wasn't the affair sort. Now Madeleina, used to men throwing themselves and red roses at her by the looks of it, was a different thing.

'She used to be a ballerina and grew too tall,' George was filling her in. 'She took me dancing with her when her boyfriend couldn't go. I was never as good as him, Ricardo. They could fly together. I only ever filled in.'

'For the demonstration dance,' it was Madeleina again, she had reappeared from behind her curtain. Immaculate, composed. Here was a woman who never sweated. Oh, my God, there's more? 'I'd like to try out our new recruit. Helen, if I could borrow George?'

As if she'd any choice.

Then she had to watch them, in the company of the old lovelies, make synchronicity. They were so familiar with each other that they must have been lovers. Helen couldn't help feeling jealous. Until that point she hadn't known how much she needed to feel attractive, capable of drawing something from men that she'd lost with her husband. It didn't matter how many makeovers she had, she'd never outshine this human wand who was spellbinding the husband of one of her oldest friends. She'd rather stitch up ten drunks than sit through this.

'Never again,' she swore. 'I'm never coming here again.' You have to, said the noble voice of her conscience, if only to keep an eye on him for Catriona.

'Let me walk you to your car,' George was offering and she was refusing, but he wouldn't hear of it. He was evidently feeling guilty for abandoning her to an eighty-six-year-old, Edith Webber, who had been Nutley cha-cha queen in 1949. And seemed hell bent on describing to Helen every detail of that, and of the demise of the current world.

'Back then,' Edith went on, 'you were lucky to have a night out. Now youngsters expect to go out every night of the week and a fight, too, at the end of it. No fighting in my day. We were too busy to fight. You a doctor, you say?'

No. George had said it. Helen would never have

dreamed of imparting this information. Within minutes of it flying around the dancehall, quicker than she ever would, the first patient had slipped into George's empty seat to discuss her piles. 'Wouldn't normally tell no one, dear, but you being a doctor, you'll understand. Any suggestions?'

Yes, but Helen was too polite to say it. She watched George and Madeleina and she listened to the ailments, interrupted only by the applause and calls for encore. They danced five. Helen watched the clock and sighed. Another ten o'clock dinner coming up. The kids would be long asleep.

'It's OK, George, I know where the car is.' And I know you want to run back inside as soon as I'm around the corner.

'No, just in case – we wouldn't want anything happening to you.'

The silence was crippling. She could think of nothing to say that wasn't an accusation.

'How far do you go back with Madeleina?'

'If you don't mind, Helen, I'd rather not talk about it.'

'OK.' She let it go, could see he was close to tears.

'Her husband, Ricardo, he died last year. She's renting this place, hasn't a bean.'

So she was going for the sympathy approach to winning George back. And with a man like George, with his old-fashioned concept of chivalry, it would work. She'd have to call Catriona in the morning. And if she did, how would she explain? She hadn't any proof yet. Physician, heal thyself: you need evidence, not suspicion. Act with reason, Helen, or all is lost in this new, mad world. This was complicated. What wasn't, these days? Helen wondered if Bea had left any apple tart – the girl had made her way through at least one since Sunday. She had a real urge to see her own family, to make her peace with Euan, make it all all right again.

'Madeleina thinks you might get better with a bit of practice,' George said. 'She's offered to take you on your own for a half-hour before the class starts. Next week. You will come next week, Helen?'

'You don't need a partner, George.'

'No, but I do need a friend.'

A man she barely knew, though she'd known him for years, needed her friendship. If she'd been a man, she might have suffered with the same loneliness. If it hadn't been for the Virgos, for Euan, she'd be as alone as George was.

'OK,' she heard herself say, and didn't know why.

He waited until she was in her car and the engine started, then waved once absent-mindedly. She saw him walk back in the direction of Madeleina Conti, then drove off. 'Don't spy on him in the wing mirror to see if he gets into his own car,' she ordered herself, as she spied on him in the wing mirror. Then she didn't have to any more. She drove past his car, parked half a mile up the street.

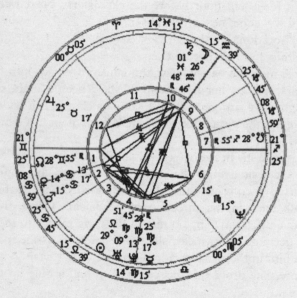

Catriona Morehampton, née Nowdy, female,
Sunday 23 August 1964 at 12.08 a.m.;
Greater London, United Kingdom (51N30'00 0W10'00)

10

CATRIONA

Saturn in the Tenth

You have a vivid imagination and you enjoy rich inner visions. The real world often disappoints you. The arts would be a proper means of self-expression for you. You love the romance of love, but the long-term future of your relationships is open to question. You are devoted to your children, should you have any. Try to realise that you, too, have the right to a little fun once in a while. Let yourself have a fling, even if you feel you have to keep it secret. You are so demanding of yourself that you tend to see the world as a cold, forbidding, merciless, unforgiving place. That's why you are someone who could go into hiding if they're not careful.

*****

Catriona sat behind the wheel of the Volvo she wished was a sports car and thought about the dust on the dashboard. One day she'd clean it. One day. The school run that morning had been doubly horrendous with her hangover – two boys, two girls and a friend who had stayed over with one of them.

She longed to go into the house and fix herself a nice milky drink. She was too organic to drink coffee. OK, the odd cup of Café Direct, but it played havoc with her *chakras*. So why didn't she go into her own house? Because Magda did not go out until half past ten and, feeling as she did, Catriona couldn't face her.

How had things got to this stage? From almost the first day Magda had arrived in their hurly-burly household she'd brought some order to it. Back then, with four children aged three to seven, Catriona had been grateful to her.

Now the only place where she had sanctuary was the Volvo, which was as nature intended her to live – chaotic, filthy and friendly. Magda could not drive such a big car and had repeatedly said this to Catriona, who had repeatedly ignored her. It was the one freedom she had from her au pair.

From the beginning Magda had run things so much better than Catriona. The debris of six people, and not one of them with a natural instinct for cleaning, had seen to it that four cleaners and five childminders had moved off the premises in Georges Avenue – named, no doubt, after the man himself – like they would never see sanity again if they didn't hurry. Then Magda had come through an agency that had advised Catriona that this was no ordinary rave-inclined teenage student with three words of English, this was a Polish woman in her mid-twenties who had decided to give nursing a break and learn English in England. Magda never did anything unless it was properly.

'We could place this woman anywhere, but it sounds like you need her most,' Edna, the recruiter who had been doing the job for almost six decades, wheezed down the phone. 'We pride ourselves, at Mother's Little Helper, on getting the right person for the right job. We've got an almost ninety-five per cent success rate, like the driving school.'

And they charged accordingly. Catriona coughed up and George protested until two nights after Magda had arrived with one suitcase, a knowing smile and two irritating pigtails, which she wore perpetually for a year until Catriona sent her to the hairdresser for fear that she herself would cut them off in a fit of loathing. Then she wished she hadn't because what had come back was a bright, funky twenty-something with no added fat. But that was all ahead of them. On night three George came home to a clean, quiet house and a cooked dinner. Catriona was upstairs on her yoga mat for the first time in months, unwinding and tuning into her spirit guides, who had left when the place had got a bit rowdy, immediately after the birth of Zoë, their last little girl. The twins, Jack and Mattie, and the eldest, Lara, had all decided to act up after Zoë's arrival, even though they had all witnessed it happen in the living room as avid spectators.

'Maybe that's why they've gone funny,' George suggested. 'I find the whole thing a bit messy too.'

George was a man who liked to be at the top end for Catriona's deliveries. No cutting the cord for him.

Catriona dismissed him. 'The children loved it.'

And they might have, but they didn't love Zoë – until Magda. Magda had spoken to each child seriously in simple kiddy English, which was all she knew at the time (two years later she was fluent, wouldn't you bloody well know it?) and had come to Catriona to explain the children's fears. 'Lara, she think she will have to be old now, because she is the big one. The twins, they think, Where is the other baby? They don't like Zoë because she make the other one go away.'

That night Catriona spoke to the children individually, while Magda occupied the others with bedtime stories. They had taken to Zoë from then on, and also Magda – who continued to read them stories. 'Is it all right? It help my English.'

Magda continued to make George perfect bland meat dinners. Catriona couldn't bear to since she was vegetarian, a woman who could reproduce the entire Crank's cookbook – and all her kids wanted was things out of packets and tins in the shape of teddy bears and rockets that were as near to food as men are to living on Mars. On the third night Catriona Morehampton, née Nowdy – there's a reason to go along with tradition and change your surname to your husband's – produced a lentil and spinach pie with cheesy potato topping and found no one wanted to eat it. She conceded that she wasn't going to win on this one. The only result would be that she'd eat her own home-cooked food five days in a row.

'Don't worry, love,' George had patted her back in the

fatherly way that made her want to rip open her top and say, 'Look at these.' 'All kids want additives. Then, one day, they realise Ronald McDonald's not half as good-looking as their mother. And not half as good a chef. Same hair, though. Ha-ha,' he laughed on his own.

Catriona continued to cook for herself.

Magda continued to clean as if it was all she ever wanted to do. She even took over the shopping so that Catriona could get back to some of the workshops and classes she had forgone for so long.

Magda made their house a perfect world. Catriona tried to overcome her irritation with the pigtails, the freckles and the figure unruined by childbirth. But the niggling, the naggling, never went away. She knew now it was dislike. At the time of Magda's arrival she'd been too tired to recognise it.

When she finally had the energy to do things for herself again, there didn't seem any need. The only responsibility she managed to hang on to within her own family was taxiing the kids. Even then Magda provided her with a laminated timetable of their events, 'to help you, a little'.

Catriona couldn't complain, because Magda compensated for all her separate failings: her disorganisation, her inability to clean and her dislike of the routine that children need. By the time Magda's year was up Catriona was counting the days to her departure. Then Magda told her she would be staying for another year, it had already been arranged.

'How did you manage that?' Catriona asked peevishly, wishing she could unpeeve herself and remember she was paying this woman, who was only doing her job.

'I rang agency and I ask George for letter saying you like me.'

It was amazing the way Magda always lapsed into broken English when speaking about the arrangements she had made for herself.

'Why didn't you ask me to write the letter?'

'You went to the course on Inner Light in Diddlesbury.'

Magda sounded hurt and, for the millionth time, Catriona chided herself. Her children and husband loved Magda – because they looked like the Brady Bunch now instead of the Clampetts – so Catriona swallowed her bile and found a smile.

After all, she had been an actress. Once.

Two years. Magda had her full working visa now. She could go anywhere, but she stayed. To help Catriona a little.

Catriona was afraid of her au pair, afraid of the raw egg Magda would make her drink for her hangover with some potion stuff that would, of course, cure it, afraid to go inside her own house and see Magda performing better yoga than she could to the strains of Dvorak. Why had she taught her yoga? Because in the beginning she had wanted to be nice to her. That had probably stopped because over the past two years Magda had seemed to want to become Catriona Morehampton. Wife of George, mother of Lara, Jack, Mattie and Zoë. She'd even taken to following Catriona out into the garden, which had been her last refuge. To help with it a little.

She'd lost her ruddy dairy-farmer's-daughter look and become slim, lithe and stylish. Catriona had started to look like the dairy farmer's wife. But she didn't feel a bit round and jolly – she wanted to murder.

It had been hard to recognise herself in the past few years. Cat Nowdy had never had a problem with being happy and lucky. She had two parents who had stayed together and loved her. Her friends were lifelong, particularly Bernadette, who she'd grown up with and who was never afraid to tell her the truth. Cat had always liked that. Bernadette had started on the lipstick when she was six and added mascara at eight. Bernadette made everyone believe she was gorgeous. And her firm conviction was that Cat was too. They'd take the best men together and get the best jobs and the best everything. They'd live in style.

'And we'll change our names as soon as we get married, for the first time. We ought to have about three husbands each. The first ones should be rich, the next ones should be cool, and the last ones young. When we're old and scabby and no one wants us any more. We'll have young lads who we keep in style.'

Bernadette Bender was also cursed with a surname from hell. It was another thing uniting them against a cruel world. Except, if Catriona was honest, it had never been cruel to her. Bernadette, a widow's daughter, had to struggle. Cat got everything she wanted.

Cat, easy-going, too talented to work, it might be said, went along with her friend's vision and ambitions. She was happy in the passenger seat, letting Bernadette drive the open-top sports car. To get in and turn on the ignition herself would have led to consternation. At discos Bernadette did the pulling. Out shopping Bernadette did the choosing. They were polar opposites in size and shape so they never had to fight over wanting to wear the same thing. The same went for boyfriends. Their differences made them even better for each other.

Until *The Elves*. A school play, written by Bernadette Bender, with the help of Alan Dempsey, the English teacher. Starring Catriona Nowdy and Tom Dulman.

The chemistry between Cat and Tom, even though both were wearing tights and pointy ears at the time, made the play a success. The school had to put on two extra nights.

Cat and Tom became the coolest couple in school.

Bernadette, the writer, the orchestrator of this fabulous beginning, was left in the wings. With a huge crush on the married, not interested and far-too-old Mr Dempsey. And a space where her best friend used to be.

Now Catriona, the woman Cat had become, fingered the piece of paper with the name on it of one of her friend's lovers, and couldn't hold back the excitement at this chance to act again. To be something other than a woman who had given away potential at the first obstacle. She knew that Magda was the new Bernadette. A driving force in her world. A driving force that couldn't get to grips with Volvos. The big difference was that Magda didn't like her, at all. Catriona suspected she hated her. Nothing she could put her finger on, just the way she would stare when she thought Catriona wasn't aware of it. Catriona was always aware, she'd been trained to be aware in theatre school.

Bernadette Bender and Cat Nowdy had stayed friends through the *Elves* incident. Cat had to put up with Bernadette's bitchiness about how great it must be to be popular. Bernadette had persevered in phoning and calling for Cat to walk to school, and put up with her friend's long absences at break times, weekends and just about any other time she could get to fumble with Tom, a good-looking boy, but a boy nonetheless. Bernadette was holding out for a man, no spots, no penchant for heavy metal, no desire to kick pigskin. A man with means.

When they left school Tom was already history. Cat went to do her drama course and became Catriona. Bernadette did arts and became disillusioned, left before her second year was up and lied her way on to a magazine with clippings from another journalist in another country. She changed her name to Dette, her age went up by five years and she had lived in NYC.

Catriona had been as scared for Dette on her first day as she was on her own first night, but Dette survived the way Dette always would. They both became successful. Then it went wrong.

Catriona saw the damage that the much older – and so streetwise he was heading for a cardboard box on the Embankment – Joe Morgan was doing to Dette. Dette saw that Catriona had had it too easy and was heading for a fall when the first disappointment landed.

'Just be prepared for the teeth kicks, love. You're in the most vain job in the world after all,' she'd warned. Their new mate, Rorie, a woman inseparable from jeans and jumpers, who'd been at college with Dette and had aspirations to direct, agreed. Their even newer mate, Helen, a trainee doctor, had also agreed. Watch out.

Catriona had nodded easily, not listened easily. They were all Virgos. They were all paranoid. She prided herself on being the least Virgo-like, almost a Leo. She had the mane, the fire and the easy cat grace. Go with the flow. Life doesn't have to be a struggle for everyone.

She passed auditions, worked hard, did well, got more auditions, worked hard, did well, got a leading role, worked hard, did badly.

It felt like someone had taken something she needed to keep breathing.

'That's approval, honey. You've never had to do without it,' Dette pointed out. 'The rest of us are cast into a lack of it about twice a week.'

The rest of them, assembled in Angelo's, had agreed. Catriona didn't. Catriona couldn't. It was too frightening to have people say those terrible things about you. To watch you fail so miserably. She cast about for a more suitable role, an easier one. Found it in George. Bernadette's words came back, 'The first husbands should be rich…'

'I didn't mean marry the Bank of England,' Dette snapped when Catriona announced her intention. 'You'll die of mint poisoning. He's too boring. Don't do it.'

She was still the chief bridesmaid at a flouncy affair that made Mr and Mrs Nowdy over the moon and Catriona a bit sick. But that was because she was two weeks pregnant, wasn't it? Luckily – for George's mother Lydia was into keeping of appearances – little Lara was not born until her tenth month. A large, lazy baby with a look of contentment that showed she was just like her mother. Someone who could do anything she wanted, be anyone. Lara still had the luck. Her mother had lost it.

Catriona looked at the piece of paper. Why would a gorgeous bit of rough like Martin Hardiman, Dette's latest squeeze, fancy a lumpy old fart like her? He was a house-painter-turned-set-designer currently making a splash in the West End with his realistic backgrounds to those gritty dramas that made her feel stupid, common, thick, like Dot Cotton in a Beckett play.

Martin Hardiman was the kind of man they wrote up in *Time Out*, in the same way they'd written off her one and only West End appearance.

But she didn't allow herself to think about that nowadays, much.

In the draw for seducees she had wanted someone who wouldn't make her feel more inadequate than she did already. Why lie? There was only one she really wanted, she couldn't risk pulling three times and arousing suspicion. The first time Catriona claimed to have drawn out her own husband. Second time she had to stick with who she got.

She caught sight of her auburn hair in the mirror and the fine features that were showing the shadows of something else she could not put her finger on – apart from a desire to do away with Magda.

Catriona née Nowdy now Morehampton was catching glimpses of the disappointment that was tightening and straining her face. Most of the time she was too busy to realise how far she felt pushed out of her own life. When she'd first got pregnant she saw herself as a matriarch. Now she felt like she'd be imposing if she slept in the dog basket. Even the Labrador liked Magda. Maybe she should start wearing the discarded pigtails and it might beg her for a walk instead.

The door to her own home opened. Catriona found herself sinking down in the driver's seat. A slight woman with one of those annoyingly fresh faces that might be twenty of fifty years old marched out and turned the

Chubb lock. She took a step back and surveyed all the windows to make sure they were closed. Magda was very security conscious, treated the house as if it was her own. When Catriona had bitched about this George had accused her of being a snob. It was Magda's home as well, after all.

'Which one of us went to public school and belongs to the class of people who used to lord it over ethnic minorities?' Catriona snapped. 'Whose mother calls Magda "that little Polish person"?'

'Me,' George agreed, 'and mine. But this is her home, Catriona, while she's here, and you know perfectly well if she didn't treat it like that you'd be complaining. She does everything to please you – I hope you know that.'

Catriona knew she had no allies, so she'd stopped.

Magda was walking towards the car with the determined smile that made Catriona want to slap her. She was looking better by the day, even her body was tidy, clad in Gap casuals. Her feet were in brand new trainers. Catriona, overweight, dressed like a bag-lady – anyone looking at them would have sworn she was the matronly cleaner and Magda George's trophy wife.

'I am going to shops,' Magda said. 'I get chicken. George, he likes chicken on Wednesday. So fussy.' She raised her eyebrows, conspiratorially.

'Great,' Catriona smiled grimly. Make sure you get one with feathers so you can pluck it to perfection. Wearing something wenchy.

'For you there are veggie burgers in the freezer,' Magda continued, and Catriona realised she was not going to go until Catriona got out of the car. Catriona hated herself, but she got out.

'Would you like anything?' Magda called, as Catriona walked towards the door Magda had just locked. Why had she bothered to when she'd spotted Catriona in the car?

'No,' Catriona called back, with a false brightness that threatened to blind her. 'Just you to go away,' she whispered, on the other side of the door.

Now she had two choices. She could go upstairs and do her yoga like a good girl, or she could eat the ice-cream that was waiting in the freezer to make her feel better. She headed for the kitchen.

11

Sugar and daytime television. Catriona switched on the set in the kitchen and got busy with the ice-cream. It was a family-sized tub but it wouldn't touch her sides. Her greatest pleasure in life was pure vanilla. Five minutes later, the end of the ice-cream tub was in sight – and with it would go all sense of pleasure. She was beginning to feel niggles of guilt. A serene waifish figure appeared on screen. 'Waifish guru spells wolfish money-spinner.' Dette's warning voice in her head. Catriona ignored it. She was willing to pay or listen to anyone who would make her feel better.

Waifish was fifty-odd, talking about her discovery of a new mind-body technique to achieve inner harmony and happiness. Dette was right.

'Not another perfect skinny person,' Catriona snapped. She'd gone from a healthy size twelve to a sixteen at a squeeze in ten years. Where was Hollywood gossip when you needed it?

She grabbed the remote control and was about to

snap it when she heard the interviewer, who specialised in oily questions and inappropriate knee-rubbing of hapless guests who had to promote themselves on his show, ask slyly, 'So, Dawn, you have the perfect life?'

Dawn eyed him with the coolness of one floating far above his tactic. 'No one has the perfect life. I'm not proposing that by using my techniques you achieve perfection. What I'm saying is, you look for contentment with what you have.'

'Oh,' the gritty little eyes of the interviewer lit up, 'so your system's the same as anyone else's, then? What you're saying is "Buy my book and you'll be no better off. But I will."'

Catriona gasped; Dawn had obviously got up this guy's nose.

'What I'm saying, Malcolm, is you have what you have and what I try to do is teach you to make the best of that.'

'Which is OK for you, since you're now a millionaire.'

'No, Malcolm, I'm a multimillionaire, and I won't patronise your viewers or you by saying I don't enjoy my wealth or that it doesn't mean much to me. But I will say I was just as happy nine years ago when I had nothing. Ten years ago I was a fat, disappointed woman of forty, married to someone like you and doing time because I was afraid to leave my home and the financial security of my marriage. My husband didn't like me and my kids probably didn't either. I know I didn't like myself...'

Catriona found herself sinking into the kitchen chair again. Her fingers released the control and her eyes were glued on Dawn's. For years she had been swallowing new-age remedies to find something that filled the hole inside. They never did. But this sounded real.

'...so I left him and moved into a bedsit. My kids came with me because he didn't want them full time. We were happier in that one room than we had been in our detached bit of London suburbia.'

She would leave now. Leave boring George and tyrant Magda and find somewhere in Paddington with flock wallpaper and candlewick bedspreads and—

'...I took the name I was given, Dawn, and I decided to live up to it. I put the Dawn Principles into practice, hence the title of the book, and my kids were happy and I was happy, and we didn't go on three foreign holidays a year. We went to the park and fed ducks. We made pictures for our flat because we couldn't afford posters. We collected stones and twigs and leaves for ornaments. We walked all over the place and when I finally got money out of my miserable ex – don't worry, Malcolm, it's not libellous, the judge called him that – we bought a two-bedroom house and we didn't leave one of those twigs or leaves behind. We lived every day. Now, that's all I'm offering to people and it's very simple and it might not be everyone's cup of tea, but so far one million people have found it to be. Because I'm a bestseller in six countries, which is why I'm on your show.'

'So,' Catriona urged the television, 'what does it all boil down to? Give me the words that will help me to change my life.'

'It comes down to this.' Dawn spoke directly to the camera, as if the infuriated host was not there. 'Tell yourself the truth and act on it. Whatever situation you find yourself in, don't lie to yourself about it. For instance, I don't like you, Malcolm, and haven't done since you put your hand on my knee before the cameras rolled. That means I don't have to put up with you if I don't want to. And I'll make sure I don't have to.'

'Well,' the interviewer looked sweaty. 'I—'

'People will either hear what I have to say or not hear it. But I will urge everyone watching to think of,' she glanced at her watch, 'ten forty-nine a.m. on Wednesday, August the second, as the dawn of their day and the rest of their lives. Whether you buy my book or not it doesn't matter – enough people have already for me not to care.'

And then Dawn was gone and the interviewer had moved on to a soap actor who wouldn't have minded having his leg felt, or anything else, if it got him work.

Catriona got up from the table and – maybe it was the sugar and fat working a high – she didn't feel hung-over any more. She had to do something quick before a feeling she hadn't had in a long time vanished.

By the time she got to the bedroom she and George had shared for eight years she had run out of steam. She couldn't leave him and make them all move into a horrible bedsit. Dawn's husband sounded like he was mean and cruel, but George wasn't any of those things. He never disputed a penny with her, would give her more if she'd asked. He loved his kids in a formal kind of way. They were used to a splendour she'd never had as a child. It would be cruel to take them away from it. A bee in a jar of honey, she was. Suffocating in sweetness.

'Come on! Think! What else can you do when the first day of the rest of your life dawns?'

She did the yoga salute to the sun, which made her a bit queasy what with all the ice-cream, but at least it was a bit of exercise. She had a shower and washed her hair, then threw open her wardrobe and put on, for the first time in a long time, a bright red linen pair of palazzos and a fresh white shirt. She wiped off the four-month-old nail varnish on her toenails and gave herself a manicure and pedicure. By then it was almost one and she heard Magda's key in the door. Her heart gave the habitual two skips and a sink, but she got out her mental pump and puffed a bit of determination into it.

'If it wasn't for her I wouldn't have the time to do all this to myself. I'd be running around with a Hoover or a duster, or feeling guilty because I'm not,' Catriona said to herself on the way down the stairs.

Magda stood at the bottom, carrying the shopping that contained the food she was using to win Catriona's husband's heart. But instead of that annoying smile an open mouth was staring up at her.

'You look,' Magda spoke slowly, as if she didn't have the words Catriona knew she had, 'different.'

'That,' Catriona smiled, 'is because I'm not in a track-suit.'

Magda's annoying smile crept back, 'But you did not do yoga?'

'On the contrary,' Catriona smiled the same annoying smile, 'I did.' OK, it was only for ten minutes, but that ten minutes had made all the difference now in this, the first round. Maybe. All of a sudden, her self-confidence wilted, but then she saw Dawn's face again and it got her going.

What had she always been good at? Acting. Well, that was what she'd thought she'd been good at until the West End reviews. One had said she made the prostitute she'd played look like a dubbed version of Pollyanna. She'd been awful. Insipid in what was supposed to have been a passionate piece full of sex and darkness. Pirandello, and she'd played Pollyanna. 'Frightfully English,' one review said, and she wasn't. She was Irish – well, London Irish. Her mother had dragged her off to the Irish clubs and got her entered in the Feiseanna. If she'd been born ten years later she'd have been the star of bloody *Riverdance*, but when she was hoofing, Irish dancing was about as trendy and graceful as middle-aged punks gobbing at a Sex Pistols tribute band.

She'd failed at her major breakthrough part. Seven months later she'd married George after a whirlwind romance and cast herself in the role of earth mother. She'd played the part for eight years now and it was satisfactory enough if she accepted the fact that she did not love her husband.

She'd married George because he was everything she ever wanted – gorgeous, a fantastic provider and he'd told her she was the perfect woman for him. Also, he had a surname that was not Nowdy. Catriona said goodbye to that and hello to the ten times more sophisticated Morehampton. In her mind's eye she saw a glistening return to the stage, after an easy labour and six months of breastfeeding, with a brand-new name and attitude. When Helen had challenged her on giving up her name she'd blamed George, saying he made her do it.

When Lara was six months old Catriona couldn't bear to stop breastfeeding. She loved her daughter and the cloistered world they lived in. She called her agent to say she needed another six months off.

'Fine.' The agent had had to be reminded twice who Catriona was. She'd never called again. Catriona could never hustle. She'd said goodbye to the struggling actress and hello to a huge house on Georges Avenue – George's inheritance after the death of his father. His mother had an even bigger palace just round the corner in Campden Hill Road. His sister had fallen out with her father and been written off with nothing.

Catriona couldn't believe that a girl from a two-bedroom terrace could end up with this. But then, there had been a price – her own dreams.

In the beginning she didn't have to think about that. She was too busy playing house and mother. Besides, she and George had a relationship that satisfied them, cemented by Lara. The twins did not bring about the same results. Catriona became preoccupied with the children – there were three now rather than the planned two. Then she'd accidentally got pregnant with a fourth. That was when things had really started to unravel and she and George had lost whatever it was they had had, if they had ever had it.

If she was not an earth mother, what was she? Someone who had never succeeded at what she wanted to do.

She and George had a working marriage, but she would never have seen it as one that was as satisfactory as Helen's until recent events. She kept trying new things to find some way of expressing herself. Her hobbies were a source of amusement to her friends.

'Does any woman on your road ever do anything but try to find herself?' Rorie asked. 'The rest of us are all trying to get rich enough to buy a house where you live.'

Even Helen, trustworthy, fair Helen, would raise her eyes to heaven when Catriona went on about how boring her life with George was.

And Dette, as always, had the final say. 'Well, you were hardly meant to be a Mildred.'

*****

Magda was watching Catriona, who was watching the garden sparrows.

'Why are you dressed?' Magda asked her, as if Catriona never put on clothes.

'I am…' Catriona had to think. 'I'm going to look for some work. I think it's time I earned a little money.'

Magda was stupefied. She saw Catriona as one of those privileged women who went from tennis to lunch to salon to home to cocktails to dinner to bed, first with a lover and then with a husband who paid for it all. At least, that was what her life would be when she finally managed to ensnare George. And it felt like they were moving to a final stage in that. Catriona, her employer, wasn't right for him. She was frightful, fat and fitted in nowhere in the great man's life.

Twice Magda and George had had to rearrange the furniture back when Catriona had gone through a feng shui phase and moved it to improve the *pa kua* of the household. Instead of thanking them, she had burst into tears. 'Why didn't you just leave it?' she'd wailed at her husband, who was grey from a twelve-hour day and a two-hour stint at sofa upheaval. 'The lines were perfect for inner harmony.'

'Darling, we couldn't get in or out of the sitting room and two of the bedrooms. The furniture was blocking the door.'

'I left space, I know I did! You just never let me do anything. You always have to spoil things. I hate you! You don't know anything about spirituality. It's all money for you.'

'It's all money because we need money,' George had said quietly.

'Oh, that's it, rub my face in my lack of earnings! I have your children to take care of.' She wouldn't look at Magda when she said that.

'I know, darling, I never said you didn't.'

'You don't have to.'

Catriona had stormed out of the room and into her bedroom, the one she hadn't been able to get into two hours earlier. That made her even crazier. She bawled her eyes out. In the kitchen she could hear Magda and George. She was making him cocoa. His night-time drink. They talked in low voices for an hour.

That was marriage for you. Women yearn for a long-term lover; men desire a life-long mother.

'I'm up for auditions,' Catriona heard someone who sounded just like her say to someone who looked just like Magda.

'How do you do this?' Magda even sounded interested.

'I have phone calls all the time, from old friends trying to get me back to work. Yes. Old friends.'

Well, Rorie was a stage manager and Martin, Dette's boyfriend, was a set designer. They were bound to know someone. Which would give her the chance to start seducing the man who, before her New Dawn, had seemed out of her league. If she needed to oil her acting skills she could try them on Martin and maybe put some truth into what she had just told Magda.

That was what Dawn had said. Tell the truth at all times. The phone rang. It was Dette. She'd lost her job.

'I don't believe you,' Catriona cried. 'You've been there for years. Sue them.'

'Nah,' Dette sounded light as a feather on the other end of the phone. Maybe it was the shock. 'They should've sacked me years ago. I've only ever been trouble for them.'

'Trouble and a huge readership,' Catriona defended her friend. 'Your column's read by anyone who's anyone in beauty.'

'That's what I told you,' Dette laughed. 'But thanks for repeating it to me.'

'So, what are you going to do now?' Suddenly Catriona had an awful thought. No job meant no money and no money meant Dette might come to stay with her again, as she had when her marriage had failed. Whatever happened, Catriona did not want that. The experiment had cost her a fortune in home improvements. Dette had much higher standards than she did.

'The problem is,' Dette had said at the time, 'I'm supposed to live in a place like this and you're not. You don't have any interest in beautiful surroundings.'

Catriona had laughed because she couldn't have agreed more. But the joke had worn thin when Dette had a three thousand pound sofa delivered to get the right look for the drawing room, as Dette called it, or telly room, as Catriona called it.

'Don't worry,' evidently Dette had read the silence, 'I'm not going to come and live with you again. No, I'm going freelance. Money's better and time's my own.'

'Well,' Catriona got enthusiastic, 'I just saw this wonderful woman interviewed on telly and she'd make a great piece for a woman's magazine.'

'Oh, yeah?' Dette didn't sound interested, but Catriona persisted. She wanted to make sure Dette had something to do when the shock hit her. What if she dissolved again, as she had when her marriage ended?

'OK. Give me her number,' Dette relented after Catriona had given a blow-by-blow account of the interview.

'I've only got the one from the programme,' Catriona offered it to her. 'I only saw her for five minutes and already I'm thinking of going back to work.'

'You're what?' Dette said.

'I'm going to phone Rorie this minute and make her meet me for lunch.'

'Cat,' Dette's smile could be heard in her voice, 'you've no idea how long I've waited for you to say that.'

12

'...I know I should be grateful for my life and my children. But the problem is they're not my job any more. They're Magda's. She does it all better than me. Everyone,' Catriona started to cry into her cappuccino, 'does everything better than me.'

From a date with destiny to reality check. That was what coffee with Rorie had given Catriona. The fairy dust had been bound to wear off some time, but she hadn't been expecting the low so soon.

Rorie, who had spent a good portion of the meeting telling Catriona a few home truths about herself, climbed down a little. 'Come back with me and we'll see if my director's about. You never know. Then I'll get you Martin's number.' Rorie had been annoyed because Catriona hadn't even tried to hide who she'd drawn. 'We decided not tell each other who we were lined up with. Now I only have to figure out who the other two are chasing to know the whole plot, don't I?'

'Yes,' Catriona agreed.

'And, of course, one of the other two is chasing my man, aren't they? Since you're not.'

'Yes,' Catriona agreed again. 'I'm sorry. I just wanted some help with this. I don't know if I'm up to it.'

The hangover was catching up with her again. She wanted to eat a plate of chips but Rorie was dragging her out of the café and into the theatre where she worked to meet the director who she now couldn't face approaching.

'Come on.' At least Rorie was kind to her as they walked at an unreasonable pace to the stage door. Why did stage managers always walk so fast? 'Nigel will be having hernias.'

Five minutes later, after the quickest of hellos to Nigel Blunt, the director, before Rorie dragged him off to other things, Catriona was on the street with Martin's mobile number in her hand.

If it wasn't now, it wasn't ever.

'Hello, Martin?'

'Hello, who's this?'

'Catriona.'

'Catriona who?'

'Catriona, Dette's friend.'

'Ah, Dette's friend.' He obviously still didn't have a clue who she was. Catriona could feel a tub of Häagen Dazs coming on, to eat on the Tube.

'Oh, I know, one of the birds with the same star sign.'

'Yes, that's right.'

'Well, what can do I for you, mate?' Martin was an East End boy. How was she going to get someone who called her 'mate' to fancy her? Any minute now he might offer to fix her motor or do a spot of decorating for her.

At a knockdown price, mate.

'Martin,' Catriona put on her chatty voice, the one she used with the kids, her bright-and-breezy-when-inside-a-chill-and-desolate-wind-is-blowing voice, 'I was wondering – you work as a set designer.'

'I do, mate. And I'm working right now.' He was busy and she felt even more inadequate because she was not.

'Well, I'm an actress, and I'm looking for work. Do you know of anything going?' Feeble.

'Not on this production. It's all male for a start and it's set in a Russian gulag for another thing. I'm up to my jockeys in grey masonry paint and chains.'

'Understood,' Catriona was already fishing around in her purse for Häagen Dazs money.

'They're all bald too. You've got lovely hair. But if I hear of anything, later, like, I'll tell Dette.'

'Thanks,' Catriona could have choked.

'And I'll see you Saturday,' Martin said cheerfully.

'Saturday?'

'For the dinner.'

The dinner at which she was supposed to seduce him. She'd need a second tub, maybe Ben and Jerry's for a little variety.

13

Catriona and George were the first to arrive at Angelo's, because George was with Catriona. If she was on her own she was almost always last.

'Why don't you drink at the bar with me, while you're waiting?' Angelo was looking at George, as usual. George had to spend a penny, first thing, as usual. In case he got caught on the inside of the table. Angelo's tables were too small for anyone over six feet and he was six three. He felt like an elephant in a Mini.

'Angelo, stop eyeing my husband up and tell me I'm gorgeous or I'm never coming here again,' Catriona reached for her gin and tonic.

'Sorry, darling. You look lovely too, but not as lovely as your husband. A god he is. With a mortal tailor. Why do you let him wear chinos? His behind, it needs a better cut to show it off. The shape of his shoulders in that T-shirt – it's criminal.'

Catriona laughed. She wished she could look at George and see what Angelo saw. She knew he was gorgeous, but her eyes always seemed to find his nostril hair, the bags under his eyes, the curly hairs in his untrimmed eyebrows. 'Angelo, please help me. I've got to chat someone up this evening. I've got to make him want me. I feel sick. Stage fright – haven't had that in years.'

'Catarina.' She loved it when he called her that. 'You got to realise, what you don't see in your husband is what you don't see in you.' He never messed about, Angelo. The truth was the truth and it belonged right between your eyes. 'You got beautiful eyes and skin and a lot of this beautiful hair. You got hips and the man who don't like female hips is like me, gay. You just take another gin, dear, and do your magic. Make it a part, like you had when you were an actor. And what you wear, it's…' Angelo stopped '…a little wrong. But it's good, for your cleavage. You give a little of that to the man and he's going to ache for you to be his lover. To know it all, that is the burning of the man. To hide it all, that is the job of the woman. It makes mystery. That way. And love.'

Catriona watched him, mouth open. 'You sound like a director.'

'Fellini, only director for me, Catarina. Now, your husband comes back and I need to make him eat my globe artichoke.'

George caught the end of this, reddened, as usual. 'Why does he always have to say things like that?'

'Appreciation. And he's right.'

'You think so?' George was looking right at her, with something in his eyes that made her want to look away, something hopeful.

'I think so.' She patted his hand in a motherly way that made him want to rip his shirt off and say, 'Look at this!'

But he wouldn't be able to find the buttons afterwards. And he'd have to sew them back on. Or get Magda to do it. Wonderful Magda, he didn't know where they would be without her.

Dette and her skinhead painter boyfriend came in. A new nostril ring and one in his eyebrow too. George made sure the women sat between them, he didn't have a lot to say to Martin Hardiman. The father in him wanted to tell the young man to grow up. He certainly hoped their Jack wouldn't come home looking like that one day. He wouldn't stand for it. Who was he kidding? His children would do what they wanted. He was soft. Even in work he'd been passed over for the top promotions because he couldn't kick people in the teeth. And he had the ability, he was sure of that, with numbers. It was hard being a soft man when men were supposed to be tough. George had learned that from dealing with his father. A man who'd gone to his grave without saying the word 'sorry'. George made sure he said it every time he did the slightest thing to upset his children or wife. They might not respect him for it now, but he hoped that would come later. And he knew one thing – they might not see as much of him as he would have liked them to, but they weren't afraid of him.

No. They didn't dread his key in the lock and they didn't know that to disobey orders was to face a slipper across the backside. George Morehampton, a man of privilege.

Catriona might not be what every banker needed in a wife, but she was a blessing as a mother. Not once had he ever heard her raise her voice to the children. No matter how out of hand they were, she had her Moomin

Mamma voice and ready arms for hugging. A huge heart. It made him glad to think his kids were in such good hands during his long hours away from them. Magda, too, looked after them well for all the things Catriona couldn't give them. Routine, order, a clean uniform on Monday morning. It was the perfect household, George felt, except that he and Catriona never seemed to be alone in it. Even in bed there was always a body – each child had a designated place. The twins and Zoë between them, Lara along the bottom. Usually by seven each morning every space had been filled.

'It's sad there's no room for Magda,' Lara said once. George had laughed. Catriona didn't.

He knew Catriona felt inadequate around Magda, but she felt inadequate about most things. He'd love to be able to speak to her about it, but he was afraid of insulting her. He seemed to do a lot of that. Public school gave you perfect Latin and no understanding of the female mind. So much more complex. George, he was happy with whatever life gave him as a lot. Wasn't he?

Catriona didn't love him. He knew that. Right now she was leaning across Dette and having a heart to heart with Martin about Russian gulags. What? Catriona, who couldn't even bear to watch the news, was discussing the best methods to portray torture in an artistic backdrop.

George wondered who'd won the football. 'Any idea who won tonight, Martin?' he asked.

'No, mate, but probably United. Always is.'

'Stop pretending you know about football. You're a nancy,' Dette elbowed her boyfriend. 'The nearest you've got to balls is the ones you've been attaching to chains in your studio all week. And stop talking about torture, you two. It's Saturday night – the hangover belongs to tomor-row.'

'Hang about – I support Spurs, and I'm not overdo-ing it,' Martin held up his hands. 'I've got work tomor-row. Set's got be ready for fitting on Tuesday.'

'My God,' Dette's eyebrows rose. 'He's twenty-five and his hell-raising days are over.'

'Not over, Dette,' Martin was annoyed, 'just not while I'm on a project.'

'Oh, project now, is it? It used to be a slap of paint, but now it's a project.'

'Stop it, Dette,' Catriona whispered, so Martin wouldn't hear. 'Just because you lost your job doesn't mean you can slag off someone else's.'

'Says the woman who hasn't worked for years. Unless you call growing your own herbs an industry.'

'Now, ladies—' George attempted to intervene.

'Ladies!' Catriona spun round. 'What century are you living in, George?'

'OK, now we have to cool it,' Martin, the youngest by a long chalk, was the voice of reason.

Rorie arrived with John, apologising for being late. 'John was writing.'

Spat over, Dette and Catriona eyed each other. Dette was so brutal sometimes, it was a full-time job standing up to her. The older her friend got, the more bitter she seemed to be. If they hadn't known each other for so long would they even bother seeing each other? Catriona wondered. The thought made her sad. Then Helen and Euan were taking the last spots at the table and it was time to order and after the main course Catriona found herself beside Martin.

'Thanks for sticking up for me earlier,' he said before she had even sat down. Catriona looked nervously at Dette, who was at the far end of the table. 'She's a handful sometimes.'

'I've known that since I was nine. But she's worth it, Martin,' Catriona couldn't not defend her. 'You have to see behind the hardness. She's led a tough life. And she's so little. It's her way of making sure she doesn't get walked over.'

'Walked over! I'd like to see anyone try. I can't even climb over that barbed wire fence she's got up. I should stick her in the set. That's the right effect. Bloody impossible she is.'

Catriona looked at him. 'She wasn't always like this.'

'Who is?' Martin sniffed. 'Life's hard, you get knocks, you get up. It's my way. We get on well, her and me – she's better for me than any other bird I've been with. But she's hard, Catriona. She don't give a stuff about me sometimes.'

You wait, Martin Hardiman. You wait fifteen years, although you think it's only ten. See what happens to you. Maybe you'll think that tough old bird you once went out with was right to keep every man at arm's length.

'And what about you? Do you give a stuff about her, Martin?' Catriona reached for her wine glass. It was going to be a long night. At the end of it she could see Dette being dumped again. What was the point in making the effort to seduce this man, so much younger, who clearly hadn't the patience to hang around long enough to figure Dette out? Then again, God hadn't the patience for that.

'What do you think? Do you think I'd bother my mother's arse talking to you if I didn't give a stuff, mate? I know she's kind, she's the best, until you get to be her boyfriend. I spent ages chasing her and when she gave in I thought she'd get a bit softer. But she's worse.'

'So, I take it you're not going to stick around?'

Martin looked at Catriona. 'I'm trying.'

Catriona pulled back. 'Sorry, you're quite right. I jumped the gun there. It's just that, being nearer forty than you are thirty, I see things a bit differently.'

'Don't pull out the age thing again, mate.'

'Don't call me mate. My name's Catriona.'

'All right,' Martin grinned. 'Dette's mate, then.'

Catriona smiled. 'If you'd seen Dette when she was twenty-five, you'd know something. She was going to do everything, run her own magazine, open a clothing catalogue for small women and write a novel. She didn't smoke, can you believe it? And she—'

'Met and married a tosser.'

'She was already married to him. The tosser met someone else and she left him. She bought her first packet of fags that night.'

'Why did she leave?'

'Because he told her to. One of the reasons he gave, apart from the fact that she was too clingy, was that she was too fat. She hasn't eaten a proper dinner since.'

'Bastard.' Martin's cheeks were red. 'I'll bloody find him and punch his bloody lights out.'

Catriona stopped. With the piercing and the clothes, the beer instead of wine, with the talk and the look of a lad, she hadn't even bothered rating him, but she envied Dette for the chance to ride a young buck while she was stuck with a man in pinstripe pyjamas. Here he was, giv-

ing a shit when so many men hadn't bothered. Wouldn't
it be ironic if in her search for total freedom from men –
and Martin seemed a perfect candidate for that role –
even his surname suggested a bloke on the make – Dette
had found someone capable of loving her?

Then he belched. 'I hate restaurant beer. They should
sell proper draught stuff.'

Across the table Dette pointed her fag at him, 'Watch
your manners, Hardiman, or I'll put you outside with the
other pigs.'

'Nah,' Martin went back to his conversation as if
nothing had happened. 'I'd never treat her like that.'

The plates were being cleared away. They were swap-
ping places. Catriona wouldn't mind, but she'd barely got
to eat anything, and if there was one thing she hated it
was a missed dinner. Still, it wouldn't do her any harm.
The truth was, over the years she had felt herself widen
on Angelo's chairs. Now they felt uncomfortably small.
Until her divorce Dette had been a cake compatriot.
They'd wolf a Swiss roll each in a single sitting. They'd
put on extra cream and feck the begrudgers. 'Let this be
dinner,' they'd say. 'All the major food groups. Who needs
broccoli and spuds and fish when you can eat something
proper?'

They never did it now.

'Thanks for the chat, Mum.' The group was moving
places, leaving Catriona behind, confused, lost in her
own thoughts. Martin was talking.

'Mum.'

It was meant to be a joke, to be endearing, but it left
Catriona needing an urgent visit to the loo to sit in a
cubicle and cry, silently, into a stuffing of loo roll.

14

'Dette?'

'Yes, Catriona.'

'You free tomorrow?'

'You know I am, Catriona. The world of leisure yawns ahead of me.'

'Then could you take me out and give me a going-over, like you did Helen? I'd pay you.'

'Do you think, honestly, that I would accept money?'

'Sorry, I just didn't want to think of you with no money and I need help, please, before your bloody boyfriend calls me Mum again.'

Silence.

'He did. Call me Mum.'

'Well, he'll get it when I see him again – if I see him again.'

'You had a row then?'

'That's an understatement. An eruption. A Vesuvius would be better. He kept banging on about my barbed-wire fence. Fecking eejit. He's just a young lad playing at being a sensitive man and nailing the knickers of as many gobshites to the wall as he manages to win over.'

'Are you sure you have that right?'

'I am sure. Sure I'm sure. What other reason is there for him to go on about wanting to get closer to me? What's he going to do? Marry me? When he's finished working on Russian gulag sets, he's off to design an urban orchard for *Three Sisters*, the New York version, only it's premièring in London. Starring Renée Zwiggy-zwaggy, Drew Bummymore and Julia Rabbit. Save me from the skin and hair that will fly over dressing room number one.'

'You're jealous,' Catriona stated.

'No, darling. You're jealous. You'd give anything to be one of them. And I'd give anything to be a fly on the wall when Martin picks one of them off.'

'Who's to say he will?'

'Well, if he doesn't, they will. A dab hand with a hammer, a paintbrush and wonderful in the sack. He can nail them in all manner of different ways. No, the writing's on the wall. I'm glad it's somewhere, because it's certainly not on the first page of my novel.'

A jingle went off in Catriona's head. Dette was talking herself out of Martin. Dette had never talked herself out of anyone since Joe. She just walked, and talked afterwards about how crap that last one had been. If I just sit here silently for one minute, Catriona thought, I wonder what will happen.

One minute later Dette came back with an admission. 'OK, I am jealous about the *Three Sisters* thing. But that's hormones. Every woman has them.'

'He was talking about you, how much he liked you,

last night,' Catriona said gently. 'Just before he belched.'

'Another knicker-nailing tactic – tell the best friend how much you like her.'

'Maybe. Dette, are we best friends still?'

'Course we are. Don't be stupid and don't mess with tradition. You and me are a tradition. We mightn't be all over each other but I'm there for you. Now, fuck off and let me not write my novel. See you tomorrow, outside Covent Garden Tube. Don't be late. If you're late, see you inside the Cartupon Coffee House. If you're more than an hour late you won't see me anywhere at all.'

'Thanks, Dette.'

'Don't thank me now. Do thank me if I manage to get you an appointment with Jude the Coiffeur. He's got all three sisters hammering at his door for the snip.'

15

'I did it!' Dette raised her espresso in triumph as soon as Catriona came through the door of Cartupon, fifty-five minutes late, with apologies and a threatened heart attack. Dette brushed aside her breathless excuses. 'Forget it. You're always late and you're never willing to accept it's your desire to make an entrance. I did it. I got you Jude! He's round the corner and he's waiting. Now or never, he says.'

They belted out the door and raced through the first fog of shoppers to land in Covent Garden. Jude was filing his nails and chatting to staff, one elbow on the reception desk, one eye on the books. By the day's end his salon would have made three thousand pounds. There was a lot to be said for going on *This Morning* to talk about Renée, Julia and Drew. His new mates. So new he'd never met two, and he'd spun out his one encounter with Julia like an old lady's set 'n' style. What little there is, make it look a lot. Give it height. Give it drama. That's entertainment and that's hairdressing. The two were made for each other. Jude the Coiffeur loved his world and all he'd done to build it. It was because he was in such a good mood that he'd given in to Dette's phone call. Might be time to change his mobile number now. A lot of C-list types had it. And word was she'd been sacked. His junior heard it from a junior on *Madame* magazine. Hard to believe, if it was true. She was like him, a survivor.

'Morning darling,' Dette kissed the air either side of his face. He did the same either side of hers. 'Here's your patient.'

Catriona Morehampton. He hadn't seen this kind since he'd styled Kate Winslet's hair for the *Titanic* retro clothing spread in *Vogue*. Jude was used to seeing women so thin they weren't there and when a real one walked in he was taken aback. This woman, cat-green eyes, tawny skin and wine red hair, would have been lying down naked, posing for artists, in the last century. In this one she was probably going to Weight Watchers and crying every night on the scales. Here was someone who was meant to be curvy, meant to be placed on a chaise longue.

'Hello, Guinevere,' Jude took Catriona Morehampton's hand and kissed it. 'Lovely to meet you.'

Two hours later they were still chatting and the chaise longue at Reception had four skinny bums jostling for space and waiting for their gold-dust appointment with the god of hairy things.

'You live on Georges Avenue. Fabulous! Is it three or four storeys over a basement?' Jude had both his hands on

Catriona's shoulders. They hadn't cut anything for half an hour. Dette's eyes rose to heaven. How much longer was this going to take? They still had the shops to do, and Dette was hoping to persuade Catriona to buy her something, since she was so broke and Catriona was so rich.

'Well, my husband has four storeys over a basement.'

'That's the way. Women like you should be looked after by their men. Nothing wrong with that I say. You do anything before you got married?'

Catriona clammed up. 'Nothing much.'

'No,' Dette sighed. 'She was only a successful actress.'

'That's the way,' Jude smiled. Catriona was fitting in well with his image of her – a Grace Kelly type, gives up a glittering career to marry a rich title and lives a life of leisure, wears diamonds to dinner, doing flowers and embroidery, holding balls. 'You got a ballroom in your house?'

'No!' Catriona held up both hands in protest.

'Well, she does, actually,' Dette advised Jude, 'but it's currently a games room for four spidery children.'

'My father- and mother-in-law used to have parties in it in the fifties,' Catriona offered, 'Lords and ladies sat down to five courses. Then a bit of bridge afterwards for the ladies. Smoking for the men. We've still got a smoking room.'

'You do?' Dette and Jude answered at once.

'Well, it's got the washing machine and tumble dryer in it now, but it was a little den, with a pipe rack, leather armchairs, backgammon boards, card table, drinks cabinet and all sorts. George's father lived in it. Mainly because he couldn't stand to be near his wife. The only things that united those two were their snobbery and loathing of anyone who didn't have cash. 'His mother, Lydia, hates me,' Catriona confided.

'Because you're young, like she once was,' Jude sighed.

'And broke,' Catriona insisted. 'Thank God I never met George's father. Lydia's bad enough. I've been looking up her nostrils for the past decade.'

Dette sniffed. 'At least you and Jude escaped the poverty trap.'

'Why, Dette, you broke? I thought you'd be worth millions with all the free make-up, and you said yourself you haven't paid for a holiday since 1991.' Jude snipped at Catriona's hair, careful not to catch anyone's eye. The chances of Dette admitting the truth were as skinny as she was. If he saw one more bony woman today, and he was bound to see plenty, he'd have to make them eat a bacon sandwich with lard while he cut.

'I got the sack.' Dette surprised herself as much as Jude and Catriona. What was this? She'd have no clout now her secret was out.

'Idiots!' Jude exclaimed, with the right amount of outrage and surprise. 'You're the number-one beauty writer.'

'Well, I managed to piss off the number-one advertiser. Keats was wrong. Truth and beauty aren't one and the same.'

'Very literary.' Jude checked his watch. Dette and Catriona both knew the score. Is that the time, Unimportant People?

They got ready to leave.

'What are you doing? Did I say go? I haven't even begun to blow dry here yet.'

'Sorry.' Both of them said it.

'We know you're busy,' Dette offered. 'I am too, I'm freelance now. Doing loads of stuff for everyone.' She'd got it in before he asked.

'Sure, but hang on a sec or two, will you? I want to get this one right. Now, I just want curling tongs, or whatever fancy name they got on them now.'

'You didn't take much off,' Catriona was examining herself in the mirror. 'But it's lovely all the same,' she added hastily.

'You didn't take any off!' Dette was insisting. 'What's the story?'

'I just trimmed and curled cos I know that to do any more with this fabulous hair is to ruin it. Your other mate – the one with the ginger? Well, she don't suit the belle look. But you do. You go straight to Merchant Ivory when you get out of here and tell them I sent you. Proper English lady you are.'

'I'm Irish, as it happens.'

'Don't matter. I'm talking about the English look.'

Dette was nodding as if an atom was being split. Her brow furrowing, 'Great line, Jude. I'll use it in my piece, and I'll get the Palm Court at the Waldorf for the pictures.'

'No! Get a drawing room, a red drawing room with a chaise longue. I'll lend you mine. I'll lend you my drawing room.'

'At your house?'

'Yeah, I got a proper period house. My mother knew a thing or two about what to hang on to, she did, with all that pawn stuff. It's in Spitalfields. When you could buy

those houses for spit she bought it. My old mother. I tell
you what, if you don't mind, Catriona, when they're
doing the pictures I'll do a few sketches.'

'You're an artist?' Catriona's eyes brightened.

'Well, I wouldn't go that far. I do paintings, but they
don't pay – no art does unless you want to plonk a farm
animal in formaldehyde. No. I like old-fashioned art. I go
to the National Gallery all the time, you know, just round
the corner. Keep hoping I'll meet some nice man who
likes pictures too. Never do. They're all pimply students
and poncy professors.'

Dette wondered. She'd been a contact of Jude's for
over ten years and had never got past the leather trousers
and styling mousse. Mind you, it was all there if you
wanted to see it. His passion for Liberty-print shirts, the
antique dentist's chair. The Rubens' replica hanging over
his mirror. Maybe he'd even painted it.

'Yeah, that's one of mine.' He caught her eye on it.
'Don't tell anyone, and I won't tell anyone you've been
sacked.'

Deal. Except that, in the world they operated in,
everyone kept everything secret by telling only half the
world. That way the secret-holder never got to hear that
everyone else knew.

'How much do I owe you?'

'Well, seeing as you're rich, one hundred and fifty,
please.' Jude was still a businessman.

'You just paid one hundred and fifty for a quarter inch
trim,' Dette stated baldly, when they were on the street.

'Worth every penny,' Catriona looked at herself in the

same window Helen had paused at. She touched her hair and her face, as Helen had, as if she was seeing it for the first time. 'I've got a period look. I've got a look! I'm all right as I am. I thought it'd take a bulldozer to make me over.'

'I hate to say it, but he's right. The Häagen Dazs habit paid off for you, love,' Dette smiled. 'Sophie Dahl, eat your heart out. Or eat something. Catriona Morehampton's the new you.'

'Better than Cat Nowdy, eh, Dette?'

'No. She's no better than Cat Nowdy. In fact, I'd say until the past few days she's not been a patch on her.'

'Don't, Dette. I can't help it if I turned out the way I did.'

'You didn't turn out any way. You stopped turning and got stuck. But don't worry. So did I. So did Helen and Rorie, if they're honest. We're not a Virgo Club, we're a Virtual Club. I think the faithful-men test is just what we all needed. A chance for us to do things differently. Who knows? We might not need to get sozzled at Angelo's twice a month any more, once we work out what's happening – what's really happening – to us. I sometimes think those lunches, all of us together, hold us back. We don't have to change, the rest of us are all there, running like mad to stand still too.'

'Please, don't say that, Dette. Sometimes the only thing I have to look forward to is our lunches. Everything else in my life belongs to someone else. Don't dismiss it just because you don't need it as much as I do.' Catriona started to cry.

'Now, stop that!' Dette ordered 'You're trained to act up. I won't cry in public, I won't.'

Catriona wailed. 'What happened to us, Dette? We used to be such good friends. Everything's changed. We were only supposed to change our last names. We changed everything. Too much.'

Dette's eyes were full too. She grappled in her bag for a fag and something, anything to distract her. 'You don't know how many times I've thought that. Ever since you went off with that weedy Tom Dulman after *The Elves*, I always seemed to be coming after you in everything, Cat.'

'You said you didn't mind.'

'I didn't, I really didn't. You being so lucky used to persuade me that one day my life would change and I'd get what you got so easy. Happiness. Even when you married George Twit, I thought you'd go back to being lucky. And you did. Because George Twit loves you, and he's loaded, and all he wants to do is make you his princess and cushion you from absolutely everything, and I'd give anything to have someone like him, Cat. Instead I fell for an old-soak hack who cut me up, and now I'm with a man fifteen years younger who'll hop off one day with some young one with big tits and bright teeth and no nicotine stains on her fingers. I hate me, Cat, and I hate smoking.'

Dette stamped out her fag and tried to dry her eyes.

'I want to live in your house with your children and be you! I can't stand the way you run it down, or snipe about George's need to have his porridge at seven on the dot. If I could make Martin love me enough to stay, I'd hand-make him croissants at any time of the morning. I just want to be loved, Cat. I want Jude to love me and welcome me with open arms, like he did you. I want him to paint me and to be my friend and bring me to the fabulous première of *Three Wagons*.'

'Martin will bring you.'

'If he's still around. If he's not on a plane beside Ms Famous and a job designing the set of her latest film.' Dette's mascara was running down her cheeks. So much for the number-one waterproof mascara voted by Dette Morgan, the voice of British beauty. Ex-voice, ex-everything.

'I look at my future and I see no man, no baby, no house, no job. I'm frantically trying to write page one of my crappy novel and I can't think of a crappy thing except where are my fags and where is that glass of wine? And it's only nine in the morning Cat! I'm turning into my ex-husband. I'm turning into everything that made him a failure and me a failure for loving him. Bitter, drunk and desperate enough to call a boy my boyfriend when I should be going out with his father – if he wasn't a happily married butcher in Billericay.'

'Bernadette, that's where you're wrong! That boy feels for you, I know he does. So what if he's fifteen years younger? Ralph Fiennes is with Francesca Annis.'

'Ten, Martin's ten years younger.'

'OK, ten. Believe the lie. I know your real age and I know you, Bernadette. He's mad about you and he's going prematurely bald anyway so he'll look the same age as you in two years' time. Promise! You're good at skin preservation and you're good at self-preservation. If you knew how much I've craved your balls over the years. If I had half your courage I'd still be acting and I wouldn't have taken some poor old number-cruncher for a crutch husband. I'd be in bed with Ralph Fiennes right now, not a man who thinks eating the kids' Ready Brek instead of real oats, when we run out of them, is a risk—'

'There you go, putting him down again. And Ralph

Fiennes. You're fixated. If you knew where he lived, you'd stalk him.'

'I would not. He lives round the corner from us. And I don't. Except for the one time I parked outside his house, but I was waiting for Magda to go out. And I can't do anything *but* complain about George. He's boring!'

'He's not, Catriona. He's trapped, like the rest of us.'

Silence. Passing shoppers, sneaking snatches of their conversation.

'I know. I'm horrible. I suppose this means you won't come clothes shopping with me,' Catriona whispered.

'You suppose wrong. I'd rather go shopping with you now I can be honest with you.'

'Instead of bitching at me?'

'Instead of that.'

'OK. Let's see if honesty works both ways. You're forty next month, Dette.'

'So are you.'

'I'm not. I'm thirty-nine.'

'So y'are. Well one up for you, then.'

'No one ups any more. Let's help each other. We could both use some of that right now.'

Eyes met and smiled after a long time not meeting.

'I suppose this means I won't be able to blackmail you into buying me a frock I saw?'

'You never have to blackmail me. I'll buy you two.'

Catriona's mobile went. 'Not a child right now, please.'

It was Rorie. 'Catriona, can you get to the theatre on Monday at one? My director would like to offer you a job.'

Hug-phobic Dette hugged her without a thought for

who was around them. 'You see? Your luck is something the rest of us would kill for! Now use it. What time do you have to be there?'

'One.'

'We have two hours before the shops shut to get you the perfect Merchant Ivory outfit.'

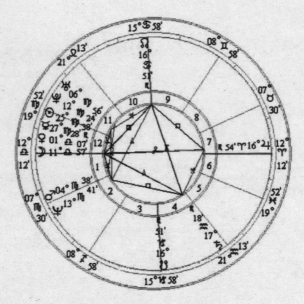

Bernadette Morgan, née Bender,
Thursday 19 September 1963 at 8:20 a.m.
Greater London, United Kingdom (51N30'00 0W10'00)

16

DETTE

Jupiter square Midheaven

You have high aspirations for yourself, and are likely to have the wit to attain them. Be careful not to allow your personal pride to stop you asking for help. Your downfall will be swift and sudden if you think you're infallible, or that you do not need the assistance of others to make your plans come true. Whatever you expect from life, expect to be surprised. You know what makes you happy will be what you saw from the start. The question is, can you remember you saw it?

*****

You can never be too rich or too thin. Dette lived by that motto, attributed to the Duchess of Windsor, her role model. Another divorcée. Since Dette's own divorce she had made her mind up never to think another serious thought. Life would be frivolous, about bubble bath and tanning cream, lip gloss and eyeliner. Affairs, no love. Affairs were great – you got all the thrill of early sex, none of the boredom of running a home, none of the pain of him leaving you.

The poor would have to forget she had ever been one of them. She went to her mum's house with bags full of make-up and her mother would just thank her kindly and put them with all the other unused Chanel, Clinique, Bourjois and Elizabeth Arden. Once they'd gone together to a Christmas jumble sale, a place where Dette used to get her clothes in the old days, and she'd seen all her pricy cosmetics on the tombola stand, being raffled at tenpence for a spin of the wheel.

'Mammy!'

'Ah, Bernadette. Now don't be giving out to me. I can't be using half the mucky stuff you gave me.'

'Muck! That Dead Sea mask is fifty pounds a pack!'

'Well, you can never tell how stupid some people are going to be when they've plenty of the stuff out their own back garden. And all the world that's starving, including you. Now will you have some of them Rice Krispie buns?' Mrs Bender headed for the cake stall. 'You used to love them, once upon a time.'

'When I was five, Mammy, I'm thirty-four now.'

'You are in your back. You're thirty-nine. Stop lying to

me about your age. Didn't I do thirty-six hours in the labour ward on you? Will you have your dinner with me, before you go off gallivanting?

'Will you have something to eat?' her mother would say as if it was the answer to everything in the world. Once upon a time it had been. Until Joe had told her the truth that had hit home harder than anything else. Or maybe it was because she'd latched on to the lardy-hip thing to blot out the other things he'd said.

But we don't talk about that.

These are the Virgo Club taboos: don't talk to Helen about the time Dette voted Conservative because she liked the look of the candidate's canvasser and had him call back more than five times, don't complain about the NHS, the boring nature of worthy causes or discuss fashion with any degree of seriousness.

Don't talk to Rorie about why she stays with John, or directors, or confidence. She doesn't have to, she should have been one and she hasn't got any.

Don't talk to Catriona about the latest hot actress, au pairs, or express any degree of cynicism about the healing power of crystals.

Don't talk to Dette about Joe the Soak. The only thing he gave her was a good surname to replace Bender. Morgan, more sophisticated, a better byline. At what price? Don't, for the life of you, bring up how useless he was or how the Conservative canvasser turned out to be married to someone, well, a lot more conventional than Dette. 'She wore pumps, for God's sake!' Dette exploded, after the wife had confronted her at the launch of strawberry bath products in Fortnum and Mason. 'Pumps! What Diana was responsible for! And I never go out with married men. I'm not like Rorie!'

The Virgo Club taboos were skirted with the ease and eye avoidance you would associate with years of seeing the same people.

'We know each other. And we know what we don't want to know about each other,' Dette said to herself as she watched London out of the train window. Grey, smelly London. She'd lived nowhere else and still she never felt she fitted in. And last night. All that booze and deciding to shag – sorry, not to shag, to seduce – her friend's man. Who'd she get? She couldn't remember. She'd look in her purse in a minute when she wasn't feeling so greasy. The hangovers were getting worse. Not even the six-cups-of-coffee cure would drive them away now.

Forty next month. Unbelievable.

Dette was murderously late for work and she had to meet with the boss. She'd managed to snag her tights in her haste to put them on. Her false nails had a habit of doing that. But the ones underneath were so bitten she could never have displayed them in public.

'Shit,' she spat.

The morning-after-the-lunchtime-before was a feeling familiar to Dette Morgan.

'What is the most important thing I need to know?' she'd asked Joe at the features department Christmas party on her first job as an editorial assistant on a national magazine. A lucky break. Eighteen masquerading as twenty-three, with a full CV when the nearest she'd got to the magazine world was a summer working in WH Smith's. She'd been beside herself with fear that she couldn't pull it off. But she had. Beautifully. Thanks to a summer spent reading and pilfering articles from Stateside magazines. She had balls. She had a laugh that made others laugh with her, a great sense of humour and plenty of talent.

'The most important thing you need to know?' Joe, the famous journalist, the only man to interview the Queen, repeated her eager question. 'The art of being not drunk. You can't do an afternoon's work without it.'

She'd followed his instructions faithfully through two bottles of Chardonnay and gone back to the office. She'd typed the same sentence over and over again, furiously and inaccurately. It worked.

Many lunchtimes and several dinners later she ended up in bed with Joe when she should have been at a desk typing the same sentence over and over again.

A few months after this he surprised her so much by asking her to marry him that she'd sobered up instantly. What she hadn't realised was that Joe Morgan was drunk at the time. Because Joe always was.

'I know what I am, Bernie.' He gave that lopsided grin that made it look like his face was going to slide off somewhere without him. 'Someone like you deserves a lot better than me and you could even reform me.' No one else ever called her Bernie. They'd have lost both their legs.

Even though she was only twenty-one when they exchanged vows, she was sure she could change him. He was forty and unchangeable. She hung on through all the carousing and infidelities because there was never going to be another like Joe Morgan and there hadn't been. He knew everyone there was to know in town, made tabloid copy as well as wrote it. He didn't think twice about coming home with a beautiful piece of jewellery for her, or flowers, or a plane ticket to spend a weekend in a

European city, but he never had enough money for the rent. Whatever life had been with him, it had not been as exciting since.

She'd caught him in their bed with the magazine's latest editorial assistant, the new her, five years after they were married. There had been many more editorial assistants before then and since. But that was the one that had persuaded her – Joe had not meant to marry her, he just hadn't the heart to back out of it once he had proposed. If Dette hadn't left then, she never would.

Then he'd turned nasty. 'You let yourself go, Dette, turned lardy. What did you expect?'

The only thing she had taken from her marriage was his name. She shared this relief in losing her maiden name with Catriona, and they both avoided the subject with Helen, who was irate at the idea of women losing anything to men, even things they didn't want.

Dette was now beauty editor of her magazine. The promotion had come from overwork when she had no other way of forgetting about Joe.

Her true self, the one her friends met every first Tuesday, was hidden under a ton of skin preservatives and the camouflage of a designer wardrobe.

'Small, blonde and the only woman who can be caustic about face creams,' another journalist had dubbed her. Advertisers were always complaining about her copy and her savage remarks about their products. But the readers loved her as mascara's answer to Jeremy Clarkson. She wrote about her subject with the truth it always seemed to lack: 'No,' she'd once replied to a reader's query. 'There is no difference between that lipstick and the one you can buy in the pound shop. Oh, sorry, there is –

about twenty-nine pounds.'

They didn't sack her because she was an institution, and because when she found a product that was good, she wrote that it was very, very good and the Morgan seal of approval was sought-after by beauty firms as much as it was disputed by the ones she had disparaged.

She hadn't told the girls yesterday because Helen's problem had been much more serious. But this time she might have pushed things too far. A serious slagging-off, of what had turned out to be a major new account, had set the phones hopping all last week and much of this one. Even though it was only Wednesday Dette could not wait for Friday. True – a minimalist fragrance for women, alleged to be an 'Essence that brings out the essence of you' – had had Dette retching at the first squirt: 'The makers of True will want me to be honest, or they would not have called it so. So here's what I think: True smells like poo. And the only way to get rid of the reek is to douse yourself in Domestos. Don't wear it. If you're unlucky enough to have bought or been given it, it does kill all known germs dead. And it might just finish you off.'

When Ducky, her editor and friend who'd championed her through other storms, cancelled their habitual Monday lunch and avoided her eyes, she began to worry. Inside a small voice said she had gone too far. A smaller voice still was almost begging something to happen. Something different. She was fed up with being a caricature, an institution. She wanted to be ordinary.

Dette was London Irish and her mother, who'd brought her up after her dad died suddenly, had filled her with a sense of longing for the home place, Athbeg, a country town. In her secret heart she fantasised about moving there. But she knew this would never happen. She had no way of making an income. 'Where's the opportunity to work with make-up there? A chemist that still sells Tweed? I don't think so,' she had once told Rorie when she urged her to try to make a go of it in Ireland.

'Ah, you don't know what the place is like now,' Rorie gave up. 'You could have a great life. Meet someone. Maybe.'

The last word gave it all away. Over the years the girls had watched Dette turn into Joe – she only ever had lovers who would not last long.

Martin was not allowed to leave so much as a toothbrush in her flat.

The only reason she was even going out with him was because, right now, she was feeling more lonely than usual and, ever since she'd met him at the opening night of one of Rorie's plays, he'd pursued her. Like most of those East End boys, once he'd decided he wanted something he was all out to get it. She wasn't sure she was even comfortable with him. There was something about the way he looked at her, the things he said, that cut a little too close to the bone. For instance, the night before last, she'd allowed him to stay after they had made love because she was too tired to send him home. She'd woken that morning and he was studying her face. 'What?' she snapped.

'I was just thinking. You look younger without the war paint.'

She'd turned on her side away from him. 'I am what I am.'

He got up shortly after that and whispered a quiet

goodbye to her from the door.

She whispered into her pillow, 'Battleaxes don't work without it.'

It had taken an almighty effort to get out the door this morning. It didn't help that this hangover was ten times worse than normal. But on her way out, she realised, it was more than the hangover – the Noise was back again.

The Noise.

It would have to wait until after she'd seen Ducky.

Dette's boss, Ducky, liked her. He would miss the gossipy lunches, her loyalty, but he could no longer be loyal to her and keep his job. She had been offered his job several times and always turned it down – there would be no free lipstick and too many migraines in proper editing. 'No, I'm happiest around smelly things.'

'What'll you do now?' he asked.

'Well, if you'll allow me, I'll take two suitcases from Fashion and empty the beauty-cupboard contents into them.'

'And I'll buy you lunch at Nobu as a final fling. And we'll still do Mondays.'

'Not today, Ducky,' she couldn't keep the tears out of her voice. 'But don't rule me out for next week, when I'm poor and you should have forgotten me.'

'Now that,' Ducky smiled, 'is not possible. You are unforgettable.'

'And unemployable. No one will take me as a beauty editor now. Not when House of Fart refuses to deal with me.'

He didn't know what to say to that. She'd helped him

when he was a horribly hetero man trying to get a job as the editor of *Madame*. She'd helped him get his first job there as her assistant. When he'd asked her why she had taken on a former employee of *Welding Monthly* she'd explained it was pure sexism. 'You're hefty. And I like that. You have a willy. I like those. But don't worry,' she had held up her hand, 'I'm not after yours. I see the happily married look on your face. It would be fun to work with a man. I've never had the privilege.

'Now, start off by pretending to be gay, in a quiet, straight way, of course, all restraint, Armani suits and Calvin casuals, and call yourself Ducky instead of Dave. That'll have the fashion houses in your pockets. And the fact that you might just be straight will have the beauty-house women hoping you might be. The only men they meet in the course of their work are research scientists with pebble glasses. Be gorgeous, be an enigma and you'll go far. You big jock, you.'

'You did so much for me, Dette,' Ducky Simpson, editor, carried her cases down the stairs like a porter after she had flounced out of the office, as they had prearranged.

'Remember, we're having a temporary disagreement. Don't let them know I'm sacked for a couple of weeks. Until I've sorted myself out.' She'd instructed her own removal like it was a major event.

'What about doing makeovers for the magazine, like you used to? Use a different byline, though, just for now.'

From anyone else it would have been a deliberate put-down. From Ducky it was a desperate attempt to give her a way to earn a living.

'Right now I'll say fuck off to that. Next week I'll be grateful.'

The cab pulled up. Ducky put her cases in and fired a fifty at the driver. 'Take her wherever she wants to go.'

'All the way, ' Dette mustered, 'as usual.'

17

Dette hopped out at the Tube, lugging her suitcases. The cabbie gave her Ducky's cash reluctantly. The truth was that fifty pounds was all that would come between her and total darkness by Friday. The electricity people had already called to cut her off.

She walked past a struggling mother, dropped her cases and grabbed the end of the buggy. The mother, coping with a runaway toddler, was grateful.

I've left five thousand quid's worth of cosmetics on the landing, was all she could think.

'Why can't they put in a lift?' the mother complained, and Dette managed to look sympathetic without saying anything, a London trick, before sprinting back up the stairs. The only thing that could make her move so quickly was make-up.

'Why?' she pleaded to the grey sky which did a good job of ignoring her. 'Why today?' The Noise grew, and her headache took over her whole body.

God, Dette grimaced. It has to happen, doesn't it?

Just when you've negotiated puberty, learned to manage your monthly cycle without committing murder in the middle of it and can look forward to a quiet decade before menopause.

The Noise had become an uncontrollable jangle that could mean only one thing – the body clock's bugle call.

Its first toot had sounded as she'd taken her thirtieth birthday cards down from the mantelpiece. That was five years ago, since she'd faked her age by five years.

Dette and a baby. For that she would need a man to stick around longer than two weeks.

Helen and Catriona never shut up about kids, talking a language they learned at ante-natal classes that Dette didn't understand. 'I can see the only way I can join this club is to get a foetus of my own.' They were horrified at her even thinking she was mother material. That was when she had learned to act disinterested about the subject. Her confidence was dented.

Catriona and Helen had brandished their awful, unsightly, uncomfortable symptoms – stretch marks, swollen ankles, dark skin patches – like weapons against Dette and Rorie, who were staving off nature with the help of Schering or Durex and steering well clear of Persona.

Then, a few years ago, Dette held Catriona's daughter, Zoë, who'd been born on the living-room floor. She feigned disgust, 'Placenta and antique Persian don't mix, Cat.'

But she'd thought, I want this. It was like wanting the moon.

Nothing got rid of it. Now, as she hopped off the train and began a fifteen-minute totter in impossibly high heels which helped her to make just under the national average of five foot five inches, Dette Morgan knew she was envious of all women who put on two to four stone in under a year.

'OK, when I get home I'll go outside and howl at the moon for a while. Will that do you?' she pleaded with the jangle. She fished in her bag for her keys, found the piece of paper. John. Yuck. The problem would be fighting him off once he got a sniff she was trying to seduce him. The man was that sad, terrible thing, an ageing Lothario. Like Joe, only she'd been too young to see it in him. Let's face it, like she could be described now.

A strange thought crept into her head, the way strange thoughts do when you should be preoccupied with something else. So now, your new career is seducing one of your best mate's man. And getting pregnant.

What if she got him to make her pregnant? It would be a sure-fire way of knowing who the father was without the father ever wanting to be involved in the child's life.

She was jobless, had no way of paying her mortgage and she was planning to have a child on her own with a friend's lover.

And what about Rorie?

'I'm doing her a favour. He's never been right for her.'

'He's never been right for her – and you want him to father a baby. What kind of future is that for a kid, and for your friendship with Rorie? She's your most practical friend. She got you your flat, and she'll give you the money for your bills until you sort yourself out.' The muffled voice of Dette's conscience found a loudspeaker.

'She never has to know, or him. He won't have anything to do with my baby. I'll be father and mother to it.

And Rorie deserves a lot better than a man who spends half his life with his wife and half with her.' People on the street were looking at her, having a conversation with herself. 'And I'll write a novel. And it'll be a bestseller and once I have enough for me and my baby I'll give the rest of it to Rorie. To become a director with.'

Already she was talking about 'My Baby', saw herself writing pieces for parenting magazines. She couldn't stop the thrill of excitement that this might be something that was supposed to happen, written in her stars. She might even start believing in the horoscopes she read.

18

'So that was when I decided the man who can write the definitive play hasn't been born yet. Maybe, just maybe, if I work hard at it, I'll be that man. But what am I talking about? You're a writer. Beauty products, stage plays, it's all the same. Words, Dette. Words.'

Patronising twat. If John Edwards really meant it he wouldn't have made the point three times in the half-hour she'd been forced to listen to him. If Dette wasn't careful she'd have to eat her dessert to avoid falling asleep. How the hell was she going to let this creep – who'd talked about nothing but himself and his craft, when everyone knew he hadn't written a readable word outside the shopping lists he left for Rorie – impregnate her?

It was hard enough sitting beside him – the thought of sex with him made her want to be sick. She could easily imagine the sensation. Hang on now, she wasn't pregnant yet.

Things were haywire, her job gone, makeovers so she

could earn next month's rent, asking Martin to please stop belching into the face of her oldest friend. Angelo feeling George's leg. Helen and Euan not talking. What a Saturday night.

'Please tell me the Scarlett O'Hara will be enough to make this fecker succumb. I can't bear to be nice to him.' She fixed her cleavage in her favourite red dress as she had a conversation with God, who, as usual, was shocked at Dette Morgan's peculiar brand of morality. Her mother had called round to her flat that morning, with a miraculous medal and a pint of holy water from her once-a-year pilgrimage to Knock, in the west of Ireland, followed by a fortnight in her hometown.

'Everyone in Athbeg says hello to you, Dette. They're all reading you in the magazine. There was a run on Max Factor thicker lashes after you giving it the thumb's-up. They say Dowling the milkman buys everything you recommend and pretends it's for his wife, but we know he wears dresses in that caravan in his garden.'

At that point, Dette ran to the toilet. Sick at the prospect of telling her mother, who was so proud of her daughter 'writing in the picture books', as she called them? Or was it the Friday-night send-off the *Madame* staff had forced her to have, for old times' sake? String-fellows, they'd ended up in, the only place they'd let them into for free. Dette stuck into a drunken conversation with a suspender-wearing waitress studying law, the rest of them singing 'She Will Survive'.

'This has to stop,' she told the toilet bowl. 'I want to be puking for the right reasons.' Back out to mammy who was cooking bacon and eggs. 'I'll never manage those.'

She ate two lots, and then dinner at Angelo's on top

and now she was halfway through her dessert and John was still talking about the postmodern state of drama and damaging effect of *East Enders*.

'I dunno. I like Phil Mitchell.' Mind you I would pick the world's most dysfunctional male, wouldn't I?

'Well, you've got the younger version in loverboy over there,' John's eyes were fastened on her newly arranged breasts. She wanted to slap him. If the kid ended up looking anything like him she'd have trouble bonding with it. This was a bad idea, a very bad idea.

Hang on now, Dette, remember what you're here for.

'What you need, Dette…' John's whisper had taken on what he must imagine was a seductive quality. But he'd had garlic mussels for starters. Come on, do what you've done before. Pretend he's human. '…is a mature man, who can appreciate you.'

'You know what, John? You're right. Maturity, that's what I should go for.'

For a moment John froze. Dette prayed he would back down, as lechers often do. But not this one. She wanted to shout across the table to Rorie, 'You see? He's not worth the steam of your pee. And I'm going to let him get me pregnant. What's wrong with me? Are my hormones really this unreliable?'

Instead she stuck on an enduring smile and let him drift back to his favourite subject: him, his writing, him, his students, him, his health problems, him, his wife's ridiculous demands for money, him, his unruly children. 'John, I'd love to talk more, but we've got to move on now, do the final switch. Look, Angelo's serving the liqueurs.' Thank God she'd be next to Euan. Even if he was unfaithful, at least he was interesting, and unassuming, and funny.

'A shame, when we were getting on so well.' He was so full of it he'd forgotten all the times she'd lorried into him on her friend's behalf, all the brief nods and tight hellos when they met on the stairs of the block of flats they both lived in. All the indications that she could not stand him.

'But you know what, John? I'd love to read what you've written so far. It sounds fascinating. And I could give you an honest opinion.'

His face clouded. Dette's honesty would not be what John Edwards, playwright, was after. More of a fawning, pawing, cloying, flattering approach, he'd want.

'I'm sure to love it.'

His features cleared at the prospect of future adoration: 'Well, why don't I bring the script to yours?' he beamed. Then whispered into Dette's cleavage, 'And the wine.'

'Friday,' she pushed the prospect as far ahead of her as possible. 'Why don't you call around on Friday night?'

They both knew nights were out for Rorie, who worked at the theatre.

'Well, if I'm going for this, I'd better get the plumbing checked,' Dette turned off her laptop and hopped out of bed. The novel she'd started work on was pretty far advanced. She had no ideas, no plot, no title and not a sentence written. Her only future means of payment was taking Rorie, who dressed like a butch lesbian, to the shops and buying her a new look. Then getting the three other Virgos photographed and selling the features to Ducky. She hoped he was still feeling lousy over the whole sacking thing.

She flicked open the *Yellow Pages* and had a look at the gynaecologists' section. Harley Street, that was where she needed to go for the initial consultation. She didn't have enough money, but once her cheque had bounced she'd be far, far away in West London. She dialled.

'Mr McCauley's rooms. Can I help you?'

'Mrs McConnell here.' Well, she couldn't relinquish all her Catholic leanings. If she was going to try to become a mother, she was going to try to become a bit more respectable. Maybe buy a pair of pumps. 'I'd like to book an appointment with you to see the doctor.'

Thursday. Two o'clock. It'd be an excuse to get out. Martin wouldn't twig she'd lost her job if she was still out and about. She couldn't understand why she'd told everyone not to tell him. What did it matter? If he knew she was broke, he might be tempted to feel sorry for her, or he might do what all men did in the face of desperation. Leave.

'It's about time I let the boy go,' Dette said to herself. 'Things are getting too complicated.'

19

'I'm thinking of showing you the first three scenes tomorrow night so you get a representative picture.' John had used the interest Dette had demonstrated on Saturday night as an excuse to ring her and confirm Friday, while boring the knickers off her for an hour about his new play. Dette was clock-watching. Harley Street by two? She'd never do it. 'And I picked up a bottle of Châteauneuf du Pape.'

'Do what?'

'Wine.'

'Isn't that expensive?' You tight fart who never buys Rorie anything.

'It's worth it. You're worth it. Isn't that what the hair-oil advertisement says?'

L'Oréal, old deaf lad, L'Oréal. Did he think this was empathy? 'Great, lovely, thanks, John. See you tomorrow, thanks, John. I'm sure it's fascinating, sounds amazing, John. Bye.'

The Noise came with her on the train. It was beside

itself with excitement, church bells ringing rather than fire-engine sirens. She couldn't help feeling nervous, smiling, sick, full of anticipation for getting there, full of desire to get off the train and go home. Visions of a three-year-old John lookalike boring her with the finer details of Barney the Dinosaur and how he'd do a much better job of bringing the character to life if he were only the script editor filled her head.

'Could you not think of someone else to donate their sperm?' Her conscience had grabbed a loudspeaker again.

'No. Everyone else is too risky. Even Martin. You can't tell what a twenty-something might do if he found out he was going to be a father.'

'Well, if you want no risk, why not go to the sperm bank?'

'I haven't got two hundred quid. Now, shut up. This donor is the devil I know. He's got some modicum of intelligence and he's not bad, if you like short Welshmen. And he's a crap father, so we won't have to have any running battles over custody.'

'Why don't you just jump the gun there, Bernadette Bender? Who's to say you'll manage to get pregnant?'

'Shut up! I ovulate on Friday. The one regular thing about me is my period. And I'm not going to drink a single drop before then.'

'What about the fags?'

'They don't affect fertility, they enhance it.'

'No, they bloody well don't.'

The train pulled in at Waterloo. Dette hurried for the Underground. 'Fine, then! See if I'm serious or not.' She threw her freshly opened cigarettes at the nearest homeless bundle. Knowing full well there was another packet in her bag, since her habit was a forty-a-day extravagance.

'Well, Mrs O'Connell, you're in perfect working order. In fact, it's so perfect I'd give you an A plus.'

'Thanks, Dr McCauley.' It was hard to be relaxed with a man who'd just given her an internal.

'Don't thank me, you've done the hard work. I look forward to seeing you on the labour ward in eight months time.'

'The what?'

'From the dates you given me, you're four weeks gone.'

This wasn't real. She wasn't really taking out her diary. 'Actually, Doctor. I mark my periods in red pencil in my book. There's no red pencil mark for last month.' She flipped back four more pages. 'Or the month before. I never noticed.'

'Well, then,' Mr McCauley, who didn't mind being called Doctor even though he was a consultant, who had kids of his own and had seen thousands come into the world in all sorts of ways, 'you're three months pregnant.'

'But you don't understand. I hadn't even started trying. I've been drinking my brains out and smoking.'

'Well, you obviously have a hardy little baby in there who very much wants to be born.'

'No. No, I don't.'

'Yes. Yes, you do.'

'But it'll be born without something. I'm so unhealthy, never took folic acid, nothing. I did have broc-

coli yesterday and I ate a Shepherdess pie a few days ago.'
She was panicking.

'Mrs O'Connell.' The consultant got out of his chair
and came round to sit on the edge of the desk. He took
her hand and stared into her eyes, 'This practice pays for
my other work with the dispossessed. I've seen some terrible things, babies born with a drug habit. Whatever you
think you've done you haven't done half what you could
do. And you'd be surprised how resilient the little souls
are. Now, go off and feed yourself. Don't smoke and
don't drink, if you can help it. If you can't then don't do
it to excess and the chances are you and the baby will be
fine.'

'Doctor, I don't have any money to pay you. But I'll
get it, I promise. I just thought you were a rich idiot. I
didn't realise. And I'm not Mrs O'Connell. I'm not even
Mrs McConnell. You got my false name wrong. I'm not
Mrs anything.'

'Well, now, there's two surprises. One for you and me.
Let me correct you by saying that I am a rich idiot. And
don't worry about this consultation. It's on the house.
Just tell the receptionist I said so, or she'll pull the net up
on you.'

Three months pregnant with a twenty-five-year-old
artist's baby. What an achievement. Still, there was a huge
wave of relief that she hadn't had to seduce John. Though
she would still have to find out if he was willing to give
Rorie an excuse to kick him out. It would have to be
quick before her bump started showing. She thought of
all the wine she'd consumed in the past two months. The

little thing would be a pickle. But then, she hadn't had even a trace of morning sickness. Well, she hadn't thought it was morning sickness. Automatically her hand reached inside her bag for a fag. She found her pearl lighter and passed it and the unopened packet of cigarettes to a beggar.

She ran into a public park, sat on the nearest seat and let the crying commence.

'I'm sorry, little baby,' she rubbed her stomach. 'What a start you've had. From now on I'll eat all the right things and I'll move so you can have proper fresh air, but don't be born with problems. I'll never forgive myself.'

Helen. She had to tell Helen. And Mammy. She had to go to Mammy's for her dinner.

The following night John Edwards left Dette's flat and limped up the stairs with an unopened bottle of Châteauneuf du Pape. 'She wants me really,' he said, when he'd drunk it all by himself in the darkness. 'I know she wants me.'

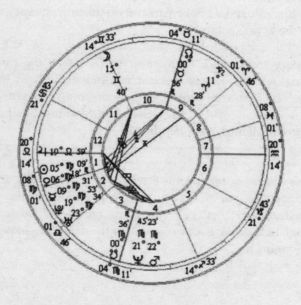

Rorie Marks, female, Tuesday 29 August 1967
at 5:06 a.m. Baldoyle, Dublin, Ireland
(53N24'00 6W08'00)

20

RORIE

No Planets in the Sixth
This might indicate a lack of direction, but in no way does it signify you lack talent. You need to compensate for this void with some serious thinking. Most people concentrate on the future too much. You are guilty of the opposite. The more unhappy you are, the less you want to know. Work-related issues are not usually paramount concerns for you. Of course, outside influences can temporarily upset this balance, causing you to devote more time and energy to these parts of your life, at least on a temporary basis. On an occasion such as this, your greatest opportunity will arise.

*****

Rorie sighed at the backs of the departing actors who were heading as usual for the pub after rehearsal and had, also as usual, not bothered to invite her. Stage managers never got told where the party was. Their job was to spoil them by pointing out to the actors that they had to be up for work the next morning. As the director's representative on Earth, cast and crew treated her like (a) the stool pigeon, (b) the carthorse and (c) the skunk.

Not that they would treat her like that to her face. To her face she was God, or at least the daughter of, because she was seated at the right hand of the director. Actors had occasionally asked her permission to go to the toilet.

She wished she'd known that before she'd decided to take this route in the business, or had it been decided for her?

Yes, like most things. For someone who had always wanted to be a director she lacked the vital ingredient – direction. All her life, it seemed, there had been someone to make her decisions for her. Her mother had told her to get an education so that she did not have to rely on any man for money, so she had. Then her best friend Helen had told her London was a better place to study than Dublin so why didn't she come over with her? So she had. Then John, her tutor and lover, had suggested they set up home together – from Monday to Thursday. So she had. Her affair was cool when she was in college and pathetic now that she was nearly thirty-seven. He commuted back to Wales for weekends with his wife, two children and dog, leaving her with her guilt and a goldfish for company on lonely Sundays.

In her career her first boss had said she was a brilliant organiser and it would be best if she concentrated on that. She had come home to John, enraged at such dismissal of her artistic capability, and he had gone silent, too silent. 'You agree with him.'

'No, it's not that. It's just—'

'Just what? The plays I directed at college were very good – you said so.'

He looked away.

'Does this mean that I passed because you were sleeping with me?'

He hadn't answered directly and she'd gone for a long walk during which she had answered for herself. It looked like she was not cut out to be the next Jane Campion.

Maybe that was why her friends from childhood and college days meant so much to her. Helen had been there for as long as she could remember and, in fairness, Helen had never gone along with John or First Boss in their theories about her. 'It's nonsense, Rorie! You've been dissecting plots since we watched *Jackanory* together!' Helen then was in the forensics and pathology part of her medical degree, everything was about cutting things up. 'You're made to be a director.'

'A lot of people end up with sad lives in show business because they thought the same thing. I'll concentrate on what I'm good at. I'll still be successful.'

'You just won't be doing what you should be doing.' Then Helen left it, because she could see how hard it was for Rorie to put on a brave face. And Rorie kept her best friend's insistence that she was good director material as a secret jewel to be examined at times when she felt low for not trying to be what she had always wanted.

It amazed Rorie how someone as bright, as outstanding as Helen would want to be her friend. Helen had laughed when Rorie had once admitted it. 'You should see yourself.'

'What do you mean?'

'You have the whole thing, Rorie. I'm a clever clogs, but you're clever and lovely. Everyone likes you.'

Rorie had argued, 'You're too busy achieving to notice men. I wish I didn't notice them. I'm always falling in love. You're too clever to fall in love unless it's with the right man.'

'Yes, yes, yes,' Helen had pushed aside what she considered a dull subject. She only considered it dull because she had Euan. 'I have Euan, I don't need to notice anyone.'

It had been like that since college. Euan loved Helen. Helen loved Euan. That was one area of life they would never have a problem in. They were so sure of each other.

And Rorie had John, who she was never sure would return on Monday. Needless to say, Helen did not like John. Needless to say, none of her friends did.

What was she doing with a father of two children who were not her own? In the beginning it was because she had loved him. In the middle it was because she had had other things to think about – stage management was all about problems. The ones at home never seemed as critical. Now, towards the end of their relationship, or that was what it felt like to her, she had a sneaking suspicion that she was doing John's wife a favour in keeping him occupied for over half the week.

Rorie Marks hated decisions.

Having John had always meant not having to have

someone else. Who she might love more. Who might leave her. Rorie knew where that came from: a father who had left behind a kind, talented, fabulous mother when Rorie was thirteen. She looked like that father. She could look at photos of herself and see the man who had never bothered to contact his daughter or wife again. For all they knew he was dead.

At least John had never been in danger of leaving her. His was the perfect arrangement, for him, for now. She was the icing on his cake, or maybe the cake now that he saw more of her than he did of Janet, his childhood sweetheart who had got pregnant by him at seventeen and hung on to him because he refused to let go of his Welsh-valley roots.

Rorie had told her friends the reason she stayed with him was that he was more likely to stay than most other men, but they would not believe her.

'He won't be there when he retires! He'll be back in Fargavenny with his wife, children and grandchildren by then,' Helen pleaded with her.

Helen had Euan until death did them part. Euan would never run out, sell up, move on from anyone he loved. He was a bitter-end person. Rorie loved him. She'd come to accept it; it was as natural as drawing breath.

Eight months ago that had changed. He'd betrayed Helen and, for Rorie, it was as if he had betrayed her too. Euan was the only man Rorie trusted. Over the years she had grown as close to him as she was to Helen. They were her family, apart from her mother.

Almost as soon as Euan had left the house that day, Helen had phoned her.

'He's been having an affair.'

'I'm so sorry.'

'Can you believe it?'

'No one can believe it until it happens to them.' What else could she say? How could she say she already knew?

'Can you come round?' Helen had finally been forced to ask.

'I have to go into the theatre. Noël and Nigel are having another bloody tiff. But I could meet you before we have lunch, at Angelo's, before the others come.'

'No. I have to wait until he comes home at lunchtime. Bea's out. The kids are at school and playgroup. I'm by myself. I told Mrs Moore not to come.'

She should have gone round, but she'd hoped it would go away, disappear, leave things as they always were.

And she couldn't face the fact that she'd betrayed Helen, too, with her silence.

So Helen had accosted her in the ladies' at Angelo's yesterday. She knew Rorie too well not to realise she was holding something back. This was a mess. How could she explain to her oldest friend that she had kept silent to limit the damage already done? Rorie did not like change. She wanted things exactly as they were.

That was why she had suggested the fidelity test. She knew Euan wouldn't ever do it again. It didn't matter about the rest of them. Catriona didn't even like George, much less love him. John was not really hers and it would give her a valid excuse to say goodbye to him. Martin was a joke – even Dette would admit that. Nothing would change that should stay the same. Only the things that needed to happen would happen. Rorie would say goodbye to John, Dette would get sense and start fishing for someone her own age, Catriona might even find the courage to go out on her own or find some way of living with George that made her less complaining.

Then Rorie had drawn Euan's name from the hat. It was what she hadn't counted on. From the way Helen looked at her, she sensed Rorie had. Rorie felt already things could never be the same between them. The last thing she needed to be doing now was seducing her best friend's husband. Not least because she was in love with him, always had been since Helen had introduced him.

That was another reason why John was the answer to Rorie's problems. John stopped her staying completely in love with her best friend's husband. Over the years she had come to love Euan safely, like a brother. At least, that was what she told herself. Even if, now and again, she felt something else, she knew it was contained.

'*Rorrieee!*'

The director was looking for her. Rorie got up from the desk in the cramped cubby-hole that was laughingly called the office of this fine West End production. The budget had been blown on lavish sets, which meant, as usual, Administration lived on the crumbs. She even had to buy her own manila folders. And, to make matters worse, the play was touring in a month's time. She wouldn't even be around to rectify things with Helen if the situation between her and Euan went on for too long.

'Rorrieee. The parlour scene's teapot has gone missing again!'

Rorie thought the drama happening in her life was a lot more interesting than this play, one of the worst she had worked on in years.

'The green room's filthy.' The director followed his

voice into her office. Nigel Blunt had a habit of bursting in and living up to his surname. A frustrated actor – Rorie knew the type. Should be on the stage rather than directing from the wings. 'And there are no biscuits. There have to be biscuits or Noël Coward,' the writer of this epic, which was playing to a half-full house after only one fortnight, 'will have a fit again!'

Rorie did not bother to say these tasks were the assistant stage manager's job to do. They hadn't got one. No money. She took out the Mr Muscle and the cloth she kept in her drawer for such occasions and the packet of Cadbury's Fingers, which she'd eaten most of this morning in her hung-over state, and went back to work on a play that she might have directed better, if she'd the confidence.

'Don't forget the Milton – we don't want anyone losing their voice.' Nigel ran after her with a bottle of sterilising fluid to wipe over the Green Room tables. 'And did you sort out the budget deficit yet? How are we getting along with that?'

Great. So she was the accountant and the cleaner. What was her boss doing?

'Nigel, I told you. To break even we need to play to a three-quarters-full house. We don't have the numbers to make it work.'

'But you can make it look good on paper, Rorie. At least that's what your references tell me.' Nigel burst out of the room. He was the only director Rorie knew who wore a tie. When he was making a particularly underhand comment he fingered it. He had fingered it just then. In this business you were only as good as your last production. If your director decided to tell the industry you were useless, then you were. So far, Rorie had emerged from each play with her reputation intact because she compensated for most weaknesses. The directors took the credit and she got the recommendation for the next job. Nigel was bad at his job but good at hiding it. The problem was, when you got to the West End you couldn't hide it any more. He was a sinking ship and his tie manipulation told Rorie he was taking her with him as first officer.

Just then Noël Coward came in. He had changed his name by deed poll ten years ago, as a publicity stunt. That had landed him work as the new master of farce. He even wore hair oil and a cravat and shopped in retro stores to get the look right. Real talent lay behind all the gimmicks – the difficulty was that he had a problem with Nigel's lack of it. But since both men were bitchy queens, they took it out on Rorie rather than each other. She was the go-between who had the choice task of delivering messages they didn't want to give each other face to face.

'Tell him,' Noël said to Rorie, ignoring the fact that she was smearing Milton into the shape of a tie on the glass-topped table, 'that three of the cast did not know their lines last night. How can this happen in the second week? He should be all over them like a rash.'

'I think he knows,' Rorie reasoned.

'So what is he doing about it?'

I don't know. Rorie wanted to say. Ask him yourself. But to do so would only make matters worse. Why did her whole life seem to be about keeping schtum?

'Well, find out and report back to me. Otherwise I might have to talk to him myself and you know what will happen if things get to that point.'

It'll be more interesting than what's happening on

stage, Rorie thought. To each other's faces Nigel and
Noël were luvvies of the highest order – Noël admired
Nigel's ties, Nigel admired Noël's cravats. It was sick-
making. In the real world neither would survive. Both
had City boyfriends who kept them financially secure in
Clapham and Islington, respectively. What Rorie Marks
needed was a City boyfriend. A George. What she had
was a miser.

'Well, Noël, it's a pity you can't have a word with each
other. I have a lot to do around here without the transla-
tor duties,' she snapped. This was the hangover talking.

Noël looked like he was ready to launch into her when
her mobile rang. It was Catriona. She never phoned
Rorie at work. Catriona preferred to ignore Rorie's work
in theatre because it reminded her that she didn't have
any.

'Rorie!' She sounded unusually bright. 'Are you free
later on?'

'I have to work through because of yesterday.' Nigel
had already hauled Rorie over the coals for disappearing.
Even though Tuesday was her official day off.

'Oh, come on. Please! Just fifteen minutes. If I don't
see you today I might not have the courage to ask you
tomorrow.'

Rorie was intrigued. Things between her and
Catriona had been strained lately. But she did not want
to think about that now.

'OK. I'll do cappuccino with you, darling. And we'll
talk about how you can help me with our budget situation.'

Nigel and Noël, both standing over her now, backed
off when they heard her arrange to meet someone who

might save the production finances and their professional skins. An hour later, neither murmured as she put on
her coat and went out the door. Rorie smiled – she never
did cappuccino and she never called anyone 'darling'.
Maybe Catriona could ask George to look over the figures. She'd never been any good at maths, especially lying
maths.

'I want to get back into acting.'

Rorie looked at her. For this Catriona had got dressed
up, come across town and made her take time out of a
busy day for something she could have told her on the
phone.

'You do? But—'

'I know. I said it was a profession for fools and full of
them, and for hypocrites trying to find new degrees of
falsity, and for snakes and lizards and reptiles and
rodents and – I want to be one of them again.'

'You do.' Rorie was matter of fact. 'And what can I
do?'

'Nothing. You're a stage manager,' Catriona still had
an actor's arrogance. But Rorie knew this hid her deep
insecurity. It wasn't hard to spot. All actors were the
same, unless they were humble. The humble ones had
real confidence, enough to know it was just a job.

'But,' Catriona continued, 'you know directors. You're
working with Nigel Blunt at the moment, aren't you?
And Noël Coward? I was wondering if you could give
them my CV and photo and see if they had a small part
in *Your Latest Fiasco*?' The unfortunate name of the new
production.

'But we're touring in a month. Our opening wasn't all it should have been,' Rorie saw Catriona's face crumple. 'We have to go to the provinces to hide the fact our play stinks.'

'Oh. I wouldn't have cared, Rorie, one line would have done. Just to get me started. Just to make me feel like I can be good at something again.'

Rorie was horrified to see tears roll down Catriona's face and even more horrified to realise that they were doing the same down hers. Both looked at each other and burst out laughing. The rest of the café's occupants looked disgruntled.

'What are you crying for?' Catriona asked Rorie.

'Oh, same reason as you. Hangover, hormones, how-did-my-life-get-me-here?'

Before she knew it Rorie had promised she would arrange for Nigel and Noël to have a look at Catriona. She knew exactly how to persuade them.

'You're a great friend.' Catriona looked so grateful Rorie almost felt guilty for the other thoughts she had going on in the back of her mind about how to persuade two pillars of the theatre to look favourably at a footstool. 'I know things haven't been great between us. I know I've been jealous that your still working in the business.'

So she had no idea that Rorie had been avoiding her.

'I know you've been avoiding me lately,' Catriona might be self-obsessed, but she was not stupid. 'I think it's because I've been even more jealous recently. I just couldn't find my way out of this depression. It's Magda, she makes me so—'

'It's not Magda, Catriona,' Rorie had to interrupt. 'It's not because I feel your jealousy. I didn't even know you were.'

'If it's not those things,' Catriona looked frightened behind her carefully made-up face, 'what is it?'

'I know, Catriona.'

'Know what?'

'I just know.'

'How long?'

'From the beginning. I saw you.'

21

'But if you knew why did you not say something?'
Catriona was gripping the table.

'Euan also told me it was a once-off. He came to see
me after it happened. He's not interested, Catriona.'
Rorie was pale. This was hard work. First there had been
yesterday's emotional outbursts, and today she had to go
through more confrontation. No wonder she avoided
emotional mess outside theatre hours. Work was draining
enough.

'Why did you not say anything before now?' Rorie
could see Catriona was still suspicious of how she had
come to know of her affair. 'Why did you not say anything to me?'

'Because I couldn't see what good it would achieve.
Things were already rocky between Helen and Euan. I
didn't want to hurt them any more than they had been.
Especially Helen.'

Catriona blushed. 'I won't have you portray me as the
guilty party here!' She almost stood up now, but Rorie
pulled her back into her seat. 'Euan was more than happy

to oblige and it was not just a one-night stand. I love Euan. I want him still.'

'And what effort has Euan made to be on his own with you in the past eight months?'

'He can't get away. He has to mind his children while Helen goes off to be a world-dazzling doctor. He puts his children first, which is more than I can say for my own husband.'

'This is my point, Catriona. You don't want Euan! You want someone who is not George. If you have Euan you'd soon realise he's just the same as George, a man who has a lot of responsibility, trying to get through life as best he can.'

'And who are you to preach? What have you been doing for the past fifteen years?'

'I know this *because* of what I've been doing for the past fifteen years,' Rorie's voice was raised now; she didn't care who heard her. 'I know what it's like to be in a relationship where there is no responsibility. I know it's not half as good as having to pay bills and make ends meet and put up with each other stealing the duvet seven nights a week rather than Monday to Thursday! It's lonely what I do, Catriona.'

'Not half as lonely as my marriage,' Catriona said quietly.

'No – twice as lonely. John doesn't love me as much as Euan and George do their wives. John has never cooked me a Sunday breakfast and we've been on holiday once, Catriona, in fifteen years.'

'Well that's your choice, Rorie.'

'It is, and I know it's a lousy one, Catriona, which is why I'm still your friend, even though you tried to shag my best friend's husband. Because I know how easy it is to make these mistakes.' The tears were streaming down Rorie's face now, and this time there was no stopping them with laughter. 'Which is also why I haven't said anything. I just wanted it all to go away.'

'I'm sorry, Rorie,' Catriona said softly. 'I only came here to ask for a job or at least a chance of one. I had no idea you knew. Otherwise I'd never have asked to meet you.'

'I'm glad you did. I would have had to talk to you about this anyway at some stage. You know Helen suspects me?'

Catriona shook her head. 'I was afraid she suspected me. That's why I asked so many questions yesterday.'

'Rubbish! You wanted to find out who else Euan had been seeing.'

'It wasn't me.'

'It wasn't anyone.'

'Oh, come on, Rorie. It must have been someone.'

'How can you know that?'

'Because he's already been willing to do it once, with me. Dette's right. If they do it once they'll do it again.'

'If I need relationship counselling, I must make sure I book Dette. She's so good at it.'

'As good as us,' Catriona smiled sadly.

'No, you eejit. You're not as bad as me and Dette. We only recognise men from Planet Bastard.'

'I don't know about that, Rorie. Martin seems to be nice to her.'

'He's twenty-five, Catriona, and he's about to work with three of the world's most beautiful women, in a lavish production that makes my budget look like what you'd spend on a children's party.'

'True, but at least he likes her.'

'George likes you.'

'I know. I wish I liked him back. I just find him—'

'Boring, repetitive.'

'So, I'm the same myself.'

'Yes. On that subject.'

'I'm sorry Helen suspects you, Rorie, it's not right.'

'Well, it's as well she does. At least that means our friendships have some chance of surviving all of this mess. But I can tell you, Catriona, if she ever does find out, that's curtains for you and her. Helen's not the forgiving type. That's why she's putting Euan through the mill. At least if she goes on thinking it's me she might give our friendship another chance.' Even as Rorie said it she felt it was not possible, but what made her want to take the blame? Maybe it was all the times she had thought about what it would be like if Euan was in love with her instead of Helen. Maybe she deserved punishment for those.

'Euan deserves it,' Catriona countered. 'It's not just me he's had an affair with. I wasn't the one he took into their bed.'

'He didn't take anyone into their bed,' Rorie repeated, looking at the coffee going grey as it went cold. 'It was just like he said to Helen.'

'Oh, come on, Rorie! That's such a childish excuse it might even be true.'

'Not half as childish as trying to shag one of Helen's friends in the back of a Volvo,' Rorie's eyebrows arched; Catriona went silent. 'But I have to admit,' Rorie relented, 'it was pretty childish. He says he can't tell Helen anything but the truth now, even if the truth stinks. He's afraid if he tells another lie he'll be caught out.'

'How come he tells you all this?' Catriona was jealous

of Rorie's intimacy with Euan. After all, she had been persuading herself for eight months that she was in love with him, since the New Year's Eve party where they had left Angelo's together and Euan had driven a drunken Catriona home. In her car. Helen had been on call at the hospital. George had gone home early, because 1 January was a working day for him. Whoever heard of a man leaving a New Year's Eve party early? Still, that was Catriona's problem.

Rorie's had been that she had left the party a half-hour after them, on her own. John was in Wales, where John always was over Christmas and New Year. Since she lived near Angelo's she had decided to walk. She had seen them in a pub car park, just off the main road. They were not discreet. Euan must have had as much to drink as Catriona, or was Rorie making excuses for him?

She had walked on, as if nothing had happened. But she had felt Euan freeze and pull himself off Catriona. If she had not seen them, Rorie was sure it would have gone all the way. The next day Euan had called her and come round to see her.

'Please don't tell Helen.' He had not begged, just asked.

'Why?'

'Because I don't think we'll last if you do.' He had left it at that.

'OK,' Rorie agreed. 'Just don't mention to Catriona that I know either.'

'So I left it,' she explained now to Catriona, 'and I hope always to leave it, because if Helen finds out who it was it's going to be even worse for her. At least she's always known I was in love with Euan. If she thinks you're after him as well things will get very complicated.'

'What? You and Euan?' Catriona was stupefied. 'How come I never realised?'

'Because there's nothing to realise except that Helen is the only woman for him and you would be doing everything, as I am, to save their marriage.'

Rorie's mobile rang, Nigel and Noël wanted to know where she was.

'Somewhere not there! I'll be back when I'm back,' Rorie snapped, and hung up. Then she took on Catriona. 'You can do two things for me. Then I have to get back to my no-use director and get this no-use play to make some headway or I will be out of a job too, just like Dette.' Catriona had filled Rorie in on Dette's morning.

'I saw you pulled out of the hat twice yesterday. That's the last stroke you're going to pull to get near Euan. I want you to make sure Helen's marriage is saved. Give her all the help you can.'

'Yes, I will,' Catriona was filled with Rorie's sense of purpose. 'I don't suppose, on that subject, that you have Martin's number, do you?'

Rorie sighed, 'You're not supposed to tell me who you got.'

'Oh, don't be silly, Rorie,' Catriona sighed back. 'I can tell you now it's only a one-shot thing for me with this boy. He won't have any interest in me.'

Rorie glanced at the time. 'That's it, I have to go. Now, the second thing I want you to do is this. Get George to look at these figures,' she handed over a self-bought manila folder branded 'Nightmare', 'and see if he can give any kind of assistance at all. In return you get a job interview.' Catriona was in no position to argue.

22

Rorie was glad when the rest of the week passed without incident.

All this intrigue. It seemed as if she was the only one not part of it. She was waiting until Saturday to make a play for Euan. A pretend play. In fact she'd already decided to tell him what was going on. Rorie had recognised that diplomacy only led her to trouble in this instance.

'Rorie! Could you come and read this?'

John had stayed up this weekend. Not at her request – never at her request. He had had some writing to do. A few years ago he had had some success as an angry young man. The problem was he was now fifty-five and angry middle-aged men are usually wearing cardigans and writing letters to the local paper. John was writing plays from what he called his direct experience. Another problem – it had stopped being direct years ago when he actually *was* working class.

Now he drank good wine and lectured to adoring students who regarded his one successful play – *How Red*

Was My Valley about, guess what? Socialism. In, guess where? Wales – as a classic. The problem about being perceived to have written a classic is that you become one yourself. John Edwards was an institution. No one wanted him to write anything other than a sequel to *How Red Was My Valley*. Once a gay-rights organisation had asked him to think about writing *How Pink Was My Valley* but John was strictly a man in the macho mould. Women, lots of them. At one point, Rorie had found his charisma catching. Now she realised he only had one angle – the broody writer who goes off into a world of his own. It made him mysterious. But Rorie had been with him long enough to have solved the mystery. The world of his own featured only one person – John Edwards.

When he stayed up for the weekend now she almost found it an inconvenience – a few years ago it was like all her birthdays had come at once. He expected her to stay around to feed and water him while he worried over his words. She was his stage manager. When had this happened? Ages ago. When had she realised? Only recently. Martin, the house-painter who she got a job as a set designer, had become a friend. So much of a friend she was dismayed when he and Dette started seeing each other. Not because she fancied him – younger men were not her type – but because Dette would chew him up and spit him out. They had been pals in a chummy way, until Dette.

For the past few months, since Martin had begun seeing her friend, he'd overstepped the mark with comments on John. 'What do you see in him, Rorie?'

'Don't you start! Everyone asks me that.' But only when they know me well enough.

'And what do you tell them?'

'I tell them he's kind, which he is. And it suits me, which it does. If they ask any more than that I tell them to mind their own business.' She was joking, but her voice held a warning in it.

'You might tell me to mind mine, but all I can say is you're a now person, Rorie. You're great. And you're with a has-been.'

'Martin, that's enough!'

'It's not. He's lived off the glory of one play and he holds you back because he's afraid of anyone going forward. I met his students at the Russian thing. He'd block-booked them into one of the previews. We had a pint with them afterwards. Not one of them was an original thinker. It's like he squares off all the talent so it doesn't threaten him.'

'Change the subject, Martin.'

But she'd known it was true. John had stopped being the dynamic writer who taught on the side and had turned into the bitter teacher who wished he could write. She felt sorry for him, but she didn't like the sound of what Martin had said about John's students. She had never seen that side of John, as far as she was concerned he was always honest and fair. In fact that was his favourite phrase: 'It's only fair.' He had used it when he put the proposition to her that they move in together.

'It's only fair to tell you, Rorie, that I won't leave Janet or the kids. I want to make sure they're looked after.'

She had loved him so much she accepted it. Monday to Friday morning had been better than nothing at all.

'Yes, love. I'll be with you in a moment.'

She put down the bills she was paying. John never had time to do them.

'Rorie, what took you so long?' He was wearing a cardigan, he wasn't writing the play. John never used computers, he liked her to type up his scenes after he had completed them. She could see it was a letter to the *Gazette* about the parking bays at the front of their flats. He never stopped moaning about them. 'Dear Editor, for the past six months cars have been parking willy-nilly outside my front door.' Except it wasn't his front door. It was hers.

The paper he handed her had a key scene between two miners' wives whose husbands had been made redundant. She raised her eyes to heaven. The nearest John Edwards got to a miner these days was when he walked past a jeweller's window.

'Well?' He handed her stuff he'd done that morning, before the parking letter had become more important. The parking letter would be better written.

She was expected to read it in front of him, so he could watch her reactions. She hated this, because she had to act enthusiastic, even though what was on the page was rubbish – a clichéd conversation with extra clichés thrown in in case you missed one. The problem was she had tried once to be constructive, to help him make it better, but he had dismissed her, 'You're not a script editor, you know.'

She had grasped that he wanted only her adoration, the kind she had given him when she was a star-struck nineteen-year-old. Nowadays she gave it to him out of habit.

'It's great. Keep going. Now, you know we're going to dinner with the others tonight?'

'I can't. I'm on a roll here.'

'John, you promised. It's not often I ask.'

'I can't.' He was brushing his hand through his hair, patting it over a tiny bald spot he thought no one had seen arriving. It made her feel sorry for him. John's looks really mattered to him. Hers had always been a reminder of her absent dad and she disregarded them, although now that she was in her thirties and still looked in her twenties she was glad. The luck of the gene-pool draw. She felt a bit sorry for whoever was going to seduce him. He was so insecure they might find themselves with more than they bargained for. As she had.

'Well, I'll go alone, then,' she told him. What would the others say? What about the plan?

'But I need you here, to read this.'

'I have to go out, John. I'll read it when I come back.'

'OK,' he smiled, an insecure smile that made her uneasy. 'I'll come with you and we'll get back to this when we come home, do a late-night session like in the old days.'

The old days had featured a lot of writing and a lot of sex. That hadn't happened in a long time. Now she thought about it, it had not happened at all in six months. John Edwards had gone without sex for six months. His lust was legendary. It was funny, though – the full lips and square jaw, the masculine brow, the parts of him that made an attractive whole – she found it hard to notice them now. It was only when she stood back and looked that she remembered what had made her want to make love to him the first time on his office desk and anywhere else afterwards.

'We'll be there by eight and home by eleven.' She heard herself promise to humour him and wondered how she'd got to be the stage manager of her own relationship.

She drove to the restaurant, although it was only a fifteen-minute walk. She wanted to keep a clear head. John had never learned to drive. He sat in the passenger seat, notebook on lap. 'I think my main character should drum his fingers on the table, like this, to signify his impatience.' He did it on the dashboard.

Rorie found it hard not to show hers when he persisted. Also, he habitually changed the station from the Chill Out channel she liked to the Golden Oldies Show, which she would cheerfully have blown up.

'The results, love, got to get the results. Might have won the pools.'

John had done the pools since he was a boy. It kept him in touch with his past, he said. 'My main character. He should do the pools, right Rorie?'

'Yes, John.' Like the last three main characters had.

A silence. She would normally have filled it with wife-like questions about his work, but she was not his wife, she thought.

'So,' John spoke awkwardly, 'how's work?'

'*Your Latest Fiasco* is my latest fiasco,' Rorie sighed.

'That's what you get for working with Nigel Blunt and Noël Coward. The nearest those guys have got to meaningful theatre is going to the *Rocky Horror* together. You ought to work on more serious material, Rorie. These West End things are staged for the tourist market.'

Rorie wanted to point out that at least they entertained people, unlike *How Drab Was My Valley* parts two to twenty-five. But as usual she left it.

Why am in this relationship? She had thought it at least once a day for the past year.

'Because you're too exhausted to do anything about

it,' Helen had said to her when she confided to the Virgo Club. 'You need to get a few months off everything, work included, and decide what's happening in your life.'

'I can't, Helen. Mortgage and stuff.'

'You can ask John to cover it for awhile.' Helen was a great one for solutions. Then she had seen Rorie's face. 'He doesn't help you with the mortgage, does he?'

'He's got his wife and kids to support.'

'And you're supporting them too by paying for him.'

'I don't mind. I'd hate to think of his family doing without.'

'They do without him Monday to Friday,' Dette had chipped in. You could always rely on Dette for the cold facts. She never saw the need to dress things up.

It had been enough to spark off one of Rorie's guilt trips. She often thought of Janet with her two children, waiting for a husband who never let her come up to London. On the few occasions she did John always moved back into his rooms at the university. Surely Janet smelt a rat. Rorie had hated her for putting up with the situation in the beginning; now she felt she knew why. John was a lot to put up with seven days a week. She felt she had something in common with the woman she knew only through a single wedding photo that used to sit on John's desk, accusing her of things she was more than guilty of.

'John?'

'Hmm,' he was still drumming his fingers on the dashboard, having dismissed her entire career in a sentence.

'What does Janet look like?' she asked as she pulled into the car park at the back of Angelo's.

'Like a wife,' John snapped. 'You know I don't like to talk about it.'

'What does a wife look like?'

'Dowdy.'

'What do I look like?' Rorie was asking him, but also her eyes with calf lashes in the rear-view mirror. She was wearing a dress tonight, felt naked without her jeans. If she was supposed to be seductive, she had better look the part, she'd thought. But it worried her what Helen would think.

'You...' he smiled lecherously while he grabbed at her before she had a chance to open the car door and pulled at her dress, '...look like a girlfriend. Now, do we have to go in there or can we go somewhere more private?'

'We have to go in there.' She pulled up her shoulder strap and pushed open the car door.

23

'What's with the dress?' Euan smiled at Rorie, filling her glass.

'I thought I'd scare everyone with me footballer legs.'

'You don't have footballer legs.'

'You've noticed then?'

'Yes.'

Rorie caught Angelo looking across at them. He turned the gauge on the Gaggia machine so that it hissed loudly.

'How are you, Euan?' She glanced down the table to make sure Helen was out of earshot. Helen was immersed in a conversation with George. A first. They normally never knew what to say to each other. All change here.

'I'm OK, Rorie, thanks for asking. I'm OK except I can't sleep and I have an awful feeling I'm going to lose her.'

'You're not. Don't be so stupid. She's cut to ribbons about this and you can't blame her. Give her time.'

'We went to the counsellor on Friday. She said we needed more disclosure in our relationship. How can you get a woman who hasn't mentioned her own mother and father for over ten years to disclose how she feels about anything? She's so reasonable with me, Rorie. I feel like a patient.'

'It's her way, Euan. She's coped with everything life has thrown at her.'

'She's driven.'

'Yes, but only because if she wasn't she'd be working as a contract cleaner with her mother and two of her sisters.'

'That's what they do? I didn't even know that much.'

'I'm from the same place and my mammy knows her mammy. But Mam hasn't mentioned anything in a while about the Larkins. I think since she moved on a few roads to a smaller house. She hasn't heard as much about them.'

'Why haven't you mentioned Helen's family before, Rorie?'

'They're not my family, Euan, and it's not my place to be filling in her husband on a past she left behind. Now, eat your pasta. It's gone cold.'

Conversation was uphill for a while. Rorie wondered about mentioning the latest development, but she was afraid someone might be listening, though they all seemed not to be. Dette in particular had donkey ears.

Angelo came to clear the plates. 'Rorie, message for you. Nigel.'

'It's my one Saturday night off a month. Nigel can swing.'

'They don't have a leading lady any more. Lavinia's upset about the padding you make her wear. Nigel says he knows you will help.'

'Well, she must've gone on or he'd have phoned more than once. I'll call after dessert, and if he does call again say I haven't arrived. Take another message, please. I need some time away from that bunch.' Rorie rubbed her face. 'I'm so stressed.'

'I haven't helped things.'

'No, you haven't, pillock. Have you spoken to Catriona?'

'She hasn't called me for a long time. I feel embarrassed to. I wasn't exactly the perfect gentleman with her. More a drunken scut.'

'I don't think she'll be bothering you again. I had a word.'

'You told her?'

'I had reason to. That's all I'll say for now. Can I have a cup of tea with you some time?' Euan and Rorie never drank cappuccino. They preferred old-fashioned blended leaves, strong enough for a spoon to stand up in.

'Celtic on the box tomorrow. I could call over?'

Rorie looked at Helen. For the first time she felt uncomfortable saying yes, even though this was something Euan and she had done many times over the years. They'd even gone off together to Glasgow for a couple of games. Stayed overnight once. In Euan's old house. Not once had it crossed either of their minds to do anything other than go to bed after *Match of the Day*. Everything had felt as right and normal then as it felt wrong now.

'OK.' She had to talk to him.

'Shall I tell Helen?'

'Why'd you ask me that, Euan?'

'Because I don't want to cause any more trouble between you two.'

'How do you know there is any?'

'Come on, Rorie. Any other time you'd have been over at our house during the week. Specially since Helen's having a bad time. I'm to blame for all of this. I'm sick of myself.'

'I can't deny that you should be. But I'm in no position to judge.'

'So, should I tell Helen?'

'You know what, Euan? That's up to you. A lot of things are up to you. It won't be a problem anyway. John's writing.'

They'd have to keep the sound down. Euan's eyes rose to heaven. He and John hated each other in that male way – openly. 'I'll take the kids swimming, then I'll call over. We'll catch the second half together.'

Angelo was back. 'Nigel says you must phone him or he will come over here.'

On her way back to the table after the call John pulled at her sleeve. 'Can we go soon, Rorie? You driving? I'm a bit squiffy. Be good for the writing, loosen me up.'

'Sorry, John, you'll have to make your own way home. I've got to go to the theatre.'

She ended up driving him home first on her way to persuade a leading lady who was known for walkouts not to leave a play that had been pasted. Even before the reviews she had had to be persuaded to don a twenty-pound padded suit. Now any excuse would do.

*****

Euan and she sat on her sofa, not because they wanted to
sit together but because there was nowhere else in her
tiny sitting room. Celtic were winning and it seemed like
something was going right again. They cheered at the
third goal and cursed themselves for not putting on a bet
at the bookie's, another Rorie and Euan tradition. Their
beer – Bishop's Finger real ale – was unopened. Rorie
had only bought it as a token to another tradition. Euan
had brought round another couple of bottles, for the
same reason.

'Where's John?'

'He had to go out this morning. Said something about
research. Won't be back until after dinner.'

'Referee! Why don't you just put on a Aberdeen shirt?
So, how'd it go with the leading lady?'

'Badly. I got her to say she'll be there Tuesday afternoon for a discussion. But I had to take her to a posh
restaurant where those three witches are going to be
lunching, rumour has it.'

'What – *Macbeth*?'

'No – Chekhov, starring half of Hollywood. Lavinia
wants to be seen there. I had to slip the maître d' a hundred quid. And every penny counts on this production!
It's a bloody nightmare. I'll have to talk to Nigel about
getting Catriona a job. At least then I could burden
George for accounting help. The production saved
money by hiring a trainee bookkeeper. I don't think the
kid can even count.'

Celtic won three–two.

'OK. We've two choices. Celebrate or discuss,' Euan
stretched.

'Discuss wins, I'm afraid.'

'Shite.'

'Has to. Euan, Helen thinks it was me.'

Euan's face fell. 'No. She knows you'd never do something like that to her. I don't believe this! It gets worse with every passing day. I don't believe what I'm causing. Never, never did I mean this to happen.' He was on his feet now, pacing. 'What can I do?'

'Nothing.'

'But I could tell her who it was.'

'If you do I'll never speak to you again.'

'Jesus, Rorie. I'm only trying to help.'

'That won't.'

'But your friendship means a lot more to her than Catriona's. You're her family, for Christ's sake. You know more about her than I do.'

'About her, yes, of her, no. Before this happened if you'd asked Helen what was the one thing she could count on, she'd never have said me first. It was always you, Euan. From the word go. She had more kids for you.'

'Don't throw that at me, Rorie. I'd never have made her have them.'

'Exactly, which is why Kelly and Joyce are such a gift.'

'You're not afraid to blackmail. Do you think I could feel any more shite than I do already? Please don't give me any more reason. You know I'm going to the counsellor Helen set up, on Friday morning?'

'I thought you were going together.'

'We will, but we do one session each on our own. I told her immediately that I'd had a fumble in the back of a Volvo and I was trying to put it right with my wife. I told her I felt like a sleazy shite. She said that was for me to feel and she also asked me to consider what events led to the affair. I told her it wasn't an affair, just a fumble in the back of a—'

'Euan, don't do that. That's so male, to be so specific. You were unfaithful. It doesn't matter why, how or where.'

'But that's where the counsellor says I've got to take a step back. Affairs are caused by circumstances, and two people cause those.'

'I can't listen to this, Euan. It's not my place. Talk to Helen.'

'I haven't seen her to talk to her.'

'Then make time. It's your relationship, not mine. There's one more thing. You've got to hear it.'

Rorie told him. Her idea and why she'd had it.

'And you picked me?'

'I did.'

'And Helen agreed to this.' He was on his feet again, having only sat to hear what she'd said. 'That has to be the worst. What a thing to do to other human beings. And what did you think it would achieve?'

'I thought it would achieve exactly this. You would never agree to sleep with anyone. I just wish someone else had picked you to prove that. There's a question over whether Helen will believe us. I know Catriona was a slip-up. The others, me included, are going out with people they don't know about. We're all waiting for Mr Wonderful and making do with Mr Just About. Except you, Euan.'

'Rorie, for fuck's sake, that's nonsense.'

'It isn't, Euan. Why do you think Catriona fancies you? Why do you think I love you? Even Dette likes you and there are precious few men on her list. Mind you, you're off it at the moment. For obvious reasons.'

The sofa found Euan again. 'What did you just say?'

'You heard me. Jesus. Don't make me repeat it.'

'I swear I never knew.'

'Well, I'm glad of that because I never wanted you to.'

'I don't believe you.'

'Euan. I'm not going to feed your ego by explaining my feelings for you. Will you just drop it? And open the beer for us.'

Two bottles later they managed to speak again.

'I must try this bastard thing more often.'

'Shut up, Euan.'

'Seriously, women don't respect men who are nice. I never once didn't call a girl when I said I would. And I always let her down to her face if I didn't want to see her again. The only thing *that* got me was slapped.'

'And Helen. It got you Helen.'

'Ah, come on, Rorie. Helen hasn't shown any interest in me for years.'

'Since the kids were born she hasn't had time. And she might not appear to show any, but she loves every bone of you.'

'Which is why we haven't slept together in four months.'

'Euan. I do not want to know this.'

'Well, I didn't want to bloody well hear you were in love with me. Now we can both be embarrassed. Who am I going to watch the footie with now?'

'Most men would find it great that someone secretly loved them. What's wrong with me that you don't?'

'What's wrong is you're my mate. More of a mate

than any man has ever been. We drink our tea exactly the same way, we drink the same beer, we love the same team. We laugh at the same jokes. Jesus, Rorie, maybe it's you I should've married.'

'Don't say that.'

'I've certainly more in common with you than my wife.'

'If you tell me now she doesn't understand you I'm going to have to kick you in the balls.'

'Helen never gets my jokes. She's never watched a Celtic game in her life.'

'She drinks tea.'

'Only after ten coffees.'

'Have another beer. Then go home. You're pissing me off, Euan.'

'You know what, Rorie? You've never pissed me off, not once. The only thing that annoys me about you is that prat boyfriend of yours. Rent-a-parent. That's all he is. And he's not even a good father to you.'

'I don't want to talk about it. What I do want to do is swear you to secrecy, over the UEFA Cup, that you won't mention you know to any of the others.'

'I don't think it's fair, Rorie.'

'It doesn't matter what you think. It's what's happening that counts. And I'm trying to help you save your marriage is what's happening.'

'Well, put like that, what can I say but OK?'

SEPTEMBER

24

Catriona arrived at Angelo's well before her one-thirty lunch date.

'You look so feminine, so Catarina!'

His words poured over her like honey. Embarrassed, she curtsied to show off her Edwardian-lady-meets-post-modern-woman garb, then pulled up a stool at the counter.

'Coffee, quick – I'm about to expire.'

'Not on my carpet, not in my restaurant. You never drink coffee. You drink weeds that can kill you more quickly and you say it is herbal tea.'

'Not any more. I'm back to the need for old-fashioned harmful stimulants now I'm back in the workforce. This job is driving me crazy. The pressure.'

'Rorie says you are very good with the play.'

'Hah! Does she?'

'Yes.'

'I bet it's just that George is good at helping with her accounts.'

'No.' Angelo's voice was serious. 'Rorie does not lie.'

'You're right. Sorry. I find it hard to take compliments and you gave me two to handle at once. Now, give me coffee. I suppose Rorie told you about the strop I threw at the start?'

'Rorie does not say any bad things about anyone except John, and also Rorie.'

'And even then she's only ever joking about how awful he is.'

'This is no joke,' Angelo poured himself some coffee. 'I think he is good at making her feel bad. I think it will be hard for her to say he must go.'

'Oh, I don't know, Angelo. One day the stage manager in her will come out and she'll shift the scenery, which is what I'm hoping to do with Martin in a few minutes' time.'

'He is your choice, from the game?'

'You know we're not allowed to say. The new Catriona keeps confidences.'

'So why are you meeting him?'

Martin arrived, smiling. 'Hello, mates. Any chance of a cup of that? I just left two Hollywood queenies screaming for dressing room space and I got no place to put the bleedin' scenery equipment. "It's not my job," I told them. I said, "Get Rorie over here. She'll sort it out. Stage manager needs sacking."'

'Which ones were screaming?' Catriona and Angelo both wanted the gossip.

'Now, you know I'm contractually obliged to keep schtum about what a bunch of bleeding self-obsessed nightmares they are. They'll all be bleeding bald, there's that much hair flying. Tell you what, Cat, you could do with going over there, hanging around a bit. You look bleeding gorgeous.'

A far cry from the Mum comment of four weeks back. What a lot could change in a little time. 'Thanks, but no thanks. I'm up to my neck on Rorie's production.'

'Oh, sorry to hear it,' Martin sighed. 'It's a stinker, so I believe.'

'Well,' Catriona couldn't disagree, 'at least it's work.'

'Anyway, let's hope it closes. That way you and Rorie can move to *Three Sisters*.'

'You might be the hottest set designer, but you're not a director. Stop offering us jobs you don't have to offer.'

'Your table's ready,' Angelo pointed to the one nearest to him.

Catriona raised her eyebrows and mouthed, 'Nosey.'

Angelo stuck his into the air and led them, with ceremony.

'Who did your hair?' Martin wanted to know. 'Sorry, rude question, but it's lovely 'n curly. You're prettier than them starring in *Three Sisters*. Only it's *Two Sisters* now. One of them's on a plane to New York, I bet.'

'How do you know?'

'Cos I read the tabloids, darlin'. Drew Barrymore weren't happy with getting changed in the ladies'. It don't help the production's got too much money. It's like it's no one's job to be doing anything and everyone's getting paid a whack. I tell you, Cat, you show your face at that theatre the way you're looking and you might get the part. We open in October, and so far we got one and a half leads in a three-lead play.'

'Thanks for the compliment, Martin.' Dette was right, he knew exactly how to build a woman up, make her feel better about herself. A bad sign if you were a woman who wanted him to stay. 'I prefer being backstage now.'

Catriona loved this. Talking shop, working lunches.

She'd even been less obsessed with perfect Magda in the past few days. Maybe because she had more of a life herself. And she'd only eaten a bowl of ice-cream once in the past fortnight. Jude was unhappy about it. 'Don't go skinny on me, darling,' he said with a brush between his teeth and another on the canvas. She'd been sitting for him two evenings a week. 'I like you just the way you are.'

So did she. For the first time in years. George wasn't getting on her nerves as much. They'd spent a few evenings together going over Rorie's accounts. And having something to work on with each other had given them something else they hadn't had in years – common ground. He'd even tried a few mouthfuls of her goat's cheese tart and pronounced it delicious, leaving Magda's lamb and roast potatoes for Magda to notice uneaten.

But that wasn't how it had gone in the beginning.

'That's not what I heard in the beginning,' Martin had almost mirrored her thought.

'Well, I was a bit off the rails awhile ago. I've seen sense now, and what's what.'

Catriona would never forget the look on Magda's face when she came home armed with shopping, her Jude hairdo and the announcement that she was going to be an actress again. The fairest thing to say was that the opposition was threatened. The sense of victory this gave Catriona was out of proportion, but at least it was a foothold out of the depression her days had seemed filled with for as long as she'd lacked purpose.

'You are going to be famous again?' Magda asked.

'Not quite.' Catriona fetched up a modest laugh from a dusty repertoire. Good practice for tomorrow. 'But there's talk of the production touring. Who knows what will happen then?'

'You are going to leave the country?' Magda took it a step further than Catriona intended, but a little fantasising in that direction wouldn't hurt Catriona's confidence. At this moment she was so nervous that a one-line part seemed too big a job.

'Well, perhaps New York. But we'd keep you on, Magda, to look after things in London.'

'But what of George?'

'Oh, George will have to take a short sabbatical, or an extended holiday. Come with me to Manhattan to mind the kids.' Catriona made herself leave the room while she was still talking. Since she couldn't seem to stop.

'I think I took things too far there.'

Still, Magda wasn't to know that. Until three hours later when George stormed into the TV room. 'I hear you've landed a big role – and we're off to New York! You might have thought of letting me know before you told anyone else.'

'Sorry, George.' Catriona had never seen him so angry. She attempted to whisper, 'It's not a big role. In fact it's small. And it's not New York we're going to first, it's Surbiton.'

'Well, you might have told our au pair that. The poor girl is downstairs with red eyes, begging me not to send her back to Poland.'

'You can't do that anyway, she has a full visa now. You see? She twists things. And I told her she'd be kept on.'

'I didn't even know you were going for auditions. What about our children?'

'I'll still be here for them during the day, and you'll be home at night.'

'But if it's touring surely you'll have to stay overnight in places?'

'I hadn't thought of that.' Magda would have a field day getting her claws further into Catriona's family. 'No, I'll commute every night. I promise, George. And we don't go out for a few weeks anyway. Right now it's in the West End.'

'Doing badly, if the reviews were anything to go by.'

'You read them?' Catriona was more than surprised.

'When Rorie's got a play on I do. I always look out for her plays. But this isn't the point. The point is you should have discussed it with me.'

He sat down as if he would fall. Catriona looked at the clock. Eight thirty. She saw how tired he was and was about to say 'Eat something', when Magda walked in.

'George, you must eat something. It is waiting in the kitchen. It is hot now. You need hot food after a long day. I have poured wine.'

'Thanks so much, Magda,' George sighed.

'Yes, I couldn't agree more,' Catriona looked at Magda. 'George, would you like to eat in here with me, on a tray?'

'No, Catriona. In case you haven't noticed Magda was up with the kids giving them breakfast. I don't want her moving my meal. She's already had an even longer day than I've had.'

They both left her. Catriona was about to say that she'd been with the kids at breakfast. She'd just nipped out to get milk because it was raining and, much as she disliked Magda, she hadn't sent her to the shops in it. And she had been going to put his food on a tray for him and bring it up herself. But it would seem childish and only make those two stronger allies. So she followed him downstairs to have a rant she didn't mean to have, but couldn't stop herself. All this energy should have been used for tomorrow's audition.

'What's that supposed to mean, George?'

'What it says. You don't do a thing around here, Catriona. That girl keeps this entire house going.'

'When I said I'd have your children I did not say I would clean up after us all as well. And I want to cook for us, but no one will eat my food.'

George pushed his roast chicken and mashed potatoes into him. 'I'd make better mash!' Catriona hissed. 'But Miss Perfect insists this is the way you like it.'

'You know how I like it, Catriona? On time. I love your food but it never comes on time! I need to eat on time. I'm a busy man who has very little of it.'

'I can't help it if I'm not a robot.'

'Are you saying I am?'

'Yes!'

'I am a robot because I have to do things by the clock. I have to perform so I can keep my job and support this family. I have to have regularity.'

'You have to have regularity because your father insisted on it and your mother insists on it even now when she no longer lives with you. You've never done a crazy thing in your life, George, have you?'

George was silent, bent over his food. He sipped some wine, and for an awful moment Catriona thought he was going to cry. What was wrong with him? George hadn't even cried when his children were born.

'You don't want me to work. That's what this is about.'

'It's not the work, Catriona. I'm happy for you to do anything you want. That's why I even buy my own clothes. I try not to put pressure on you to do anything. So you'll do what you want. So you'll be happy. And you're never happy, Catriona. Maybe when we first married I might have thought it better for you to stay at home, but that was only because it was what I was used to.'

'You weren't married before, George.'

'No, it was what worked for my mother and father. That was what I imagined I'd need.'

'Your mother! Let's not get started on her. You do everything she says. I can't understand why you did marry me. I'm so obviously not what she wanted for you. Four grandchildren later and I'm still not good enough. A dead husband and a daughter who never sees her and I'm still not good enough. Eight rotten Christmases just how she likes them and I'm still—'

'I married you because I wanted you more than I've ever wanted anything. And it's made me even less likely to gamble now.'

That hurt like hell.

'Why?'

'Because I've failed so miserably. I loved you so much I felt if I worked at it as hard as I knew how it would come right. But even a fool like me realises nothing is enough if you're not the right person for somebody. I wouldn't care what Mother thinks if I knew you loved me. But you don't. And I live with it. For our children.'

George's interruption took the anger out of her. She wanted to give him some comfort. He looked lost, over the cold food in the cold kitchen. She wanted to make him eat more than the few bites he'd taken.

'You should eat now. Keep your strength up.' For a

moment she thought she'd said it. Then she realised Magda was there, behind her.

George shook his head, 'It's too late. I'll get indigestion. Mightn't sleep. Big day tomorrow. All of that.'

He got up and left them both. She went up the stairs after him but hadn't the courage to follow him into the bedroom, so she went back to the TV room. And then she smelt the Ovaltine and toast. Magda would drop it in to him. Magda had remembered.

'I'm a selfish cow,' she said to the screen. 'Only getting what I deserve.'

The following day she found she was still a fantastic actress.

Nigel Blunt and Rorie Marks told her the job was hers from tomorrow. She asked if she could see the script, at least. 'I haven't been on a stage for over eight years, you know,' she smiled.

'And you won't be now,' Nigel Blunt snapped.

'I'm sorry, but you're offering me a job?'

'As Rorie's assistant. And Rorie assures me your husband will help us with the accounts. We need his help. Otherwise you can forget it.'

As soon as Nigel left the room Catriona let her have it. 'You might have told me!'

'I had no idea you were expecting anything more than I could offer,' Rorie watched her.

'But assistant stage manager? Why don't you just ask me to do the cleaning?'

'I will, Catriona, because that is what an assistant stage manager does. Now, if you're not happy with it, you don't have to take it. I can't believe what a snob you are.'

'Fine. I'm a snob with a full acting CV and a diploma from RADA.'

'And you're only as good as your last job. Which was?'

Catriona stormed out but hadn't even left the backstage alley before she realised.

Back again.

'I'm so sorry. I just got carried away in my own head. I'm sorry, Rorie.'

'Good. The pay's two hundred and fifty pounds a week and no complaints. Deal is, I give you a glowing reference if you glow for me. And I'll lie and say you had a small part. Now go away because I'm still angry with you.'

What she hadn't bargained on were the kids and Magda and George, who had come home from work early, who never came home early from work, waiting for her. She had to act then. Had to. 'I can't believe how delighted I am. My first job in so long. And the role's made for me.'

'It is a housewife, the part?' Magda asked.

'No, it's an artist's model,' Catriona was not lying entirely. She had just begun to pose for Jude Mackenzie.

The children hugged her and asked when they could come to see the play.

'And I – I would like to see it too,' Magda made her request formally, almost in writing.

'We'll all go! We'll make a proper night of it!' George was carried away with excitement. 'We'll hire a limousine to take us to Surbiton and back. Take a picnic for the back of the car.'

George, planning an extravaganza. She looked at him and the tears began to fall.

'Why are you crying?' he asked, as if he was one of their children.

'Happiness.' If it was, it was almost choking her.

Then she asked George for a word. In their bedroom, the last private place. And she whispered to him what had happened, about the accounts. And another small thing, she would also be a stage manager, on duty from four every evening. Could he be home by six, and could he help with the books? She hadn't the heart to tell him there was no part.

'Never mind. A start's a start, Catriona. I'm sure your appearances will more than make up for the backstage work. I'll do the accounts for you too, save you the hassle. A talent like you shouldn't be number-crunching.'

He was trying harder than ever. Or maybe she was seeing it. And it was all based on fresh air. If she had to shag Nigel Blunt or get Angelo to shag him she was going to get some part for one night in whatever draughty community hall this crappy play ended up in. She would make her lie a truth. 'But you're too busy to do the books,' she whispered, in case ears were outside the door.

'I'm never too busy to help you.'

'George, thank you so much. I'll repay you for this. I will.'

'A wife shouldn't have to repay her husband. To see you happy is all I want.'

And she had been. The weeks flew by and even Rorie had to hand it to Catriona that things were done without her having to open her mouth. Jude made up for the lack of attention she got in the theatre with all that he lavished on her during the sittings. Silks, fresh fruit, a proper Regency chaise longue to recline on. A beautiful robe to wrap herself in, and slip off only when she was comfortable. There was real comfort with her artist. He had no interest in her sexually. And he kept saying, 'Rubens would have loved to get his hands on you. Pity I'm bent as ninepence.'

Life got more interesting; the children seemed to want more to do with her. Even the dog wagged his tail when he saw her. She was always singing. Magda couldn't sing.

For all these reasons Catriona Morehampton was able to say to Martin Hardiman, the boyfriend of her best friend, that she was happy to remain backstage for the rest of her life. But she should also mention she was an understudy for the lead, only because she was the right size.

'That's about right. You'll make a better fist of it than that anorexic old turkey Lavinia,' Martin supported her.

'And I should add I'm also understudy for all parts under three paragraphs of female origin.'

'Well, bound to get on, then, aren't you? Break some-one's leg.'

'Look, Martin. I've two things to ask you.' She cut through her lasagne verdi and to the chase, 'The first is unorthodox and the second less so. Which would you prefer first?'

'The very unorthodox, I suppose,' Martin had sat back in his chair. 'Get me in the mood for the second,' he was flirting. Cheeky bugger.

'First, I'm wondering if there is any way in the world you would like to sleep with me?'

'Where?'

'In a bed. Would you like to have sex with me in a bed? At night-time? With no one knowing?'

'Bloody hell, Catriona,' she noticed he wasn't calling

her Cat now. 'I mean, I wasn't chatting you up when I said you was gorgeous. You're a lovely bird. But no. No thanks, I mean. You're Dette's mate. I wouldn't do that to Dette.'

Catriona smiled uncertainly. 'And you're turning me down just because of that? Because she's my friend?'

'Don't be daft, man. I'd turn you down if you was Julia Roberts. I'm with Dette, that's all there is to it.'

'Just as I thought. That's absolutely brilliant.'

Martin burst out laughing. 'Bloody hell, you're a strange bird.'

'Sorry, I was just testing you to make sure you weren't going to mess her around.'

'That's a bit sneaky, isn't it?'

'No, Martin. I'm not a bit sneaky – at least, not any more. That's why I invited you here. No lies, no hassle, is my new motto. If you'd said yes I'd have called Angelo over to ask you to leave. She's worried, Martin. I can tell she likes you.'

'How? I can't.' He sat forward, serious now.

'Because she hasn't dumped you. She's been trying but she hasn't found a way to do it. She's too old for you she thinks. Don't take it personally.'

'Listen, mate—'

'If you call me mate once more you're meat in Angelo's kitchen.'

He raised his hands. 'Well, you got some balls with the new job, Cat.'

'Cat you can call me. I liked it once. Mate you can't.'

'I've got a strange feeling this conversation's going to be a lifelong memory for me. My bird's ma— friend asks me to shag her, then tells me my bird's trying to dump me, then asks me not to read a lot into that. I'm glad we got that sorted. There must've been magic mushrooms in this pasta.'

'You are twenty-five, Martin. Why aren't you playing the field?'

'I love her.'

'You don't know what love is. You're a child.'

'I'm a child? Who's just asked her friend's boyfriend to sleep with her and told him he's about to be given the elbow?'

'Sorry,' Catriona murmured.

'Then let's get a coffee. Because you're the one's drunk too much at lunchtime. My business is me own. If I love a bird fifteen years old than me, then that's for me to decide. Not you. Cat. Mate.'

'You know she's forty?'

'Course I do. I saw her passport when we went to Vienna for the weekend, snuck it out of her handbag. Knew she was cagey about it. So my girlfriend's five years younger than my dad, I don't care.'

'Well, good for you,' Catriona said softly. He meant it, she could see.

'I suppose this is a bad time to move on to my second request?'

Martin shook his head, silently.

'Good, I hope you won't say no to it, for Rorie's sake. Will you make us a touring set for nothing? We've no money, the play's crap and Rorie's at her wit's end. There's no budget and the designer hadn't been told to factor it in with her original build.'

'Blimey. I'm flat out on *Three Sisters*.'

'I see.'

'But it's for Rorie. Rorie got me first job. I'll do it. I'll have to do it in me evenings.'

'Great stuff, Martin.'

'OK, now, you're done talking I'm starting. There's something I want from you and, let me tell ya, it's not half what you've asked of me.' Martin leaned forward and Catriona sat back.' Tell me, what was she like as a kid? She never tells me anything.'

Catriona popped a kiss on his cheek as they were coming out of the door. 'Dette's lucky to have you. See you Saturday for the birthday bash.' For the first time in years, Catriona thought, she and Dette had a lot to celebrate.

Across the street Dette watched them. She waited until they'd turned the corner together before going into Angelo's.

'Hi. I was going to have something to eat in-between meals. In keeping with my new-found appetite. But I've just lost it. Can I have coffee, decaffeinated?'

Angelo poured and watched her. 'Dette, there is no need to worry.'

'I've changed my mind. Get me some garlic bread with extra cheese, Angelo, and I'll make you realise you need a woman in your life.'

Angelo laughed and went to the kitchen to make it himself.

25

Angelo came back with her garlic bread. It was steaming hot and the hole in her stomach cried out to be filled.

'Gorgeous, yum-yum.'

'The woman who for years will not allow me to put olive oil on her salad eats it with extra cheese now, Dette?'

'So I got a life. I saw my magazine past and my habitual dieting for what it was.'

'You are not ill?'

'No. Yes, I mean.' It would help explain things. The others, Helen apart, had all been advised she was on a six-week detox plan, courtesy of a new health-and-beauty guru. They'd swallowed it like good wine. Dette was known to be a victim for all things fashionable. And if it meant she was no longer smoking fags they were happy to go along with her. Catriona had even hugged her again.

'Stop it now!' Dette ordered. 'That time out shopping was a one-off. This is not the start of a new touchy-feely friendship.'

The others had waited for Catriona to be hurt, or to retaliate, as she normally did. But she just laughed. There was an ease between Catriona and Dette, an intimacy that hadn't been there for years. Which was just as well because Rorie and Helen didn't seem to be anywhere near their usual selves with each other. Or maybe that was because Dette knew them so well and had always, if she was honest, been a bit jealous of their friendship. But that was before she and Catriona had found their way back to the place they'd lost years ago. Now she realised that what she'd thought of as jealousy was a yearning to be as close as she had been to her best friend. She'd tried to talk to Catriona about the awkwardness between Rorie and Helen, see if there was something she could do to help. But Catriona had backed off. 'I don't think we should interfere, and us speculating will only add fuel to the fire. Let's leave them to get on with it, will we?'

Dette had left it. A bit stung, and just as well because she'd been on the verge of telling her best mate her amazing news. But something had stopped her. She'd wanted time to get used to it. Change wasn't something she'd encouraged in a long time and the idea that anyone other than Helen – who was bound to secrecy by her profession – knew might mean her mother or even Martin found out. All in good time. She'd wait until she was past the sixteen-week mark. Then she'd have a scan, to check that her little foetus was properly formed, since she'd led such a ridiculous lifestyle for a pregnant woman. She was still not convinced that everything would be all right.

And she had waited. And she was now almost sixteen weeks. And her scan was next week. And Helen was going with her. And her boyfriend was having a fling with her best friend since childhood. She'd almost prefer him to be seeing a Hollywood icon. It would be a talking point to be dumped for Drew Barrymore. She could have made a fortune too, with the tabloids, dressed in a smock, highlights growing out, in front of a tower block with no working lifts.

This was her future – a buggy and the benefit office. Or home to mammy. Mammy wouldn't mind, but she just couldn't. Mammy's dream was about six months away. Next year, 1 January, she would be retiring as dinner lady after some forty years in the school where Dette and Catriona had been pupils. Then she was going home to Ireland. She was an institution. There would be a glowing send-off. If Mammy found out she was pregnant she would not only put off Athbeg but retiring too.

'Well, at least I'll get the makeover money. Better persuade Rorie out of her jeans asap.'

She took out her mobile and phoned Ducky, the bread was safely inside her tummy and her baby was having a nice big feed. Her fingers ached to curl round a fag, her lungs longed for a big draw of nicotine. Then she felt the place where her baby was and found the strength not to smoke.

'Ducky, darling, how about supper at a place only you can afford this week? I need work, lots of it, and I've got some glowing ideas for you…What are they?' Dette was thrown on to a spot marked with a huge X. 'I've three drastic makeovers lined up and a story of an artist who is working on the set of the new *Three Sisters* play and a woman who makes people think it's the dawn of their lives,' she dredged up Catriona's idea. Fuck them! If they were going to cheat on her, she was going to use them for what she needed.

On her way out the door, in the newsagent's beside Angelo's, she saw a sign for a car-boot sale. Its clientele were in for a knockdown-price cosmetics bonanza this Sunday. But first, she had to find out if her baby had arms and legs.

The following lunchtime Helen was waiting for her outside the foetal-assessment unit.

'Thanks, Helen.' Dette was pale, she hadn't slept for worrying what this might bring up.

Now Helen was smiling at her, pointing to what was quickly becoming obvious through Dette's clothes. Her eating like a horse had given her a tummy, a baby in a tummy. In just four weeks the transformation had been marked. She hadn't let Martin near her in a fortnight. It hadn't been easy and now it wouldn't be hard to keep that up. Next time she saw him he was for the chop.

This wasn't real yet. Another life growing inside her. How had it got there? Forty next week and still confused over the facts of life.

'Dette, it won't matter now, but was it you?' Helen's voice was quiet. They were the only ones in the monitor room, waiting for the scan operator to return.

'Me what? Oh, my God! Was it me shagged your husband? Thanks for the confidence boost! It shows how much you think of me.'

'Sorry, I just had to ask. He won't tell me who it was, so it has to have been one of the Virgos. What would it matter if it was someone else? He'd be able to tell me then. I thought you and he might have had a wild fling. It's either you or Rorie.'

'Why not Catriona?'

'Catriona's not Euan's type. He doesn't like needy women.'

'Well, it's definitely not Rorie. She loves the bones of you. And it's not me. Do you think I'd tell you I was pregnant if I was pregnant with your husband's child? You're not the brightest member of the medical profession, are you?'

'No, but I'm struggling with so much, Dette. I don't think I can live with not knowing.'

'Knowing won't help, Helen.' Again Dette's voice said she had been one of the women to find that out.

'It will. I like dealing with facts, not mysteries. It'll stop me imagining how much better she is than me.'

'Have you asked the other two if it was them?'

'No.'

'Well, that was too honest even for me.'

The scanner came in.

'Thanks for coming off lunch early, Karim. It's just that I know this one,' Helen rubbed the top of Dette's head. 'Would have lost the baby with worry if she'd been allowed to sit in the queue all afternoon.'

'Folic acid!' Dette was mumbling. 'I've eaten more spinach than Popeye in the last four weeks, will that do?'

The scanner passed over her Vaselined belly and on the screen a lot of swirling and lines everywhere. But no baby.

'It's gone – I can't see it. It's gone,' Dette gripped Helen's hand, hysterical.

'This isn't a pre-shoot Polaroid, Dette. Let Karim get on with his work. Lie still or he won't see anything.'

Dette lay like the meek lamb she wasn't, her eyes pinned to the screen, her hand gripping Helen's.

'Look,' Karim's finger pointed to the screen. A little flashing O.

'What's that?' Dette near-screamed. 'The hole in its head from all the booze I drank?'

'It's the heart, Dette,' Helen was rubbing the back of her hand, soothing.

'The what? I haven't got one of those. It doesn't take after me, then.'

'Shut up, Dette, and listen,' Helen pointed to the switch Karim was about to flick.

And then the room was filled with a beat that took over Dette's entire body and her eyes swam with water, just as her little baby was doing now, somersaulting over and over. Living.

'And very healthy,' Karim said.

'The spine is straight, the limbs intact. It's only a two-dimensional picture, but it's a perfect one,' Helen added.

'My baby,' Dette whispered. 'Hello.' Nothing would beat this feeling, nothing would stand in its way.

Ducky had used up his three-month advance booking for the Ivy, bless him, the lunch he'd meant to have with his wife, and he was still pleased to see her.

'You won't be so smiley when you watch me eat enough for ten men,' Dette kissed his cheek – instead of the air as she usually did. Close to tears in front of the man who'd sacked her only four weeks ago. If she wasn't pregnant, she was mad.

'You're pregnant!' Ducky's eyes were shining.

'How could you know? How could you see?'

'I've had four babies, or my wife has, and I can always tell. It's my trick at parties. Well, unless I think someone doesn't want to know. I was once kicked out of a dinner party because the husband was sterile. Speaking of which, who is the father?'

'There isn't one. Let's face it, poor kid, there's barely a mother.'

'Stop it, Dette. You mothered me and half the magazine. You're missed, you really are.'

'Enough for you to give me my job back? Relax, Ducky, only joking. I don't want it, honestly. I'll be too cumbersome with this and the other things I've got on the go. Let me tell you about my ideas.'

'I don't care if they're crap, I've commissioned you to do all of them. And I'll call Justine, my friend who edits a maternity magazine. Get you a pregnancy diary slot. That should keep you going.'

It might have kept an ordinary person going. Dette lived up to her name where finances were concerned. She'd always laughed them off before, saying they ought to be the same colour as her lipstick. 'Thanks, Ducky, but I'll have to write ten magazines to pull me out of my situation. I've lived beyond my means, darling. Got too many bad habits from my ex-husband.'

Ducky laughed. Joe Morgan was known to every journalist. 'You'll survive, Dette.'

It was nice that someone who didn't have to thought so highly of her. It made her feel like she could cope. Then she remembered. She didn't have a choice in the matter. There was a cold rush of fear, then a huge flip in her abdomen.

'Ducky – my baby just moved.'

Ducky, the rugby-playing, suburb-dwelling, children-and-wife-loving editor of the most chic women's magazine on the market, started crying with her.

'Something is telling me, very strongly,' Ducky was also quite psychic, or thought he was (he did the psychic page under a different name, and sex, in *Madame*), 'that this is the making of you, Dette Morgan.'

He was right, she realised. She was going to provide for this child, just like her mum had for her.

She believed him for that night and most of the week but, come Saturday, when she was trying to find something to wear for her annual joint birthday party that didn't tell anyone what she was, or why she was, or who she was with, she knew it would be a struggle. Martin would have to go. Tonight.

The doorbell rang. She went to answer it, hoping it wasn't Martin; he was the last person in the world she wanted to see. Then she realised he was the second last. John Edwards was outside.

'What the hell are you doing here?'

'I didn't like the way it ended up between us last time.'

'Neither did I, and if I have my way everyone'll know about it. Now get out of my face and take your wine with you, it didn't work last time and it's not working this time, prick.'

26

Helen arrived early, as she had for the past four weeks. As she hated herself for doing because it had become obvious to her that George Morehampton and Madeleina Conti were lovers. She knew she should tell Catriona. But she couldn't. Why?

Because Helen Larkin had found her feet and those feet were in love with George's. They weren't entirely separate from the rest of her, either. Helen's feet were the only part of her as yet being unfaithful, but the rest of her was well aware that this was a giant crush that existed, most likely, only in the ballroom. George's size elevens did all the right things for her eights. Madeleina was full of praise for their partnership. 'Your height, your movement! You're made for each other.' She clapped her hands with the encouragement that made Helen only want to try harder and longer.

And then there were George's blue-grey eyes, his quiet smile and occasional whispers. Just a few words, thoughts as they came to him, he was lovely. Why did upper-class Englishmen think being boring was better than being themselves?

'This is a treat, Helen. I feel so relaxed with you. My goodness, you're coming on. Tango. Aah.'

It was the dance they both loved. No one knew better how to keep to the point and stay there than Helen and George. Focus was their forte. This was only week four and Helen could already bend so far back her head reached the floor.

'Supple, Helen, you are so supple,' Madeleina called. No wonder, once upon a time, she'd been good at lying-down sports. 'Flexible, George, you are the flexible one, now flex those arms and hold her like you never want to let her go.'

Yes, please. Last week she'd been due to work on Tuesday evening and she'd called another consultant to switch shifts. 'What happened, Helen? Someone die?'

Switching shifts was something she had never done. She'd even taken her colleague's Saturday. It didn't mean seeing any less of the kids because she worked through the night and slept until midday Sunday. But then she'd had to go in to work on Sunday evening too.

Why am I doing this? She'd thought at the time. I'm so wrecked I won't be able to dance.

But she was. The problem was stopping. And that Madeleina still hogged George for the demonstrations, and the pensioners insisted she share him for the ask-me-ups that finished the night. For the final dances Helen always ended up leading Edith Webber, who she'd warmed to.

'You're a pleasure to watch, dear,' Edith gushed. 'Such a lovely couple you and George make.' Helen glowed. 'And him and Madeleina too.' Helen glowed a bit less. 'Mind you, he'd make an old sow like me into a silk purse, a man like him.' Helen was properly punctured. By the time she went to her car there was no spark left. George always walked her to it, then turned back in the direction of Madeleina's. Even as she got into the car she began counting the minutes to next week.

Her epiphany had happened only on the second night of classes, after the disastrous first week. She'd turned up at seven thirty at Madeleina's request, intending to warn her off George, say she'd have no hesitation in telling his wife if a rat was sniffed. But when Madeleina came out from behind her curtain, beautiful, graceful as ever, her eyes were swollen. Whatever she'd been crying about she didn't wish Helen to know. The smile she switched on was brilliant, professional. Helen hadn't the heart to quiz her.

'Helen, darling, let us turn the duckling into a swan.'

She didn't say ugly, that was not the implication, but Helen felt insulted. Still, she sensed Madeleina was speaking to the truth in her, the place beyond politeness. This was a genuine offer. A sincere wish to bring out something that Helen knew little about in herself.

'I want to help you, if you want help.'

Helen found herself whispering, 'Yes.'

'Good,' Madeleina was brisk. 'Now. I will be the man and you will let me lead you. I will tell your feet what to do and we will thaw the ice in your spine, entice your hips. Give you joy! But first, you must let me put my arm round your waist. Try not to flinch, darling.'

Two tall women met eye to eye. The cool of the green took on the warm gold of the hazel and found itself melting.

One. One, two. One, two, three.

She fell backwards on the first step.

'Sorry! I wasn't expecting you to go into reverse.'

It was a fiasco at first – twenty-five minutes of wrong turns, trips, bumps and frustrated apologies. And all the time Madeleina smiled and never once did she show a hint of impatience. Helen Larkin was tired, hungry, lost and close to tears for the hundredth time.

Then she got it.

Her feet found the pace. Her hips loosened and her ribcage wanted to go where her hips went, and her hips wanted to be where those feet were, doing whatever they were doing. The feet knew where to go, her head knew to let them, and without a single comment from Madeleina they glided through a waltz.

'And stop.'

That was it. Madeleina pulled back, gave a satisfied nod and smiled.

'You could at least clap,' Helen smiled back.

'If I start now I won't stop. You'll improve so quickly from now on.'

'How did you know it, Madeleina?' Helen had to ask. The high she was on could only be compared to holding her children in her arms for the first time.

Madeleina was walking behind her curtain again. 'Because I am trained to see. I knew your rigidity was in the head only. Your body wants freedom from that,' she called. On her own, in the great big room, Helen began to feel the Conti spell slip. She hadn't really executed a waltz without fault in less than thirty minutes. It had been Madeleina's magic. She wanted Madeleina to come out again, bring it back. It was as if Madeleina had heard. She came back with a towel round her neck.

'Madeleina, what's going on between you and George? I came here to ask and I have to ask it.' She felt uncomfortable putting the question. It seemed a betrayal. It was a pity, she liked Madeleina, who had an air of independence she identified with strongly.

Madeleina's eyes were full again, not with tears, but with a sadness that made Helen want to say, 'I feel it too.'

'George hasn't told you?'

'No.'

'Then I can't either, except to say there is nothing but history. Don't be afraid for your friend. Think about yourself, Helen, I would say, and what you're doing here.'

Then she was gone. Helen did think about it, and stared at the door, waiting for the reason to walk in. George arrived ten minutes late, purple, apologising as if it were a mortal sin, dodging old ladies' smiles and outreached hands to get to Helen's side. 'Major crisis at work. Sorry.'

'Don't worry. I know you're punctual to the point of death.' Helen surprised him by slipping an arm into his. He had imagined she'd be livid and mortified, if not already gone home, since last week had been so miserable for her.

'Helen has a surprise for you,' Madeleina smiled at him. It had less warmth, but it was still brilliant. She was hurting, Helen could see it. But she was clapping her hands now, putting on a record, no CDs or cassettes. Madeleina despised them. Vinyl was fitting for the place anyway, it added atmosphere and vintage. There was certainly plenty of that already. It took everyone back, even Helen – to her early teens and some forgotten sense of longing.

And when she and George faced each other she discovered that this was what it had been about. She had once been normal – she had desired romance and a tall dark stranger to dance with. Life had given her a freckled, sandy-haired kind heart. She was scared by how quickly she was losing sight of, or touch with, what she felt for Euan. Helen was not the sort to forgive betrayal. She knew it was her greatest fault but she couldn't do anything about it. Especially now that she was experiencing its first sensations. Too much pleasure in it. The thought of Euan going through this before her, and carrying it through, made her want to weep and at the same time find him and kill him.

The music began; George bowed and took Helen in his arms. And Helen surprised him.

It had been a beautiful evening and there had been two more since. It was a contained crush only because George was oblivious to it. What was it Catriona had said once? 'If you put him in a room with a Meccano set and a naked supermodel he'd ask you to get some clothes for the lady, and begin building.'

And they'd all taken her word for it. Obviously they'd seen him cleaning his forks and knew he ironed his own ties from Catriona's reports, and witnessed him working out the exact breakdown of the bill on paper napkins with his ballpoint pen. But that was because they always asked him to work it out. No one else could be bothered. And now she thought about it, he always chipped in the missing extra without drawing attention to it.

Madeleina. The feeling of playing second fiddle was another that Helen was not used to. But her emotional state would not be able to contain a full-blown affair, she was sure of that. Once or twice she'd thought of getting medication, but the dancing was now doing that. It was another reason why she did not want to know about their old affair – she'd have to stop coming here. Her rational mind also saw that Madeleina had a lot more time for George than Catriona had, she treated him with more respect. And there was no doubt his money would help her. If she was a gold-digger Madeleina was a bad one.

After having been blinded initially by Madeleina's beauty, Helen had begun to regain sight and pick up some pertinent detail. The elegance hid a lot, but Ms Conti's clothes were worn and although her shoes shone to perfection they were patently old. The house was shabby and though it held traces of former glory Helen could see it wasn't far off being condemned.

Last week she'd made the discovery. On her way to the loo she'd taken a quick look behind the red curtain and seen the single bed, the Baby Belling stove, a bookcase, the record player. The bathroom didn't even have a shower.

Madeleina Conti's living circumstances were far beneath her persona. The fall had been long and hard, no doubt of that. If George was or had been her lover, why was he not giving her some much-needed financial support? Why was Helen thinking like this when she wanted him so badly, well, wanted sex with him badly or at least an exotic, erotic tango? Why was she thinking like this when she valued Catriona's friendship so highly and now, to confuse matters, felt such an affinity with her dancing teacher? Helen had to admire that this woman, on her uppers, was not gunning for George in a bigger way. If anything, she was ignoring him. A woman of her

class knew how to do hard to get, but if that was the strat-
egy it would mark her down as pathetic. Washing in a
kitchen sink, sleeping in a single bed behind a curtain.
You don't do aloof if a rich and gorgeous man wants you.
And George Morehampton was the one making the
puppy-dog eyes here. Staring at Madeleina in a way that
made Helen want to poke him in one of them and stand
on his foot. Even Edith had noticed it. 'Never mind, dear,
it's you that takes him home.'

They'd given up trying to tell everyone they weren't a
couple. The pensioners were either deaf or keen to show
they were not stupid.

'Madeleina, she's the sort of woman all men fall in
love with, dear, just a bit. But she's an illusion. Like a film
star, dear, like Audrey Hepburn. She's a real lady, but
there's a secret there, dear, you trust me on that. You –
you're all there. A big doctor and all. You done good for
yourself, dear. George can see that. And she's a lot older
too, dear. Once you reach a certain point looks don't
hold.'

Excuse me, I happen to be gorgeous too, especially
with my new one-hundred-and-fifty-pound hair. You just
don't realise it because I have to come here in flamingo
fancy dress. I must get some new pumps that aren't pink,
and a black dancer's leotard and you'll realise how lovely
I am too. And elegant and—'

Helen didn't say it. Edith and she finished their final
set. At the last note George was over to her side.

'Are you ready to be walked to your car, Ms Larkin?'

'I am, Mr Morehampton.'

September evenings are made for falling in love. A
last touch of summer and a first suggestion of autumn.

The odd falling leaf, a sense of losing Paradise. She wanted the walk to the car to last. He was polite, and she polite back. But at the car he spoke. 'Helen, thanks for coming. Thanks for dancing with me. Thanks for not asking any questions. Thanks for being a brilliant friend and ally. Wait until you see Catriona's face on Saturday when she's dancing with me and I'm not falling over her. You'll get your reward.'

In all the Madeleina speculation Helen had forgotten the point, to surprise Catriona on Saturday night. So she wasn't even second fiddle. Third in line to tango with a stuffy English banker. What a place to end up.

'That's my reward?' she couldn't help snapping.

'No, that's not your reward. Your reward is this.' He held up a piece of paper. South Sheen and Nutley Amateurs' Night. Prizes. 'A naff trophy could soon be on your mantelpiece, Helen. Madeleina thought we should enter, but she wanted me to tell you. She was afraid you'd not be confident enough. She thinks we'll do well.'

It was next month. He did not want to stop the classes. He wanted them to go on for at least another month. She would still be dancing with him in four weeks' time. She would be first in line to tango with Mr Morehampton in four weeks time.

'I'll see.'

He was hurt. But he was diffident. 'Good. Think about it. I'd like to do it.'

Then he was gone. She sat in the car. She couldn't drive off without seeing him again, saying yes, with more enthusiasm.

She ran back to the school. The door was open. She walked in. The door to the ground-floor-bedsit-cum-ballroom was open. They were sitting on the single bed in each other's arms. Both of them were crying.

She left and ran back to the car, crying too. She had to get home, had to see Euan. Find out where all that love had gone in such a short time. Only it hadn't been a short time, had it? It had been a long time ebbing away, unnoticed, a night tide.

The speed limit was easy to break at this time of night. But the police were not interested when they pulled her over. 'That's three points for you, Madam.'

To add to the other six. Helen was a hopeless driver. Three more and she would lose her licence. It didn't matter. She would get home to Euan and he would make it all better, the way he used to.

She opened the door at speed. The way she saw it, right now, she and George were playing at romance in a ballroom. Or at least she was. There were two partners back home about whom they once had felt similarly, but too many children were in the way now. Too much work had been put in to this relationship to let Euan go so easily, after one possible transgression. She might even cut back on her hours. See if it was possible to get an overstretched department to do without her more so she would not have to do without her family. The mess of the hall, coats piled on top of coats piled on top of shoes piled on top of dirty laundry. Discarded bits of food. It dragged her down, but she pushed it aside and carried on through the hallway to the kitchen. He was on the phone.

'I know. Listen, I'm sorry I've been so removed since the time, you know, that it happened. I didn't treat you very well afterwards…I'm sorry. I feel so guilty. I want you to know that. You're a good woman…'

A pause. She should go in now, before she heard too much more. Too much. He always called Rorie a good woman. You're a good woman, Rorie. She's a good woman, Helen.

'So am I. For the time being…I know Helen's told you all…Yes…Great. I'll see you Saturday at the birthday do.'

He hung up and went back to loading dishes in the dishwasher. She should go in. She didn't go in. Suddenly Helen was in need of sleep. It was only just after nine. But she was already a couple of nights down. Right now she was too tired to know more than that she was correct in thinking it was one of her three closest friends. Most likely her closest. She felt foolish in her white tracksuit and pink pumps. She couldn't go to their room, so she had to go to Bea's and collapse on a spare bed without sheets.

'Magda? Have you seen George?' Catriona came clattering into the kitchen, fresh from a sitting, full of Jude the Coiffeur's tea and compliments. Her bladder was bursting and her arms were aching from holding them back over her head. And her head wasn't too far from exploding with all the work she'd done today at the theatre, and it wasn't over yet. She had to go over a set of figures with George. She hoped he'd be OK with that. She was in no mood for sweet-talking.

'No. He is not home yet.'

'But it's eight thirty. He's never late beyond eight fifteen.'

'It is work. He called to say. He will be home at ten.' Magda sounded delighted to be able to report it. You don't even know what's happening with your own husband.

'I'll just have a wee and then call him. The children?'

'They are all in bed now. We waited a little for you.

But they were too tired.'

Shut up. I'm home most evenings and up at cockcrow so they don't miss me too much. 'OK, thanks for that, Magda. Why don't you just take time out now and do whatever you want? I'll look after George's dinner.'

'No dinner tonight, he is eating in the office. He brought extra sandwich. I make soup for him too. Put it in Thermos flask.'

Childlike grammar meant only one thing with Magda – a dig at Catriona for not looking after her family the way Magda could.

'I'm sure it was all delicious, Magda. You never get time off from being an archangel, do you?' Catriona found herself saying. Magda was still staring when she left the room to hobble for the downstairs loo.

With the relief from her empty bladder and bursting now to sort out the figures, Catriona picked up the phone in the hall and speed-dialled First Investment.

'Is George Morehampton there, please?' she asked security.

'Who?'

'The head of group finance? Senior company member who's been working in the building for almost twenty years?'

'Sorry, missus, I've only been here twenty minutes. I'm a contract man.'

Silence. She was switched through to George's voice-mail. He must be on his way home. But he'd told Magda ten. He was never inaccurate in time or weather forecasts. She redialled. 'Me again. My husband is still in the build-ing. I need to speak to him. Please can you go to his office in person?'

'He ain't in the building, missus.'

'How do you know? You only came on shift twenty minutes ago.'

'He ain't in the building because no one is. All four floors are lights out. Not even a cleaner left this evening. I'm on me tod. Hang on, you're not one of them robbers are you? Casing the place. We did that in the training course…'

Catriona hung up. Faced the wall. There was a picture of her, George and four beautiful white-blonde kids with light tans – they all had their father's skin – on the Cornish coast one glorious summer day. They were leaning against a whitewashed wall and laughing. Everyone was laughing. It was twelve months ago. She studied the picture for five minutes. Then she blocked her number ID and rang Rorie's house. Rorie answered. She called Dette's. Dette answered. Then Helen's. Euan answered.

'Euan, Catriona here.'

'Hi, Catriona, how are you?' She could tell from the note of reserve in his voice that he didn't want to know. He was just being friendly. Euan was always that.

'Great, Euan. I started a job.'

'I heard, from Rorie.' Not Helen, then. 'It's wonderful. Good luck with it all. Could be the start of something great.' Optimistic. He was always that too. Catriona had thought at one point he could make her that way.

'Is Helen in, Euan?'

'No. Extra workload at the hospital. She'll be back by ten.'

'That's right.' Straight into acting mode, casual, light. 'She said something. I forgot. I'm always forgetting things. You know.'

'I know. Listen, I'm sorry I've been so removed since

the time, you know, that it happened. I didn't treat you very well afterwards.'

'No. You didn't.'

'I'm sorry. I feel so guilty. I want you to know that. You're a good woman.'

'I'm beginning to see that. I'm also a married one.'

'So am I. For the time being.' So he was being open about the problems they were having. 'I know Helen's told you all.'

'Euan?'

'Yes.'

'I hope you sort things out. But I really have to go now.'

'Great. I'll see you Saturday at the birthday do.'

She phoned the hospital, held on for five minutes before someone in A and E answered the phone with a bark.

'Is Helen Larkin there?'

'Ms Larkin is not rostered tonight. She's here tomorrow.'

They hung up without waiting for a nicety. Which was good. She didn't have one.

27

Rorie found each stair was an Everest. It seemed hours since she'd eaten or even sat down. Things at the theatre were at crisis point. Nigel and Noël were not even capable of giving each other the luvvie treatment. They were at the baleful-glances-of-hatred stage. She was up to her neck in flapper dresses, which needed altering since the wardrobe mistress had decamped to Twickenham to work on a big-budget movie. Lots of Edwardian crinoline, lots of money. Rorie would have done it herself but she didn't know one end of a needle from another. That was because she needed glasses. She hadn't time to get glasses. Last night at dinner she'd complained to still-writing John, who'd smiled and reached for her hand. 'Don't you worry. Rorie always finds a way. I'm concerned about the midpoint of my play. It seems to lack the dramatic punch.'

Rorie so badly wanted to give him one and say, 'Wake up you self-obsessed moron. I no longer love you and am trying to find a way of kicking you out.' Right now she was too knackered, but the day was coming.

If it wasn't for Catriona helping her out she might already have lost it. Over the past few weeks having her on board had turned what would have been an impossible situation – failed play, pissed actors, frightened writer, stroppy director – into just an unbearable one.

'Don't get in a flap about the flappers. I know how to stitch in a straight line,' Rorie had been delighted to hear Catriona say.

'But the cast wants—'

'Fuck the cast. They got paid this week. You didn't. They'll wear what we put on them.' Catriona had never been one for bad language. Pressure had produced in her a tongue of which any dock prostitute would have been proud. Catriona had firmly joined backstage in bitching about the actors. Rorie loved her for it.

Three days ago they'd been sitting in the green room eating all the biccies, knowing at some stage they'd have to go to a corner shop to replace them, when Rorie had burst out laughing.

'It's my bloody birthday.'

Catriona had laughed back. 'It was my bloody birthday six days ago. I was too busy to remind my husband and kids.'

No one had remembered Rorie's either. They shared a look that said, 'We have each other.' And Rorie went back to unpicking seams, and Catriona to sewing them.

Now, heading up the stairs to her flat, thinking she'd never get there, Rorie wondered if John would at least have put the kettle on, and knew he wouldn't. She knew it was beans on toast again and the opening credits of *The Bill* before she fell asleep on the sofa. She hated *The Bill*, but she never had the energy to get up and turn it off.

John would be writing in the study, which was her

second bedroom. Everywhere would be a kip. And it would remain so until November, when she was out of *Your Latest Bloody Fiasco*. If not earlier. If it didn't sell, it wouldn't stay open.

Not even a card this morning. Maybe one had come in the afternoon post. She was just about to step on to the return to the second landing when she saw John walk across it. At Dette's door. In more ways than one. She heard Dette say, 'Take the wine with you, prick.'

Rorie creased up with silent laughter. She hid in a doorway, just as well as Martin walked past at that very moment. He didn't look happy. He headed down the stairs for the pub at the speed of light. He had the bottle of wine she'd noticed that morning under his arm, she thought the Châteauneuf du Pape had been for her birthday. Was almost grateful that it wasn't, for the first time in a long line of gift-free birthdays. At least she'd have her beans on toast in peace. Inside the door her post was still on the floor. John's footprints were on it. They might as well have been on the back of her neck. Three bills and a card. From her mother. Thanks, Ma.

Inside was a cheque for fifty euros, which Rorie would never get round to cashing, and three photographs, two grainy and taken at a distance, of men. One celebrity head and shoulders of the latest Irish phenomenon at the box office – Colin Farrell.

'Oh, no!' Rorie groaned. Rorie's mother had been playing *Blind Date* private detective since she'd seen a programme on television about a mother who had found a husband for her daughter in exactly the same way. Some people watch too much Discovery Channel. Ma was of the firm opinion that Rorie needed to marry and marry someone (a) Irish, (b) alive and (c) soon.

Every so often these parcels would arrive and she had to make her decision on which one she liked best so Mrs Marks could put the target On File. On File meant Under Observation, which meant Mrs Marks, who knew everyone on the estate – and in fact in the whole of Ireland – went about gathering information on her subject. To make it to the choice-of-three stage the men had already been ascertained as single. After that they were put on the good-enough-for-my-daughter checklist. They almost always were. A criminal record was the only thing that put Mrs Marks off. Since Rorie had turned thirty Mrs Marks was no longer fussy. The game had been going for eight years and not once had Mrs Marks progressed things to the date stage, but it didn't mean she was giving up.

Mrs Marks loved Rorie more than life itself. Her desire was to see her married and settled and then she could die, deserted and happy. Mrs Marks had been to England to stay with her daughter on many occasions and not once had she met John, or known of his existence. She came for weekends and for summer, Easter and Christmas holidays, when John was with his family. John never answered the phone in the house in case it was Mrs Marks. On the one occasion he had, Mrs Marks had quizzed Rorie for a full year on the nice Pakistani man she'd spoken to.

Rorie loved her mother more than life itself and never wanted to disappoint her, as her father, the pig, had done. So she never mentioned anything that wasn't about how great she was doing and how far she was going and all the famous people she was meeting. Mrs Marks saw that finding a husband was the only way she could show all this welter of love she had for her great girl, who'd done so well at school and in life without a daddy.

Rorie hadn't phoned home in weeks. She cooked her beans and burned her toast and forwent falling asleep in front of *The Bill* to sit on the tiny hall stool in the tiny hall, which still managed to be cold, and dial Ireland.

'Hiya, Ma, happy birthday to me.'

'Indeed, love! Lovely to hear your voice. I tried earlier today but you must have been working.'

'I was. Very hard. Still wish Jack Lemmon hadn't died, he'd have been perfect for this lead.'

Mrs Marks loved Jack Lemmon. 'A gentleman you can tell', was how she described him. It was amazing how many times Jack had starred on the West End stage in Rorie's imaginary world. In reality he'd been only once and Rorie had been his stage manager and discovered that, yes, he was everything her mother thought he was and so she'd been happy to keep bringing him back for fictitious shows that were not *Your Latest Fiasco*.

'Indeed, I'll never forget him for the photo. It's still here, Rorie.' Mrs Marks had got it in 1990 and was still talking about it. It was on her mantelpiece. It would be there for as long as Mrs Marks breathed.

'Did you get the ones I sent you?'

Here we go.

'Yes, Ma.'

'Three's a possibility.' Mrs Marks always marked the back of the photo with a number. 'He's not your type physically, but who's fussy when they're your age? He's his own butcher business.'

Rorie only ate fish. 'Great. Ma?'

'Yes, love, only I wish you'd call me Mum. It's much

nicer. It's what Mrs Bridge's children call her.'

You're her cleaner, Ma, and I've called you Ma for thirty-five years before you started working for her. 'OK, Ma, I'll try. Listen, why'd you send me a picture of Colin Farrell in this latest bunch?'

'Colin who?'

'Colin Farrell, the actor.'

'Oh, him. Because he's an actor.'

'So?'

'So you're in the acting game. And he's single. I read it in the paper. And he's Irish, sounds like he's making a way for himself. He'd be grand for you. Phone up one of your friends and get them to introduce you to him.'

'I work in British theatre as a stage manager, Ma. Colin Farrell works in Hollywood as a new god.'

'I was only trying to help. What about the other ones? Any joy there? Number Three is the ticket, I'd say.'

'He's hidden behind a bus stop.'

'Well, I have to take these photos surreptitiously, love. I don't want them thinking I'm funny.'

'What about me? Do you want me to think you're funny?'

'Stop it. I'm only trying to help. Now, pick one.'

'No.'

'You know what happens if you don't.'

'Please, Ma.'

'Mum. And I'm not listening. I don't go to all this trouble for nothing. Are you sure you're not lesbian, Rorie?'

'No, I'm not. Why d'you ask that again?'

'There's a lovely lesbian moved in next door. She's a creator at the museum in town.'

'A curator. I think you mean curator.'

'Well, she's a good job and she's no girlfriend. I asked her had she anyone.'

'Sorry, Ma, I'm heterosexual.' And stuck with it.

'Grand so. Pick a number and let me get on with it.'

'Three.'

'Thanks, love. And you'll thank me one day.'

'I hope I won't have to.'

'Not every man is like your father, Rorie. That's all I'm trying to help with.'

'I know. You're sweet. How is Mrs Larkin, Ma?' It suddenly occurred to Rorie to ask – for Helen more than for herself.

'I kept meaning to ask you, Rorie, to ask Helen for me. Since the stroke five months ago she's bedridden. They moved out of the area. Don't see as much of them.'

Rorie had to sit down. She was sure Helen didn't know. Even though they weren't seeing each other as much, Helen would still have told her. 'Is she going to get better?'

'No, love. Not after her husband going so quick. They never got on in life and then she found she couldn't live without him. She told me that at the funeral.'

'You never told me Mr Larkin was dead.'

'Seven months. Sure I forgot and I thought Helen would have told you. The family said she couldn't be there because of work commitments. Though I know, all's not right there, Helen should have come home.'

'That's right.' She didn't want her ma to find out she didn't know a scratch about the Larkins. And off Mrs Marks went, oblivious, on a mission to find out as much about Number Three as possible.

Rorie put the phone down. If she'd thought she knew

Helen she now realised she didn't. Her father had died and she hadn't bothered to tell her. Maybe not even her husband. It wasn't just cold behaviour, it was freezing. No matter how far you're removed from someone, if they're your father and they die, you mention it.

I hope she doesn't let the same thing happen with Bea.

She had to phone. She couldn't tell Helen straight-away, phoned Euan's mobile. In their bedroom Helen watched his mobile ring and saw Rorie's number flash up. She didn't answer and left the room. Euan came chasing out of the shower to get it, saw who it was, answered.

Bea, downstairs, saw Helen outside her own bedroom door listening to Euan's conversation. For the past three nights Helen had been sleeping in her room.

'Rorie, how are you? Yes, I'm alone. She's downstairs. No, she can't hear me.'

Helen went downstairs. She didn't want to know the rest. In the kitchen she went straight up to her oldest, most estranged daughter, put her head on her shoulder and cried.

28

'Happy Brithday to Us', the banner read. A dyslexic friend of Rorie's had made it ten years ago and no one wanted it changed. By the end of the evening the spelling would be correct. Every first Saturday in September, five courses served over four hours. The first food was on the table after eight, last nibbles served at midnight.

A jazz band, who weren't above doing a few Abba numbers, provided the entertainment and the night usually ended up with the children in sleeping bags upstairs in Angelo's flat and the diehard adults cooking Sunday breakfast in the kitchen. Sixty could be squeezed in at a push, with a postage-stamp dancing area, and winched out by four in the morning.

Everyone helped Angelo in the afternoon, and not as much as they were supposed to. Someone would always think it was a good idea to open wine and by five-thirty, when everyone rushed home to change, the world was a fuzzier place. Dette would bring her outfit to change into in the loos and quietly go around on her own arranging

the flowers and tables to her perfect standards. 'My associates are the kind who put sugared almonds at the
kitchen sink, chocolates on the stairs, fairy lights round
the bog. They make places perfect for one evening and
that's what I do. I'm not having my bash looking like a
tinker's wedding.'

She liked it and so did the chef, who invariably ended
up with Dette in the ladies' just before everyone arrived.
Passionate coupling was a great inducement to him to
produce great food. Dette regarded it as a service to the
diners. This year was different. He smiled at her hopefully as she fussed with the cornflowers and sprinkled con-
fetti on the pressed white tablecloths.

'Not this year, my darling,' she blew him a kiss.
'Things are complicated.'

He shrugged his shoulders and raised a spatula to her.
The man didn't have a word of English and didn't need
it.

John's arrival on her doorstep yesterday had freaked
her out, he'd looked like he was going to burst in on her
for calling him a prick, but then Martin had come up the
stairs.

'What are we going to do?' John looked over his
shoulder.

'Let him in?' Dette suggested.

'If you blow me out for that twat I'll want to know
why, Dette.' Martin had said it with more than a smile
and less than a meaningful look. So even he thought
she'd shag anything. Well, it'd make life easier for what
she had to do.

'What do you want anyway?' she snapped.

'How d'you mean?'

'To eat. Pasta? Takeaway?'

'Dunno, don't care. The question is, what do you want?'

'Both. I could eat you as well I'm that hungry.'

'Sounds good to me.'

They'd had a wonderful evening. Particularly good since they hadn't seen much of each other that week or the previous one.

'Sorry about that, Dette, work's gone mad. I've paint-ed enough fucking cherry trees. This Chekhov bloke, he liked his orchards.'

'That's all right Martin.' She'd been glad of the space – known it was time to say goodbye to him. Having a few nights to herself let her work up to it. But he was such easy company. He made the food, he put the telly on – he even poured her some Amé since she couldn't stom-ach wine.

And he didn't drink either.

'I don't mind giving it a miss for one evening.'

When she woke up it was almost one and he'd allowed her to use his shoulder for about two hours. He was sitting in a way that was obviously not comfortable for him and looking at her in a way that wasn't comfort-able for her.

'OK. Now it's time to say goodbye and thanks for all the fish.' She gathered herself up and her strength. Appropriate since they'd had a feed of tuna and pesto pasta. Omega three, the pregnancy book said, great for foetal growth and brain development.

'Dette?' Martin spoke softly, just before she did. 'Is there anything you want to tell me?'

'Yes. There is.' She looked at him and the cold dread

at what she was about to do was upon her. As she'd already long decided, there was no alternative. But there was no alternative. He was too young for children and she was too old for messing. It had to be now. If it was now he would never have to know. The baby heard the thought, kicked. Hard. Don't be stupid, Mother. Tell him. Tell him I'm here and that he's my dad, put his hand on your belly and make him feel it too. Tell him even though he's a young stud fifteen years younger than you, and with more opportunity ahead of him than you have behind you. Tell him that you love him.

Listen, darling, you're a foetus, you know feck all. I tell him and you and I will be up all night crying with how fast he runs out the door and down the street. Or maybe he won't. Maybe he'll play daddies until he realises what he's saddled with. We're better off with each other. I'll manage fine. You'll be worth it—

'Dette?' Martin broke into her thoughts.

'What?'

'We haven't made love in four weeks.'

'So?'

'Well we used to be at it like bunnies. I wondered if you'd gone off me, that's all.'

'No, no, Martin.' Say yes. Say yes now. 'It's just I'm going through a life change at the moment.' It should be Catriona Morehampton on this sofa. What was Dette Morgan doing pulling out navel fluff?

'Have you joined AA?'

'What?'

'You haven't drunk in a month, Dette. I've never seen you without a drink in the six months we've been together. I want to know, have you quit?'

'Yes.' She said it as quietly as she could. If the foetus heard, it might expect her to stop for good.

'How are you managing at work? I know journalists drink reservoirs.'

And how are you managing to get on with my oldest friend? Dette could still see him and Catriona coming out of Angelo's. As per the rules of the game, she wasn't saying anything.

'Oh, I'm not seeing much of them. I'm working from home now. Mostly.'

'Since when?'

'Since I decided it was better for me, I'm changing a few things, you know, about my life. Now shut up and watch *Frasier*.'

Ducky was negotiating a severance deal for her, pretending she was threatening him with solicitors so the company might cough up a few thousand. Since he'd found out she was pregnant and below penniless, he'd phoned every day. His wife was getting together all her old baby equipment and they were going to give it to her. Just shows – you do someone a favour... She didn't know why she was being so secretive with her other friends, just knew she had to be for now. The independence forced on her by a dad's early death and a husband who couldn't support himself had made her wary. Lean and you might fall over.

'Good. I'll support you, too, in that. You know, if you need anything. But I know something else is up, Dette. When you're ready you let me know.' Martin looked away, embarrassed by his offer. They weren't the most intimate couple. In six months she hadn't even found out how many brothers and sisters he had. There was no suggestion of meeting parents on either side. They both knew what an odd couple they made. 'And another thing. Let me just say this. I know you're a touchy bird on the subject so take your time chewing me legs off. I don't give a stuff about age. I like older women a lot more than I like birds me own age.'

After that, saying goodbye would have to wait until tomorrow.

'Do you mind, Martin, if we just go to sleep?'

'Not so long as I'm kipping here, no.'

Now tomorrow was today and today was six-thirty and Angelo had wandered back in to look at Dette's party décor. He was in his lightweight suit. No one wears suits like an Italian. Dette whistled. 'Armani?'

'Top Man,' Angelo whispered. 'Do not tell anyone.'

'Looks Armani on you.'

'Thank you. Beautiful.' He spread his arms. 'This place, you have magic.'

And that, along with twenty other things behind it, made her cry.

He brought her to a seat. From the kitchen the chef looked over the saloon doors with concern – he was well ahead of himself on the starters. Angelo waved him away with narrowed eyes. His arm round Dette he whispered in her ear, 'Would you like whiskey? I have some nice whiskey.'

'No.' She looked up, mascara on her cheeks for the second time this month. Apply ten brands and bawl, measure results out of ten. Sell to *Madame* to pay mortgage. 'I'd love warm milk, though.'

Angelo nodded and went to froth and steam some with the Gaggia. He sprinkled chocolate and cinnamon on top and drew a smiley face. She laughed. 'They'll be here any second.'

'They'll be late,' Angelo promised. 'No one comes before seven-thirty. Now, tell me. Tell me what is wrong.'

'No, I will not. You might gossip.'

'Dette,' Angelo's tone sharpened, 'I do not gossip about my friends. Tell me, what is wrong?'

'Isn't it obvious? This is my fortieth birthday party – you tell anyone that and I'll kill you – and I'm four-and-a-half months pregnant by a man who is only slightly older than my foetus.'

'You're pregnant! Dette! This is wonderful!'

'You think so? The toyboy, who I've had the wisdom to fall in love with, is providing cherry-tree backdrops for three of the world's most beautiful Eves. Apart from that I saw him walk out of here on Wednesday with my oldest friend and snog her on the street.'

'They did not snog, they embraced.'

'Embracing is worse. Catriona's classy enough to embrace. I'm the sort men snog.'

'You are just being insecure, Dette. You feel hopeless, you feel no good at anything.'

'That's because I'm not. I can't write about anything other than foundation. I don't drive because I'm scared. I don't swim because I don't like water. I can't drink or smoke any more. I used to be brilliant at those. I'm getting fat and you haven't offered me any cake yet to help me get fatter. You're supposed to offer crying women cake, especially on their birthday.'

Angelo shook his head. 'I will get some cake and you will get some advice from me. Tell Martin. He feels the same for you.'

'No, Angelo, he thinks he does. He's playing at serious

relationship. The only long-term one he's had is with his comics.'

'You don't tell anyone else you are pregnant?'

'Helen knows. The others are too wrapped up in West End drama to notice anything much. I haven't even heard from them, so I haven't been in touch. Keeping myself to myself.'

If Catriona had noticed Dette hadn't been in touch, she didn't show it. All she talked about was her new and very exciting job as Rorie's slave. The two of them were thick as thieves. Dette made the jealousy vanish elsewhere, along with all the other negative emotions that were damaging her unborn child's psyche. She laughed, 'Funny, Angelo. Me and Catriona are trading places. She's swearing and drinking all the coffee that exploited plantation workers can produce. I'm reading articles on channelling *chi* to the womb.'

'You are still the same woman, Dette. Smart. Be smart now.'

He was speaking and she was only half-listening. The pace of change was so rapid she kept having these out-of-body experiences, or maybe it was a pregnancy symptom. She watched herself now, drying eyes, producing compact, doing a quick repair job, receiving warm embrace (classy kind with extra comfort) from Angelo, sitting at her place, watching Helen arrive, alone. Standing up again to greet her. Helen saying, 'You have a week or two before everyone knows without you telling them.'

The others came alone too. And everyone apologised for being late. Seven, they were supposed to be here at, seven-thirty they turned up. For fifteen years or thereabouts. Would there be a sixteenth?

The ritual was cocktails and present-giving. Angelo had already been primed to give Dette an alcohol-free one. But the atmosphere was different this year. They were all much quieter. Sobered up after the afternoon's drinking and cleaning Angelo's place, determined not to get drunk again. But with the heavy nature of silence, with the reasons not to speak freely, there seemed no way through but to ask immediately for a second round to loosen their tongues and minds artificially. Angelo didn't offer to join them, as he always did, but made an excuse to go to the kitchen.

'The chef, he is not his usual self. I need to find his bottom and kick it, since he will allow me to do nothing else with it.'

Rorie broke the silence, 'Well, I know that you're all dying to see what I got you. And I'm dying to see what you think of it. It's been a tough year on us all and I don't know if it's going to get any easier. So I went the whole hog and bought us these—'

She produced four envelopes. Each contained a voucher for a wash, cut and blow dry at Blow Job. The table became what it had always been, animated, exclaiming, interrupting each other.

'You idiot, how can you afford this? That's six hundred quid you've spent!' Dette started.

'He gave me a discount. I told him who my mates were. He looked like he wanted to kiss me when I said who I was. And another thing, I invited him this evening. Hope you don't mind me crowding in on your mate, Dette, but he's a right laugh. Kept me in stitches about all the *Three Sisters*. He's the only man who's had Julia Roberts, Renée Zellwegger and Victoria Hazlet in one go.

And he'd much rather have Angelo! Speaking of who, I think we can sprinkle a bit of fairy-dust there? What d'you think?'

'Brilliant.' Dette didn't have to find enthusiasm, it was there, bursting out of her. 'I wish I'd thought of it.'

'You haven't got the money to be doing this,' Helen said quietly. 'Why are you doing it, Rorie?'

'No reason, Helen, but the one I just gave,' Rorie's joy cooled.

'I see. Thank you. I'll enjoy using it.' Helen was too polite.

Dette and Catriona looked at each other – someone say something, move things on.

'It'll be great taking you in there.' Dette nudged Rorie. 'I've got you booked in for Wednesday anyway, the makeover feature. We can do all the preparation in one afternoon.'

'The makeover feature.' Rorie's face fell. 'I completely forgot. I've got a logistics meeting with Nigel and Noël. We're off in a week. I can't, Dette. Sorry, sorry, sorry.'

'Now, Rorie, I can cover that.' Catriona waved her hand. 'I know exactly what's involved. Please, get your hair done and buy some new clothes. You need some Dette magic.'

Dette and Rorie smiled at Catriona, who felt like she'd never felt before in this group, or hadn't for a long time. Useful.

'Well, while you're all adoring me, could I give you my present?'

She handed out another four envelopes.

'What? No lava lamps?' Dette enquired, as she

opened hers. Then let out a sigh, astonishment, disbelief. The giving had gone mad this year. 'Five hundred pounds in an account in my name?'

She looked up to see all the others had the same.

'Now, don't go thinking I'm as generous as Rorie. I'm rich. Or my husband is. It was his idea. Since I've been doing the show's accounts with him I've begun to understand the value of money. George gave me the idea of an investment account that offers bonuses to long-term savers. It's fascinating,' she watched the blank faces. 'Well, it's fascinating to me. I want us to save one hundred pounds a year for the next two decades so we can take a holiday together when we retire. Or when we're all over sixty, whichever happens first. I was only going to put in a hundred pounds. George opened them and put in the rest. They're with his bank, so there's no need to produce the relevant documents until next week. Now, if you could please pass on your birth cert and/or passport and/or driving licence, I'll get them copied and return them to you.'

Catriona, who knew nothing of worldly affairs and hadn't wanted to, arranging financial futures.

More brandy needed. Dette had a small Bailey's, with extra milk, whispered to Angelo. It would help with indigestion. Catriona, survivor of three pregnancies, each with nine-month nausea, didn't notice. She was high on involvement. Dette wondered if she cashed the five hundred pounds would George rat on her.

'Well, you'll all be surprised to see that I, too, have envelopes,' Dette produced her present out of the Prada bag she was considering pawning. She was rewarded with a gasp as loud as the other two had been.

'The Dawn Principles, a day-long workshop, October the tenth. Dette!' Catriona raced over to hug her, forgetting Dette was touch-phobic. 'I can't wait to meet this woman. It must have cost you, this.'

'Nah, it didn't cost a penny. If Dawn's not media savvy then her publicist certainly is. A feature in *Madame* to include four distinct impressions of the day swung it. If I'd had six hundred nicker, believe me, I'd have bought them. But I brought these too.' Inside four beautifully wrapped boxes was a selection of her finest free products. 'Last lot of goodies, I'm afraid, girls, so use sparingly.'

'Well, I'm a skinflint,' Helen apologised in advance. 'I just bought something I thought you'd all like. And I like it myself, I have to say. It's funny we all bought ourselves a present this year. Here, amazingly, are four envelopes.'

This time they were A3 and inside each one was a personal astrological chart.

'They're from Astro Info. I found them on the net. I got one for Bea, too, for next week when she turns eighteen. She showed me the site this week.'

'You and Bea? Talking?' Dette laughed. 'There must have been a major planetary shift there, Helen.'

There has been. She's supporting me as I lose my husband to my best friend. I haven't told her he's having an affair or who with. I've just told her I feel like my whole life has been wasted effort. 'We seem to have found some common ground. Must be her maturing.'

'Or you getting younger, Helen.' Rorie, mindful that bad news was only two days away, tried to compliment her. Euan and she had agreed Helen should have this birthday party, then tackle her on Monday with the details. The details Euan had found out by ringing Ireland. He would fill Rorie in later this evening in a quiet moment.

'Now that the pressies are out of the way, can we talk about some business in hand?' Rorie suggested. She wanted Helen to have more good news. From the sound of it, from Euan's account, things between them were disintegrating. She wanted to stop it soon. 'The fidelity test. Will we give a progress report?'

There had been one at the last Tuesday lunch, but nobody had done much then. Surely by now things were more established.

'OK,' Helen looked at Rorie. 'Let's hear a little.'

'Not so much it'll spoil our dinner,' Dette pleaded. The others looked surprised. Dette was never one to shrink from something. Everyone now knew who was after their man, though they didn't mention it. They could also make a healthy stab at who was after everyone else's. You didn't need to have George's head for maths to figure it out.

'I think we should agree to tell one another everything by a fixed date,' Helen's rational side had come out with the suggestion. The irrational said she wanted enough time to have sex with George, so please build that into the equation.

'OK,' everyone agreed.

'Let's not mention it till the first lunch in October,' Dette suggested. By that time she wouldn't have anything to hide herself. 'Except to say, has anyone got anything awful to report that they can't bear to keep to themselves?'

'No.' A chorus.

'Then let's enjoy our birthday. We'll speak again on the first Tuesday in October.'

'OK,' everyone agreed.

But they wouldn't have to wait that long.

29

The first guest had arrived. George, looking nervous, wearing a dinner jacket.

'Well, George, you'd give God a run for his money.' Dette was the first to say something.

'Thought I'd get a bit dickied up for the occasion. Took an hour with the bloomin' bow. Magda did it in the end.'

Did she now? Four minds thought.

'Anyway, Catriona. Can I have a bit of a word?'

George pulled her aside. 'Look, I asked Mother if she'd drop the kids here later, in a taxi.'

'George!'

'No, listen, darling, I wanted an hour or so on my own with you. To give you this and have a drink, without having to charge after the four scraps.'

Catriona looked at the tiny package he handed her.

'It's late, sorry, but that's only because we didn't see each other on your actual birthday. You were being paint-ed.' Did she hear jealousy?

Catriona opened a box. Inside was a moonstone necklace set in silver. It was Catriona. Never before had George managed to buy anything that was Catriona. She had enough gold to keep an Essex girl in multiple orgasms, and she never wore any of it. This had cost half the price and was worth more because of the thought that had gone into buying it.

'Beautiful, it's beautiful.'

'I had it made for you. It's what I thought you would like.'

'Like? I love it.'

'Good, good.' He didn't know where to put himself. So she put her arms round him. And Helen watched.

People were arriving thick and fast now. Catriona wanted to try it on, but there were some new best friends coming from *Your Latest Fiasco*. Rorie was amazed to see the lighting and props people saunter in. 'Bloody hell, Catriona, they never have anything to do with me!'

'Have you ever asked them, Rorie?'

'No, but they never ask me either.'

'Because they're afraid of you. And they're also aware that if you aren't left to get on with things they're out of a job soon.'

Martin came up behind them, 'Wotcha. Where's my fat girlfriend?'

'Did he really just say that?' Rorie asked Catriona.

'He really just said that.'

'Does he expect to live?'

'Come on, I think she looks great now she's put on a bit. And she's not fat, she's just me girl.' Martin pulled back from the glares.

'Well, Martin, let me just be me and say if you breathe a word to her about being fat when she's only just turned the corner from anorexia, I'll stuff your Amstel neck where it can't be seen,' Catriona pointed her finger to the relevant place.

Catriona was known to be a member of Peace People and this new line in violence brought a smile to Rorie's face.

'I get the message. Now did you get mine, Cat?'

Rorie's eyebrows rose at Martin's question.

'Yes, and I don't want to talk about it now.'

'Fine, be a cock-tease all night. I don't care. I'll wait for ya. I'm not proud.'

He saw Dette coming out of the ladies', the inside of which she now saw twenty times a day, and sauntered over to her.

'Looks like your seduction paid off,' Rorie whispered. 'Is Dette in for a let-down?'

'I'm not going to say, Rorie, because you told me not to. Remember?'

'Yes, but that was when I was being sanctimonious with you. Now I'm so curious I won't be able to enjoy my dinner.'

'You will, because you're holding on to the wrong end of the wrong stick. He's mad about Dette. And he's a brilliant bloke. I'm happy for her.'

'You are?'

'Yeah, she's struck gold this time. Let's hope she knows it.'

'Well, what was all that about phoning you?'

'We're doing a bit of business.'

'He's my mate. I've known him five years. You're my

mate. I've known you even longer. Tell me what's going on.'

'You see, Rorie? That's the stage manager in you. Put your nose away and let people do what they have to do without trying to control it.'

'Fine, but don't tell that lot anything about me,' Rorie pointed to the *Fiasco* crew, who were waving. 'Especially about John.'

'You're ashamed of him, aren't you?'

'Yes. Wouldn't you be?'

Euan and Bea arrived with the children. Helen wanted to get up and kiss them, but she was still winded from seeing George in a dinner jacket and giving his wife a present. It was her birthday in a couple of days and she knew she wouldn't be getting anything because she had told Euan that if he gave her something he would be trying to buy her back. Now she wanted to be bought back.

As soon as he came in he'd glanced at Rorie. Rorie looked up. Bea came straight over to Helen. 'How're you doing?'

Helen had already told her oldest daughter how much she was dreading this evening, and having to pretend to be on top form. 'I'm better than I expected to be. That's as much as I can manage.'

'Can you manage some wine?'

'I can always manage wine. And you?' Bea was eighteen next week, it was time to loosen the stranglehold, admit her daughter had been getting drunk since she was thirteen. At least now she would be doing it legally.

'No, thanks.' Bea's refusal could have knocked Helen over with a feather.

'I hope you're not doing this on my account, Bea.'

'Stop it. I don't want any. Now, can I sit beside you?' Bless her. She knew that sitting beside Euan would only make her tense. Bea had surprised her with how mature she'd been on the subject of why the spare bed in her room was suddenly occupied by a mother who spent most nights weeping as quietly as she could. Not once had she demanded to know what was going on, although she'd said, 'If you need to tell me anything, if you want to talk about what's going on with you two, then I'm happy to. Don't worry about upsetting me.'

'Please, Bea, I can't at the moment.'

'OK. No problem.'

Helen had never noticed how patient her daughter was, the space she was prepared to give her. She looked back at a lot of incidents between them now with regret that she hadn't credited Bea more. Bea didn't take sides either, she was as affectionate with Euan as she was currently being civil to her mother. Helen and Bea had a long way to go before affection.

'Doesn't George look bloody gorgeous – even if he's overdone the dress code?' Bea asked her mother.

'Catriona's got a surprise coming tonight,' Helen was amazed at how light she sounded in saying it, conspiratorial, even.

'Lucky woman,' Angelo had come over to give Bea a hug. 'I wish someone would surprise me with George.'

At that point Jude Mackenzie walked in. He was wearing a canary yellow suit, with a T-shirt featuring scenes from *The Wizard of Oz* and wearing ruby-red sparkling winkle pickers. He was not Angelo's type, judging by the look on Angelo's face.

Jude marched over to Rorie, threw his arms round her like she was someone he'd known all his life instead of someone who'd spent thirty minutes in his salon collecting four vouchers.

'Hiya, Butch, my name's Sundance. Wanna swing?' The band had just started up, right on cue.

'Hiya, Jude. I told you last time, I'm not gay.'

'Then let me do something with the hair and let Dette do the rest. You need a look.'

'What?' Rorie laughed. 'You mean like yours?'

For a split second, Jude looked unsure. 'Am I overdoing it d'you think?'

'Yes, yes you are.'

'Good. You told me there was totty. I dressed to be noticed.'

'Well, he's noticing you all right.'

Jude looked across the room at Angelo, who was looking across the room at Rorie.

'My God, that's him,' Jude sat down suddenly.

'You know him?'

'Course I know him. He's the man I'm going to marry.'

Angelo looked at Helen and tilted his head to one side.

'Rorie thinks I will sleep with *him*?'

Helen nodded.

'She is barred. I am going to bar her.'

Helen tried not feel delighted by this.

'You can't bar her, she's your oldest customer,' Bea said.

'I can. If I have to speak to that man I can—'

'Angelo,' Bea butted in, 'don't talk to my mother about these things. She hasn't a clue. Go over there, be polite, take a drink order. Then leave.'

Helen was still listening to 'my mother' – the first time Bea had called her that in a long time.

Angelo walked over to the table where Roric was gassing with Jude and also Catriona. Both fawned over Jude like he was their favourite gay man. Fickle tarts.

'Well, hello.' Jude extended a hand with French-manicured quarter-inch nails in Angelo's direction. Angelo barely palmed it, then asked, 'Drink?'

Jude leaned on his rejected hand and smiled prettily. 'A double brandy. I need something medicinal.'

'And we'll have singles,' Catriona rallied in support, 'to accompany our single, very available friend.'

30

'That didn't go very well, did it?' Jude turned to Rorie.

'I'd say that's an understatement.'

'Sorry, I thought I was being charming.'

'You were. It's just that you're a bit over the top.'

'How d'you mean?' Jude asked, mystified.

'I mean you'd make Graham Norton look like Sylvester Stallone.'

'No!'

'She's right,' Catriona nodded. 'It's not Angelo's cup of tea, really.'

'Well, pity about him,' Jude snapped. 'I'd have been doing him a favour.'

He stormed off to the loo.

'Oh dear,' Rorie whispered. 'I hope this doesn't mean I get a hatchet job on Wednesday.'

'How's the love thing going?' Dette joined Catriona and Rorie.

'About as well as the relationship between the royal family and the tabloid press,' Rorie sighed. She sighed even more when Angelo came back, slapped the drinks on the table and stormed off, as Jude had.

Rorie chased after him. 'Angelo, come on! I was trying to help you find a boyfriend.'

'The only thing this man and I have in common is we are gay. I am insulted, Rorie.'

'I'm sorry. I don't understand why.'

'Imagine Rorie, how you would feel if I brought in some man who wears medallions and has a hairy chest and expected you to fall into bed with him.'

'I don't know. Anything's a step up from John.'

'I am looking for a boyfriend, Rorie, not any boyfriend. This man is Danny La Rue.'

'Danny La Who?'

'A big queen, a Liberace. I want a Gianni Versace, someone who has style. Not this. I want what I offer.'

'Angelo, this man is London's most sought-after hair stylist. He's the one who's done all the hairs of the Hollywood ones over for the play. And he's done Helen's. And Catriona's. And Dette's. And next week he's doing mine.'

'So he is a man who cuts hair and wears terrible clothes. Pah!'

Rorie took a step back, 'I had no idea you were such a snob.'

'Well, if you think standards are snobbery then maybe that is why you are with John.'

Angelo regretted it the minute he said it. But it was too late to apologise and anyway, he was Roman. Romans have to be fed to lions to make the word 'sorry' part of their vocabulary. Even then one lion wouldn't be enough.

*****

Rorie went off in the direction of the toilets and decided to pop into the gents' to see how Jude was doing. He wasn't in there. He was in the ladies', taking off his make-up with toilet paper.

'Sorry, Jude. He's a rude bastard when he wants to be.'

'Well, not your fault, darling. I suppose I came over a little strong.'

'I wouldn't say that. To be honest, I think Angelo's afraid. He's not had much success with men, believe it or not. They seem to see him as a meal ticket.'

'Not surprising. He runs a restaurant. I know what you mean, though. I get a lot of it myself. Snippy little shits trying to make me fall in love with them so they can steal my clients. Last one – the one I married in Vegas? He took my sofa with him. My sofa! The only reason he didn't get anything else is my neighbour called me up and said there was a removal truck outside my house.'

'Really? I wonder what my man will do when I finally work up the courage to kick him out. He's never bought so much as a lightbulb for my place and he's been there fifteen years. And he's unfaithful.'

'So who's the grubby little mistress?'

'Me.'

'You? Sorry. I don't believe it.'

'Why?'

'You don't look the mistress type.'

'Well, I've let myself go, can't be bothered any more. I used to be hot.'

'Still could be.' Jude was standing back from her. 'It's well camouflaged, but it's all there.'

'I could say the same about you. Now, let's go and get some food and maybe later, if you're lucky, we'll have a dance.'

'Sounds good to me. Your boyfriend. Where is he tonight?'

'Writing. Otherwise he wouldn't even be around. The weekends are for his wife traditionally. If he came along tonight, though, he'd be obliged to acknowledge it was my birthday and be forced to give me a thing called a present.'

'You want to get him out of your life, darling. It'll be hard, you know. He's got rights now. He's been living with you for so long. Even if he's got a wife. I know. I fought a court battle with my ex, and he was living with another sugar-daddy by that time. He got a lot more than the sofa he stole. I swore never again – a man my own age or older and with his own means. But it won't be your friend, I'm afraid. Now, come on, let's have a party.'

Rorie felt a cold wash of fear. The brandy didn't help. For years she'd thought of herself as a woman without any rights to her lover. Now he had them over her.

The band went into instrumentals as the first courses were served. George went up and had a word with them.

'What's he up to?' Catriona asked Angelo, who was sitting beside her.

Angelo shrugged. He wasn't up to much conversation.

As soon as the first-course plates were taken away, George cleared his throat and stood up. 'Catriona, would you do me the honour of dancing with me?'

'Eh, no thanks, George. Maybe later.'

George sat down again. Angelo nudged Catriona.

'Don't be rude. He wears a dinner jacket, he buys you a beautiful present and he asks you to dance. Accept.'

'OK.' Catriona stood reluctantly and took George's hand, 'Come on twinkle-toes.' In her experience George had two left feet and two right arms. If he was trying to woo her, he was trying hard. She hoped it wasn't guilt for the fling he might have had with Helen. But then, she'd flung herself at Euan. And if she was honest, she had Helen to thank for being able to see George in a different light. And since she'd let go of her own disappointment about life, started to get on with living it again, she was seeing just how lucky she was.

And for all of these reasons she stepped on to the floor.

'I hope you don't mind, Catriona, but I've asked for something specially.'

The band struck up a tango. Catriona looked at him. 'I can't dance to this.'

'You can. You did dance at drama school, remember? You were always telling me how good you were at it.'

'I might have been lying.'

'Don't worry. Just follow my line and lead. It'll be fine.'

She did. It wasn't fine. Catriona lurched through it miserably. If anything she was worse than Helen had been on the first night. Everyone watched her miss the turns and then, when she failed to bend backwards and George nutted her, someone laughed. Rorie glared at the *Fiasco* crew. Already Catriona couldn't face work next week.

'I'm sorry, George. Can we sit down? I just don't feel like finishing this.'

'Yes,' he whispered, red in the face. 'Yes, of course. I'm sorry, darling. I took some lessons. I automatically assumed you'd be brilliant at it.'

There was a faint, half-hearted ripple of applause, led by Helen, as they moved off the dance floor.

She was going to shout at him, but out of the corner of her eye she saw Angelo trying to hide a dozen red roses under the table. He must have meant to present them to her at the end of the dance.

'I thought it would be romantic,' George was still apologising.

'It would have been if I'd taken the lessons with you. That was just embarrassing. And I've a bruise on my head now. I hope Jude can get round it at the next session.'

'He's painting you, Catriona, not photographing. Of course he'll get round it.'

'Jude, he is painting you?' Angelo pointed at Jude, who was chatting to Rorie. 'He is the one?'

'Yes, I already told you. Interested now, are you? Well, too late, you blew that one.'

'And me, have I blown it?' George asked humbly.

'No, you haven't. I've had worse experiences.'

At this point their children arrived with Lydia Morehampton, who was as keen on babysitting as the French are on giving up wine.

'I hope you've ordered food for me. Without it I shall wilt, looking after all these children. The chauffeur,' Lydia never called them taxi drivers, 'was going to charge damages.'

'Mother! I didn't think you were staying,' George could not hide his horror.

'She always does,' Catriona hissed.

The children ran to join Helen and Euan's girls at a children's table and Lydia took Catriona's seat, between George and Angelo. George moved up so there was room for Catriona on his other side.

'Of course I am, I haven't come all this way to go home again. Angelo, darling, how are you?' They met every year at this party. Lydia made a note of never missing it. Catriona had made a note never to invite her after the first year, when Lydia, among other things, had advised her not to waddle like a dairy animal when she was pregnant the first time. 'It's not good to let oneself go as you have.'

The next day Catriona was admitted with high blood pressure and Lara had been born weeks later by Caesarian section since it never went down. She never forgave Lydia. But, then, Lydia had never forgiven her for marrying George when a dozen Arabellas and Ginnys had been bleating for him.

Now Lydia was reaching across the table to open the jewellery box. 'My goodness, this must have cost a fortune. But it's not a special birthday, is it? You're only forty-three or something.'

'Thirty-nine, Lydia.'

'Really, darling? Already? Never mind. One day those children will be less of a nuisance and you can begin to make yourself decent. It's the only way to hang on to a husband nowadays. I know. Albert loved me to his dying day.'

'Dad had at least two mistresses that I know of,'

George whispered in Catriona's ear. 'They used to come round to the house and look for money. Mother always gave it to them to go away, didn't you, Mother?'

'Eh?' Lydia strained to hear.

'I said you always had a wonderful way with Dad, didn't you, Mother?'

Catriona grinned. George never stood up for her publicly, because as far as he was concerned it fuelled Lydia more. This was one of the few occasions he'd offered support from the wings. Whatever was happening to George, she liked it.

Helen couldn't stop herself feeling over the moon. The failure of George's surprise had given her some hope. Of what she couldn't admit to herself. For the first time in years she felt alive. You felt alive on Scafell. You felt alive when he married you. You've forgotten Helen, forgotten too quickly.

Dette came up to their table. 'Honey Bea!' Dette was the only one who got away with calling Bea this – and it was only because she was of the opinion it would be Bea's stage name when she made the successful transition from model to singer/actress.

'Hello, Dette,' Bea smiled.

'You're wearing the dress your generous mother bought you, with my eye on the proceedings.'

'I am. D'you like it?'

'I do. Wear it next week when you see the agency.' Dette's present to Bea was a meeting with Assets, an old contact of hers. Dette had had to threaten to reveal his girlfriend's whereabouts to his boyfriend if he pulled out of it because she was no longer the one employing his models every week for shoots.

'Oh, yeah,' Bea did not fall over herself.

'What's this oh-yeah business? Is this opportunity not the Holy Grail you've been chasing since you were twelve?'

Helen was watching them.

'Yeah, but modelling's just one of the things I'm considering right now. You have to have other skills, don't you, Helen?'

Helen nodded, could have kissed her daughter. But she didn't do kissing.

'Suit yourself, ingrate. But make sure you turn up. I had to put myself out for this.'

'I will, Dette. Thank you, I will.'

'Here,' Helen handed Bea her envelope. 'Early birthday present.'

'A horoscope chart!' Bea pulled it out of the envelope. 'Thanks. The fact I have a chart might even mean I have a future.'

'Come on, now,' Helen touched her daughter's arm and Bea did not flinch. 'You've got the world at your feet.'

'Have I?' Bea looked at her.

'Yes. You've everything ahead of you and nothing to tie you down.'

'That's right. I want to go and say hello to Rorie. Is that OK with you?'

Bea was no fool. But Helen was wiser. She knew this was a test, to see why the oldest family friend was having least to do with them, these days. Rorie was talking to Jude still. 'Of course. Give her my love, tell her I'll catch up with her later.' There was no point in giving a worried girl any more to think about. Especially one who was turning eighteen this week. Helen had to bear this herself until the time was right.

'You could come over and speak to her yourself?' Bea asked.

'I will, once I've been to the ladies'.'

She went in and shut the cubicle door. If she could just live in here for the rest of her life she'd be all right. Outside this door she was not speaking to her best friend. Hiding another friend's increasingly obvious pregnancy. Relating to her daughter for the first time in years. Rejecting her husband's every attempt to make up with her. Fantasising about the husband of another great friend. It seemed her head might explode.

Euan came out of the gents' and saw that Helen was not around. He immediately made his way to Rorie and ignored Jude's smile. Bea couldn't believe how rude Euan was in making Rorie get up and leave the table to speak with him somewhere else.

'I'm sorry, but there'll be few other chances since we're supposed to steer clear of one another now,' Euan apologised. 'I called Ireland today. The number's right. Your mother should have been a private detective.'

'She is,' Rorie said drily.

'I spoke to Helen's sister, Eunice – what a name!'

'I knew her growing up.'

'Well, she says Mrs Larkin's been in hospital six weeks and, although the stroke hasn't affected her speech, she hasn't got out of bed. The doctors reckon it's grief. Mr

Larkin, Paddy, he was buried only a few months ago. I can't believe they didn't want Helen there, Rorie. Eunice couldn't say whether her mother had called her or not. I explained we weren't telling her because she's going through a personal crisis at the moment and we wanted to be sure of the facts.'

'Which are?' Rorie enquired.

'That I had to ask a woman I'd never met if she knew whether my wife's father was dead. That my wife won't speak to me other than to communicate tasks about our children. That she's in Bea's room and I'm in the spare bedroom and nobody is fucking sleeping in our room. I don't want to be there without her, Rorie, and she doesn't want to be there at all. That my wife's mother is in hospital dying of a grief-related illness and I don't know whether or not to tell my wife. Happy birthday by the way, Rorie.'

'Thanks, Euan.'

'Is there anything I left out?'

'Your wife suspects you of having an affair with her best friend. You actually had a fling with another friend. You recently found out that her best friend was in love with you for years.'

'Was?' Euan looked at Rorie.

'Was.'

'Good. I don't even have that to boost my ego any more.'

'It was never meant for that purpose.'

'I know, Rorie. But it felt good. That's all I can say. A woman like you loving a man like me.'

'You're forgetting I once loved John Edwards.'

'Ah, yes, I wish you'd not reminded me. Where is he?'

'Writing.'

'As he always is when you need to be looked after.'

'Stop it, Euan.'

'I have to. Helen's on her way back,' Rorie turned to face her.

Helen walked towards them. If they were brazening it out, so would she.

'How are you two doing?'

'Great. Just discussing the match against Barcelona,' Euan offered.

'Let me see, that's football, isn't it? I'm sorry you don't have anything else to talk about. It's not a conversation I can join in.'

They could both see Helen was swaying.

'I hope dinner's soon,' Rorie rubbed her belly. 'We all need it. Soak up this alcohol.'

'I don't want mine soaked up. It's nice to feel numb to all that's happening,' Helen snapped. The waiters came out of the kitchen with food on trays. Everyone went back to their table, as if nothing had happened.

After dinner the dancing started in earnest. Bea watched Helen down another glass of wine. 'Helen, easy now. I'm the one supposed to binge drink.'

'That's the young for you, want to keep all the fun to themselves.'

Helen hadn't taken her eyes off George. He was busy talking to his wife, then his mother, never both. Tomorrow morning he'd have a crick in his neck. Angelo was sulking over his food. Nobody was talking to him.

'Do you know doctors drink and smoke to excess more than any other profession, Bea?'

'Except modelling. And journalism. And stage management. And assistant stage management.' Bea was eyeing up Helen's associates. 'I hope you don't get into this state at every Virgo Club lunch.'

'We get into worse, love. Far worse.'

'Maybe I'll join.'

Helen smiled at her. 'You're always telling me you're Libra.'

'Maybe I might stay this side of the cusp.'

'Take my advice and don't, it's not as much fun as it looks. You're better off being balanced.'

31

George got up to go somewhere, anywhere, for a breather and saw that the seat beside Helen was free.

'Thank God. The sparring's threatening to break into ten full rounds.' He pointed to Catriona and Lydia. 'Care to dance?' He said it casually. She accepted the same way.

He swung her on to the floor as the band flew into a fifties big-band tune. They didn't notice the other dancers moving away until the floor was clear. By then they were enjoying themselves too much to stop. It wasn't the magic of their tango but it was very passable ballroom. Dette and Rorie caught each other's eye, mouths open. Euan and Bea stared at each other in much the same way. Catriona knew then exactly what her husband and friend did with their Tuesday nights. Lydia commented, 'Now, that's a lot better than what I saw you two up to when I came in. Catriona didn't turn as she elbowed the red wine glass into Lydia's lap. The shriek didn't make the band or the dancers miss a beat. Lydia ran for the loo and Catriona didn't follow.

Catriona stood up to catch the air that seemed to be missing from her lungs. She grabbed Lara as an excuse. They went to stand in the porch, Lara chatting about the five kinds of ice-cream Angelo had provided for the children. She shared her mother's passion for it. It was a gene thing. Catriona had surprised herself by refusing her share. Something big was happening here.

'I can never really decide which is my favourite.'

'Why don't you list them all, from one to five? Let's work it out properly,' Catriona was happy to work it out forever, if it meant not going back in there.

'Vanilla, one. Chocolate, two. No. Chocolate, one. Vanilla, two. No—'

Her conscience threw in a point of information. You've a short memory, Catriona. Two months ago, six weeks ago, you couldn't stand to be near him. You've never stood in the way of your au pair trying to get into his horrible Y-fronts. (Maybe he'd thrown those out along with his other diehard habits.) Be honest, the only thing that concerned you about Magda was that she'd take your financial security.

And my children! She was acting like I couldn't do anything for them.

No, Catriona, *you* were acting like you couldn't do anything for them or yourself. She just convinced you you were right.

'That's not true,' Catriona snapped.

'It is, Mummy! I don't like rum and raisin.'

'Oh, yes, Lara. Sorry sweetheart. You're right. So that means it won't ever make your top five, so you can stop worrying about that one,' Catriona stroked her daughter's fringe to either side of her forehead. Saucer eyes, the same bright blue as her father's, stared up at her. Trust. My mother can make everything OK. It hit Catriona like a train. Her daughter might allow her au pair to run her day-to-day affairs, might love her daddy, but Catriona was her rock, not afraid to cuddle her like a baby and give her safe harbour. She did it for all her children – she was doing it with Rorie now because she was seeing her in a different light. She was seeing the vulnerability that the woman had to let out because her job was so stressful and her home life so empty. And Catriona had it all. And George was part of the all. He was not fiery but he was capable – and he was capable of loving her and right now for some reason he was doing what he could to show her that.

The actress in Catriona wanted the applause she could hear for Helen and George. The mother in Catriona knew she was good at instinct, intuition and nurture. The sidelines were no longer where she'd ended up. She was choosing to be there. She had George. Helen wanted him. Catriona wasn't stupid. Helen wanted the romance of dancing away from a life laden with responsibility. Catriona wasn't going to let him go. And she would win, because she realised she had never treated him well and he had never left. For the rest of her life she was going to make up for that.

He never had the opportunity to leave before. He's got at least one now. You might be too late. This wasn't conscience talking. This was reality. She could see she had a fight, but for the first time in her life Catriona had ambition for something.

'Strawberry. I love strawberry. It's not fair to put it third, it should be first, or second, but what about. This is very hard, Mummy.'

'I know that darling. We've got to keep thinking. And then we'll find a way.'

Lydia stormed into the porch.

'You did that deliberately.'

'Yes, Lydia.' Catriona continued to look out at the street, her arm round her daughter, who shrank close to her. 'I can only say in my defence that it wasn't premeditated. I plead provocation. The way I feel right now, I could drown you in a barrel of wine. So please, leave me alone. We're working out about ice-cream here, and we're very, very busy.' Catriona was trembling, but her voice wasn't.

Lydia stayed her ground. 'If you can speak to me like that in front of your daughter, my grandchild, you show your true colours. I'd rather my son had married a tramp. But, of course, he has. You see that woman in there?' Lydia pointed to Helen. 'She has what is known as class. You have none. I said it the day I met you and I say it now. If it weren't for the children he'd have left you years ago.'

'Yes, Lydia. Thank you. And good night.'

'Grandmother's very angry with you,' Lara whispered.

'She is.'

'She's always angry with you.'

'She is.'

'And you're always angry with Daddy. And Magda only tries to help Daddy. You're always angry with her too.'

'You're right sweetheart. But not any more.'

A few yards up Lydia hailed a black cab. It was then that Catriona saw the shadow in the doorway. As soon as

Lydia got in and drove off, it emerged and walked towards Angelo's.

Instinct told her to sit down. She pulled Lara on to the bench beside her. 'Where were we? Strawberry, chocolate, vanilla, what else?'

The woman stared through the window at Helen and George. Catriona could see her, but she couldn't be seen. A tall woman in a long black coat. Black hair swept up in a chignon that said the wearer never had to visit a hairdresser to keep it that way. The coat was open and underneath was a white linen dress, and a necklace, made almost certainly by the same jeweller who'd made the one George had given her.

Immaculate. Elegant. An Audrey Hepburn lookalike. It might have been the last scene in *Breakfast at Tiffany's*. She was smiling, a Mona Lisa smile, and walking on down the road, a passer-by observing the party. A passer-by who had glanced into a porch, seen a face she recognised and glanced away. Catriona thought of George's words, 'My mother gave at least two mistresses money to go away.'

32

Midnight, the witching hour. Children still ran wild and the diners were all full and still drinking, though fast approaching falling-over stage.

Catriona and Lara were cold – the nights now had the autumn chill and they'd been in the porch for a long time, during which George and Helen had never sat down.

As soon as Catriona came in, George pulled back from Helen and bowed, pointed to the gents, mouthed to Catriona, 'See you later.'

Helen, glowing, came up to her. 'Hope you don't mind me borrowing George. I love dancing and he's very good at it.'

'It's the first I knew,' Catriona watched her, 'that either of you liked dancing. You meet on Tuesdays. That was something I did know.'

Helen couldn't hold her eyes. 'We haven't done anything. It was all about surprising you. George thought you'd like it, after you were upset about him not celebrating your anniversary. We did some classes. To get him up to speed. He thought you'd done it in college, dancing.'

You're gabbling, Helen. I'm the gabbler, you're the cool one. I must remember that I tried very hard to have sex with your husband. My actions caused all this. I must appear and be forgiving. Kind. That is my job now. A kind, gracious winner.

The naff song by The Drifters came into her head. Save the last dance for me. It was hers by right, and she'd have to make sure she held on to that right.

It looked like the band was winding up soon. And when George came from the gents'.

'I figured that out, thanks, Helen,' Catriona kissed her cheek. 'I wanted romance and you got it for me. I'm grateful to you.'

'OK,' Helen seemed embarrassed. 'Are you OK, Catriona? You look pale.'

'Well, I've just spilt a glass of wine all over my horrendous mother-in-law, and then I saw a ghost. A ghost of Audrey Hepburn.'

Catriona had decided to come clean, in part. Why let a woman know you're her adversary? Why let her know you're watching her every move with your man, particularly because you know how easy it is to want the husband of a best friend? Let her think it's not her you're concerned about. Let her know how far down the list she is.

Madeleina. Helen knew she should say something, right now. She couldn't. If she blew George's affair, her dancing days were over. She couldn't give them up just yet. And she couldn't give up George just yet. If she played it

right, casual, open, then Catriona might agree to let them
continue with the classes. It was part of the contract.
Seduce until the first Tuesday of October, then report
back. Catriona would have to agree. And Helen could
dance at the competition.

'Isn't that what Dette said once? She saw George having lunch with someone like that?'

'Yes.'

'What are you going to do?'

'What wives have done for centuries, for all time.
Nothing.'

'Oh come on, Catriona.' Even Helen was surprised.
'At least try to join the new millennium. Women don't
have to take that crap.'

'I'm not taking any crap. I know he wants me more
than her because he's with me more than her. I know she
wants to challenge that and I'm waiting until she's ready.
When she's ready I'll be ready.'

'How do you know?'

'Because she tried to come here tonight. Soon she'll
be ready to talk to me and I'll be ready to listen.'

'The question is, how did she know?' Helen asked
Catriona and herself.

'George must have had to tell her for some reason,
and I'll find out what that reason is.'

Helen watched Catriona. Never had she seen this
kind of assurance. She didn't need a Dawn Principles
day. She had already achieved something, she had left
behind the fear that strangled Helen. The fear of being
who you are without apology. Helen saw in that moment
that Catriona had the beauty of a bygone age. It was what
Jude was painting. And she also had its wisdom. Helen
was the willow type, had the kind of looks that were so

fashionable now, but she'd rather have been the earthy one. The one who knew how to wait and what she was waiting for, and how to offer herself. If Helen came on to George right now she'd mess it up, with her obvious need to be loved and romanced, wined, dined and celebrated for being feminine. A and E doctor seeks chaise longue, the chaise Catriona Morehampton was lying on, without any intention of moving. It made Helen sick to realise how pathetic she would have seemed to George, if she had been foolish enough to make a pass at him. 'I admire you, Catriona.'

'Thank you, Helen. I'm glad someone does. Now if you don't mind, I want my husband to dance with me. I might be a lot better second time around.'

Helen watched them. The music slowed and they didn't try to dance. They moved and he had his eyes on her all the time. And she looked at him the same way.

'Good to see those two getting on,' Euan said, at her shoulder. 'I never knew you could dance like that.'

'We never went dancing anywhere. I'm tired, Euan, I don't want to stay any longer.'

'Neither do I.'

But Rorie's still here. Talking to her theatre cronies and Angelo, finally, after freezing him out all evening over his behaviour with Jude. Helen felt a yawning loneliness. Her best friend was far away and her husband was in the same place. Bea was with Rorie and waved to them.

'We're going,' Euan called to her. Helen was glad, she hadn't the energy even to say goodbye. A general wave would have to suffice.

Kelly and Joyce were sad not to be sleeping upstairs

on Angelo's floor. But Catriona and George came up as all the kids were protesting to Euan and Helen.

'No, we're going home too, guys. Daddy and I are very busy and we need to get a proper sleep in our own bed,' Catriona said to the children, but she might as well have said it to Helen.

Dette sat down beside Rorie and Bea.

'It's the first time I've ever known a Virgo Club birthday to finish at just gone midnight. We're normally here for breakfast. What's going on?'

'Old age,' Rorie smiled. 'We're not able for it any more. And the ones with kids have other commitments. We've no idea what it's like, nor are we likely to.'

I will soon. Dette felt the fear needle her again.

'Bea?' Martin had just finished dancing with Dette. 'You got any more life in you than my old lady?' He pointed to the floor.

'It was a joke. Don't do a number on yourself,' Rorie hugged Dette. Dette, for once, didn't visit the Arctic; she leaned against Rorie for a while, and they watched Martin and Bea.

'Look at them. They look like a couple. I look like his auntie.'

'You don't. But keep telling yourself that and you'll behave like one. I need to talk to you.'

Dette sat up straight again, turned round.

'Earlier on Jude told me something. John's been living with me for so long he might have rights to my property. My flat's all I've got, Dette. Even Ma lives in a council house. I have no other security. If I kick him out I might have to buy him out.'

'Aren't you forgetting something? Aren't you forgetting his wife and children?'

'That's what I've been thinking about. I've never seen
a picture of Janet, or the kids. Apart from his wedding
photo I wouldn't even know she existed. He kept that
photo on the desk. I had to make him take it down when
we had sex there. What if Janet doesn't exist? What if he
got some dumb actress,' she looked around nervously, in
case Catriona was listening, 'to pose for a picture like that
to keep eejits like me from wanting more? Now I cannot
imagine wanting less of him. But then? Then was a different story. Now? Now I'm done for, Dette. No court
would believe I thought he was married and gave him
rent-free shelter as his mistress.'

'Shut up. You're drunk. You're reacting. You saw a
wedding photo.'

'He could have got someone to stage it with him, to
keep students from making too many demands.'

'Rubbish! No one would be so thick they'd fall for
that.'

'I was, Dette,' Rorie said quietly. 'I never questioned
him.'

'That's because you knew there were children
involved. Go to Wales. Find Janet. Find out. Don't torture
yourself like this.' Like I'm torturing myself watching
eighteen-year-old Bea and twenty-five-year-old Martin.
What is a thirty-five-, fuck it, forty-this-year-old woman
doing with a bloke that young and tasty? I need a shrink.
I need a drink. I can't have one. I'm having the young
bloke's baby. It'll come out and say, 'Wotcha! Where's
Daddy?' Daddy won't be there.

Rorie was a goldfish, moving mouth, her words
drowned by Dette's thoughts.

'Sorry?'

'I said I can't go to Wales. I'm up to my neck with the play.'

'Wales is open on Sundays. Plays aren't. Go to Wales tomorrow.'

'I don't have an address. I won't be able to get one by tomorrow.'

'Then go next Sunday.'

'Maybe. I saw John called in to you last night with more of his play. Has he tried it on yet?'

'Rorie, we don't talk about this until October. Stick to the rules. How come the *Fiasco* cast turned up?'

'They were elated after the full house tonight. Catriona's brainwave. Bus in a load of pensioners, give them free tickets. Build play's profile. Great idea.'

'Yes,' Dette raised her eyebrows. 'She's had a lot of those lately.'

'What's that supposed to mean? I thought you two were getting on like a house on fire again.'

'We are. Doesn't mean I don't see things. Listen, I saw Euan battling out of a snog with her in the gents' last New Year's Eve here. She followed him in there and I followed her.'

'Dette, you don't know what you're talking about.'

'I know exactly what I'm talking about when I ask why you're letting Helen decide it was you. She's already challenged me about it and she's told me she suspects you, not Catriona. And it doesn't take a scientist to figure out your Helen's latest cryogenics project.'

'I thought Helen would forgive me quicker than anyone else. Not that I've admitted to anything.' Now I'm glad I haven't because Helen couldn't forgive her own father enough to attend his funeral. Poor Euan. Keeping that phone call to Ireland to himself, watching his wife glide around with George Morehampton.

'If it comes to it, Rorie, tell Helen,' Dette pleaded. Without drink she was much softer. 'You've been friends a long time. Don't lose that out of a stupid sense of honour.'

'To tell you the truth, I'm not doing it for Helen any more, or Euan. I'm doing it for their kids. I don't know what it was like for you, Dette, but when my da walked out on us it nearly killed me and Ma. I was Kelly's age, and it still hurts, thirty years later. He never came home for my birthday party and even now, at my thirty-sixth, I look around for him, in case he decides to turn up. All my life I've been afraid to make choices because of it. What if it's the wrong one? What if John leaves me before I leave him? At least when he's with me I know he'll have something to do with his kids. I thought of his kids when I was in love with him and now I'm thinking of his kids because I'm not and I wish he'd go.'

At a moment like this Dette needed a fag. 'I don't miss my dad any more. In the beginning I wanted to die – doesn't mean I don't think of him sometimes.' Dette looked at Martin and felt his child move again. Once it had started it wasn't going to stop. A night owl, like its mammy. Dette thought two a.m. was time enough to go to bed and two p.m. time enough to get up. Life had to work hard to persuade her different. Martin. Tell him. No.

'I suppose I knew after a while that it wasn't his fault,' Dette went on, 'and I was thirteen. I got a lot more of him than you did of yours. And I know he loved me to bits. Just like I thought Soaky Joe did.'

'He was replacement daddy, then? Like Euan's always saying John is for me?'

'You must be joking! My dad was big and burly and he never let my mother go without a penny. Joe was thin as a rake, green from drink and left me with a six-thousand-pound Visa bill.'

They were both laughing. They were both crying.

'You know, Dette, I'd have preferred it if my dad had died. It's horrible to know he didn't love me enough to stay. Or Ma, I love Ma the most of anyone in the world. And she stuck around for me.'

'Still sending you husbands and baby bars of Cadbury's chocolate in the post?'

'Still doing that. She's old-fashioned, Ma, and I'm more like her every day.'

'So you're sending her potential stepfathers?'

'No, feck, no. She's old and mad. That's why she gets away with taking pictures. I'd be arrested for stalking. Anyway, I believe the right man will come along, just as I believe that once kids come into an equation couples have to put their own lives on hold. Kids need two parents. Growing up without a da was like growing up without an arm, even after everything Ma did.'

Dette started to sniff. I'll tell him tonight. Rorie's right. I've got to give the kid a chance to have a father. If he thinks he loves me now, he may go on thinking it. I have to try.

On the table Martin's mobile rang. At two in the morning? The caller ID was Vicky. Dette showed Rorie who said, in stage-manager mode, 'Answer it.'

33

A cool American voice: Harvard meets Broadway. New York with no knobs on. Dette could see the Central Park penthouse, the driver opening the door, the concierge opening the door, Tiffany's doorman opening the door, Donna Karan greeting in person. Dette saw herself lumbering up her two flights of stairs in her 1930s trust-housing block to the flat she was lucky to have.

'Hi there. I wonder if I could speak with Martin, please.'

'Who's calling?' Dette reached for Chelsea posh, but her voice cracked and she sounded like Eliza Doolittle fighting it out with Fergie.

'Victoria Hazlet.'

The replacement for Drew Barrymore. Never out of the papers since her arrival in town two weeks ago. A nominee for a best supporting actress Oscar after her first film. Father a close friend of the Kennedys, runs a successful law firm, mother a former model – of the Chanel variety, not pictured in patio-furnishing catalogues. Result: the kind of genes that make the media dub you the new Grace Kelly.

And she was on Martin's phone. And he'd worked a lot this week and hadn't seen her. And he had never mentioned Victoria Hazlet except to say, on Friday night, that she was a great gal, not a bit up her own arse.

'Martin, darling,' Dette shrieked into the receiver. 'Call for you.'

Martin bounced over, blowing kisses to Bea, who continued to bop around on the dance floor with the *Fiasco* crew, 'Wotcha! Victoria!'

It was amazing how any-old-iron he sounded when an American dream was on the other end of the line. Calling from Park Lane, past midnight.

'Jet lag gotcha still? Can't sleep? Cahm on dahn.'

Dette could see the remake of *Mary Poppins* – Martin as a big Dick, Victoria doing perfect received pronunciation.

'That awright with you, Dette, lovey?'

He never called her lovey – must be because she'd called him dahling.

'Sure, Martin, sure.' You bring a woman nearly twenty years younger than me with tits and arse of steel, and money to burn, to my birthday party. I'll sit here, forty and pregnant with your kid.

Twenty minutes later she came in with the kind of dress she threw on and others paid a year's salary for. Not a hair out of place, not a suggestion of black root. Natural blonde as well as everything else.

'Vicky!' Jude bounced over and threw his arms round her.

'I'm sorry, you are?'

'Jude.' Jude stuck on his professional, brilliant, that-didn't-matter smile.

'Oh, yes, the hair guy. I'm seeing you Tuesday. Might not be able to make it. Might have to be Wednesday at eleven instead.'

'Sure,' Jude fawned.

'Surely not. You're doing Rorie that day.' Dette said.

Jude put on a Rorie-can-wait face, but Victoria slipped into real-person mode, 'Oh, my gosh, you've someone else booked in? A friend of Martin's? That's fine. I'll stick with the other appointment, just shift some other stuff around. Agent stuff, gotta speak to them some time.'

Martin came racing back off the dance floor with Bea holding his hand. Dette saw the look Victoria gave their clasping.

'So, this is your girlfriend? The one you were telling me about?'

'Nah, this is her niece. That's me girlfriend.' Martin pointed to Dette.

'Hi,' the polished smile didn't hide the shock. The tasty set designer was going out with an auntie.

Why had she worn floral? She might as well have a tea pot and scones in front of her, and a *Women's Weekly*. Victoria was clocking the situation, categorising it. Very soon time for Dette to go home. 'Well I'm not really her aunt,' she found herself saying. Bea looked hurt at that. 'But I might as well be,' she added. Dette was nothing without her loyalty. It was the only thing she had left. That and her baby. And her mammy. And her friends. And her kind ex-boss. And five thousand pounds worth of make-up to sell at a car-boot sale tomorrow.

Ten years ago a thoroughbred like Victoria Hazlet

would have been stamping on the likes of Martin Hardiman to get to titled men. Now that tough and urban was trendy she was desperate for a Guy Ritchie so she could do Madonna. And Martin was tumbling into it with his trademark young-boy enthusiasm.

He was just about to sit beside Dette when Victoria slipped into the seat. Jude very quickly took up the one on the other side, keeping a practised eye for paparazzi outside the window. Victoria turned her back on Jude and got stuck into Dette, 'So, you're in cosmetics, Martin tells me.'

'Yes, I'm an Avon lady.'

'What's that?'

'I run a company in Stratford-on-Avon.'

'Where Shakespeare was born?'

'Yes. We make soaps with pictures of William Shakespeare on the front.'

Martin, on his hunkers between the two of them, froze. 'Vicky, what can I get ya?'

'A Velázquez, please.'

'He's a painter,' said Martin, in an I-know-that voice.

'So am I!' Jude found his elbow into the conversation was shoved right back in his face.

'Oh, yeah, we did him in art history. I graduated in that before I turned to acting,' she turned to advise Dette. 'It's what makes Martin and me get on so well, the art thing. He's been a real friend to me since I got here. I've been kinda lonely. Just broke up with someone special before I came.' Jeffrey Rodgers, the speedboat millionaire. Everyone knew it, everyone pretended not to. Angelo joined the table, sat beside Jude. Jude ignored him like he was being ignored.

'Are you the waiter?' Victoria asked him innocently.

'The proprietor,' Rorie overcame her early-evening spat with Angelo.

'Our angel, he is, Angelo,' Dette doused him in syrup. Rorie winced.

'So, how do I get a Velázquez?' Victoria asked everyone, like someone should know.

'I'll do barman, for a laugh, if you let me Angelo.' Martin smoothed over the queen's demands on the hoi polloi. 'What's in it, Vick?'

'Dry white wine, pinch of bitters, twista lemon, soda, olive,' Victoria said sweetly. Martin-is-my-hero smile. Pass the bucket, if I have to drink that and look at this, thought Dette. She decided not to say it. Instead she said, 'Hazlet, isn't that a kind of cold meat? Processed? Cold cut, I think you call it?'

'Not in America.' Victoria did not do sarcasm or if she did she was practised at not flinching. 'Anyway, it's pronounced Hazlé. We're Normans, Daddy says.'

'In the bloodline of Wisdom?'

'I suppose, yes, that might be right.'

Rorie glared at Dette, then glared up behind her. John had just walked in.

'I finished up and thought I'd come along to join the party. Grace you with my presence, but I can see you're already graced.' His eyes found the valley between Victoria's breasts. He was good at finding valleys. 'I'd love a cold beer, Rorie. Writing's thirsty work.'

'And Rorie would love a dry white wine since it's her birthday party,' Dette said, into John's eyes. He looked away.

'Of course, that's what I meant. Wine for the birthday girl, coming up.'

'Wait. You're a writer?' Victoria smiled. 'Of what?'

'Plays.'

'I'm doing one at the moment,' Victoria said as if no one would possibly know. 'Theatre's where it all really happens.'

'You can say that again,' Rorie sighed.

'Rorie's the stage manager I told you about, who should direct. Rorie's brilliant,' Martin was back, putting the glass in front of Victoria. Dette's was empty, but he hadn't noticed.

'Oh, yeah. Martin said you've got real talent. Just have to find the vehicle for it. I'd love to work with a female director some time. The business is so male dominated.'

Which is why you get exactly what you want, you little fawn princess thing. Dette beamed the words across to Rorie, but Rorie was too busy glowing with wine and compliments. Dette knew she'd lost an ally.

'Call me when you've got a project you think I might like,' Victoria gushed.

And her agent will make sure she never sees it.

'Really?' Rorie was luminous now.

As was John, who had received no such offer. 'I might send you my new play, if you're interested. There's a good female part in it.'

'Yes,' Dette smiled at Victoria. 'John's very good at female parts, aren't you, John? Rorie, didn't you say you weren't feeling well a while ago? How are you now?'

Rorie looked snotty, then remembered what she and Dette had decided. If John was here then now was a good time to go searching. 'Just tired. I'll go home, I think, after this drink.'

'But I just got here! I stayed the weekend for this!' John had forgotten he hadn't arrived until one in the morning.

'Oh, don't worry about coming with me, John. You stay and enjoy yourself.'

'If that's all right with everyone else, I will. Any food, Angelo?'

'What do you think this is? A restaurant?' Angelo snapped.

Bea and Victoria got talking.

'You really could be a model.' My God, the woman knew how to work a crowd. Slip the compliments to the ones you want to know, alienate the rest with innocent, but lacerating, observations. You wouldn't wind her, her stomach was rock hard with working out, for a start.

'Yes, I'm sctting her up with an agency.' Dette flexed her own flabby abdominals.

'Which one?'

'Assets.'

'They're my old place. I still do a few shoots with them.' Like Calvin Klein last year. And Versace this. They all wanted Victoria. 'I'll make a call to Davina, just to strengthen the case a bit. The more support you got, the better.'

The owner. Only God knew Davina. Dette knew someone who was doing her a favour for using a coke-riddled model who was out of a job if someone didn't get her photo in somewhere so she could pay for her rehab.

'Will you?' Bea's eyes shone. Then it was as if she remembered something. 'Thanks,' she whispered, and turned away.

'Hey, Bea, why don't you take Vicky out some time? She ain't got no mates her own age here. Poor kid needs

looking after – keep all the ones wanting a piece away
from her. What d'you say?' Martin gave Victoria and
Bea's shoulders a simultaneous squeeze. Martin, everyone's mate.

'No problem. I'd be honoured.' The stars were visible
in Bea's eyes.

'He's so nice, your boyfriend,' Vicky said to a dull-
eyed Dette. 'He just treats me like a normal person. Not
many people do. Except the ones who knew me before,
you know.'

Before you grew to six feet, before you had the waist
of a wine bottle, before you had legs longer than the
Empire State, which your daddy probably owns. Before
you turned up outside the Chinese Theater in Chanel
white for the Oscars, then dipped your hands into
cement wearing Prada black the next week. You're a
cloud-nine commuter and the ground's only for visiting,
just like us normal people.

'Yes, Martin sees people for what they really are,
warts and all.' Hopefully one would appear on her chin
tonight and ruin her life, or at least keep her off the cover
of *Vogue* for six weeks.

'Yeah, he's taken me to some real places. We went out
to Walthamstow for real jellied eels. Yuck. Marty loved
them.'

Marty. I hope they were alive when you ate them. 'Ah,
yes, the eel and pie shop. We go there all the time.'

'Gosh, really? Marty said he found it hard to entice
you past EC1. You're a real West End girl, he says.'

'Does he? Well, I'm doing a car-boot sale tomorrow in
Essex. How East End is that for you, and you're a New
Yorker, right?'

'Sure thing.'

'Bet you've never been to Rikers.'

'Actually, no, but I plan to, just as soon as I go back. We're deciding whether I should play this NY chick whose boyfriend is accused of murder. He doesn't even get free legal aid, so she has to sweat up and become his representation. With Daddy being a lawyer, I think I got some background there.'

'Of course, your father has never represented anyone like that, has he?'

'Yes, he has. He runs a charity called Law Connection, which has top lawyers take on worthy cases for nothing.'

So they make the cover of *Time* magazine and even more money out of it.

'Admirable. Admirable.'

'You bet it is. Say, you want to dance?'

'No, thank you, Victoria. I'm a bit of a wallflower this evening.' There are a dozen salivating males out there delighted to wobble round you.

'Nice talking to you, Dette.'

'Likewise.'

While they were dancing, Dette called a cab. She'd been planning to ask Martin for his help with the boot sale. At least, the loan of his car.

Don't be a fool for pride. Go up and ask him. You've been going out six months. You're entitled to Sundays together.

No, we're not, Junior spoke up. You've never allowed this man to plan more than one date in advance. You've kept him at leg's length since the beginning. You've never made demands or asked questions about where he's been and who with. The Dette golden rule does not break now you're up the duff. Joe Morgan was the last man to make you cry, and you're going to ruin a track record if you ask Martin for something he can't give. Besides, if you ask him to stay over tonight he may want to have sex with you and you've managed not to for four weeks. I will jump and Daddy will bolt. Your hormones will betray you. What are you doing walking over there? This is not on.

Still, she found herself on the edge of the tiny dance floor, trying to catch Martin's attention, but he was too busy with Bea and Vicky, his new best friends.

Above the music Victoria hollered in Martin's ear, 'You still taking me to the Tower tomorrow?'

Dette turned away, like she'd forgotten something. And she had. To leave. She waited for the cab outside.

As it arrived, so did John. 'Can I cadge a lift home?'

'Only if you pay half the fare.'

'Fair enough,' he said miserably. It was still better than paying full price. And it was only round the corner.

'Where did Dette go?' Martin asked Angelo. Angelo was watching Jude cha-cha with the remaining diehards.

'Home. She went home.'

'I thought I was staying at her place tonight.'

'Then you were assuming. Do not assume anything with Dette.'

'Now, hang on a minute, mate. If anyone's cooling off it's her. She won't—'

Before Martin could finish Victoria was there.

'I'll run you home, Stephen's coming for me soon.'

She stood at Martin's shoulder – actually she was over it, being two inches taller than him. Stephen was her limo driver, on twenty-four-hour call.

'Thanks, Vick.' Martin went to say something else to Angelo but thought better of it.

Everybody went home. For the first time in ten years. Angelo wondered what he would do with all the breakfast food he'd bought. Jude was at the bar, finishing a drink.

'Looks like it is just you and me,' Angelo said. He poured two brandies, to toast a peace offering.

'No, it doesn't,' Jude Mackenzie didn't give second chances. His cab honked the horn and he was out quicker than Dorothy left the Emerald City.

Angelo looked at himself in the mirror behind the bar. 'You make yourself sad. No one else is to blame.' He switched off the lights, poured the brandy into one glass and went to bed.

34

Rorie clipped open John's briefcase, a Pandora's box. She knew the combination because she'd been watching him fiddle with it for years. Somehow she'd always known she'd use it. Inside she found five *Playboys*, a sheaf of essays and half a Mars bar. A photo of him with Neil Kinnock. Only John would keep half a Mars bar and a photo of himself with a man who never made prime minister. Rorie almost felt sad for him; she found his address book. It was that easy. Under E: 'Janet. 14 Manor Street, Fargavenny.'

In the taxi home Dette sat as far away from John as possible in the hope that the ten-minute drive would be over in five. She was boiling for a cry. He had downed five beers in an hour and was stinking of the leftover garlic bread he'd sneaked out of Angelo's kitchen. She was overtired: the thought of an eight o'clock start was torture, but she had a mortgage to pay. So this was what it felt like to do real work for a living. And fighting off John Edwards was proving another full-time job.

A sharp corner gave him the perfect opportunity to lunge, which took her and the baby by surprise. Both jumped. John's spidery digits recoiled in horror. 'My God,' he said, after a shocked silence. 'Well. Loverboy left a little bit of himself behind before he went on to Hollywood.'

'I'll knock your block off if you tell anyone. In fact, I'll tell everyone you're the father. Now, if you don't mind being a gentleman for once in your life you can pick up this fare. That's all you'll be picking up tonight.' She leaned forward to speak to the driver. 'I'm pregnant, he's paying. If he doesn't you can beat him up and I'll tell any court he set on you first.'

Inside the door she picked up the phone.

Rorie answered the phone.

'He's on his way up.'

'It's OK. I've got everything I need.'

'One thing, quickly. I need your car keys tomorrow morning.'

'OK,' Rorie hung up at the sound of the door opening.

'Who were you on the phone to,' John was white with anger, 'at this hour?'

'Answering machine. My director was drunk after the show. Wanted to make a meeting for tomorrow. Emergency.'

'It's always an emergency with you. I suppose you have to go straight to sleep now? No chance of a bit of love. Like the old days.'

Rorie felt afraid for two seconds. Then something took over. Dette was down the stairs. If he tried anything she'd bolt there.

'No, John. No chance at all.'

The next morning Dette and Rorie met on the landing.

'Keys.' Rorie handed them to Dette. 'I don't want to think of you driving Mercy.'

Mercy was Rorie's old Beetle. It was exactly the same age as Rorie. Both made in the sixties and both just about alive in the new century.

'Mercy will be fine. I never drink and drive.'

'That's the problem. You've never driven for years because you've always been drinking.'

'True, but it's like riding a bike, isn't it? You never forget. I'll drive carefully.' I've good reason. 'Now, good luck, darling.'

'Same to you.'

Rorie sat on the Cardiff platform. As soon as she'd drunk this cardboard coffee and eaten the lumpy lardy thing that was passing itself off as a pastry, she was getting back on the same train she'd arrived on. This had been a huge mistake, mainly because the connections didn't work. If she didn't stay over she'd never make it out to Janet's house. The alternative was missing the Monday meeting, which was an emergency now and Rorie had better be there because she had called it. For the entire cast and crew. She'd gone over Nigel Blunt's empty, fat, talentless, conniving head to do so. Everything depended on it.

Hang on. Everything depended on *this*.

She took out her mobile.

'Hello,' Catriona was sleepy. George was mumbling in the background, loving mumbling. On a late Sunday morning. Rorie could see the breakfast tray, the papers, then the kids piling in. The life she'd given up on having before she'd even tried for it. Imagine! She'd actually had the arrogance to feel sorry for Catriona, seen her as a cop-out. She was loved. Every one of the Virgo Club but Rorie had tried for that kind of happiness. She'd chosen John and a bit of wishful thinking about Euan. Even Dette, serial shagger, had some hope of an eejit wanting her for the rest of her life. She'd been the one to say about love, 'You have to keep cracking on at it, because if love doesn't work we're out of a job. The human race has little enough going for it without losing that.'

'Hello, is anyone there?'

'Catriona, it's Rorie. I won't be at the Monday meeting. Something very important has happened. Whatever happens, I need you to handle it for me until I get back.'

'Rorie! I said I'd tackle Wednesday for you. Tomorrow everyone's going to be there, I can't do that.'

'Can't means won't and won't means won't try.'

'Where are you?'

'I'm in Wales. I'll tell you when I get back. Call Dette and say if she does anything to harm Mercy I'll kill her. I'm closer to that car than any man. Someone, you or Dette, call Helen and make sure she's OK. Euan has bad news for her today. Don't call her until this evening. Give him time to tell her. I'll try and call myself when I get this thing over with.'

'OK OK, I understand. You're running all our lives from Wales.'

'No. Just my own. Now I really do have to go.'

Rorie didn't wait for the goodbye. She walked out of the station and into a waiting taxi, the only waiting taxi. 'Fargavenny, please.'

'Pleasure.' The driver sensed her mood and didn't say a single word for the rest of the forty-five-minute journey.

'Excuse me? Miss? We're where you wanted to go?'

'Yes. Can you wait for a moment, please?'

'Pleasure.'

Number 14 was a red brick terraced house among many. But it was the most individual. A stained-glass panel had been fitted to the front door, which had been painted cherry red, like the window frames. A tiny front garden was filled with tubs of autumn shrubs and late-summer flowers. The doormat said, 'Welcome', under a rainbow.

Rorie stared and, as if the door knew, it opened. A woman in her early fifties, wearing a sky-blue turban and a long flowing lavender dress, looked out. She was the woman in John's photo. Beautiful still. For a split second she met Rorie's eyes, then shut the door again. If she knew Rorie, she didn't want to.

'I think you'd better take me back to the station, please.'

'Station, is it? Pleasure.'

'Wait.'

'Wait, is it? Pleas—'

'Don't say pleasure again.'

She got out of the car and knocked on the door. The thirty seconds it took felt like thirty years. The door didn't open, and she'd decided only to knock once. Each knew who was on the other side. Just as she was about to walk down the path again, it opened.

'What do you want?' Janet Edwards sounded tired.

Rorie shook her head and raised her hands.

'Come in, then.'

'You picked a good time. The house is empty for a few hours,' Janet handed over a strong brew with great calm.

'Thanks,' Rorie took a sip because she felt very cold all of a sudden.

'What are you doing here, Rorie?'

'You know my name.'

'I should do. You were cited as co-respondent in my divorce case. Put the cup down, Rorie. I can't believe that's a shock to you.'

'When? When did you divorce?'

'Ten years ago. I take it from your reaction you're still living with him?'

'Yes,' Rorie whispered. What did he do from Friday to Monday, when he left her flat?

'And you didn't know I was no longer his wife? You were served with papers, you know.'

'Was I? He must have intercepted them.'

'If you didn't know, he's been telling you he's coming to Wales still, at weekends and holidays.'

'Yes. Where does he go?' Rorie asked the question like a child.

'To the next opportunity. He'll always have a next opportunity, until the women no longer want him. That's his nature.'

Two hours flew. Janet told Rorie she'd stayed with John for the first five years.

'I was putting the children first. Until I realised when he was around they had to compete with him for my attention. And he wasn't worth that. John doesn't like children. He's not seen my two since the divorce became final.'

'But he does support them financially?'

'Are you kidding? I had to give him half the house to get rid of him. We moved here – this isn't a home you'd buy on a lecturer's salary, but it's a lot happier than the one I was in.'

'He'll look for half of my flat, then.'

'I shouldn't doubt it.'

'I'm as bad as him, living with him so long.'

'I used to think you were. But you're not. Years ago I hated you. But I know now he has a way of working women who are naturally generous, who want to give away all they have at the expense of themselves. I wanted to do things with my life, and I thought he'd do them with me. I went up to London on the train once. About six months after he stopped me coming up to see him there. I got a good look at you. You were a foxy little thing. I felt like a long lump.'

'Don't say that, please,' Rorie said.

'I don't think it any more. I have it all, Rorie. And if I'm honest, and nowadays I always am, I have you to thank for it.'

'Me?'

'I would have wasted a lot more years on him.' Janet looked at the clock as she spoke. 'Look, you have to go now. The kids are coming round for tea and I don't want them meeting you. They don't need this and, come to think of it, neither do I. Good luck. You deserve it after the years you wasted on him.'

*****

Rorie checked into a hotel room, climbed on a bed, slept like she was going to die.

Her phone went. It rang off and started again immediately. She was so tired she didn't even have the energy to reach out and answer it. Whoever it was, her life was more important right now.

In London Helen left a message Rorie wouldn't get until the following afternoon when she finally switched her mobile on: 'It's me. I can't believe you knew my father was dead and my mother was in hospital and didn't tell me. At the moment I never want to see you again. I also really need to talk to you. Neither Bea nor Euan seems to understand why I can't go home to Ireland. I need you to come over and explain to them, Rorie, what it was like for me in that house. You remember. You're the only one who knows what it was like. Please, Rorie, will you?'

At twelve the next day Rorie surfaced, only because the maid rapped on the door for kicking-out time. She got onto the train and sipped coffee, feeling like she'd been beaten up. *Your Latest Fiasco* felt a long way away and very minor in terms of fiascos. She stopped herself turning on her phone to find out what was going on. All the problems would wait.

The lighting man, Don, was the only person backstage at the theatre. 'They've all gone. Nigel resigned and so did our leading lady. He's off to do another production. She's off in a huff because he was supposed to do it with her, used it as an excuse to dump this. Clever of her. The rest of us need the wages we're owed. *Fiasco*'s fucked. Unless your *protégée* persuades the writer she can direct it. That's what she's off doing now. I'll tell you one thing. What happens backstage in this play is a lot more interesting than what goes on out in front.'

'Where are Catriona and Noël Coward now?' Rorie was amazed at how calm she sounded.

'In Brown's, lunching for the last three hours.'

'Don, call everyone, can you? Get them back here for six or they don't get paid for this week.'

'I think that'll persuade them. I was only here to see what stuff I could nick.'

'You won't have to nick anything. This play is still touring and you can tell them all that, if I have to pay them personally.'

35

Catriona put the phone down on Rorie and turned into George's back, slipping an arm round him.

They had been drifting off to sleep having made love in a way that Catriona had forgotten they could – in fact, she couldn't remember if they ever had. Then Rorie had called and one of the kids had run into the room – thank God they'd finished what they'd started – Catriona couldn't help but be excited at the prospect of running the show tomorrow, as well as being nervous about it. 'Looks like I'm going to be in charge for a lot of this week,' she whispered to George. 'I hope I'm up to it.'

'You've run this home well for many years, Catriona.'

'No I haven't, Magda has.'

'Oh, she's the nuts-and-bolts person, but you're the one the children turn to. You've given them the confidence I never had as a child, Catriona. It's worth its weight in gold.'

'Really, George? You really think that?'

He turned to face her. 'Of course I think that. I know

we've had problems for a long time, but I could never fault you on how you are with the children. I wish Lydia had been half the mother you've been. Then I might still have a family of my own instead of a sister who never wants to see her family again and a mother who wouldn't know how to praise an Olympian.'

Pressed against him, she thanked her lucky stars that things hadn't progressed with Euan, or any of the half-dozen men she'd had crushes on since she married George. She was grateful that he'd put up with the way she'd dismissed him over the years. Something had shifted that countless New Age courses and consultations hadn't managed to move – she knew now that as long as she hated herself so much she could never have respected any man who loved her. The kids were different, they hadn't chosen her. George had, and that was the biggest reason why she rated him a fool. He was everything a woman could want in a man, but he couldn't make up for her own personal disappointments because he couldn't provide her with personal satisfaction. He'd killed himself trying in the beginning – overcome his public-school reticence to talk about his emotions at a Heartfelt Centre Weekend, which featured a few lentil-eating, sandal-wearing men and George in his chinos; he'd witnessed the home births of three of his children when he'd rather have sawn off his own leg.

Then he'd given up and become worse than he was even when she'd first met him. He'd shut down and coped with what had to be done, ignoring all signs of crises. Emotional upset would have disturbed his routine.

Now Catriona was going to have to disturb it without upsetting him, by getting him to give up his mistress and all those bidding to replace her. Somehow she'd have to find a way to get Magda out of the house and replace Helen as his dancing partner. Then she'd have to get hold of Audrey Hepburn and advise her that Tiffany's did not want to ask her to breakfast any more. She better move on to lunch with someone else.

For now she must exercise patience. The show had to go on the road and she had to go with it. Let Helen try fancy footwork and Magda make as many dinners as she liked, Catriona knew what had just happened in their bed didn't happen to just anybody. The only serious contender was Ms Hepburn. And she was the one she had to watch. As her eyes closed she could hear Magda chiding the kids, in her polka-dot Polish voice. She was clearly not happy with George and Catriona still being in bed, and was taking it out on the kids.

Catriona got up. 'It's all right, Magda, have the day off.'

'But George, he has paid me extra.'

'Keep it.' Because you're not keeping my husband.

When he woke up George came downstairs barefoot (the last time she'd seen him without his socks was at the Heartfelt Weekend and that was because he was made to take them off by group vote). He hadn't brushed his hair either. George never left the bedroom without brushing his hair. The kids were running in and out of the garden, enjoying the last of the summer weather.

They rushed up to George when he came in, hugged him and filled him in on all the important things they'd been doing with their mummy, then raced off to do more important things.

'See?' George's eyes were twinkling at her. This was a

private moment. George and Catriona hadn't had a private moment since the birth of Lara.

George's mobile phone rang conveniently. 'Could you grab that, Kate, sweetie? It's beside you.'

He hadn't called her Kate for years.

Helen's name came up on the screen.

Catriona smiled. 'It's Dette, I gave her your number for when she can't get through to mine.'

George, a bit afraid of Dette at the best of times and terrified at others, was only too happy to let Catriona take it and wander into the other room.

'Hello?'

'Hi, it's Helen.'

'Is everything OK? You don't sound well.' Catriona remembered what Rorie had said. Helen sounded like a cracked plate.

'Not great, but I don't want to complain. I was hoping – is George there? I need some financial advice.'

Financial advice, on a Sunday morning?

'He's with the kids in the garden, a bit busy at the moment. I'll get him to call you. Do you want to leave a message?'

'No message. I'll see you both soon.'

Helen was a pushover. Magda might be more hassle. Audrey made the ring a little crowded. Still, life was a lot more interesting than it had been for many years. And Catriona had a growing confidence that she could come out on top. She could see George still loved her, however little she deserved it. She could see all she had to do was appreciate him and what she had. And then there was tomorrow.

*****

Tomorrow was today. Catriona hadn't been able to sleep since five. One of the children had climbed into their bed then and she lay there, eyes open, looking at the ceiling.

'Come on,' she pleaded with herself, 'you've got to get another hour at least. By nine you'll have fed and dressed four children, dropped them off to their various places and be sitting on the Tube to work.'

To work. It still felt great to say that. OK, now the money had run out she was working for nothing, but she was contributing and being recognised for it. The recognition in one area had made her see what she had to offer in others. Her kids loved her. Her garden loved her. Her husband loved her. Her au pair no longer frightened her. The *Fiasco* crew loved her, and the cast had a growing respect for her because she could talk to them in actor-speak. Lots of reassurances peppered with 'darling'.

At five forty-five she slipped out of bed and went to have a hot shower, to compensate for lost sleep. As she ran her hands over her body she no longer felt the awful sensation of hating it. So much so that at the last sitting Jude had convinced her to pose naked. They'd fought about it for weeks.

'Come on, Catriona! Get your kit off! I'm not into women – you know that.'

'Look, Jude, I'm a trained actress. If you asked me to strip in Trafalgar Square and dance in the fountain I'd do it, if it had artistic merit!' It was wonderful to take the piss out of her former profession, and its way of persuading itself that nudity was art if it paid.

'Then do it now.'

'I can't at the moment. My tits make Erica Roe look flat-chested, and the rest of me is too blobby for Mr

Blobby. I'm not sexy – I'm lumpy. I don't want my lumps committed to canvas. I won't even have a family photo done because I look so matronly.'

'Matronly! You're a bleeding goddess! The Greeks made statues of women like you.'

'Well, today they'd give me a calorie counter and a "before" part in a cellulite commercial.'

Over the weeks she'd changed since she'd less time – make that no time – to obsess on her body. And on Friday she'd posed in her pelt. And loved it. Now Jude was giving out to her, 'You're losing weight. Don't turn into a skinny arse before I finish the picture.'

'I can't help it. Rorie and the rest of *Fiasco* have me run ragged.'

By nine-thirty she was at the stage door. There was nothing like turning up for work at a stage door again. She wouldn't have minded if she was the cleaner. Hang on, she *was* the cleaner.

'Mawning, Cat!' Joe the doorman had taken to calling her that. She liked it, and the way it was catching on with everyone else.

'Mawning, Joe. Where's everyone?'

'In the green room, moaning that there's no milk.'

Catriona lifted the carton out of her plastic bag of bits, featuring rubber gloves, Domestos, chocolate biscuits and a sandwich for the lunch hour she wouldn't have.

'Think of everything, don't yah, missus? Hope you got an answer for today's conundrum. By the way, the party was great on Saturday night. Thanks for inviting us.'

'No problem. Make sure you thank Rorie too. It was her bash as well.'

'She didn't invite us, did she? Bear with a sore head, she is. Good luck upstairs, anyway.'

'Why, Joe? Do I need it more than usual?'

'Put it this way, they're all up there waiting for Nigel and Nigel ain't coming. He left this letter for Rorie to read to them.' Joe held up an envelope.

'Rorie's not in this morning.'

'Then you're the ASM, you'd better have it.'

There were twenty-one stairs and a corridor between the stage door and the green room. In the time it took to climb them she'd read the letter, digested it and decided what she had to do.

As soon as she opened the green room door the crew looked up from their tabloids, the actors from their broadsheets and Noël Coward from his bone-china cup, 'Milk, Catriona, there's no milk for morning coffee. Also, there is no stage manager or director. I wonder if you would care to rustle up those as well for this vitally important meeting that they, and you, have chosen to be late for.'

Catriona put milk and biscuits on the table.

'Now, someone can open that – or do you need me to break the foil seal for you as well? I've got important news.'

'Excuse, Cat,' Jonathan Blake Thompson, the male lead, young and in danger of growing old starring opposite Lavinia Delmont, the female lead, who was the most famous and worst thing about the play as it stood. 'But there's no point in addressing the chicken until the head is present.'

'Jonathan,' Catriona liked him. He talked a lot straighter than most luvvies. 'I'm afraid our chicken is now headless. As of today Nigel Blunt is no longer our director. He has begun work on his first Hollywood feature, a remake of *Brief Encounter.*'

'But we were supposed to work on that together. I was to update the original Noël Coward screenplay! It was my idea!' Noël sat down in the chair as if he was never going to get up again.

'And I was supposed to recreate the Celia Johnson role!' Lavinia shrieked.

'Well,' Jonathan laughed, 'I definitely didn't get asked to do Trevor Howard.'

'Who'd've asked you if we'd've got Ralph Fiennes? I brought Nigel Ralph! I got Ralph on the project! They'll probably give my role to Julianne fucking Moore again, like they did in the *End of the Affair.* This is a fucking fiasco. I'll have to call my agent.' Lavinia was foaming at the mouth.

'It'll never work without me,' Noël was whispering to himself, drinking coffee, without milk.

'That's it!' Lavinia Delmont stood. 'I'm not spending another minute here. My career is already compromised, my talent has been ignored. Goodbye, everyone, and Catriona,' she addressed her understudy, 'I hope you know more lines than you did last run-through. You're hopeless, and even then you're better than this script.'

Catriona sat down in the chair Lavinia had just vacated. She'd forgotten that was her job along with everything else.

Jonathan came up and squeezed her shoulder, 'If you're half as good at the lead as you are at getting the biccies in, we'll turn this play right round.' But even he had plans to slip out and call his agent to see if there was anything else doing. A guest appearance on *The Bill* would do. Something told him there was nothing doing. *Fiasco* had cut off all other offers. He was stuck here, like the others, paying his rent.

'Where's Rorie? For God's sake, where's the stage manager?' Noël looked like his cravat was cutting off the blood supply to his head.

'Rorie's in Wales, for personal reasons.' Catriona spoke to the floor. They'd have to get a proper actress in, she wanted to stay this side of the curtain. Mind you, the chances of the play making it to Surbiton were slim – she might be joining a dole queue tomorrow.

'By that you mean she's on a jolly with that stumpy excuse for a writer John Edwards,' Noël spat. 'Typical! I always said she was rubbish. It's her and Nigel's fault I'm in this mess.'

'I'm not here to comment, Noël. But I am deputising for Rorie,' Catriona said.

'Deputising? You've only been here two minutes. You make the tea. You don't get milk on the table in time. And you're deputising for one of the industry's seasoned stage managers?' Noël was apoplectic. The need to blame someone had forced him to target the messenger. 'I've a good mind to walk too, only I wrote the damn thing. My name's on it, no matter what. My name's featured in all the terrible reviews. Can I help it if this cast and that director couldn't interpret my material properly?'

'No, Noël, you can't. But, then, I do think a lot of what's gone wrong here is that your work has been translated to stage unedited.'

'You what? How dare you?'

'I am aware of your considerable talent, of course. But every play that débuts has to be edited by cast and director to help it meet stage requirements. It's textbook theatre-school stuff. You, well, you're brilliant, naturally. But you're not in the glare of the footlights. For instance, the train scene—'

'What about it?'

'It's hard for such a small cast to simulate a crowded station and a narky ticket collector and a reuniting couple. It would have been simpler if you'd just changed the time from evening rush hour to last thing at night. The actors could've worked at the atmosphere instead of competing with a BBC soundtrack of Waterloo at five p.m.'

'She's right,' Jonathan nodded. A ripple of assent ran through the gathering.

'Thank you. I've also been looking at our other problems and I've got some solutions. Big ones. We need a complete reshape, fresh impetus and talent for the tour. First date is one week, and we're ready, but we're not polished. I've got Martin Hardiman to work on our touring set.' Everyone oohed, Martin had won an award for his work.

'Victoria Hazlet will cameo as Roberta on opening night, five scenes only and a lovely lot of publicity for us.' Catriona had heard from Dette that Martin was as thick as thieves with her; she hoped he loved Dette enough to pull it off. 'Of course, we'll have a new female lead soon. We have a dramatic new director on board, whose name will be released this afternoon. Most importantly, we have the money because we have a new producer.' She'd have to talk to George, get him at work, tell him she needed to borrow money from him.

By the time she'd finished talking the crew were still dubious, but the cast were sold on the chance to resurrect *Fiasco*. Noël was looking at her as if he was in love with her.

'Now, take the rest of the day to consider this. When Rorie gets here this afternoon we'll call everyone, set a new meeting and reveal our new schedules. OK?'

'OK.'

'What about lunch, Catriona?' Noël stood up. 'Or at least brunch, at Brown's?'

'I was about to suggest it. There's a lot we have to talk about.'

They were still there at three o'clock. She wanted to get back so she could tell Rorie what had happened. But nothing doing. Noël was determined to tell her his whole life story, including details of the stitching used to tack up his French poodle after it was cruelly run over by a moped while he was walking her before college.

'It was terrible to watch it, Cat – I can call you Cat, can't I?

Can I stop you? Catriona nodded. 'Yes. Like I was saying, Noël, I would be perfect for the job, if you'll endorse the appointment with theatre management. I've got the right approach for dealing with both cast and crew and, like I've said, I've got the new producer on board and the Hazlet cameo's just a formality to be finalised.'

'Oh, yes, oh, yes, I think you'd be perfect for the job, Cat. I'm just worried about Rorie, that's all. How will she react? Is she up to this kind of news?'

'Brilliantly. I know Rorie. She's a brick when it comes

to stuff like this. A talented brick, a very talented brick. You can depend on her.'

'Depend on me for what, Catriona?' Rorie was suddenly standing by her left shoulder, where all devils sat. The angel on Catriona's right had disappeared.

'Sorry, Rorie, we were just coming back to the office to tell you.' Noël rapidly excused himself to the loo, living up to the surname he'd chosen by deed poll.

Rorie immediately sat in his seat at the table for two, picked up his half-glass of wine and drained it. 'Tell me that Nigel's resigned, Lavinia's run away and you're the new director with a flood of new money and star appearances?'

Catriona sat back, mouth open and closing.

'Don't bother, sweetie. I don't want to hear excuses. I know you've a lot of those. I've heard enough of them over the years.'

'Rorie,' Catriona said, as quietly as she could, but it was still too late. Half of Theatreland was having a good listen. 'I'm sorry you found out like this, but I had to take over. You left me in charge.'

'I didn't ask you to promote yourself over my head.'

'I had to, I had to impress everyone enough to make sure there was a possibility they'd turn up for this play. This play is all I have, Rorie.'

'Wrong. It's all I have. You've four children and a husband. As of today I have no one but my old ma and my last job, which was this one, before I had to resign in disgust at one of my best friends taking my opportunity away from me.'

'I thought you didn't like stage management,' Catriona said miserably. 'I thought I was organising things so well.'

'What? What d'you mean?'

'I thought I'd be a good stage manager.'

'Not a director?'

'No. I've got Noël to agree to get the management to give you that job. I was going to be your new stage manager.'

'I don't believe this! Don said—'

'What?'

'Nothing.' Rorie thought quickly on her feet. 'You really think Noël will let me do this?'

'I know he will or the show closes – without my husband's money and other things I've promised that I haven't got yet.'

'Like what?'

'Like Victoria Hazlet to do an opening-night cameo. Dette said she was all over Martin at our party. Martin's doing the touring set, by the way, for nothing. And I told them we had an amazing new prospect as director.'

'And they're so used to working with egos they thought it was you.'

'Oh, for God's sake, I couldn't direct my way out of a paper bag. I've let an au pair run my life for two years. I've hidden behind my husband for a decade. It'll be many a day before I direct anything. But you—'

'I'd love to do it,' Rorie admitted, 'but I haven't got a single director's credit on my CV, since college.'

'You have now. I got Noël to agree to let you be the director of most of what he's worked on up to this. And it was all wildly successful. I've written out your CV in longhand and I'll type it up when we get back to the office. You just have to sign it.' Catriona held up some napkins.

'You're amazing.'

'No, you're amazing. If you hadn't kicked my arse I'd still be wearing it out from sitting down.'

'Well, for my part you've assisted me on the worst job in my life and been the only thing that made it bearable.'

'Ahem.' Noël had returned now that the storm had cleared. 'If we could leave the love-up until later, we three have a lot to discuss. I have to say I'm not convinced by you as director, Rorie. I think we should—'

'There is no think-we-shoulds,' Catriona said firmly. 'The only way any of this works is if you put Rorie in creative control. I'll run everything else. The two-hundred-thousand-pound stump-up is conditional on Rorie Marks directing. You have no choice in this, Mr Coward, and only one opportunity to make this *Fiasco*, your fiasco, work.'

'It's a Faustian deal.'

'It's a heavenly deal. She's brilliant. I'm brilliant. Now, let's get on with it.'

'Agreed.' Rorie had decided to give Catriona a rest from swinging the punches. 'When we get back we tell the cast it's all systems go and you and I, Noël, will tackle the script straightaway. Cat,' even Rorie was using it, 'you see if we can push all the dates back a fortnight. It shouldn't be a problem with two of the venues. They're not even theatres. We took what we could get. Noël,' Rorie eyed him, 'let's aim to open first week in October. Gives us time for a complete, and I mean complete, rewrite. It needs to be cut by at least ten pages, and that train scene is set at the wrong time—'

Catriona's eyes told Noël not to dare mention she had said the same thing.

*****

Later that night George nursed a brandy. 'I can't believe you did that, Catriona, without even calling me.'

'I did call you but you weren't in your office. Probably out ballroom dancing.'

'I don't do that at lunchtimes, I do it on Tuesday evenings, and you said you didn't have a problem with me and Helen being partners, especially as you're so busy with the play. The play you have said I will give two hundred thousand pounds to.'

'Don't be silly, George, I only want you to give twenty thousand as a first instalment. By the time Rorie reworks it and I handle the production side it should be going swimmingly. Martin's helping!' She thought she'd push a button. But George had his banker head on and his banker head said he'd be better off flushing notes down the loo.

'You're getting a credit as co-producer. Think of it as a new venture, George.'

'I suppose. But it's not how I would choose to invest.'

'You're not investing in the play, George, you're investing in me. Our house is worth five million pounds. You're always telling me it's half mine. Well, I want twenty thousand pounds of my share, please. I'll give it back to you. If I have to go out cleaning I'll give it back to you. Don't make me beg. There's a lot at stake here, not just me.'

George looked like she'd trodden on his corn. 'What if we no longer lived in this house? What would you do then for money?'

'We own it, George. Well, you own it. We'll always live in it.'

'OK, twenty thousand pounds. No more, Catriona. We have to watch what we have.'

'Thanks,' for making it so hard, you miserable bastard. We have a huge income and millions in assets, and you make me crawl.

He wrote the cheque there and then, in silence. She didn't thank him again, went upstairs to bed and felt the familiar leaden feeling of aloneness. When it came to money George Morehampton hadn't changed a bit.

Downstairs George looked out the window at the street-light; it shone even though a light was going out in his world. 'George,' Magda was behind him, all of a sudden. 'Would you like more brandy? You look so tired. A lot of work you have to do, George.'

'Thanks, that would be nice.'

When he turned round she'd poured two glasses.

'I hope you don't mind?'

'Not at all. But to be honest I'd prefer a little privacy, Magda. Take it up to your room.'

Magda left like her clothes were on fire.

George picked up the phone and dialled. 'Madeleina. How are you? Are things still bad?'

He listened while she told him. 'You must let me help you. I'll give you half of everything I have. It's yours. You must let me help you.'

Five miles away Rorie was busy. Busy with plans for her great and glorious directing career. Her first job was to direct someone to exit, stage left. She ran from the Tube station, saw Mercy in one piece on the forecourt, thanked

God for that. John would be at evening tutorials on a Monday.

She had forty-five minutes.

She got into the flat, opened two cases and piled all she could find of his into them. Except for the blue paperweight. That she put into her drawer to send to Janet, from whom it had been stolen.

Then she got his manuscript. Typed two words on the last page so far: 'The End.'

She put his cases outside the door. With a small note of her own: 'I went to Wales to see your wife. I never want to see you again.'

The twenty-four-hour locks company pulled up their van at that very moment.

36

Euan put Kelly's hand into Bea's. 'Can you take this little one out for a while big sister? I've got to speak to your mother.'

Bea sniffed and nodded. Helen had just torn a strip off her for puking in the kitchen sink. 'I can't believe you don't learn that bingeing is a mad person's game. You might as well hammer yourself over the head and get rid of the brain cells that way.'

'Leave her be, Helen. Can't you see she's not well?' Euan said softly.

'Leave her be? Have you ever dealt with a cirrhosis case? Have you seen what a jaundiced, liver-failed, pickled-skin drunk looks like?'

'Oh, Helen, will you stop taking it out on him? He's not the one worse for wear.' Bea moved to Euan's side. As she always did.

'I don't see any point in continuing with this any more. You two just gang up on me, that's all you ever do. It's two in the afternoon. My daughter just got out of bed and vomited in our sink and my husband says I've got the problem.'

'No, Helen, we've got the problem,' Bea sighed, 'and it's you.'

Kelly had already left the room to drown an increasingly familiar sound with a Tellytubbies video. She didn't even like the Tellytubbies, they were too young for her. Joyce was squirming in her chair to get away from the noise. Euan picked her up and handed her to Bea. Both left the room.

'Helen.' He wondered at how difficult it had become to say her name, to speak to her on anything. She was so defensive he had to edit every word before it came out. And that meant he said little these days.

'What?' she snapped. Even saying her name was enough to set her off. Was it what he'd done that had caused this reaction, or had she been ready to snap for a long time? He'd failed her, expecting her to cope. Somehow he had to stay calm, somehow he had to deliver the news.

'Would you like some tea?'

'No, I'd like some answers. Who did you fuck? Why did you fuck? When and where did you?'

'I think you should have tea. I need to speak to you.'

'I don't want to speak. I want to go to sleep and not wake up.'

'For God's sake, what's brought this on?'

'As if you didn't know.'

'I've told you, it's in the past. I won't reveal who it was because it would hurt you even more.'

'You don't have to reveal it. I heard you on the phone on Friday.'

'On Friday?' To Euan it felt as if years had gone by since then instead of only forty-eight hours.

'To Rorie.'

'Yes, yes, I spoke to Rorie. About you, Helen. Since you've decided never to speak to her again and to blame her for what happened between us, since you insist on thinking that your best friend would have sex with me behind your back—'

'I know it was her. I heard you. I know it was her.'

'You're off your box, Helen, and there's not a lot I can do about that. I can't defend myself, but I'll defend Rorie. She's a—'

'Good woman? You're always telling me what a good woman she is, Euan. How good a woman lives with a man for fifteen years who is married to someone else? And if he wasn't there she'd be after you.'

'You knew she loved me, then?'

'Yes, as did you.'

'That's where you're wrong. I only found out recently. She said she was trying to make you see sense, and she told me why you suspected her of having an affair with me.'

'What else did she tell you?' If Rorie had mentioned the fidelity test, Helen was ready to ring round and isolate Rorie from the rest of the Virgo Club. It was almost an exhilarating prospect. This way I can keep my friends and never have to see her again.

'Nothing.' Euan caught himself in the nick of time. 'She thought it would help things if she came clean.'

'I'd say she's picked the right time – a time when John's on his way out the door and she knows you and I are falling apart. Come in, play the confessor, get Euan's sympathy, then persuade him to leave his wife and kids.'

'Helen,' he had his calm voice on, the voice that she knew there was no arguing with, 'if you slander her once more I will personally see to it that you don't get a chance to do it again. Rorie Marks looked after your child for nothing while you studied. She was the first to congratulate you on every promotion and the first to console you when things went bad. Right now, she's sitting somewhere, up to her neck in a lousy life, still finding the time and space to worry about you. And on the basis of something you thought you'd heard, and your own bad maths of assumption, you've decided she and I have been at it behind your back. You're not worth her friendship, in your current state of mind, and you're certainly not worth all I've given you.'

'And what exactly is that, Euan?'

'My absolute devotion to the point of foolishness. I went along with things as they were because I knew how much it would upset you to change them. I've put your career and interests before my own. I've compensated as best I can for your complete lack of time and interest in your eldest daughter's welfare and happiness, and I've lived with the prospect that you'll do the same with Kelly and Joyce when they get to an age when they can challenge you and what you stand for. And you need to be challenged, Helen. I've done you no favours. I should have done this years ago.'

He doesn't love me. My kids hate me. I'm fantasising about a life devoted to tango with an investment banker who already has a wife and a mistress.

Bea walked in.

'Thank God that's over,' she said. 'The girls are watching another video. I know you don't approve of too much telly,' Bea looked at Helen, 'but they're upset.'

'Actually, Bea, it's not over,' Euan said. 'I need you to be here when I say this. Can you come and sit down?'

Both of them were shocked when Bea burst into tears. 'Please, Euan, don't leave! I know she's a narky bag and she's decided you're the world's worst, but you're all we've got, Euan. We love you, even if she doesn't. Please, please don't go. I can't stand it. It's not for me just, it's for them.' Bea pointed to the door behind which Kelly and Joyce were watching television. 'They need you around. She'll have to get over whatever it is that's making—'

'Bea,' Euan stood up to comfort her, rocked her in his arms, 'I'm not going anywhere at all. Your mother is.'

I should be there, I should be doing that. He fucked someone else, maybe not Rorie, but someone, because I haven't been available to him in the right way for years. And now I don't even know if I can love anyone, let alone him.

'Bea, Helen. Rorie rang me on Friday. She'd been on the phone to her mother…'

Ireland, this is going to be about Ireland.

Somewhere she heard the name Eunice. Her sister. Somewhere she heard the words 'dead', 'father'.

He's dead. He died. No one told me. Bea never had a father. I never had a father.

'And your mother, Helen, is very, very sick. You need to go there right away.'

'I'll go with you. I want to see them, Mum. They're my family. I want to see my grandmother. Kelly and

Joyce have a grandmother. I want to see mine.' Bea was crying saying this, Euan was crying. Helen was stone.

She stood up. 'I have to go to work now. We'll talk about this later. I have to get changed and go to work.'

Upstairs she sat on the bed into which her husband had taken someone else. Upstairs she looked out the window. Rorie. She had to speak to Rorie. Rorie would know.

Rorie's mobile rang once and went to message. Three times. She must have turned it off. She hates me that much. I've been horrible to her. Everyone hates me. She knew for two full days my dad was dead and she never told me. I could kill her. Even if she could kill her, Helen still had to speak to her. She called back and left a message.

Downstairs she could hear Bea and Euan talking in the kitchen.

She got dressed slowly, as if someone else was doing it and she wanted them to get a move on. Most of her life seemed to be about waiting for other people to get a move on. It was the same when she came down the stairs and got into the car – she had to do it slowly or she wouldn't do it at all.

At the hospital the admissions clerk inside the front door asked if she was OK.

Two nurses, one junior and a registrar all asked the same question. She gave the same answer.

Fine.

Her beeper went as soon as she got to her office. No time to put on her white coat, her extra skin. She went as she was.

On a table was a sixty-eight-year-old man, heart attack, flat-lining.

'Resus—'

She called for it as it was arriving. She saw the shirt ripped open, the pads applied, knew she was expected to take hold of them, shout 'Stand back', demand voltage.

Someone else did all that.

No sense in helping this man when she couldn't help her own father. A woman would be admitted tonight, by the law of averages, who would be around the same age as her sick mother. If her mother died in Ireland tonight she wouldn't be there, she would be here, saving another woman's life. Her mother. She'd asked for some of the scholarship money to help with the other kids. Helen had had to say no. She had already known the margins would be too tight.

'You're no good to us,' her father had snapped. 'You got your education. Now you're fecking off on us. We fed you this eighteen years.'

'Don't, Michael, don't speak to her like that.'

'I'll speak how I want. It's my house.'

He'd not bothered to come to the boat – she'd taken the boat instead of the plane to save money.

'Don't mind him,' her mother had said. 'He's only upset you're going.'

All her life she'd heard her mother make watery excuses for that man. Grainne and Michael Larkin had never come to see Bea. It hadn't bothered Helen much. They'd never had anything to offer her, why should they have something for her children?

It didn't seem to matter that the man was dying in front of her now and that she wasn't doing anything to prevent it. Everyone had to die some time. She knew that more than most.

Somehow she'd expected to make amends with her family, or to have amends made to her. If one parent could die, and the other decide not to tell her, then why would they want her to see her mother now that she was ill too?

No sense. No sense at all.

Someone was leading her down a corridor, back to her office. She was sitting at her desk, waiting. When Euan came to collect her she was wearing a white leotard suit and flamingo pink plimsolls.

She didn't get up for nine days. Even a Tuesday night went by. Euan tried several times, but never managed to persuade her or get her to speak to anyone, on the phone or in person. Rorie came round every day and stood at her bedroom door. 'Hi, it's me, just checking on you.'

Silence.

'OK. See you tomorrow.'

A doctor came but she wouldn't take what he offered because she knew that it would move her on. She wanted to feel this. She wanted to feel nothing.

Euan came with the phone on the tenth day.

'No.'

'It's George.'

She pulled the duvet off her head and sat up. She answered.

'Helen, sorry to bother you when you're not well.' He was so polite, knew what the trouble was, wouldn't mention it. Why couldn't everyone be like George?

'OK.' She hadn't used her voice in days, it sounded like sandpaper.

'I'm terribly sorry to trouble you about this, but I've got the competition form in front of me. Are you going to partner me? It's just I have to give it to Madeleina this evening to process.'

'I didn't think Catriona would want you to continue dancing with me.'

'Catriona? She doesn't mind a bit, and she's preoccupied with the play, too busy to partner me. Do you think you can, Helen?'

Right now she couldn't feel her feet.

'Yes.'

'So I'll see you at practice tonight?'

'Yes.'

'Good, jolly good. Until then, keep well. Helen?'

'Yes.'

'Euan is awfully worried about you.'

'Yes.'

'Well, I expect you knew that. Cheerio.'

George put the phone down, looked at himself in the mirror and mimicked himself. 'Cheerio! You idiot. A woman loses her father and you say, "cheerio". She'll think you have no heart.'

Helen was standing on her feet for the first time in ten days. They were tingling. She was thinking what a big heart George Morehampton had, what a way of dealing with her. He put no pressure on her at all. Everyone else was a ton weight.

'Euan, can you drive me to the shops? I need to buy dancing things that aren't white and pink.'

'Sure.' He had tears in his eyes. 'What about work, Helen?'

'What about it?'

'Would you like me to phone and say how you are?'

'No. No point. I'm never going back.'

'At all?'

'Of course not at all, not after the spectacle I made of myself. Don't look like that, Euan. I thought you'd be pleased.'

'Helen, don't. I never wanted…I just…Anyway, if that's what you want. But I think we should—'

No shoulds need apply. You should have kept your thing in your pants. I should have gone to see my family years ago. I should have been a better mother. I should have taken it easy a lot more, had fun. I'm finished with should, I'm on to can.

'Can we just go without having to speak about anything?'

'OK, Helen. And maybe, only if you think you can, you might consider coming to Diane with me this week.'

Diane was it now? Diane, the counsellor she had booked for Euan, to get his head straight, who seemed keener in their joint sessions to probe Helen about her behaviour. At first, she had been Diane Henderson.

'She's siding with you, Euan,' Helen had said after the last session.

'No, Helen, she isn't. She's just seen me a lot more than you. She's more familiar with me.'

'You can say that again. What's her code of conduct say about that, I wonder?'

'Helen, she's not a doctor, she's a psychotherapist.'

'She's still supposed to be impartial.'

'What did she do that wasn't?'

'Try this. "Helen, I think that dwelling on the fact Euan was unfaithful doesn't move us forward. Euan is accepting responsibility for this and for all the considerable hurt it caused. If you're still in the space where you need to accuse I think we need to look at why." That practically says it's OK for you to sleep around.'

'No, it doesn't. She also said you had her sympathy as the betrayed party.'

'Only because I challenged her.'

'That's not how I heard it. I heard that she thought it was hard for you.'

He drove her to Pineapple and parked on the double yellow outside. The assistant was going to smile, then saw Helen's expression.

'I want some things that suit me. You can decide which. I'm no good at that sort of thing. And I want them sexy. I want something that doubles as a dress and a dance outfit for a competition. And I'd like nice shoes. Size eight. Please.'

The assistant barely spoke as she scurried round the shop collecting suitable items. Helen watched a female traffic warden approach Euan. Hopefully she'd clamp him. He hopped out and ran round to the pavement side. Within minutes the warden was throwing her head back, laughing. They stood there, chatting.

Only Euan. In days gone by his ability to get on with anyone used to make her proud. Helen went in and tried on a black two-piece with wrap-round skirt. A turquoise Lycra dress that came to mid-thigh but had hidden knickers to keep it from being indecent. If indecent did the trick with George Morehampton Helen would cut out the knickers. Patent leather shoes with one-inch heels that fitted like velvet, sheer skin-coloured and barely black tights that seemed to suck up her legs and spit them out longer. Two silk roses, one white, one red, to pin to her bodice, red for sex, white for chastity. She pinned the red one right in the middle of her cleavage.

When she came out of the dressing room the assistant was smiling and waving out the window to Euan, who'd opened the shop door to include her in the conversation with the warden.

'Wow! You look divine. And so does your husband. I can't even get a boyfriend.'

Euan was staring in at her like he'd never seen her before. She felt like she'd never lived before, dressed like this.

'I'll take everything. Now.'

In the car on the way home, Euan had to say it. 'I think you're stunning. George is one lucky lad to be dancing with you. Wish I hadn't flippers for feet. I'd never do you justice. He told me you were having lessons.'

'When?'

'At the birthday party. He wanted me to know there wasn't anything going on, you know, it was all above board.'

'He did, did he?'

'He did. He's a straight bloke, George, a bit too straight, probably.'

'You know what, Euan? He couldn't be straight enough for me. What I really want right now is someone reliable, who can help me understand how my life can become nothing I recognise in a few short weeks.'

'Helen—'

'And as for him being straight, you don't know the first thing about him. Nor do any of us. George has secrets and he guards them and he doesn't go round—'

'Helen, stop it.'

'You stop it. You stop picking up traffic wardens and flirting with shop assistants.'

'I wasn't flirting. I was being friendly. The warden is a granny of four and mother of nine. She does that crappy job to pay for her kids' education. The assistant was only just eighteen. She wants to do West End shows, dancing. I was being nice to pass the time.'

She couldn't eat for the rest of the day, waiting to see George, waiting to dance. Lack of food and excitement made her light-headed. By six o'clock she couldn't wait any longer and left the house. The flamingo had finally fallen over on its one leg. Here was a black swan getting out of her old Mercedes, walking to the Madeleina Conti school. An hour early. She didn't care. The door was open. She walked in because she could hear them and she knew tonight she could compete for elegance and beauty. If she'd had to throw herself at him she'd do that too. What could happen? He could say no. The world was too crowded with shoulds. She was a can woman.

He was there. She could hear them in the curtained-off bedroom. She didn't announce herself, sat in a chair, listened.

'I don't want to be here! I want to be where his bones are, George.'

'He's dead, Madeleina, and I'm here and living. And I

need you. We have to be there for each other. We're all we've got.'

'You have a wife and a family to look after, George.'

'Yes, but I need you too, Madeleina.'

'And what about Helen? Do you need Helen?'

'What do you mean by that?'

'What do you think I mean?'

'I've never laid a finger on Helen. She's my wife's friend. How could you think such a thing?'

'She's thinking it. And so are you. You don't need to lay a finger on her. You are susceptible to her, George, and she is to you.'

'Madeleina, I don't think you should continue with this. Really I don't. You're out of line here.'

'How can you say that to me? I know you better than anyone else. I know you're going to break into pieces if you keep this up.'

'I love my wife, Madeleina!'

'Yes, you do. But you have to accept that she makes you behave as you do. You need to let your armour down, George. Your life is full of nothing you enjoy and you will be broken and disappointed in your old age. That's why I won't stay.'

'For God's sake, Madeleina! Is that your answer to everything difficult? Catriona is trying hard with me now and I'm trying hard with her. You have to forgive and you have to forget. That's why you have to stay in England with me now. You're leaving for nothing when I'm offering you all I can give.'

'It's not enough, George. It's not enough to make me happy.'

It will be enough for me, George. I can take the job of

mistress. I'm good at secrets. I'm good at saying nothing and I'm good at dancing. I'll do all those things with you George. Let her go. She's already said she could never love you as much as her dead lover. I'm here and I want you more than my husband. And I'm prepared to let you keep your wife and children. It'll work, George. Perfectly.

'Hello everyone!' Helen announced herself.

In ten seconds they came out from behind the curtain. They were twins in the way they hid all trace of their conversation.

'You're bright and early,' Madeleina beamed.

'Sorry, wanted to make up for last week, for lost time.'

'I'm sorry to hear about your father, so sorry,' George began.

Don't tell me, George, I'm sick of sympathy. But do tell me what you think of this. Helen took off her coat.

George hadn't the words to tell her. But his body did the talking for the next two hours. On a dance floor. With pensioners for an appreciative audience.

That night she sat at her kitchen table and thought about what she was going to do next. If she just went to a place of her own for a few months, maybe she'd sort herself out.

Don't be disingenuous, Helen. At least admit to yourself that he'd be able to come and see you there. The way he comes to see Madeleina, who is leaving the country soon. Her conscience had a quiet word, when no one else was around.

And what would be wrong with that? Hadn't Madeleina said Catriona made George miserable? Hadn't

George offered to keep her financially if only she would stay in England?

But she was honourable. She wasn't going to take him up on it. She's told him that he's second to her dead lover and she's leaving him because she cares about what happens to him. You care about what happens to you.

What should I do?

Astro Info.

She went into the den, logged on to the website she'd bought the horoscope maps from.

Double clicked on Virgo, love, 18 September.

You are more ready for surprise and adventure than you've ever been.

Euan came in, sat down.

'Good evening?'

'Yes. I'm busy right now.'

'Too busy to talk?'

No, no – all of a sudden she wanted to talk. She wanted to say something and she couldn't believe she wanted to say it so badly. 'Euan, I think I should move out. As a temporary measure. So we can move forward. So I can stop accusing you.'

She'd never seen a man curl up and cry like he did. But she couldn't comfort him. His face was so contorted he was ugly. The sobs came out in big heaves like an animal who couldn't hide. She handed over tissues, whispered 'Sorry', but she didn't take it back. It was that nothing feeling again. There was no remorse in her.

After a while he quietened down, and soon after that he straightened up and looked her in the eyes. 'Please, Helen, don't do this.'

'I'm sorry, Euan. It has to be done, for now. I'll find

somewhere to live and be gone by the end of the week.'

And that was when his face hardened. That was when he said, 'Do you take me for a complete fool? You come back from dance class and tell me you're going to move out. You get me to drive you into town and watch you dress like you've never dressed in your life for me, and then you say you're leaving me. Well, I can tell you, Helen, you're not the one who's leaving. I am. You're going to stay here and do what you should. I know that's not your word of the moment, but it's the one that applies as far as I'm concerned. You should look after your daughters and learn what it's like to be a mother to them. I'm sick of playing both parents. You're leaving your job. I have a job. My salary pays the mortgage now. You can take care of your kids.'

He was gone within the hour and she was left with the sinking feeling that this might be the worst thing ever to happen to her. Kelly and Joyce were fast asleep. Bea was at school. She'd suddenly developed an extra desire to do well in her repeat A levels. Last year's results had been abysmal and Helen had been surprised when Bea had suggested that she resit them. And there'd been no talk of the modelling for some time. Even Dette's gold-dust offer to make an agency introduction for her birthday present now seemed not to be such an appealing package to her as it had been.

Helen was on her own. She picked up the phone to call Rorie, a reflex action. Euan was probably on his way round there right now. Instead she dialled Dette.

'Hello? Helen – are you out of bed? I've been phoning. Euan said – tell me how you are.'

'Good. I think.'

'We should meet up.'
'Yes. When?'
'Tomorrow. I'll call over to you first thing.'

At Rorie's block Euan parked and got out with his overnight bag. This was the last place he should be, but he couldn't go anywhere else. He needed someone right now and he knew Rorie was a good someone. When he knocked, she opened the door. Her face said he shouldn't be there. 'I've just got rid of one problem. I don't want another one.' But she still stood back to let him in.

37

Dette didn't even manage to surface when the alarm went off for the fourth time. Eventually Junior did a dolphin flip to stir her. 'Careful,' she yelped.

Be careful, yourself. The baby kicked again. We're going to be late.

For the past few days the imaginary conversations with her unborn child had taken on a very real quality. She almost relied on them. But sometimes the baby asked her things she found difficult to answer. Made her do things that would have horrified the old, irresponsible, live-for-today Dette. Like reminding her to get out of bed to go to an Essex (if Martin thought she never went past EC1, she was heading far beyond that today) car-boot sale to sell cosmetics to pay the mortgage.

Come on, Mum! You've put it off for weeks now. We've got to flog the gear.

'Stop talking like your father. You're growing up nowhere near the East End. If I have my way you won't meet any girls till you're twenty-five.' She loved it when it called her Mum, but it terrified her as well.

A quick burst out of bed. She caught sight of herself in the mirror. The bump had grown overnight, must have. She couldn't be this big already. She flung open her wardrobe and saw Martin's dirty shirt in the laundry basket. She must be slipping up, agreeing to get out a pesto stain for him. All these wifely instincts were cropping up. Watch yourself, Dette.

The only thing that would fit her and not cut off circulation was that shirt. Another of Dette Morgan's golden rules was never wear clothes over twenty-four hours. If anything, she changed twice a day. Her wardrobe was organised as if by a clerk with a passion for filing, all of it in alphabetical order: A-line skirt teamed with black blouse, a pair of Cuban heels. On really bad days she had consoled herself with a bottle of wine and thrown open the double doors to do a complete recategorisation. Lately she'd been too busy even to think of it. As long as she lived she'd never understand Catriona-Buckets-of-Money Morehampton never ironing a stitch but still refusing to send it all out to a laundry service, afraid of not being seen as one of the proletariat. Yet she'd lost all real touch with them years ago.

Not that Dette would either. She loved looking after clothes as much as she loved buying them. Her washing machine had cost as much as a whole kitchen. And she had a range of fabric conditioners and detergents any supermarket would have been proud of.

She threw up the ironing board, plonked Martin's shirt on it and dabbed it softly with a no-rinse stain remover she'd bought off the internet for almost fifty quid. It was miracle stuff and took the stain out straight away. Then she sprayed on leave-in conditioner and ironed. It looked like you could hang it in a shop window but she still shivered with disgust when she put it on.

Stop it, Mum! Beggars can't be choosers. Now get out there and peddle make-up for our dinners. Make sure you eat some more tuna. I love tuna.

'Well, I used to hate it, till you came along.'

Rorie was almost at her door when Dette started out on to the landing.

'Who're you talking to?'

'Myself. Who else is there?' Dette shrugged.

Rorie gave her the keys to Mercy along with a health warning that would apply if any damage was done to the old girl, then headed off. Rorie looked pale and worried. But she didn't mention a word to Dette about the pregnancy. John must have kept his mouth shut. Fear of a paternity suit is a fabulous thing. Rorie would have a big problem with the fact that Dette was determined to go it alone, she realised that from their conversation a few days ago. But she knew it was for the best. Martin's behaviour last night with Victoria was just the kind of thing that told her it would never work. And who could blame him? He was so young and if you had the choice of (a) one of Hollywood's top names or (b) a has-been hack with forty years of failure behind her, would you have to rack your brains?

At nine-thirty she arrived in the field. Mercy was full to the gills and Dette was glad the roads had been empty. Her foetus was a more experienced driver than she was. That, plus the fact that the field – which was actually a hill – was full made her want to turn back. The far corner was where the only available space was. Mercy gave out stink but Dette, fuelled by lack of funds, drove on.

It took ten goes to get into the tiny space, and it didn't help that a Nissan Micra was nudging behind to hassle her out of the way. By the time she parked dark patches of sweat showed under her arms. Lovely. There was a four-wheel drive on one side of her and a seven-seater with power steering on the other. The owners glared at her. She glared back. Mercy had been around since the sixties: she knew a lot about survival of the fittest.

The four-wheel drive was selling Far Eastern electrical goods. The seven-seater was selling Dette's pet hate in all the world after ceramic pierrots: baked and varnished dough twists with dried flowers.

'An ideal hobby for the woman who has too much time and no taste,' Dette whispered to Junior.

Shush, Mum. Your mother has one hanging in the hallway.

'One good reason why we shouldn't move back if we get kicked out of the flat.'

In an hour three blokes were the only people who had bothered to climb up the hill. And they all came to purchase Far Eastern electrical goods at knock-off prices.

'Who needs a motorised screwdriver when you can have Jo Malone body lotion at a third of the price?' Dette asked, mystified. Her baby didn't answer. It must be a boy.

Across from her an old lady was selling off some of her possessions: old postcards, an art deco lamp, some vases, lovely wall prints and a broderie anglaise shawl.

'Now that,' Dette pointed to the shawl, 'is the ideal christening accessory, if we decide we're not pagans.' Again the baby didn't answer, but Dette was sure it raised its eyes to heaven. 'I know, we haven't got any money. The Chinese saying is "If you have only two pennies buy a loaf of bread with one and a lily with the other." I'm off to get a lily.'

I'm not even going to be born for four months.

'That's hardly enough time to assemble your wardrobe – that shawl, babygros—'

Twenty minutes later, Dette came back to her stall with red cheeks and tears in her eyes. The old lady had given her the shawl as soon as she'd asked how much it was.

'If it's a babe you want it for you can have it. I can see you're pregnant, love. I had it for me own son. I don't get on with his wife, can't bear the thought of someone throwing it out when I pop me clogs.'

They'd got chatting, Dette full of joy at meeting the first stranger to recognise her condition and sadness that she might some day be this old lady. One day her child would leave her.

Gimme a chance! I haven't even been born yet, Mum.

Dette gave the old lady a hug. Things were getting weird here at the top of the hill, and with all she had in her purse she bought everything on the stall, promising to treasure it and keep it together.

'You can't afford this, love. Not with a babe on the way and no man about.'

Was it that obvious?

'I can. It's all so beautiful – you've a great eye. I'll find a place for it.' Even if it's under my bed in a box for a while.

The old lady gave it to her for a hundred quid. Cheap at the price, but it was a price Dette couldn't afford.

'I'll set off home now. You've saved me a horrible job, I can tell you. Bless you, dear. Send me a note when the babe comes along. And don't worry, you'll sell all you have on your stall if I've anything to do with it.'

The bread-twist woman was sniffing perfume when Dette got back.

'How much?'

'Fifty in the shops, fifteen to you.'

'You're right 'n all. It's fifty in the chemist down the road. Bargain. And here's one of me twists, if you want it. Nobody's buying 'em today. My 'usband moans about 'em lying all over the place.'

Dette sighed. If only she could drop the twist as quickly as this woman dropped her haitches they'd be in business. Mercy's boot would be fuller going home and she was eighty-five quid down.

The old lady had indeed told everyone on her way out. There was a sudden stampede up the hill to buy cut-price cosmetics.

The bread-twist woman did a roaring trade too. As soon as Dette put something out, it was snapped up – she was sure some were filching stuff too.

'Have you any Issey Miyake?' 'What about Giorgio Beverly Hills?' 'Mascara?' 'Ruby lip pencil?' 'Bourjois blusher?'

She had a lot of what was asked for, but it was a job keeping up with demand.

She turned round to the boot to sort out an order. The notes were falling out of her handbag – she hadn't time to organise it.

He's here.

'Not now, Junior.'

He's here, Mum. You know he is.

She turned round. Martin was there, with two people who could only have been his mum and dad.

Age hadn't been kind to his mum. She was only five

years older than Dette, maybe ten, but she looked twenty. Martin's dad looked a bit of all right still. She could see where the cheeky grin came from.

'Wotcha, Dette.' Martin was embarrassed.

'I thought you were at the Tower today.' Getting your head chopped off? Or another vital organ?

'No. Vicky was wrong about that. I never said it was today. Some other time, I said. I'm at me mum and dad's for me dinner. Rosemary and Dave. This is me friend.'

'A very good friend indeed.' Rosemary raised an eyebrow. 'I bought you that shirt for Christmas.'

'Sorry, can't talk now, very busy. Nice to meet you, see you later.' Dette tried to rush them away.

'You look a bit pushed, love.' Dette's father tilted his head. The crowd was getting forceful, threatening to knock over her rickety little table.

No. Not for a few months yet, eh, Mum?

Stop that! 'Sorry, Dave, yes I am just a bit.'

'Tell you what, give you a hand shall we?' Rosemary came round the other side.

'No, not at all. I mean—'

'Shush,' Martin grinned. 'She's a dab hand at Christmas in me dad's butcher's.'

'And we'll do bouncer, shall we?' Dave offered.

By three that afternoon Dette Morgan had made five thousand pounds and dealt with a curious police officer, who at first wanted to question her on whether these were stolen goods, but then Martin had advised the officer of who Dette Morgan was.

'Oh, yeah, I read you in *Madame* magazine. What sort of moisturiser do you recommend for combination skin?'

Dette had recommended an entirely free tub of Clinique. The officer had gone away happy.

'My word, that's fantastic,' Dette said, as she counted the last note. 'Here, I'll give you all a cut for your help.'

'No, thanks,' Dave, Rosemary and Martin said in unison.

'You're going to need every penny,' Rosemary whispered to her. And people said Essex women were thick? They were the smartest Dette had come across in a long time.

'Tell you what, Dette, want to come back to ours for dinner?' Dave asked. 'It's nice to meet a mate of my son's. We ain't seen him in so long now we don't know nothing about him. You could fill us in.'

'You certainly could.' Rosemary looked at her.

'No, thanks. I'm not hungry.'

You are! Junior cried. These is my gran and granddad, you want dinner and I want to see them.

'Aw come on, Dette,' Martin looked like he meant it.

'OK.'

One fabulous roast and apple pie later, Dette sat in Rosemary and Dave's conservatory, looking at baby pictures.

'He was a right brat – you had any yourself?'

'No, not yet, Dave.'

Rosemary brought in tea and biscuits.

'Maybe one day.'

That caused Martin to look up.

The conversation had been great over dinner. Dette liked these people. They had no pretensions and no need for them. Martin's younger brother and sister were out at a match and due back later.

'Leyton Orient fans they are, just like Marty.' Dave slapped his son on the back.

'I never knew that, Martin. Spurs you said.'

'And them too, there's a lot you don't know about me, Dette. Give us a lift back when you're going, will ya?'

'Not just yet. Stay and have a cuppa. I've a lot more I want to catch up on, love,' Rosemary pleaded. 'We'll have a read of the papers.'

The *Sunday People*, the *Mirror* and the *News of the World* were spread out on the coffee table. It was all a little bit of heaven. Celebrity gossip, tea and biccies. Until Dave started guffawing and held up page three of the *People*.

'Marty! You bagged a Hollywood bird. Well done, son. You kept it bleeding quiet, didn't ya?'

And there was a picture of Victoria Hazlet and Martin Hardiman snogging in the back of her limousine. The headline read: 'Exclusive. Hazlet Finds Happiness.'

'Nothing exclusive about that. Everyone knew.' Dette stood up. 'I really have to go now.'

She was in the car before they had a chance to stop her.

Standing in the driveway, Rosemary Hardiman beside her son, watching the Beetle bomb off.

'Is it yours, son?'

'The shirt? Yes.'

'No,' Rosemary clipped her son round the ear. He wasn't too big for that. 'The baby.'

38

If she could have cried, she would have, but she'd been so prepared for this. 'You see, Junior? Your dad's Jack the Lad and I'm not his Jill.'

There was no answer. The baby knew, too, by now. Mercy found the way home, but Dette couldn't face it. Instead she turned round and headed out on the road to her mother's place. Mrs Bender threw open the door. 'Bernadette! A surprise, and I'm in need of one since it's four weeks since I saw you last! How are you?'

'Pregnant, single and broke. Have a bread twist. It'll look as lovely as the other one.'

Two hours later, having heard the story of the boyfriend, the sacking, the pregnancy, the boot sale and the dumping, Mrs Bender nodded as if Dette had just filled her in on a normal month.

'Well, aren't you going to say something, Mother?'

'What can I say? It's done now.'

'You've said that to me since I was a child. I hate it when you say that. It makes me feel like it's all my fault.'

'And who else's fault is it?'

'And that's what you've always said as well. I hate that too.'

'Whether or not you like it, it's the fact.'

'So that's all you're going to say? I think I'll head home.'

'Bernadette, you want advice from me?'

'Of course I want advice, support, encouragement. You're my mother!'

'Well, that's a turn-up for the books. For years you've gone your own way, not eating, not doing a thing I wanted you to do. You married that eejit and you went out with a whole load of other eejits. Now you're going to have an eejit of your own.'

'Don't say that! I want this baby more than anything I ever wanted in my life. And I love the father, but he's too young and that's not my fault. That's God's.'

'Oh, you're keeping it, is it?' Mrs Bender suddenly looked different, softer. 'I thought you were going to go for one of them abortion things.'

'Mother, I'm five months gone in a fortnight. I think I'd be up for murder.'

'So, the advice. What is it you want to know?'

'I don't know the first thing about babies other than that they hurt coming out. You have to help me.'

'I'll help you all right. I'll help you by saying we sell up this house and your little flat, and we'll go back to Athbeg. There's nothing keeping us here in London. London's the last place in the world you need your child to be brought up. I only brought you up here because of your daddy's job and then the widow's pension. And, to be honest, I'm only here now because of you. Athbeg's a grand spot. Lots of lovely new houses.'

Barrett homes, Irish style. Dette shivered, but Junior was sold, Can we go? Granny will look after me while you work in the chemist, selling Tweed.

'There's no beauty parlour in Athbeg yet, Dette. You could set one up. I'll mind the child in the daytime. And you'll do well in the beauty end of things, they have some of your articles stuck up on the wall in the local hair-dresser's. You're a name there.' Mrs Bender was going for the hard sell.

Dette smiled, then she stopped. 'I don't know, Mother. It's such a big step.'

'Well, you've taken bigger.' Mrs Bender eyed her belly.

'OK, OK, I'll do it.'

'You will, I know that, and you'll stay the night and feed that child a good dinner for once. I've some leftover roast and apple pie. Don't know why I do it just for meself. I suppose I hope you'll call out on the off-chance.' Mrs Bender sprang out of the chair. Dette couldn't recall seeing her so happy.

Dette crawled into bed with two dinners in her belly. 'Bet you'll turn out to be a ten-pounder,' she said, and slept like a dead woman. The following morning the lead weight of all that had happened pressed on her. But she had to get back to the flat.

'Remember, love. We could be gone even before the child is born.' Mrs Bender brought in a breakfast tray.

'No, I'm in the system here, and my gynaecologist is lovely. He works with the homeless when he's not attend-ing to my every need.' Dette still had traces of the drama queen.

*****

Outside her block Dette sat in the car, waiting for the energy to get up the stairs. When she got it she wished she hadn't. John Edwards was sitting on two cases, outside her door.

'Well, I see Rorie got sense at last.'

'I hope you find yours too.' John's smile made Dette feel sick. Junior bucked at the sound of his voice. Not that creep again.

'Meaning what?'

'Meaning I've come to stay and if you're sensible you'll welcome me.'

'Or what?'

'You know. Martin finds out who's the daddy. Rorie gets taken to court for half her little den. You'll save everyone trouble if you let me in.'

'Pigs sleep in sties.'

'I'd watch what you say. This one wants your spare room – your room, if you keep this up.'

'You'll never get a penny out of Rorie. You're married.'

'Divorced ten years, actually. I did well there, too.'

'Well,' Dette couldn't prevent herself wanting to kill him, 'you won't come across any worse than you. You mean you'd take her to the cleaners after all she's done?'

John stood up to his five five height and squared his shoulders. 'Now Bernadette—'

'Call me that again and I'll throw you over this balcony.'

'Calm down now, easy does it. I did Rorie a favour and I'm doing you one now with this offer.'

'Offer? Of what exactly? I think the correct term is blackmail. You'll have to find someone else to victimise. I'm not the sort that gets bullied.'

'I don't think I'm bullying. You see, dear, I've been sitting outside your door quite a while now. Thinking. I'm thinking Rorie doesn't know you're pregnant. Now, why would that be? She and Martin are friends. He wouldn't touch her with a bargepole. Nor would I now. But they're matey. And she has a view that all kiddies should have daddies. She'll side with Martin straight off – now where does that leave you?'

Dette knew exactly – with a complicated custody battle. But she was facing one of those anyway. There were ten missed calls from Martin on her mobile. 'What are you proposing, John?'

'You can say I'm the father.'

'I'd rather put Lucifer on the birth certificate.'

'But what choice have you, Dette? I'll give you my name for the birth certificate, you let me move in. You have perfect cover. Of course I won't be in a position to contribute to your mortgage, but then, you're such a leading light in the beauty industry you don't need assistance of that kind.'

Dette thought on her feet, swollen though they were with all the extra pressure of pregnancy and life in general.

'You know what, Mr Wonderful? I think I'll pass, and if you don't get out of here by the time I've dialled 999 I'll have you done for assault on a pregnant woman. I know one witness who'll back me up.'

Rorie.

'Excuse me?' John was looking worried, for a change.

'Thought you'd see it like that. Now get back under whatever rock you crawled from and I'll flatten you with it.'

Inside she shook like a leaf in high wind.

Well done, Mum.

'Thanks, darling.'

The doorbell went. Only five minutes after the last caller had left, and Dette still hadn't managed to get her legs to move.

It's him, Mum.

Martin.

'Dette, what's it all about? You're pregnant with my kid and don't tell me you're not because I'm not buying it.'

'Like I'm not buying the *Sunday People* now they've told me my boyfriend's the latest squeeze of Victoria Luncheon Roll?'

'I'm not going to pretend it didn't happen.'

'How honourable of you, Martin. The picture evidence corroborates your version of events.'

'She jumped me. I was drunk.'

'I don't care what she did or what you were. It's been over between us for a while now. Just as well I saw it. You certainly weren't going to let me down gently, were you?'

'Dette, for fuck's sake.' Martin raked his hands over his shaven scalp. 'I came here to sort things out. I should be at the studio – things are going crazy.'

'What exactly did you plan on sorting out?'

'You know.' He pointed to Junior, who was practically leaping into its father's arms. Traitor. Definitely a bloke.

'I do know, but I think you ought to know, Martin – or should I say Marty? – it's not yours.'

'Aw, for crying out loud! Next thing you'll say it's that idiot's who just left.'

'It is.'

'Please, Dette.'

'Please nothing, I don't want anything to do with you.'

It went back, it went forth, and Martin ended it by standing up and saying, 'I want a blood test done when that kid's born. If you were fucking both of us it's a fifty–fifty chance it's mine.'

As he left the door nearly came off its hinges.

You'd better listen to him. Junior was insistent.

'We'd both better go for a lie-down, or you might arrive tonight.'

Dette hadn't cried herself to sleep often. It was almost a relief to have it happen. At least the pillow was soft, and Junior was sympathetic, staying quite still.

'The sooner we're gone from here, the better.'

39

Rorie was next to call, on the phone. It was near to midnight. 'I'm sorry I haven't called sooner. The play's been mad. I'm directing it now. Martin's been trying to get hold of me. He's been doing the scenery for us for nothing. He told me you had an affair with John and you're pregnant but don't know which one is the father.'

'No,' Dette whispered, 'I didn't. And yes, I am.'

'Look, I'm coming right down. I want to see your face before I take this on.'

'How can you do this to Martin? He's such a good guy, and he's cut to pieces over this.'

'Excuse me, Rorie, can I point out who was feeling whose tit in this week's *Sunday People*? Can I point out who was tonsil-touching?'

'That was a mistake. Martin loves you. He's not interested in Vicky.'

'Oh, Vicky is it now?' Dette picked up on Rorie's shortening of the great star's name. 'Look, the reality is that I said I shagged John to get Martin to back off. You know and I know that I'd have to be anaesthetised to let that happen.'

'If it's Martin's child, you should let him—'

'Rorie, please, don't turn your issue into mine. Or else my kid will end up like you, abandoned by their dad, who is too young and or feckless to take on the responsibility.'

Rorie stood up, said, 'I can't argue with that.'

'Or the picture in the paper,' Dette pointed out.

Rorie nodded.

'What about Wednesday?' Dette said it like it was a way out. 'Are we still going shopping? I've got a few ideas.'

'I can't, Dette. I've got to put this play on the map. When's the baby coming?'

'Four months.'

'Well, at least I'll be around then to help.'

'I'm moving to Ireland, Rorie, after it's born.'

Rorie's eyes filled. 'Good for you. Looks like we both got a fresh start. I just wish you'd think about—'

'I did think, Rorie, that's why I took the decision.'

The phone rang. Dette considered taking it off the hook. But it might be someone who actually didn't think she was a walking bitch for squeezing Martin out of his own child's life.

'I know I haven't been in touch for ages,' Catriona said, 'and my guilt is weighing me down so much I found myself in this little dress shop and I bought you a little dress – to say I love you, though I know you'll hate that but I do and I realise that I've been leaving you to sort out all the job stuff on your own and getting on with my own selfish life so—'

'Bring it back and get me a smock.'

'What?'

'Or lend me one of the ninety you used to wear. And a few jangly jewellery things. I'm having a baby.'

'I don't know what to say.'

'Try congratulations. It's customary.' Dette filled her in on the details.

'Dette,' Catriona was over to the flat before Dette had had a chance to say 'No, don't bother.' 'You can't have been such a twat.'

'Cat, you never read the tabloids. See if your posh corner shop has a back copy of the *People*. It shows Martin doing things to Victoria – or Vicky as you're now calling her, now she's going to help your crappy play out.'

'D'you think I'd have suggested it if I knew what she'd been up to? And you have to listen to Martin. He's mad about you.'

'Get the paper, then talk to me.'

Catriona paused, looked hard at Dette, then something cleared. 'You're doing this to get back at him, aren't you?'

'No. I made a mistake and I'm living with the consequences. Now, if you don't mind, if you've finished the judgement call, I need to get on with things.'

'What things?'

'Cancelling the makeover shoot of all of you.'

'Who said I wasn't going to do it?'

'I thought you—'

'Listen, you might have been ridiculous, and you might have used the fidelity test to give your foetus a bogus father. Now, do yourself a favour and phone Martin, sort it out with him.'

Dette looked at Catriona. In all the latest developments she'd forgotten about the fidelity test. For a while she'd thought Martin and Catriona might be at it. The confusion of this was making her suffer from morning sickness again. 'How did you get on with your test?' she asked Catriona, as casually as she could when feeling like she would vomit.

'Not bad. At all. In fact I have good news to report to the owner of the male I was checking out. But it'll have to be Tuesday when I report back. Them's the rules. And I'll see you Friday week, in my glad rags. Helen'll be there too.'

Helen, when she was up and about, called Dette to tell her she'd let Euan leave. And could Dette please come over and tidy her house for her? Helen's housework skills were suffering. As was her relationship with her three daughters, who were determined to get their father back. 'They're going softly on me because I lost my father, but they want theirs. I've got to find out a way to remove brown stains from the loo. D'you know?'

'Limescale. It's your only man. And I could say the same about Euan.'

'Don't, Dette. Not now.'

'Why? Still dancing in your head with boy George?'

'Please, Dette.'

'OK, OK, I'm feeling sorry enough for myself without trying to sort out your mess.'

'Why, what happened?'

Dette's answer was long enough.

'Are you absolutely fucking crazy? You pretended to

Martin you and John had been at it? He *is* a brown stain in a toilet. He's useless and he's unsightly and he's waste product.'

'Helen, I don't want to accuse you of calling the kettle black, but I think you have a bit of analysing yourself to do before you begin—'

'OK, OK. But please, please, explain to me your reasoning. I thought mine had gone out the window.'

'I don't want my child with a fly-by-night father. I want to be able to move to Ireland. If Martin knows it's his kid he'll take me to court, make me stay here. Then when he's old enough to want a younger woman, whether it's Victoria or not, he'll throw me and my child on the scrap heap and have designer brats. My child will be only just younger than its stepmother. It'll scowl in all the family photographs and it won't get as nice presents as the other kids at Christmas. It'll be terrible for it. I'll be in Ireland and only have the price of an orange or a lump of coal. My love won't be enough. Martin will be rich and his new brood will be living in a loft conversion with original works of art and totally unsuitable for kids. I'll wonder at what might have been. My kid will hate me when she or he comes back after the holidays to smelly Athbeg and—'

'Are you sure you don't have a future as a novelist?'

'Shut up, this isn't fiction. This is the future. I have to be realistic about who I am and what I've done. Even Rorie didn't take my claim to have shagged John seriously, but Martin did, which tells me he thinks I'm capable of it, which tells me it would never work out. I'm as likely to have had sex with John as Rorie is with Euan. Nil prospect.'

There was a pause while Helen digested all of this.

'You're right, you're absolutely right. Except for the affair. She definitely had it.'

'Oh, God, Helen. How d'you come to that conclusion?'

'She's living with Euan now. He moved in with her a few days ago.'

OCTOBER

40

Angelo laid the table in the window as normal. But nothing else was. Catriona and Rorie had been too busy to come to the last Tuesday lunch, in late September, and this one, because the play was being rewritten, recast, refinanced and relaunched this coming Saturday in a place Angelo could not believe existed – Surbiton.

'Who would live there?' he asked Rorie.

'About forty thousand people. That's enough for a week of full houses if we can get Vicky to keep to coming on for the five-scene part on the first night. She's promised.' But Rorie had somehow realised all that Vicky promised was not delivered. *Three Sisters* was a rampant success, and people who'd never been to a theatre in their lives were queuing for tickets. There were award nominations – Martin had been selected for his set and its three-dimensional effect. His use of projected film, real trees and abstract painted ones had every show in town looking for him. The Tate wanted it as an exhibit when the show had closed. Victoria had Martin now. She didn't need to be nice to his friends. But she had agreed in the heat of the moment, and Rorie had never allowed her to un-yes herself.

Rorie was not finding the project of working with Victoria a pleasant one.

'Beware of a woman who keeps using the word real,' she yawned down the phone to Angelo. 'For a start she's got an unreal idea of what "on time" means. She kept me waiting two hours for the run-through this week. Then she got into a flap about her flapper dress because it wasn't the nicest in the show. For the two minutes she's on stage we're having to make her a dress that's twice the price of the rest of the cast's. We've got to go on an hour early, so she can get back for dinner at the Ivy. And she wants to keep the dress as a genuine London souvenir. I wouldn't mind, but the fabric's Thai silk and our new wardrobe woman's from Vietnam and her fingers are worked to the bone, even with me and Cat helping her.'

'She is Martin's girlfriend now, no?' Angelo asked.

'Looks like it.' Rorie didn't want to think about that. It made her uncomfortable to see how quickly he'd switched his affections. Especially when he and she had discussed the subject on only one occasion, when Martin turned up to work on the set.

'Look, Rorie, I appreciate you being so fair to her, but I'm just going to leave it. When the kid is born I'll make sure I find out if I'm its dad, and if I am, I promised me mum I'll look after it.'

'But what about Dette? You said yourself you were keen on her, what's happened to that?'

'She got up the spout and didn't tell me. She might even have slept with that goblin you used to live with and not told me. What do I owe her, Rorie?'

'Nothing, Martin, but an explanation of why you and Victoria were all over the papers.'

'Listen, you're beginning to sound like me mum an' all. Don't get the 'ump when I say this but me and Vicky are together now.'

Rorie knew she shouldn't push it. He was doing the set for free, his girlfriend was doing the part for free. 'I think Dette loved you. That's all.'

Martin stopped hammering and looked Rorie straight in the eye. 'She had a funny way of showing it. Now, if you don't mind, I want to get this finished so I can go back to me day job.'

'OK, fair enough. One more thing.'

'What?'

'You're sure Victoria will turn up for the opening night?'

'Yes, I told ya, if I'm there she's there. She'd do anything for me.'

Rorie sensed that Martin's affection was misplaced. She'd do anything all right – to get her next job. And she was currently playing the role of posh totty seeks rough botty.

'That's what so cool about Marty.' Victoria stroked his shaven head when they all went to the pub after rehearsals. 'He doesn't care about celebrity. I could be anyone and he'd still want me.'

Rorie wasn't sure, but for one second Martin cringed before he smiled, in a way that didn't reach his eyes. One thing Dette had always done was crack Martin up with her sense of humour. Victoria, it seemed so far, didn't have one.

'I think you will be brilliant,' Angelo had assured Rorie on the phone when she'd called to cancel for herself and Catriona, who was doing just about every other job Rorie couldn't. Including the lead role. It was worrying Rorie to think of someone who had frozen on her first lead night taking up a second one with such pressure attached over ten years later. But then, they hadn't any other option. 'I think it will be a great success,' he went on. 'I will even come to Surbiton, though already I hate the place.'

'If you do then you'd better be nice to Jude Mackenzie. He's promised to do the hair on the night for nothing. He's a real sweetie.'

'And I'm not?' Angelo was miffed. Rorie was his friend, not that queen's.

'You're my number-one sweetie, Angelo, always, and I'm sorry Cat and I can't make it for lunch tomorrow, or even in a fortnight, but we're tied to this.'

'What about the fidelity test? Were you not supposed to give results?'

'I think everyone's too busy to be unfaithful right now.'

When Helen and Dette arrived at Angelo's, Angelo sat down with them as two places were free. Helen regaled them all with tales of her horoscope surfing. 'I can't stop. Every day I find something more fascinating – I'd no idea there was so much in it.' She pulled out today's reading. Her face was flushed and her eyes had a glassy quality that made Angelo and Dette uncomfortable. 'Here. Look at this.'

You'll feel good about something you did at work today. It's more likely to be something behind the scenes that you got on with quietly, rather than a high-visibility task. You deserve all the success it brings.

'I hate to point this out to you, Helen, but it's a crock of shit.' Dette's lip curled.

'How can you say that?'

'Because we're both jobless. Without prospects, darling. How can we achieve success when we're not even in the workplace?'

'You're taking it too literally! It's our behind-the-scenes things we're succeeding at. That's the baby for you, and your move to Ireland. It means I might win the competition with George in a few weeks' time.'

'Yes, yes, I see,' Angelo said soothingly. He put a hand on Helen's arm and gave Dette a warning look.

'When the baby's born you could do its chart for me?' Dette's eyes met Angelo's. 'Maybe he'll have more luck than I had.'

'Don't talk about your life as if it's written off and don't talk about it being a boy – what if it's a girl?' Helen chastised her.

'I just know it's a boy.'

'Bollix. I thought all three of mine were boys.'

'Well, dare I say it Helen, until this point you weren't that in tune with yourself? Or into prophecy for that matter,' Dette observed.

'Not fair! Just because I have medical training doesn't mean I've lost the ability to deal with mystery.'

'Really? And have you solved the mystery of why your

husband is now living with your best friend?' Dette raised her eyebrows.

'They're welcome to each other.'

'They're not lovers, Helen,' Angelo and Dette both agreed. 'You're letting a situation develop that otherwise would never happen. By being stubborn.'

'And dancing with the man who should be my boyfriend.' Angelo raised his chin.

'Excuse me? George and I are dancing in the full knowledge and consent of his wife and we do nothing more than that.' But I wish we did. He hasn't come near me even though I've worn something new and sexy every week. Madeleina was wrong – he doesn't have feelings for me. If anything he seems to have less of them, is going through the motions. The passion's dwindling—'

'And as for you,' Dette pointed a finger at Angelo, 'you should be going out with a man who cuts hair, but you were too much of a snob.'

'Stop this! That man wore make-up, I don't date men with make-up.'

'He was only dolled up to impress. You know he's painting Catriona, don't you? He's done a great likeness so far, she tells me.'

Helen's ears picked up that Catriona was in touch with Dette. It used to be her and Rorie in touch all the time. It was hard not to have a confidante any more, and so far she couldn't trust anyone else in the same way she trusted Rorie. One thing she was holding on to was guilt that on her eighteenth birthday her daughter Bea had had the present of a father walking out and a measly horoscope chart.

'I'm sorry, I'm truly sorry. I meant it to be better than this,' she had said.

'Don't worry, Helen,' Bea rushed to assure her, 'you lost your dad and your husband in the one week. I know you've other things on your mind.'

Helen was amazed at the maturity Bea was showing. If it was a tactic it was working. She needed Bea's help to get the other two girls into line, and Bea seemed to know where everything was and what everyone should be doing on what days.

'I never realised your father did so much,' Helen had admitted one day, when she'd brought Kelly to the after-noon Tumble Tots and left her with a bunch of three-year-olds and taken Joyce to ballet with a class of six-year-olds.

'Well, it's good you do now. It'll be good for both of you eventually.' The note of hope in Bea's voice was impossible to miss. 'You're both still seeing the counsel-lor, aren't you?'

'Yes,' Helen lied. She'd missed the last three appoint-ments.

Euan had called her after the last absenteeism. 'You're supposed to be trying to make this work, Helen.'

'I thought you needed a little confessional time on your own.'

'For what reason?'

'You walked out on us.'

'No. You tried to walk out on me and I gave you what I've never given you before. The harder option.'

'So, you admit staying with Rorie is a soft one?'

'I'm staying with Rorie only until I can find a flat or we sort this out so I can come home again. The longer you don't go to counselling, the longer that will take.'

'Don't threaten me, Euan!'

'I'm not threatening.' His voice broke with all the effort it took him not to raise it. She was delighted on these occasions that she felt even less, was more numb. It made her win the arguments more easily. 'If you talk to Rorie you'll realise I'm sleeping on a futon. You know how much I hate futons. As soon as I find a suitable place I'll be delighted to move on.'

'So it takes three weeks to find a flat?'

'It does when you're trying to pay a big mortgage and support your family on a teacher's salary. You have to call the hospital. They need to see you before they can sign you off on sick pay, Helen. The chief executive told me it was only a formality, they want to give it to you.'

'I don't want to go in there ever again. I told you.'

'You're not being reasonable, Helen.' He didn't say he knew that if she didn't make an appearance soon they would look on it as a resignation. He was trying to remember all she was coping with. That was hard when he saw the payments for new ballroom-dancing clothes and shoes coming out of their joint account.

'You not being here makes me not reasonable. You come home and I'll go and stay somewhere else. The kids hate me.'

'They don't hate you. But they don't know you. This was all about you getting to know them, Helen. This needs to happen if we're to progress as a family.'

Another shrink phrase from the mouth of his new best friend Diane Henderson. Rorie had better watch out – Euan would move on there pretty soon. She hung up without saying goodbye because she was tired and because she knew the bed was waiting.

Kelly and Joyce followed her into the bedroom. 'Are you going to sleep again?'

'Yes.'

'But it's not night-time.'

Helen sighed, used what was left of her energy to pull the curtains. 'Now it is.'

The two little girls stood in the doorway. Then Kelly ran out and Joyce started to whimper. But Kelly came back with two books.

'Mammy, one for me, one for Joyce. At night-times you read us stories. Or Daddy does. Or Bea. At night-time you read to us, Mammy! Mammy! Mammy!'

The shout knocked something in Helen's skull. Something that needed knocking. She forced herself to turn on the bedside light. Dragged herself into a sitting position and pulled back the duvet. 'Come on, then. What have you brought?' I'm depriving them of their dad and their dreams by hiding under my own feelings.

After she'd finished reading, she pulled them close to her and gave them the kind of hug she'd never had as a child. And the tears pushed out more for all the soreness in her heart. She had to do something, couldn't fall apart like this in front of them. Weeks had gone on with her feeling sorry for herself, clinging to fantasies about a man who wasn't hers. She hopped out of bed and pulled back the curtains.

'Morning! It's morning. What do we have in the mornings?'

'Snap, crackle and pop, with the noise,' Kelly reminded her seriously. Joyce nodded. Joyce had taken to thumb sucking. She hadn't done that since she was a baby. Helen remembered it. The closeness, the whisper of baby breath against her skin. The link she'd broken in booting back to work at the earliest opportunity. You've read the psychology, Helen Larkin. If you sort yourself out now, they'll be sorted. If you don't do it soon, they're lost. You've already lost them a father. 'I think we should go to the park this afternoon.' Helen mustered enthusiasm, though the thought of it made her want to run back to bed.

Bea came home from tutorials to find the house empty. She panicked and rang her mother's mobile. Helen answered. 'Yes?'

'Where are you?'

'At the park, having ice-cream in the rain. Do you want to join us?'

For the first time in weeks Bea smiled. 'No, I think I'll pass on that pleasure and put on some hot food for when you get back.'

That night when the kids had gone to bed, Helen and Bea had talked.

'It's great you're making the effort.' Bea was all encouragement. 'They went to sleep quickly for the first time in ages.'

'Yes, they did, didn't they?' Helen had a note of I-did-that in her voice. Surprise at the idea she was capable of it.

'Now, what about Euan? Are you going to try to see him?'

'I know I'll have to. I know I'll have to see Rorie. I just have to wait until I have the strength to behave properly. I don't want to make things worse than they already are.' Helen was beginning to see she had played a large part in making things the way they were.

'There's nothing going on there, you know, between

Rorie and Euan.' Bea was blushing. She knew nothing directly of Euan's affair. Helen couldn't do that to her. The girl had enough to carry at the moment.

'I went to see Euan and Rorie yesterday. I hope you don't mind. I just couldn't be sure of what was happening. I had to talk to someone. They're still the same, Mum, honestly. They're just great friends. And they both love you. They wanted you to know that. And me, they wanted me to know they love me too. I needed to hear it.'

Well, they shouldn't make an eighteen-year-old girl become the messenger.

'Bea,' it sounded strangled, it sounded weak, 'you are my first best girl and I'm so proud of you and what you're doing.'

'Really? Really, Mum? It's not because there's no one else to listen to you?'

That hurt. But she could see where it had come from. She could see where a lot of things had come from lately.

'Yes. I'm delighted to see how you're growing up.'

'Ah,' Bea was wary, 'you mean because I haven't mentioned the modelling in ages, and I'm knuckling down to study.'

'I can't deny that impresses me. What impresses me more is your maturity in all of this. And what I'm most grateful for, most humbled by, is your sympathy. I know I don't deserve it. I know that I've given you an unnecessarily hard time. I can only apologise for that and say I gave it to myself. I don't know how to stop it. But I'm trying, Bea, I'm trying.'

'Will you try to meet Rorie on Tuesday for lunch, like you used to?'

The plea was so deep, so needful, she had to say yes.

*****

Now Rorie hadn't shown and Helen was knocking back a glass of wine with relief.

Dette watched her. 'You know you haven't spoken for a half-hour nearly?'

'No.'

'That's OK. I don't feel that chatty myself. I wasn't even going to come today, but Angelo said you were definitely here. I wanted to talk to you about something. I need to speak to you about Bea, Helen.'

'Oh, I know what you're going to say. She's not turned up for her modelling appointment. I think she's had a change of heart on all of that, and before you say anything, it's not me behind it. She came to the conclusion herself. I can't believe how well we're getting on of late. It's the best thing out of all this mess.'

Dette sighed. No that wasn't what I was going to say and now I can't find a way to say it. So I'll leave it for another day, like I seem to be leaving a lot of things. 'OK, you're right. That's what I wanted to know.'

'How're things with selling up, Dette?' Helen wanted to know. Angelo raised his eyebrows.

'Sorry, A-Lo,' Dette's pet name for him drove him mad so she continued to use it. 'Helen wasn't supposed to mention it.'

Helen shrugged apologetically.

'I didn't tell you because I'm not telling anyone. Mum and me are moving back to Ireland. We're selling up our places and buying a little one there. It's a fresh start, for me and the baby and her.'

'So you won't be coming here for lunch then?'

It was the first time Dette had realised it. 'I suppose not. Unless I meet a rich farmer and can afford to fly over every second Tuesday. Otherwise you're all welcome to Noelle's Café on Athbeg main street. Mixed grills and roast dinners and apple tart for dessert, anything else is exotic. Exotic is bad for you...' Dette drifted off, wondering how she would cope in small-town Ireland.

A fortnight later Helen had been the only one who could attend the first October lunch. Rorie and Catriona were busy with the play, and Dette was fitting in as many lunchtime viewings of her flat as she could. Helen decided she didn't want to come on her own. 'It'll feel too sad, Angelo. Sorry, see you in a fortnight. If anyone's around.' It looked like the Virgo Club had run its course. Angelo seemed to be the only one who knew what they were giving up. Fifteen years of food, laughter and friendship. All because they had decided to push their trust of each other further than it could ever go. Of course, they would have wound up there anyway as lives moved on to different things and places. But not so quickly and dramatically. And they would have remained friends and come for reunion lunches and invited him to their new homes. Now everyone, except Rorie who'd known him before the others, associated Angelo's Place with the dissolution of the Virgo Club and the ties that bound it. He wondered what he would do without his friends. Nothing came to mind. So he decided not to be there either when the window table was filled by four other diners on the first Tuesday of October. He put on his hat and coat and went to a gallery.

Angelo found himself in the National Portrait Gallery, staring at faces, wondering if they could supply him with some answers to his loneliness and isolation. And felt someone else stare at him. Jude Mackenzie, on his lunch hour. Before Angelo could speak, Jude turned to leave.

'Wait!' Angelo's shout startled even the portraits. Jude still moved away. 'Wait!' Angelo ran after him. Caught him in the corridor. Jude wasn't trying that hard to run. 'Look, Jude, I behave very badly. I am arrogant, I am a snob, I am also alone. I want to apologise to you. I will take you to lunch, if you will let me, whenever you like. We can talk. I will tell you what a nice man you really are. If I offend you once you may leave.'

Jude Mackenzie looked at the exit. Five minutes away four skinny bums were cramped onto a chaise longue waiting for his scissors to work their magic. By the time he got back after lunch there would be eight. That was too much, even for him. All this publicity was doing his back in. His scissors hand had pins and needles by the end of the day. But here was a Roman god looking to take him to lunch, in a place of his choice – and it would be an expensive one.

He took out his mobile.

'Sandra, get the girls on the couch a sandwich and tell them I'm out on an Italian job.'

Angelo smiled, for what seemed like the first time since forever.

41

They were sitting in Nobu doing what Jude called knob-spotting.

'Look at her. She thinks she owns the place because she does a daytime doctor drama. No one who's not on the dole, a hypochondriac or saddled with children even sees it.'

Angelo smiled again – he hadn't stopped since they'd arrived at a place that was going to set him back at least two hundred pounds for a meal that wouldn't amount to a quarter of his portions. But it was worth it. Jude Mackenzie made Angelo smile.

'And see him? He did an action film that was supposed to take on James Bond and it didn't even make a dent in Basildon Bond paper. Mind you, he is gay. Mind you, so is James Bond, don't you think, Angelo? More lobster? I think I'll have a martini as well, shaken not stirred.'

Of course Jude had ordered the most expensive thing on the menu, but he'd rewarded Angelo with one or two mouthfuls of it.

'So tell me about the foursome.'

'I am sorry – whatsome?'

'The Virgo girls. What's the deal with them? They've been coming to your place for yonks. No?'

'Yes.' Angelo stopped smiling. 'Not for much longer, I think.'

'Typical women! They fizzle out on things. Not like us fickle gays.'

'No, not right. I just think too much is coming between them.'

'Like what?'

'Like life. You don't need to know and they would not appreciate me telling you. Eat your criminal lobster. Stop being so curious.'

'Ah, I see. You think if you tell me you tell London.'

'Yes. Something like that.' Angelo watched a pair of world-class athletes eat world-class fish and chips. They must be out of season.

'Well, you're wrong. I'm in the hairdressing game because I know how to keep confidences, just as well as you do. Otherwise we'd both go out of our respective businesses.'

'I agree,' Angelo was smiling again, 'which is why I'm still not telling you.'

'Bitch.' Jude camped it up. 'I'll just have to torture you with no chance of a second date.'

'You think this is a date?'

'I don't know you from Adam, you took me to Nobu, I think this is a date.'

'Jude,' Angelo said gently, 'this is an apology. A big one, I admit. But you deserve it. I was terrible to you when you came to my restaurant.'

'Oh, don't worry about that. I hear you're horrible to all your customers, except the girls. I don't know why people bother coming back.'

'The food.' Angelo held up a parcel of clam and filo pastry to look at it before he put it into his mouth. 'Mine is not as fashionable and just as good. And the bill won't kill you.'

'Now, now, the host never moans about the price of things to the one he's wooing.'

Angelo shook his head.

By dessert they'd discovered mutual passions: art, history, travel, cinema, and with each passing mouthful Jude Mackenzie wondered if this could really be it. Angelo was wondering why he couldn't fancy this skinny man with no hair who dealt with everyone else's all day. He would be perfect if he was more handsome.

Just then Jude leaned across the table and fiddled with Angelo's fringe. Angelo sprang back.

'Steady on, darling, I just think this needs to go.'

'I am Italian. Italians are proud of their hair.'

'But the way yours is presented adds years. Come back to the office, darling. I'll do a lovely thing on you in Blow Job.'

'This is what your business is called?' Angelo laughed.

'Yes, and before you turn up that Roman nose again, let me tell you it's a name that got me acres of free editorial publicity. I didn't advertise once. Every gay man and follicly aware woman in the city wants an appointment. I'm offering you one for free.'

'No.'

'OK, I can see you need work.'

'I do not need it this badly.'

'Fine, fine, be snotty and unappreciative and alone all your life.'

'Please,' Angelo's shoulders sagged, 'don't be offended again. It will bankrupt me.'

'Oh, you!' Jude laughed. 'You made a joke, so at least I know now you have a sense of humour buried under all that arrogance.' Which makes you just about perfect. Oh, God, please let him think I am.

'I can't come now. I have to go back to my restaurant, close up for the afternoon, get ready for the evening.'

'Good, then come to my house for dinner and a proper decent haircut cos you need it sooner rather than later.'

'I have a very expensive barber, Jude.'

'Who doesn't know shit. I'll show you.'

'OK.' Angelo surprised himself. 'I will come.'

'Goody!' Jude lost all sense of judgement and distance and clapped like a child. 'Now I have to go and clear my salon of cranky customers.' The first one in the queue would have waited three hours by now. And Victoria was due in this afternoon. Best not to keep her wafting in the air – for such a beautiful woman she'd produce a very bad smell among clientele if kept waiting, which would gain him some column inches and lose him the *Three Sisters* hair-consultancy job. Jude weighed it up quickly and decided to hop it.

'See ya soon, Angelo, baby. Got to bounce.'

Before Angelo could stand up he was gone. He had to admit he felt a little deflated. He called the waiter over for the bill.

'Mr Mackenzie already covered it, sir.' The waiter minced in a way that showed he and Jude were well acquainted. 'He says to come over next week for something that could change your life. Here's his card.'

Angelo slipped it into his pocket. Life had just got interesting. It hadn't been interesting in so long.

42

Angelo hated admitting it to himself, but he'd been looking forward to this evening – even though he was still no
nearer to finding Jude physically attractive, he found he
wanted his company. He rang the doorbell five minutes
before he was due to arrive. He had wondered about
walking around for a while longer, but he knew Jude
would be keen to see him. He was arrogant, he was
Italian, of course he knew when someone was on to him.

Jude took two minutes to answer and when he did he
had a paintbrush in his hand.

'Sorry I kept you waiting, I was on a tricky bit. Come
up to the roof conservatory, that's where we are.'

We was Jude and a naked Catriona Morehampton, a
beautiful ripe fruit lying on a red velvet chaise, cerise silk
draped over her shoulders, covering her lower abdomen
and falling in painstakingly arranged folds to the floor.

'Darling!' Catriona beamed but did not move her eyes
or any other muscle. She was a born poser.

'*Bella*, you are heavenly.' Angelo sighed, 'I see. You

have time to be painted by this poof and no time to eat in my place.'

'Oh, darling!' Catriona sparkled. 'I'm not jilting you. I'm just dreadfully busy.'

'And dreadfully happy?'

'That too.'

'How is everything? How is George?'

Angelo said it in such a way that Jude's paintbrush paused. He'd been waiting for this night like a teenager and the last thing he needed was a hetero married rival. It was going to be hard enough to persuade the Roman god that he was the right cupid for him, and someone like Gorgeous George would haunt Angelo with his unassailability. Jude hadn't the looks, the physique, to remain aloof and wait for men to come to him. He was peddling like mad here, offering Angelo free haircuts and letting him see his wonderful home, put together over the years on nothing but a sense of style and an eye for a bargain. Years before he had become successful, he'd turned his little corner of Spitalfields into a period palace. When other people were throwing out what they thought was junk, he was filling up his old van with it and taking it to workshops to have fixed. Just like his old mum had before him, as a sideline from pawnbroking. He did all the painting, upholstery and fabrics himself. Now he wanted Angelo to make it all complete. Like no other man had. Like all the best and most successful obsessives, Jude Mackenzie fell hard and would be floored if this didn't work out. He wasn't stupid either, he could see Angelo was going to take his time coming into the net.

Catriona yawned.

'Oh, he's OK. He's not pleased I put twenty thousand

pounds of our money into *Fiasco*, but otherwise he's pretty good. Apart from that, we're getting on better than we ever did. I'm beginning to see how much I have. You know he's ballroom dancing instead of rugby now?'

'Yes, with Helen.'

'With Helen?' Jude hoped he hadn't said it aloud, but he had.

'Oh, don't worry, Jude, it's OK. We're all good friends, aren't we, Angelo?'

'Yes, you are.'

'Are you coming to the opening, darling?' Catriona seemed to be spending too much time with luvvies. 'Can't believe there's only two days to go. Rorie promises me if I go belly-up she'll get another person to play the lead. I'm just doing the first night, that's all. With Victoria there all eyes will be on her.'

'Of course I'm coming. Will George be there?'

Will George be there? Jude mimicked savagely, hidden from the two of them behind his canvas.

'Yes, I couldn't not have him there. Will you?'

'Yes, of course,'

'And so will I,' Jude couldn't resist saying.

'And so will he,' Catriona agreed. 'Jude's styling for us, lovely boy that he is. George is dancing in the afternoon with Helen at some competition and Magda will mind the kids for the day and night, while we're busy.'

Catriona didn't want to tell Angelo the full facts in front of Jude. But she made a mental note to call him and ask for advice on what to do when an au pair suddenly sees her potential husband slipping through her fingers. The woman hadn't worn a skirt more than four inches long for a fortnight. Catriona was too tied up with the show even to compete.

But she knew once the show was up and running she'd have to handle it.

Right now she was having a hard job handling all that needed to be done. The only reason she was lying on Jude's chaise longue was because it was the only place where she was required not to move a muscle. 'And, let's face it, it's good practice for when I flop in two nights' time. At least I won't be flopping nude. Doing this does my confidence good. You know the dream where you leave the house naked and don't realise until you turn round that your keys are on the hall table? At least when I have it, after my terrible reviews, I won't be too embarrassed.'

'Right, duck, that's us for today. Another couple of sessions should do it.' Jude interrupted Catriona's clearly nervous chatter. She was feigning resignation, but you could see she was scared. Too scared to eat by the looks of things – the weight was falling off her.

'Can I see?' Angelo stood to come behind the easel.

'No, you cannot. I'm not even letting Cat see it now it's at the crucial stage. We'll have an unveiling party once the big show is out of the way.'

'That would be lovely,' Catriona stretched to release her cramped muscles. But they didn't uncramp.

'Are you staying for dinner?' Jude asked her with legs crossed that she wouldn't.

'No darling, off to see my children. I'm trying to make sure they don't lose out too much now I'm rushed off my feet. I've said once this is over I won't be doing it again in a hurry.'

Jude and Angelo looked at one another. It was obvious how much she loved it. Weaning herself off showbiz would be hard for her. They hoped *Fiasco* found its feet.

Catriona and Rorie had a lot more riding on it than money. In Catriona's case, her entire self-esteem was wrapped up in the project.

'So,' Jude shut the door slowly, 'we're alone.'

'Yes, it appears we are.'

'Come down to the kitchen, then. I've made us a little food.'

Laid out on the table was a selection of Asian dishes (never serve an ethnic minority their own cuisine – they'll always have had better) and a pot of steamed rice stood on the stove. There was nothing fitted about Jude's kitchen – each cupboard had been hand picked and painted. 'There's nothing nice about naked wood. It's like sending your granny out without clothes.' A set of pots hung from a ceiling bar. The china was all individual pieces, but put together so it looked like a set. There was beer, far better with such food. Candles. Angelo was overwhelmed he'd gone to such trouble.

'Don't worry, I threw it all together after work,' Jude breezed. And for three hours before it. 'Let's eat and then let's cut and then let's drink.' And then let's see what happens.

After dinner Angelo tipped his head back into the kitchen sink and Jude washed his hair. He didn't just wash, he caressed. And then he massaged Angelo's scalp and then he cut.

And by the time he'd finished cutting, Angelo was in heaven and had forgotten that Jude was not handsome. All he could think about was what wonderful hands Jude had and what wonderful things they could do.

He stood up. 'My restaurant…'

'Don't tell me. You have to go and close up.' Jude was knackered from the effort he'd put in. If this didn't come off he had no idea what would. I mean, excuse me, but I'm on my feet all day with hair in my face and then I come home and do yours for twice as long as I'd devote to any paying client.

'Can I use your phone?' Angelo put his new head to one side. The cut was a George Clooney crop and it suited him far better than he was prepared to admit.

'Sure.' Jude put his head to the opposite side.

'Marco, can you close up for me? Keep the keys. I collect them tomorrow from your place. On the way home. I am out for the night.'

He put the phone down with one hand and took Jude Mackenzie's with the other.

And that was how a lifelong love affair began.

43

'We're so close to opening I can't eat!' Rorie was begging Euan.

'Look, one mouthful of my fish pie and you'll dive to the bottom of the sea for the next. Great haircut by the way.'

'Thanks.' Rorie touched the wisps that felt like feathers. Jude had cut it just that day because she had publicity shots to do tomorrow, as new director of *Your Latest Fiasco*.

'Why've you got all this long hair? You don't look like the sort who wants it.'

'What's that supposed to mean?'

'Well, you're more Butch Cassidy than Lady Chatterley, aren't ya?'

'Are you this rude to all your customers?'

Jude laughed. 'Yes, cos there's plenty more where they come from.'

'If you must know, I don't wear it short in case I turn out too much like my father. And I'm not butch, but you shouldn't say it like it's an insult.'

'It isn't. It's a great look. Some of my best mates are butch. I'm not thinking butch for you. I'm thinking feather-cutting, wisps, elfin. You got a pretty face under the mop. Did your dad have that?'

'No. But I look a lot like him. When he was around, that is, and he hasn't been around since the seventies.'

'Then you got nothing to worry about. I'm not going to give you sideburns.'

'OK,' Rorie sighed, 'do it. It's worth a try.'

She winced as the first lock fell. After every other snip, she got lighter and lighter. By the end, and Jude hadn't even started to do his trademark blow dry, she was just as he'd promised.

'It's lovely.' Rorie couldn't stop smiling,

'Lovely! Yuck, don't insult me. Come up with something better.'

'It makes me look ethereal, like a fairy.'

'You see?' Jude was smiling just as broadly.

'Are fairies allowed to wear Docs? I don't have any other kind of shoes.'

'If we can get sparkly ones,' Dette spoke for the first time, 'you might be allowed one pair. The rest are going the way of the charity shop. The students, of whom you just stopped being one, will be delighted.'

OK, so Rorie was mad at Dette for letting Martin go and for using John as a reason for pushing him away. But then, she'd never have been rid of John if it hadn't been for Dette, and Dette had also been there when Rorie came to her door, just before midnight, with the solici-

tor's letter. The letter that said John Edwards was looking
for an equal share of Rorie's home since he had occupied
it for fifteen years and paid half of the mortgage.

'He's not getting your doorbell, don't worry. I'll sort
that fucker out,' Dette promised. She was now six
months pregnant and ball-shaped. 'Enough worrying
about this when you've far more important things to
think of. Like what you're going to wear for your first-
night curtain call.'

'You mean you'll help me with that?'

'Course I'll help you, if it means upstaging that bitch
Hazlet.'

'You hate me for using her, don't you, Dette?'

'Well,' Dette sniffed, 'I didn't like it, but I love you
enough to know that without her you're a burnt offering.
And if it's launching you and Cat into proper theatre jobs
then I'll be delighted if her famous mug gets you column
inches.'

'I love you for this, Dette,' Rorie said softly.

'Delighted.' Pregnant, swollen ankles, three months to
go, don't need to stand on my feet all day shopping, but
delighted.

At first Rorie couldn't bear the pressure. Fourteen-hour
days revamping a lost cause like *Your Latest Fiasco*, dealing
with the dramas of Noël Coward, Catriona Morehampton
– recently promoted from understudy and crapping-
myself-as-lead-lady – Jonathan-this-could-ruin-my-career
Blake Thompson, and I-might-not-make-it-on-the-night
Victoria Hazlet, along with a suspicious-we-might-not-
get-paid crew, she crawled into bed and that was when
the despair caught up with her.

Rorie had to see it for what it was. She'd never kicked John out because doing so would have meant she was alone. Being alone was OK if you liked yourself. If you thought of yourself as unlovable it was worth avoiding at all costs. And Rorie had. So, in her own way, she'd used John as much as he'd used her. Another great reason for not getting out of bed.

The doorbell rang after a week of this schizophrenic behaviour, which was great in the outside world, shredded inside her own world. The problem with doorbells was they rang. The problem with doors was that people could get into your house through them. She wanted to stay in this lovely warm spot in her lovely warm bed that matched her own body and was as far away from John's old side as she could get. She wanted to own a potty. Even the loo was too far away for her to want to use it. Her bladder was full to bruising. The doorbell was now being rung without relief. Whoever it was was prepared to run the battery down waiting for her to answer it.

The shrilling began to affect her vision. Even under the duvet and all five pillows she still heard it. OK, she'd go to the loo and see if they went away before she got back.

Euan.

Of course, she knew at the time she shouldn't have let him in. But, of course, she did. It was good to have a friendly face inside her own territory. She hated the sight of her own so much. So she'd opened the door.

She'd known it was going to work when he went straight for the kettle to make them their strong-as-porter tea. He was not the sort to lean.

'One rule.' She had raised a finger. 'No bitching about Helen. No she-doesn't-understand-me conversations. No discussing your home life.'

'That's not one rule. That's three.'

'Same proviso – don't make me have to take sides.'

'Fair enough. I'll be off as soon as I find my own place anyway.' He looked worn out at the prospect of finding it and all that it meant.

And he was so fair enough that he kept the place sparkling for her. He was so fair enough he ran a bath for her every evening and left her in peace to watch whatever she wanted on telly while he corrected homework. He was so fair enough he never complained about the uncomfortable futon, had dinner on the table every night and a lunch box for her going out the door.

'You don't have to do all this, Euan.'

'I'm used to doing it. I do it for my wee girls. Just be my wee girl for a few weeks, please, until I know exactly why I've lost my family.'

He said it so honestly. He wasn't looking for sympathy – he just knew how to say how he felt without labouring the point. It was scary how little she thought of John now, and when she did think of him it was always with relief that he was gone. She almost felt guilty that life was so good.

When she'd gone shopping with Dette they'd both managed to steer clear of talking about relationships and the seduction test that now seemed to have dissolved in the face of the bigger test of keeping their individual lives on track and their collective friendship together.

'Thank God you called. I need somehow to get you all together for a makeover shoot. Don't tell me you won't do it, I'm giving you expert advice here, missy. Ducky paid me a whack for these pieces upfront. I need to deliver something.' Dette stuck out her bump just to add weight to her appeal.

'It could be they're finding excuses because none of us can handle being in the same room all together at the moment.' Rorie shrugged, lifted her coffee cup.

'True.' Dette lifted her herbal teacup. Life had certainly moved on from double espresso. 'But you'd have the most reason to be pissed off. I mean, I know how you feel about children growing up without fathers and also that I claimed your ex, however oily he was, might be my kid's dad. And you still ask me out clothes shopping.'

'I'll put it like this. You know about clothes and I admire the way you're squaring up to it, Dette. It's admirable. I just wish you'd let Martin help.'

'I get you, and I won't.' Dette nodded, 'OK. So now we've mentioned the taboos, what about you and Euan?'

'He's living in the spare room and he's getting his life together. That's Euan. I'm frighteningly busy and never think about it. There's nothing going on.' I'm glad I'm too busy to let the prospect tempt me. 'He's heartbroken about himself and Helen. Bea called round the other day, I think to check up on us. I don't know what Helen was saying to her. We tried to reassure her and to remind Helen we both still want to see her, when she stops thinking we take our clothes off every time we're together.'

'Helen's gone a bit mad,' Dette pushed a forkful of apple pie into her face, which was now rounder than Rorie had ever seen it. It suited her to look real instead of like a clothes hanger. 'I'm not sure I should tell you this, but Bea came to see me as well…'

*****

On the third mouthful of fish pie Rorie found her
appetite and realised she would do anything right now to
have an uncomplicated go at Euan Clarke. But it wasn't
going to happen. Their history was so tied up with Helen
and the girls it would never survive. Right now she was
grateful for his skills as a wife. It had been a long time
since anyone had looked after her. She needed it. He read
the script, read the changes, approved them, listened to
her woes and had suggestions that worked. When he had
no suggestions he just listened. He cheered her just as
they'd both cheered on Celtic. Come on, Rorie, you can
do this. Now get on with it. The right blend of arse-kicking
and hand-holding. His whole role in life, the thing he was
best at, was playing supportive partner. How Helen had
let him go was beyond her. What wasn't beyond her was
that she wanted him to stay forever. And the need to keep
that feeling under control was what made her not say just
how good the fish pie really was.

A play was opening on Saturday that could make or
break her career. And the frightening thing was she didn't
seem to mind half as much as she should. Euan taking
her mind off work was great, but what happened when he
left, as he had to? At least it wasn't likely to happen
before opening night. She and Catriona were booked into
a hotel as a treat and Euan was coming back to London.
He'd been determined to see the show.

'I've a feeling this is the start of great things for you,
Rorie.' Just as well someone thought that because the
actors certainly didn't. They were as nervous as anything.
A sniff of another gig would have Jonathan Blake

Thompson galloping. There'd been a piece in the *Guardian*. A delightful critic had written:

> Sensation or flop? One suspects with *Fiasco* that onomatopoeia is the order of the day. Nonetheless we'll all be there to see the delightful, multi-faceted Victoria Hazlet make her second London stage début in a single month. Though one suspects it's her close relationship to fresh-faced, first-time director Rorie Marks that makes her throw the lifebelt. Rumour has it Ms Hazlet has only one five-scene appearance for one night only. It's worth travelling to Surbiton (where is that?) to see her for sixty seconds. That, if nothing else, should prompt Surbitonites to pre-book. The arrival of unknown (but for a terrible role ten years ago on the West End) Catherine Morehampton as leading actress is a question in itself. Without Lavinia in the first-lady position one might be prompted to say of *Fiasco*, 'When it was bad, it was very, very bad; and when it was relaunched it was rotten.' We shall reserve judgement for opening night.

'Great.' Catriona took it the way she took everything nowadays – on the chin. 'Panned before we even open. At least expectations aren't great.'

Where the fight had come from, Rorie was not sure, but she was glad it was there. Because she knew something that the critic didn't – in rehearsal, when Catriona was good, she was very, very good. But first nights had a habit of freezing things up, even for seasoned players.

A plus was that the piece had caused the first night to

sell out, so everyone would be paid for at least a week, but Rorie still felt the hatchet between her shoulder blades. She looked at her ticket list. A personal allocation of three. One to Euan, one to Bea, one to Helen. Helen wouldn't want one. Helen would want to be as far away from here as possible. Rorie knew that she still had to offer. When Euan was safely back in his bedroom correcting fictitious homework so he could stay out of her way, she picked up the phone.

'Hi?'

'Hi, Bea, it's Rorie. I'm just ringing to invite you to the grand première.'

'Oh, yeah! This Saturday, isn't it?'

'Yes, sorry it's short notice. I just couldn't get round to it. I told Catriona I wanted to ask people myself and then forgot. You will come, will you?'

'Sure, I wouldn't miss it. Though I'm not coming to see Victoria Hazlet, I can tell you. She got Martin to jilt poor old Dette in her condition.'

'Yes, she's pretty terrible. But she's not when she's on stage. If she saves this show I'll marry the bitch myself.'

Bea laughed.

'Your mother, is she there?'

Bea stopped laughing. 'No, she's at ballroom dancing.'

'I've got a ticket for her.'

'I don't think she'll come, Rorie. It's not about you. She has the competition on Saturday. It's marked on the calendar. I don't think an earthquake would cause her to miss that.'

Bea looked at the calendar, thought absent-mindedly that there was no exact time written against it. She decided not to say anything to Helen, about going or about the invite. It was best not to let Helen know that Euan would be there, as Rorie's guest. 'How's Dad?'

'He's OK. He misses his family and he wants to be home with you but otherwise he's OK. I was half hoping he and Helen might—'

'Yeah, that would've been good, but if I suggest to Helen that she misses her dancing – you know how obsessive Mum is.'

Mum, Rorie noted. Things must be better there at least. She hung up. She knew for a fact that the dancing was happening in the afternoon, because George was coming straight to the play afterwards. Poor old Bea, having to play diplomat and lie like that.

This was all such a mess.

Despite all that was going on, despite all that could go on, Rorie felt curiously calm. The kind of calm that comes when you know there's not a damn thing you can do about anything, so you just go along with it.

Just going along with it was going to take her to a place she could never have imagined.

44

Catriona ran a cold bath after she got back from Jude's sitting. She was so tired she knew that if it was hot she'd fall asleep and drown. She was already going under with all the arrangements that still had to be made for *Fiasco*. When the kids were small she'd been this exhausted, and then, as now, she'd felt joy at what was happening with stabs of fear about how little she was equipped to deal with the task demanded of her. Her head swam, her limbs ached and her heart raced faster than a Grand National winner. The only reason she got to sleep each night was the great hot loving lump of George wrapping himself round her, like a warm barrier between her and the world's constant questions.

Noël Coward: 'Darling, do you really think Rorie's done the right job with the script? I felt the lines she cut, like they were peas falling off a plate were very convincing ones. What do you really, really think? I'll listen to you. You have the background. You have the belief in my words and ability. And you're wonderful in the role, darling, wonderful, wonderful. But I worry you might have too much on your shoulders.'

In other words: You're cheap as chips and therefore the only option available to us. 'Well, of course I do, darling, I believe Rorie has done what was required for the audience. You know the audience, darling – it needs things spelled out clearly and moved on quickly. Rorie's got the sense across without losing the sensibility. See it that way, know I value your work more than any other playwright since Wilde in this genre. And, yes, it's my first major role and it's not of my choosing. But I feel it was written for me, darling, and I know I'll do all I can with it. To make you proud. Dar-ling.'

Jonathan Blake Thompson: 'Darling, tell me honestly, I need to know – am I good-looking enough? The script calls for dashing. Do I dash enough?'

'You dash delightfully. You are the most beautiful male actor I have ever seen or known.' And the most like a peacock.

Don the lighting man: 'We're out of milk again.'

John the sound man: 'And biccies. Where are the biccies? You can't have tea without biccies.'

'You wait right there, gentlemen. They'll be with you in a tick.' Right after I get your wages out of my husband's bank account. Right after I ask you would you like me to provide the loo paper *and* wipe your arses.

And that was just one day. Each time it got unbearable she'd go to Rorie's office, which Rorie had handed over to her, and put her fingers down her throat to rid herself of the bile she'd had to swallow at their egotism, their shallowness, their vanity and self-centredness.

*****

'Was I really as bad as them once?' Catriona asked Rorie, who was going over the script for the umpteenth time trying to find more dead wood to cut away. She'd already removed a full half-hour and was looking for forty-five minutes.

'Yes.' Rorie smiled, pushed the script away from her and stretched.

'Well, I'm glad I failed in my chosen profession, because my new one has shown me what a worthless individual I once was.'

'Not worthless, highly talented, actually. But scared. You were as scared as they are and that made you as hard as they are to calm down and deal with. That's why I have a sneaking suspicion you will be fabulous on the first night.' Because this time you've nothing to lose and that's exactly what I'm not going to tell you. 'Now, would you like tea or coffee? I have secret biccies too, unavailable to Don and John.'

'Thanks, Rorie. You know how I'm treating it? Amateur dramatics. Please don't take that the wrong way, but Dette and I did everything on every play at school. And that's just what I'm doing now. No time to be nervous.'

Rorie stood. 'I think that's a great way to look at it.' My God, she might even pull it off if she can keep that attitude. 'I'm the one person who knows that your job is much harder than mine. All I have to do is direct this mess. You have to run it and then go out front and sell it. For that, and for the chance you've given me, I'm grateful. Always.'

Catriona smiled at the door through which Rorie had

left. In her heart she knew Rorie had done a great job, but it wasn't great enough to make the play great. For that they had needed more time, talent and money. Still, they'd all tried.

And tomorrow night, Catriona thought as she jumped out of her cold bath, if they got one helpful and not entirely dismissive review it would be successful in her eyes. She already had it in mind to ask Rorie to start work on smaller projects with her, to begin working for themselves. Her loyal friend, who had taken the blame for something she'd done, needed her help now more than ever.

'How's it with Euan, Rorie?' Catriona had asked her earlier in the day.

'It's great. It'd be better if he got back with Helen, but for now it's really nice having him around. Especially now, I mean. Once *Fiasco* fiascos I'll have to help him get sorted with a flat.'

Catriona nodded and handed over a chocolate biscuit. 'That's going to be hard for you.'

'Yeah, but it's harder not seeing him and Helen together.'

For once, Catriona Morehampton was sure Rorie Marks was lying. Lying to persuade herself. Life was tough for her.

45

Dette shuddered as she got into her cold bath. Cold because she hadn't paid the gas bill. She was saving all she could for Ireland.

Excuse me, this water's freezing. Can we get out please, hygiene freak?

'Sorry, Junior.' Dette shivered as she stepped out on to a wet bath mat. 'At least it'll stop me cooking up a storm. It has to be the hormones, this nesting. Yesterday I froze two lasagnes.'

And ate practically a whole other one. I was there, remember?

'I have to keep up my strength. You're due to be born on Christmas Day, for God's sake.'

But I'm not planning on bringing a football team with me. You're putting it away, Mum – I'll be your size, if you're not careful.

'Shut up, it's comfort food.'

Why?

'Not telling.'

You don't have to. You miss my dad.

'So what if I do? I can see him any time I like, if I buy a tabloid.'

You should tell him, Mum.

'We've been through this.'

You've been through this. I didn't get a say.

'Because you're forty years younger than me and you're not even here yet. You don't know what men are like.'

Hang on, I might be one.

'I have a fair idea you are, even though they couldn't tell from the scan. And if you are, you won't be that kind of man. You'll be the kind that treats women right. And tells them how the hell they can get rid of their little flat that no one seems to want.'

For weeks now Dette had been tidying up but no one had put in any offers.

'The market's definitely slowed down, Mrs Morgan.'

'Ms.'

'Sorry, we can't understand it. You've decorated it to such a high standard, and the area it's in means it should be sale agreed by now. We'll stay optimistic.'

'You'll keep actively seeking a buyer or I'm switching agents,' Dette had snapped. In the old days she wouldn't have thought twice about being rude to such a reptilian profession, but these days she'd had to call back and apologise.

'Thank you, Mrs Morgan.'

'Ms.'

'Yes, as I say, we're trying and we're optimistic.'

Dette tied a knot in her robe. The phone rang and she did what she thought was race to answer it, but Junior thought she was a healthier impression of a snail. If you lie on your back you'll look like one too.

'Listen, you little runt, giving your mother cheek and not even born yet—'

'Hello, Mrs Morgan?'

'Ms.'

'Ms Morgan, Scatell Estates here. We're pleased to tell you we've a buyer. They're not in a chain. They want to close asap, but after Christmas will do. We told them you were expecting. They saw it a couple of weeks ago but only decided now.'

'How much?'

'Full asking price.'

'Tell them I want ten grand more.'

'What?'

'If they want it that badly they'll pay.'

'OK, Ms Morgan.'

That's greedy, Junior warned.

'No. It's desperate. I need to get as much cash behind me as possible so I can spend as much time with you as possible. I don't want to make halves of myself like most single parents have to. Why d'you think I'm moving to Ireland? Your granny's buying the Irish place with me and I want to put in as much as her.'

Junior was silent.

The phone rang ten minutes later, just enough time for Dette to make a cup of tea, put the telly on and decide to phone Scatell's back to say she'd been stupid and yes, of course, she would take the offer.

It was Scatell's. 'Ms Morgan, you should be an estate agent. They said yes.'

'Good, ask them for twenty more.'

'*Ms* Morgan!'

'Only joking. Get the contracts out as quick as you can to my solicitor. I'll sign in blood if I have to.'

In Billericay Martin Hardiman put the phone down. 'I tell you what, I had to pay ten thousand bleeding pounds extra. She's some hard nut, Mum.'

Rosemary Hardiman laughed, then passed him a bacon butty and a beer. 'I know. I saw her in action at the boot sale. She's well able, son. Well done. You done the right thing.'

'The kid mightn't even be mine.'

'But there's a chance it is, son. And you were looking for a bit of a place of your own. Now you've got it and, from what I see in this brochure, she keeps it nice. Though you might need me to give a hand with redecorating.'

Martin looked at his mum's place, all bread twists and figurines and dried flowers and swirly carpets.

'No thanks, Mum. I got ideas of me own.' Like, leave it exactly as it is.

'Good, son. Now, can you tell me what exactly is your game going out with the Hollywood skirt?'

'Oh, come on, Mum, she's from New York and she ain't skirt. Vicky's brainy.'

'Brainy where you're not. That Dette was a nice girl, the nicest I seen you with.'

'Mum, she's no girl. She's only a few years younger than you.'

'Age don't come into it, son. She keeps herself as nice

as her place.' Rosemary held up the details. 'I can see that.'

'It's over, Mum. I'm doing this so she's got the cash to go wherever she needs to go, and if it's my baby I'll make sure it's looked after. But she don't want me any more than I want her. I got Vicky now and she's putting some big chances my way.'

Rosemary stood up, thumped her husband who was asleep on the couch with the newspaper over his face. 'Dave, you're the boy's dad. What've you got to say about this?'

'Nothing.'

'Nothing what?'

'Nothing you've not already said. I agree with your mum, son. Family's family. That girl's got your baby, you better do something about it.'

'I told you both, she don't want nothing to do with me. This is as much as I can do without getting the courts involved.'

Martin had seen the details when he was out property hunting. Without thinking he went straight up to the desk. 'I want this one.'

'Are you sure, sir? Wouldn't you like to see it?'

'Nah.'

'But you were looking for a Chelsea penthouse, sir. This is only a fraction of the price. And it's not Chelsea.'

'I want it. Here's the deposit. Get it for me or I go somewhere else.'

He'd been meaning to meet Vicky and go out to some poncy do with her. Instead he found himself at Liverpool

Street and on an overground train for Billericay. He needed to talk to his mum. To his surprise she'd hugged and kissed him when he told her. He'd hoped she'd talk him out of such a rash action as buying his ex's flat. Then his mobile had rung and Dette had been looking for an extra ten grand.

Even as he stumped up, before his mother even told him he was right to, he knew he was right to.

He knew it was over and he knew it was a pity, because he loved her. But Martin Hardiman wasn't a dummy. He knew when he wasn't wanted and when he had to move on. If moving on meant he went stratospheric and straight to Broadway, as Vicky was planning to help him do, it was all the better.

Take his mind off things.

46

Saturday morning – the day on which George and Helen would dance together in the Nutley and South Sheen Amateurs and *Your Latest Fiasco* would make its touring début in Surbiton – was bright, fresh and crisp.

Rorie got up and went straight to the loo where she thought she might vomit with nerves. Instead she stared helplessly into the mirror and wondered why she had ever thought she could do this. She came out and sat down to a full breakfast prepared by Euan and surprised herself by being able to eat it.

Dette got up, went straight to the loo and then to the bagel shop.

Catriona would have gone straight to the loo when she woke up but her husband and children trooped into the bedroom with a breakfast tray and a good-luck card. It rested on her full bladder, which she ignored, as she was

a mother practised in this art. Outside the door a seething
Magda listened to the sounds of a family wishing each
other good luck in everything. From under her pillow
Catriona pulled out an envelope. 'For George (and
Helen), good luck today, sorry I can't be there, your lov-
ing wife, Kate.'

Helen Larkin should have gone straight to the loo but her
old control issues were at play when she made up her bed
and laid her black satin dress with red corsage and patent
black shoes on it. Then she logged on to the computer
she'd now moved into her bedroom so that the kids and
Bea couldn't see what a complete addict she'd become to
checking her stars on Astro Info. She read the free stuff,
then clicked on 'in-depth' for her personal ten-dollars-a-
pop reading. She charged it to her own credit card
because Euan was becoming so stingy about things.
When the bills came in she didn't bother opening them.
Who needed to know what they owed? It was already
obvious. Visa never wrote loving letters. Like bad husbands they only wrote when they wanted money.

On 2 October Uranus goes retrograde at two
degrees Pisces, making all your outer planets in
retrograde motion. Some secrets are bound to be
revealed. If you follow the planets' advice today
you'll learn ways to learn more and you'll reap
rewards. The new moon tonight gives you the
opportunity to leap faithfully and land safely. By
the time of the lunar eclipse on the tenth you'll be
taking what you learned today and changing your
life with it.

The tenth. Helen checked her diary, once full to breaking point with times and initials and reminders. Now an empty white page stared up at her but for one date. '10 October: Dawn Principles workshop.' Shit, she'd never planned to go to it, and she had to now. The stars were dictating it.

> By the sun's eclipse at the month's end your house of self-knowledge and awareness has become a mansion. You are complete in a way you have never been before.

My God. She and George were going to be together forever and the symbol of this would be the dancing trophy on their mantelpiece, a symbol of when it had all began. Euan and Catriona would forgive them in time. The kids would get on famously together and have four parents instead of just two. It would be like a French film. She finally had to answer the pain in her bladder.

Her children didn't bring her a good-luck card. She'd kept low key about the competition because she didn't want them to know how much it meant to her. But Bea, Kelly and Joyce were waiting downstairs when she finally got there, with a bowl of Special K (she couldn't afford to eat – the dress was so fitted) and a black coffee.

'Mummy, it feels like you're getting married,' Kelly said, excited. Bea looked the other way. Thank God, because Helen thought of Euan and a register office and an Italian café, and all of a sudden she felt something she hadn't felt since he'd gone. Loss. Helen, quick, move, get through this. Go dancing. Once you and George have won there'll be no stopping you, you'll be together.

'Thanks for the help with my hair, Bea. I've got to go

over to Dette's now, for my make-up. I'll see you all there.
Bea, my car keys are on the table. Drive safely. Be good
for Bea, you two. I love you all.' That slipped out as she
was already halfway down the hall. She'd taken to saying
it as often as she could. It still wasn't often enough, but it
was better than never saying it at all. Still, she didn't want
to thaw too quickly – a quick thaw causes an avalanche.

'So,' Dette stood back from her and surveyed her
achievements, 'where is the grand event on?'

'Nutley and South Sheen Workingmen's Club. It's not
grand, but it's a start. Wish me well, love.'

'I wish you well, Helen.' Dette waved to her from the
door and closed it. 'I certainly wish you that.'

The arrangement was that George would pick up
Helen and Madeleina from Madeleina's place. Bea was
driving the kids to the venue. Magda was going too, she
had the loan of Lydia's car as she couldn't manage
Catriona's Volvo. Lydia would not be attending. George
had asked her not to. He might be more nervous in front
of his mother, he felt.

As usual Helen got there early and as usual George
was already there. Nutley and South Sheen Workingmen's Club. A bizarre venue for a ballroom event, considering that half the couples were all-female. Men who
danced in this style at this level were either scarce or
dead.

Madeleina answered the door on the second ring.
When she did so her face was flushed and she was busy
doing up her blouse. Helen felt the cold blade of jealousy
and forced herself, with her lifelong discipline, to hide it
with an unknowing smile.

'Hi there. You ready for the big day?' Madeleina was puzzling because she always seemed so glad to see Helen, even though Helen was always interrupting something. Did they really think they weren't obvious?

'I'm very nervous. How's George?'

'He's OK. He's just popped to the loo. I fixed his bow-tie and he helped me with the tight seams. I just hate tight seams, don't you? Mine wobble like a drunk if I don't get assistance.'

'Yes, I know what you mean.' And I hate you for being so in my face about the fact that he's willing to get physical with you and won't touch me.

'Helen!' He was wearing a dinner jacket. James Bond, long threatened, was definitely out of a job. 'You look absolutely gorgeous.'

'Likewise.' She spread her hands and twirled as if she'd been doing it all her life.

'You just do that like you've been doing it all your life, Helen.' Madeleina put her head to one side and smiled. 'What a pity we didn't meet years ago. You might have travelled the world with me, dancing.'

'Oh, I don't think so.'

'Well, not as a dancer, but as a showgirl you'd have been stunning. You've all the height, the legs and the moves.'

'Sadly not the breasts.' Helen's were practically taped together and the silk red-rose corsage held the dress fabric in a vice grip to keep them where they didn't want to be.

'The looks too, but Helen has a great job as a doctor. She's saved lives. I'm proud to know her,' George said quietly.

'So has show business.' Madeleina laughed.

Anyway, I'm not a doctor any more. I'm much more interested in dancing. 'You really think I look OK? I got Bea to do the hair and the make-up was Dette.'

'How is Dette?' George asked.

'Huge, but in denial of the fact that she's on ten dinners a day.'

'Shall we go?' Madeleina had swung on a white velvet coat and caught the top with a black-pearl brooch. Money had once been about.

'You really belong in a stately home,' Helen couldn't stop herself saying. 'You're such a lady, so beautiful.' I feel like a slattern in me satin and slingbacks.

'Ah, yes, and I'd have died young in one.' Madeleina smiled. 'They're boring places mostly, darling. And freezing. And the company is never very good. So inbred, the aristocracy.'

'She was once courted by a lord.' George put his hand on the small of Helen's back and guided her through the door. The dirty flirt. Imagine, he'd left his wife's bed, come straight to his mistress's and now he has his hands on me just before we take to the floor. I should care. I don't care. I'm happy.

'He used to send a car for me and when I got into it, there'd be all sorts of presents. Like this brooch.' Aha. 'That was one, wasn't it, George?'

'It was indeed.'

'Pity I wasn't in love with the man who gave it to me. Life would have been a whole lot easier.' Madeleina went off into her own thoughts.

They went for a spot of lunch, as was the plan, and Helen pushed Caesar salad around the plate. Madeleina polished off a burger and chips. George had steak.

'You're eating like Dette used to.' George smiled, pointed to her unfinished plate of rabbit food. 'Madeleina and I are right carnivores, always have been, since we were little. We'd polish off half a cow between us, wouldn't we?'

'We certainly would, George.'

'You've known each other since childhood, then?' Helen fished.

They looked at each other.

'We certainly have.'

'When did you meet? Was it at the stately home?'

'No, I never got an invitation.' George grinned. 'Let's just put it this way. I was always too young for Madeleina and she never took me seriously.'

'I did! But I was so busy being glamorous. It takes a lot of work, doesn't it, Helen?' She winked, and Helen flushed to be included in such a statement. For a second she felt as beautiful as Madeleina. 'I was only ever good at two things, loving and dancing. They both require you to look your best whatever the circumstances. That's the truth. I spent too many hours of my life putting my face on and now I've only got a little of it left I have to work harder at it.'

'You'll always be beautiful, Madeleina, always.' George covered his eyes with his hands, but there was no mistaking the love in his voice.

'Thank you, darling.'

They were made for one another. Helen was in the way. Bloody horoscopes. There was no truth in them. Just then Madeleina hopped up. 'OK, darlings, you need a little time alone to say what you have to say to each other.

Work up the bond. I'm going to sit over there with my coffee and leave you in peace.' And she was gone.

'You know, Helen, I never saw you looking as beautiful as you do now. Your dress is so – becoming.'

A word that had gone out with chivalry. But it fitted the man George was perfectly.

'Thanks, George. It's a good job this is a round table because you belong at one.'

'Thank you, good lady.' He rose to the occasion and offered her his arm. 'Now, shall we dance?'

The competition was an afternoon event because the competitors didn't last well past nine o'clock at night. If ballroom dancing was enjoying a resurgence among the young it was only the old who took it seriously enough to compete in it. There were a few middle-aged couples, one or two young sprightlies, as Edith Webber, Helen's octogenarian friend and occasional class partner, called them.

George and Helen stood out. They were elegant. The other younger couples were all sequins, blond streaks and outlandish make-up, and that was just the boys, their tans as fluorescent as their outfits.

'I'm glad Madeleina told us to stick to black,' Helen whispered. She couldn't say much else because she lost her breath when he put his arm round her waist. It wasn't that he hadn't done it a lot of times before, it was that everyone was watching. It was like they were together. If it weren't for the fact that his children were waving frantically at him and his au pair was wearing what could only be described as an indecency (she was showing more cleavage than Helen), she had him all to herself. Then there was Madeleina. Thank you, Madeleina, I'll be as good to him as you were. When you finally feck off and stop getting him to straighten your tights.

Her own kids were at a table with Dette, who was watching her with arms folded over her huge bump. Dette hadn't been invited. She'd turned up as a surprise. She was sitting beside Madeleina with raised eyebrows. How would Helen explain that she'd never advised Catriona that Audrey Hepburn, who Dette had seen having lunch with George all those months ago, was their dance instructor? At the end of the day Dette was Catriona's best friend.

It was a question she'd have to leave for later. Right now, the competition was on and she was feeling, as always, competitive. George, as always, was under-confident.

'God, I feel like I've got stones in my shoes. I do hope I'm up to this, Helen.'

'George, wherever you lead I'll follow.'

When the music started, she didn't even have to try, she was there. It was a waltz, not their favourite, but she floated like a feather. George was tighter in himself. 'Everyone's watching us.'

'Everyone's watching you because you look divine and dance divinely. Love it, George. You're rarely in the spotlight and the same goes for me. All our lives we've worked hard. You got me into this dancing caper, now do your stuff.'

The shoulders went back immediately, his head went up and he did what George Morehampton had spent a lifetime not doing, he let go.

The judges tapped each couple on the shoulder when they should leave the floor. They didn't ask George and

Helen to go until there were only three couples remaining for the waltz and the rumba. But the cha-cha was a disaster, they were bumped off after only sixty seconds. If they were going to get any kind of placing they'd have to put it all into the tango.

During the five-minute interval George took it upon himself to apologise. 'So sorry, Helen. I'm like Pinocchio out there. You were great. I feel I've let you down.'

'Nonsense!'

'I agree,' Madeleina had come up behind them. 'You were doing very well out there, George darling, and your best dance is last. Give it all you've got and you'll still get medals.'

'And what about getting to the Blackpool Tower Ballroom for the Excuse Me Amateur Finals?' Maybe it was the adrenaline, but Helen couldn't help leaking out her secret fantasy. They were this coming January and she knew if they were in the top three couples they'd get a spot – and a chance to spend an entire weekend together.

George was silent, staring at the dance floor, psyching himself up. Helen went on tiptoe – there weren't many men she had to do that for – to whisper into his ear, 'So. What are you thinking about?'

'I want us to give this our best, Helen. Let's give this our best, shall we? For—'

'Us?' She said it for him as if she was reading a script.

'Well, yes, for us, but also for our kids. They're all watching. Let's show them what their mum and dad are capable of.'

Edith Webber was chatting to Magda, who was nodding politely and not taking her eyes off George. Madeleina wasn't taking her eyes off George. Dette wasn't taking her eyes off Helen. Neither was Bea, and the kids were all watching both of them, hopping up and down with excitement.

That wasn't what he had been supposed to say, but Helen figured he was surrounded by those would report back to Mummy. This wasn't the time or the place.

La-dah-dah-dah-dah!

They moved like soldiers to a beat. Rhythmic, disciplined, restrained. They knew from the first few steps and didn't even watch anyone else, just each other. Everyone, even the shabby little venue, disappeared. For five minutes Helen Larkin was sure that George Morehampton thought of no one and nothing but her and their dance.

When the music ended they were alone. There was a few seconds of complete silence. Then someone clapped, and there was a roar.

Helen looked at him. 'I love you,' she whispered.

He was looking at Madeleina. 'I always wanted to do that for her, Helen. Thanks for making it possible.'

If he'd heard he'd pretended not to.

At the awards ceremony they got a plastic-and-gold-plated ballroom-dancing trophy each, with the words 'Third Placed Couple. N and SS Amateur Circuit. 2003'.

Dette, Bea, the kids, Madeleina, even Magda were hoarse from cheering.

George shifted his trophy under his arm.

'Do I need to say it again? What I said just now?'

'Helen, I'm a bit overwhelmed at the moment. It's the first trophy I ever won. Remember I told you my dad wouldn't let me compete?'

'Yes, it's mine too. I want to talk to you, George. I

want our trophies to sit side by side on a mantel forever. I—'

'In that case I really need to talk to you. Right now.' He marched her outside.

This is it, she kept thinking. This is when we really begin.

They were beside a bottle bank in the car park. It wasn't the most romantic location and it was freezing, but it would do.

Then he started talking and almost immediately she stopped wanting to listen, because the stars were wrong for that day.

'Look, you're very attractive, Helen, and I find you irresistible – well, almost.'

'Thanks very much.'

'What I mean is, I won't cheat on my wife. I watched my mother tortured by my father's infidelity and I swore never to behave like that.'

'Oh come on! What about Madeleina?'

'What about Madeleina?'

'It's obvious you love her. It's obvious you've a history together. The only reason you're not with her is she won't let you.'

'Helen.' George was white in the face. 'I think you should just leave well enough alone.'

'I will. I'm offering to do what she won't. Look, I know what I said just now about the trophies and I'm sorry. I got carried away. I've got a much more practical proposition. I'm a practical person like you, George, you know that. I'm offering to be your mistress with a single string attached. We should dance together all the time and go to Blackpool every year. We'll get better and better. I know you have feelings for me, George. Catriona need never know.'

'Helen, you're making an exhibition of yourself. Please,' he held up his hands, 'stop. I don't want to have to end our friendship on a sour note. You're my wife's good friend. We'll find it difficult to carry on seeing each other if you continue to pester me.'

'Pester you?'

'Yes. I have enough trouble keeping my au pair's hands off me without having to tackle you as well. I don't deny you're someone I felt drawn to, but I know that will pass and that you don't really love me.'

'How can you say so? I should be the judge of that.'

'If I may say so, Helen, you're not in a position to judge anything. I'm of the opinion you're letting something of great value go from your life.'

'And what might that be?'

'Euan, your kids, your job where you do such wonderful work.'

'How dare you? How dare you preach to me? You're a cheat yourself! You keep Madeleina, and you've obviously got an au pair who's been at your underpants more than once.'

'Helen, please, stop now. You're going to regret you've said all this, truly. Let me tell you the only reason we're still dancing. Your husband thought you needed to continue with it to lift you out of this depression.'

'Yes, Helen,' Dette appeared. 'It's time we went now, before you make any more of a fool of yourself. Bea took the kids home. You and I are going for a big walk.'

And the pregnant one led away the dazed one, who was still carrying a naff trophy.

47

Dette took her straight to the Tube and straight back to Angelo's. 'First of all, congratulations on a fine achievement. You looked stunning out there. Second of all, what the fuck did you think you were playing at? For a start he's Catriona's husband. For another thing you ought to know how it feels. Do you remember what happened here in August? How hurt you were?'

Helen shook her head. 'August was such a long time ago.'

'Well, it happened, and I know that Catriona's far from perfect but the last thing you need to do is make your friend suffer like you've suffered. You know what, Helen? I was the one back then who told you to kick Euan out. Now let me be the one to tell you that if you don't get him back, you're a fool.'

'How can you say that after what he did to me?'

'Because,' Dette rubbed Junior, who was leaping about with all the excitement, 'I now know that what he did was hold you together. Without him you're a mess. A fanciful, delusional, disorganised, hopeless, dangerous, helpless mess. Now, I'm your friend and that's why I'm advising you. You're blowing it big time. Your husband is in Surbiton right now cleaning up a theatre for your best friend where her play is going on in four hours' time. You are here, in a fabulous dress by the way, drinking coffee with me and I am telling you that you are out of control. Your dad died and you did nothing, Helen. You walked out on a career you had devoted your life to building and you're doing nothing. Your husband left and you did nothing. Your mother is sick and you're doing nothing. Your daughters—'

'I get the picture.' Helen held up her hand. 'He was unfaithful. That's how this all started. He was—'

'Helen! My husband shagged a different bird every week, excuse my language,' Dette addressed her belly, 'and I managed to forgive him ninety-nine times out of one hundred. I took it ninety-nine times before the hundredth taught me. Your man slipped up once in all the years you ignored him in favour of playing doctors and nurses. He's a great guy and he messed up bad. You're messing up even worse. You don't see what's under your nose. There are people who need you, Helen. One of those people is Rorie. She needs you tonight and instead she has your husband selling programmes and cleaning stalls when you should be there. Another of those people is your eighteen-year-old daughter trying to act thirty-eight so she can give you a sister, when you already have one of those back home in Ireland that you never try to see. Do you know what Rorie and me would do for a sister? You and Catriona suck. You get the good husbands and the sisters and the jobs and the everything, and you moan, groan, moan when it all doesn't go your way. Well, I'm sick of it. I have my little baby in here and I think I won the lottery. And as for Rorie! You accuse her of something she wasn't guilty of and send your man running to the one place he shouldn't be. Her flat. She loves him, Helen, and you're rubbing her nose in it because she can never have him. She can never have him because she'll never take him from you. You should be in Surbiton, Helen. Instead, he is.'

'You forget something, Dette. I wasn't invited. Even Bea was invited before me.'

'It was an oversight. Definitely. Rorie's not a grudge-bearer.'

'But she doesn't want me there. It's too awkward for her. We haven't spoken properly for ages.'

'It might be awkward for her, she might not have spoken to you properly for ages, but she still would want you there.'

Angelo came over to them.

'OK,' they both looked at him, then at each other. 'Who did you fall in love with, Mr Happy?'

Over more cappuccino they discussed the play in general terms. Angelo was doing the after-party food for nothing. He was driving down at five o'clock. It was a quarter to now. Helen felt she wanted to cry. Dette was going with him to eat all the food on the way down then fix make-up if need be. 'I'm actually excited to be going, can you believe it? I used to be so snobby about what I went to. Now I'd go to a karaoke night in the pub if they didn't all smoke in them. Disgusting.'

Helen and Angelo raised eyebrows. Hell knows no hypocrisy like a reformed character.

'I understand you don't entirely accept the new me,' Dette said.

'Oh, you just want to pretend your life has become deep and meaningful. You're still preoccupied with appearances,' Helen snickered.

'Stop it. I'm not. I've gone all spiritual now I'm with child.'

'Maybe so, but I never met a woman with an overnight bag packed three months in advance in case she goes early.'

'That's not vanity, that's good planning.'

'Dette, I saw what's in it. What's Clinique body scrub, L'Occitane lavender shower gel and night-blue nail varnish going to do for you when you're in labour? And that nightdress! It's pornographic, not for a woman who has recently borne a child. Do you know how much blood you're going to pass?'

'Helen, stop it! I need only know so much. I'm not good with blood.'

'Well, then, you're in for a spot of confrontation therapy.'

'Catriona's giving me a homeopathic labour kit and some essential oils to help the healing process.'

'You're better off booking an epidural.'

'Typical doctor. Stand on the side of intervention before it's even begun.'

'You forget I've done this three times myself.'

'You didn't have an epidural.'

'I gave birth in hours each time, Dette, and I'm one of the lucky ones. The only reason I didn't have an epidural was because there wasn't time. You're tiny and you're forty.'

'Thirty-five.' You're right, I haven't changed that much. 'Now, can we get back to our original topic for discussion? Why are we sitting here when we should be in Surbiton?'

Put like that, Helen knew it made sense. The part of her that would have been delighted to ignore what night this was knew she had to rise above – oh, God, she was going to have to see George again. Right now she never wanted to again.

Dette's mobile rang. She held it up to Helen and Angelo before answering. Martin's name was flashing. 'Hello, spawn of the devil?' she began.

Five minutes later Dette hung up.

'Right, we're all going to Surbiton. And, Angelo, your *new boyfriend* insists you bring extra food for some dinner before it. It seems there's been a few mishaps.'

48

'Let's enjoy this, Cat.' Rorie and Catriona were in the foyer standing on either side of a promotional poster featuring Victoria Hazlet. Two hours earlier, they'd had the news they'd both dreaded. She wasn't coming. She had a sore throat. Her agent had phoned and hung up immediately. They'd tried to get hold of Martin, but he wasn't available on his mobile. He must be with her. Bastard.

'We both know *Fiasco*'s not all it could be, Catriona,' Rorie said as they took down the poster. 'Let's enjoy it for all that it's taught us.'

'Why the philosophy of resignation? It's going to be fantastic!'

'It's never going to be fantastic. We both know something big is missing. If we'd been on it from the start it might have been fantastic. What we've done, you and I, is make it not as awful as it was. It might even be a bit good. But it will be a miracle if we make it past Surbiton.'

'You could have told me that when I was booking the other five weeks of venues!'

'I'm sorry, I didn't want you to have to carry the weight of that – and who knows? Maybe Victoria Dried Brisket will turn up and go on and then we can rely on that to do it for us for five weeks of advance bookings. But she's not here, and she's not coming and, like I say, there's something big missing anyway—'

'There certainly is,' Milly, the Surbiton theatre manager, burst in. 'And I can tell you right now that it's your cheque for booking the theatre.'

'What? We give it to you out of takings – we agreed that.' Catriona was bristling. She and Milly had hated one another on sight, ever since first thing that morning when Milly had tried to send her out for coffee. 'Excuse me, but isn't it supposed to be you who supplies that? I've a small task of my own here, to go on in the leading role tonight, as well as do the job you're supposed to be doing in getting backstage organised.'

'Consider it unagreed, if your main attraction is pulling out and you're left with this.' Milly eyed Catriona. 'We want money upfront.'

'That's four thousand pounds,' Catriona breathed.

'Catriona.' Rorie was back to using her full name. This must be serious.

'We'll have to close,' Catriona said it for her.

'We don't close. The show goes on. Shows always go on. OK, the show might have to close – if all we have is you to offer, it'll be like throwing you to the lions.'

'Thanks very much. We did it to save money, remember? We never thought Victoria would do this to us. The spotlight was supposed to be on her for tonight. I was just filling in the gaps.'

'Catriona,' Rorie was now hissing, turning her gaze

right on her. 'Put on the dress Victoria was supposed to wear. You'll look gorgeous in it.'

'It'll be too small.'

'It's a flapper, it flaps. And you'll fill it nicely. Do it. The other one looks a sack on you, which is what you'll get if you don't pull this off for me. If we haven't got Hollywood we have to have the brightest new, or almost new, star in the West End, or almost West End.'

'Rorie, I don't think I can take this pressure. It was bad enough—'

At that precise moment Martin Hardiman walked in with Jude Mackenzie. 'Wotcha! I thought I'd come to support you on opening night.'

'Thanks, because your girlfriend hasn't,' Catriona snapped.

'Cat,' Rorie warned.

'So it's back to Cat now, is it? It's not you that's got to go out there and make a fool of yourself! They're expecting a Hollywood star on stage and they'll get me. I hope they don't bother to bring eggs and the critics. They'll savage me again. I don't know if I can.'

'Now, now.' It wasn't Rorie who spoke, it was Jude. 'Calm down, love. Uncle Jude's here. Put your head in that sink, if you please, and let's start off with a nice, calming head massage and then I'll give you a twenties set. Martin, get on the phone to your current girlfriend and tell her to get her arse down here. Then get on the phone to your ex-girlfriend and tell her to get her arse down here to do her best mate's make-up. And, Martin,' as he headed for the door, 'make sure you contact my Angelo and get him to bring down everybody's dinner. We're all in need of a little solace.'

'*My* Angelo?' Catriona and Rorie said together.

'And George,' Catriona said as Jude led her away, 'somebody phone George and get him down here to me straightaway. Tell him to bring his chequebook and give that bitch four thousand pounds. He's dancing, ask him how he did. I need my husband. And a cup of tea, a cup of Rorie-strength tea. And the script. I've got three hours to get myself ready.'

'No problem, darling.' Rorie kissed Catriona's forehead just before Jude poured water on it. 'Now, everyone, not a word to anyone outside. I don't want anyone, especially Jonathan Bad Underpants, knowing Victoria's out of it.'

Martin Hardiman went to the gents'. It was the one place he knew he could make calls in peace.

'Hellooo?'

'Vicky? It's Martin.'

'Marty! Are you coming over?'

'No. I'm in Surbiton.'

'Oh. Sorry I didn't make it. I was kind of wrapped up in something else.'

'That's no problem, love. I understand.'

'Really? I'm glad – there's so much pressure on me, Marty. I don't need pressure right now. I need understanding. Everything's so—'

'I understand. I understand that if you're not here before curtain up it's curtains for you and me.'

He hung up. She was still hot for him. He hoped it paid off enough for her to get herself down to this outpost in that time.

He called Dette.

'Hello, spawn of the devil! Met any more horny bitches lately?'

He smiled. She hadn't wiped his number off her phone, then. 'Hiya, Dette, you busy?'

'Busy is right. Always too busy to speak to you.'

'Listen, your mate Cat's got stage fright. Vicky pulled out.'

'Which was more than you did,' Dette said.

'She needs—' Martin was figuring out, it's mine, the kid's mine. 'I need, what?'

'I'm already on my way. Helen's coming with me.'

'Listen, Dette—'

'Save it, shithead, I'm not interested.'

'You were just as guilty.'

'True,' she said, as if it had just occurred to her, 'so I guess I'll have to be friendly to you when I see you. I'll bury the hatchet on my way. Now, get off my phone. I'm trying to get out the door. We're at Angelo's and he'll drive us.'

Martin looked into the mirror and said one word to himself. 'Pillock.'

George was finding it hard to hear Martin over the noise of the children. 'Sorry, Martin, I'm just dropping them home and then I'll be straight on my way. Tell Catriona I'll see her as soon as I can.'

'You won't see her, George, unless you're in the audience. She's going on without Victoria tonight, maybe, and she's panicking. She also needs four thousand quid to pay for something. Anyway, she's—'

'What? My God, did I hear that right? Sorry? I'll have to call you back. Zoë! Sit—'

George dropped the kids off with Magda. Lara took his trophy straight to her bedroom where she was going to keep it forever, she said. He started to change out of his dinner jacket, then thought better of it. He'd change just the shirt, let his wife see him dressed up smartly.

He was out the door again in fifteen minutes. A speed-limit breaking half an hour later he was on the M25 when the phone rang. It was Magda. 'Sorry to tell you this. Lara's not well at all.'

'Can I speak to her?'

'She's lying down, ill. You ought to think about coming back.'

'If I come back now I'll miss curtain up.'

'If it was my daughter—'

'OK, OK.'

He dialled Martin's number since.

'You on your way, then? Your missus is peppering here.'

'I'm sorry, Martin. One of our children is ill.'

'Jesus Christ – which hospital?'

'No, not that ill, but not well. I'm going home now to see her. Listen, Martin, carefully. Tell her I'm there, but I'm going to be too late to come to her before curtain up. Tell her I love her madly and I'm proud of her. Do not tell her Lara is ill. Tell her that I need to take care of some urgent business and I'll be right down.'

*****

'Business? What business is more important than me being in a bloody play I haven't had time to rehearse properly? Where's your girlfriend?' Catriona was hopping so much that Jude had to smack her shoulders.

'If you want to turn out looking like the Jackson Five that's up to you, but we need twenties here, not seventies – so sit still!'

'Look.' Martin caught Catriona's frightened eyes in the mirror. Most of the bulbs round it had blown, probably the static from Catriona. 'Vicky's coming and, believe me, so is George. He got held up, that's all.'

'With Helen, at the dancing?

'No. She's on her way down here with—'

The door burst open. Helen and Dette came in. Dette went straight to Catriona, gave her a hug that six months ago would have made her sick and now threatened to expel Junior from the womb.

'I can't believe it. This is just like *The Elves* – remember, Cat? A rotten play by a rotten writer and you were its saving grace. Now you're doing it all again and I'm here to watch. Hiya, shitface,' she said to Martin, then turned back to Catriona. 'Now, you're going to do it, you're going to do this the way you always did everything at school. Brilliantly. Without trying. By the way, your hubby won a horrible trophy with Ms Larkin over there so let's make sure you bring home a prize this evening too, OK? We want it to be a starry night in the Morehampton calendar.'

In this way Dette did what Rorie could never have done. She tapped into the past of Cat Nowdy and brought it bang up to date with the present. Remember your mum and dad are out there, and I'm out there, and

George will be out there and we're all thinking the same thing – how amazing you are.

Helen was outside, looking for Rorie, looking for something to do, when she bumped into Euan.

'Hello – you look amazing. How did it go?' He asked her.

He'd remembered. 'I won a horrible trophy.'

'That's great. You always win something. I never won a trophy.'

'What's in the bag?' She pointed to the one he was carrying.

'Sandwiches. I thought Rorie might be hungry.'

There was a silence.

'She'll be glad to see you, Helen. It's been tough on her, this job. She's really held it together but she's scared out of her mind.'

'She won't need sandwiches. Angelo's brought down a spread. He's unloading it in the green room. I thought I'd go and give him a hand. You know he's going out with Jude now?'

'Oh, good.' At least one relationship had formed successfully out of all the messing around that had been going on.

'Euan, do you think we could take those sandwiches and have a talk somewhere, if we're not needed?'

'We're not needed. Let's do that.'

They didn't eat them. It was a long, painful conversation and both of them cried. He said he could never tell her who it was and she said, now, she had finally understood why.

She said she'd like to try again. That was when he said, 'Maybe. I don't know at the moment. I'm still figuring a lot of stuff out, Helen. I let myself fade into the background and, to be honest, I think your career was the excuse. I just never knew what I wanted to do with myself.'

'Do you love me?'

'Yes. I love you and I love our kids. I just don't love who I ended up being. We need to take time, more time. I need that.'

She told him she understood.

'What happened, Helen? Why the change of heart?'

'Nothing.' Nothing had happened.

When the curtain went up Helen was sitting in the seat George was supposed to be in. She'd wished Rorie a formal good luck – and wished, too, she was capable of doing what she wanted to do, hugging her like Dette had hugged Catriona, but she didn't want to cry all over her best friend's big night. She would tell Rorie soon how much she meant to her.

Back home on Campden Hill Road, George Morehampton steamed into the house.

'Where's Lara?' he asked Magda. 'Is she OK?'

'Lara is OK now. Lydia took her and the other children for a treat. I tell Lydia I am a little bit sick. So she take the children.'

It was then George noticed that Magda was dressed in a peacock blue full-length backless evening frock, a little dressy for babysitting.

'You like my dress?' Magda twirled and raised a hand
to her hair. It had been put up beautifully, the right combination of soft tendrils and height. A real Jude job – no
hairdresser round the corner had done that.

'Lovely. Are you going anywhere nice?'

'No. Here I am going. I have made dinner for you,
George.'

'Magda, why have you made dinner for me? Why has
my mother got the—'

'Come, George, our dinner waits. I am waiting to eat
with you, George. Lara is OK, just a little bit sick. She is
with your mother and the other children. For a treat. I
have laid the table, George, all the crystal and china, and
I do it like it should be done. If you live with me, you live
like this always.'

'Magda.'

'Ssh,' she put a finger to his lips, 'I have poured
brandy for you, to relax after dancing with that horrible
lady and all that you have to do. It is so difficult for you
with this wife of yours. She never pays you attention—'

'Magda, I have two words and I am going to say them
quietly, and then you are going to go upstairs and pack
your things and be gone by the time I come home. You
are fired. Sorry, that's three. Here's another three. Get
out of my house. Sorry, that's five. I'm just a bit angry,
that's all. I am missing my wife's stage début. Sorry, that's
a lot more than five words. Two more. Get out. One
more. Now.'

George waited in the car, shaking, until Magda came
out of the house. She was shaking too, and crying.

'Get in. I'll drive you to Mother's.'

He took her round the corner and rang the bell. Lydia

answered. 'One delivery for you, and I'm here to pick up my kids.'

'George, I—'

'I don't want to hear it. You knew what this madam was up to, and you should be one yourself. I just want the kids and we'll save the scene until later.'

He took them all home and they watched a video together. George drank the brandy and phoned Martin again. 'Tell her, afterwards, that I love her madly and I'm sorry, but I had to be here with the kids. I'll tell her myself when I see her. Let her know I wanted to be there more than anything. But I put the kids first and that's what she would have done.'

Catriona was all Dette had said she would be. And by the second act, when Victoria was due to make her cameo, the show had already been stolen. And Victoria was there, with Martin holding her in an armlock in the wings, wearing Catriona's cast-off. It didn't suit her. Nothing suited her. She should never have come.

At the close of the curtain Noël Coward and Rorie Marks took a bow too, with their cast. In the green room the first champagne was uncorked and everyone clustered around the good-as-new-star – Catriona Morehampton.

Noël went round kissing everyone, telling everyone what a discovery he'd made. 'I saw in them what the world now sees.'

The critics the next morning would say the leading lady stole the Hazlet's thunder without even trying, in looks, ability, coquettish behaviour, skill and presence.

'Try,' wrote one, 'keeping this out of the West End.'

★★★★★

As soon as she could leave the green room, Rorie asked where Helen was.

She had already gone home, Bea and Euan told her, to look after the children. 'But she thought it was brilliant, and you were brilliant and she said to say she'll see you soon.' Bea's eyes were shining with happiness. Helen and Euan had sat together for the whole show and Bea had barely noticed what was happening on stage. It looked like her mother wanted Euan back and, if she did, Euan would come home like a shot, wouldn't he?

'I've got to go too,' Bea added.

'Stay for the party,' Rorie pleaded.

'No. If I wait I'll have to go back with Victoria, who's not a bit happy that her appearance didn't raise the roof as it should have, and Martin, who's barely speaking to her. I'm better off on the last train, really. And I want to help Helen. Will we see you tomorrow, Euan?'

'I plan to take you all out. You and the kids, that is. Helen's got something on.'

Bea looked downcast.

'Don't worry, love, we're doing the best we can.' He couldn't lie to her and say it would all be OK, but he made it as easy as he could for her. Rorie loved that about him.

Meanwhile, Catriona had slipped out to make a quiet call to her husband and recover from the shock of unexpected triumph. She found she would also have to recover from the shock of finding Jonathan Blake Thompson in her dressing room without his clothes on. With an erect penis.

'Don't tell me you didn't feel it too on stage? We were brilliant for one another, we were sizzling. We need to consummate it now!'

'Oh, yes, we sizzled.' She sighed. She was still stage manager, so this had to be handled with kid rather than boxing gloves, which was what she felt like using. Because we're actors we're supposed to be good at pretending to sizzle, you prat. 'But I love my husband.'

'But he's not coming. You can love him and have sex with me and he need never know!'

'That really doesn't matter, Jonathan.' She knew she was skating on thin ice here – the actor's ego was so fragile. '*I'*d know.'

'But isn't your husband a banker?' Jonathan said it with horror as Catriona tried not to laugh at his wilting member. Why were men so proud of those things when they looked so ridiculous? She placed her wig on it, gently.

'Here you go, Jonathan. It's hard to have a conversation with that thing in the way.'

Jonathan looked down, 'That's the first time any woman ever said it got in the way. Most women enjoy my penis.'

'I'm sure they do. But the fact is that we have to remain professional. We're acting together for six weeks. Let's allow the sexual tension to build, darling. Let's send the audiences straight home to bed with each other.' I'd like to be in mine right now, snoring. 'And the banker is your bankroll, darling. If you care to look at the new programme you'll see George Morehampton is our producer. Believe you me, this is a difficult one, but I'd like not to offend him by having an affair with you. The show will close without his input.' And his input is a lot larger than yours. 'So off you pop, now, there's a good lad.'

George answered on the first ring. 'How was it?'

'Wonderful. Just like you.'

'How can you say that? I should have been there, but I was—'

'Looking after our kids, I know. Forget the play, how's Lara? Is she running a high temperature?'

'No.' George couldn't believe this – self-obsessed Catriona downplaying a triumph in favour of hearing about her child? 'It turned out to be nothing at all. Tell me how you got on. My God!'

'I must say, darling, I relished every minute of the last two hours.'

'Does this mean you're going back to acting?'

'No. It just means I'm having the time of my life right now.'

Helen drove Angelo's car back to her place. The babysitter wanted to leave at eleven and she was having to motor. Even she knew she was pushing it. Leaving Euan behind had been harder than finding out about his affair. Rorie looked gorgeous. He looked gorgeous. She'd watched him be one of the first to congratulate her. It had never been Rorie – it had always been someone else. But, looking back she saw that she'd pushed them together because that was what she'd always done. Pushed away anyone who loved her.

The clip of her corsage had broken and her breasts

had flopped back to their normal position with a sigh of relief.

If I end up on my own now, I've only myself to blame.

Dette watched Victoria and Martin with a certain smug satisfaction. He was edgy and she was fuming. Their discomfort was obvious. Her little baby was fast asleep and not interrupting her with constant queries about Daddy.

Angelo reserved the nicest, most comfortable chair for her and got her to put her feet up on a stool. She felt like a queen. A sad queen because she didn't have the man she loved. But she'd lived with that feeling ever since Joe Morgan had gone out of her life. She was used to it. Catriona's mother and father came up and kissed her, and offered congratulations. Rorie came up and hugged her.

Jude handed her a nice cup of camomile tea and a plate of food.

She felt very loved.

In six weeks' time her flat would be sold. Her mother's place had been taken too. They'd agreed to spend one more Christmas in London and move in January, after the baby was born. It felt sad, it felt good.

'I'm outta here,' Victoria hissed. 'You coming?'

'OK. I just want to say cheerio to a few people first.'

'You mean your roly-poly auntie over there?' Victoria said, loud enough for everyone to hear. Then she left. Because people were looking at her. Not in the way people normally looked at her but as if they didn't like her very much. No one had given her the gratitude she deserved for pulling this out of the shit. She left the room, but she didn't leave the building. If she did that, she knew she'd be leaving Martin for good. And she wasn't prepared to let that happen. Victoria Hazlet didn't lose. Especially to a mumsy frump like Dette Morgan. She slipped into an office, and slumped into a chair.

'Hiya.'

'Hiya.'

'Wot – no spawn-of-the-devil, shitface insult?'

'No, I'm too tired and sleepy for that.'

'Listen, Dette—'

'No, *Marty*. I don't want to listen. The hatchet's buried. I wish you well in your glistening life. I hear from Rorie you're off to Broadway in a few days to set up shop. It looks good for you and that makes me happy.'

'Very gracious of you. Look, Dette, you got no job, you're up the spout and it's mine.'

Junior stirred. Shut up, Junior, go back to sleep.

'It isn't, Martin, because you'd never stay long enough to see the child grow up. But I can live with that. I'm so happy to be having a baby I don't give a toss who the daddy is.'

'You will. Remember what you always said? You can never be too rich or too thin?'

'I didn't say it. Wallis Simpson said it, and you know what they said about her? She was a miserable skinny bitch who never enjoyed a plate of grub in her life. All that money and no taste for caviar. Give me cod roe and chips any day. You can never be too fat or too poor.'

Martin laughed. 'You're a diamond.'

'I could do with one, all right.'

'Listen, I've got to go chase a haughty horse and drive her back to London. She did me a favour turning up here. I'd better do her one back.'

'You'd better. From what I hear your future depends on it.'

'Well,' Martin stood back, 'I'm delighted to see you still got the odd miaeow left in ya.' Then he did something he couldn't not do. He touched her bump.

'Night night, little lad.'

'You think it's a boy, too?' she asked.

'Of course it is.'

He walked out before she could see him filling up. Essex men don't do blubbing.

Night night, Daddy, Junior whispered, and went back to sleep.

'Angelo, can you take me home with you and Jude?' Dette pleaded.

Angelo and Jude looked at one another – they'd wanted, on the spur of the moment, to check into a hotel.

'Sure,' Angelo said.

They took her right to her door. They even tucked her in and left her some food for the next day. It didn't make her feel any less lonely.

Catriona came up to Rorie and Euan, eyes shining. 'Is it OK if I go home? George had to mind the kids. Lara wasn't too sick after all. He says he has a wonderful surprise for me.'

'Sure. I'll cancel your room. It's as well you do go home – Blake Thompson's making puppy eyes at you,' Rorie whispered. 'I can't guarantee your safety.'

'Oh, I can.' The certainty in Catriona's voice made them all smile. 'Let's put it this way. He has very bad underpants for such a good-looking little boy. And I do mean little boy.'

Catriona heard the laughter all the way home.

'Well, that leaves just us,' Euan whispered.

'Euan, I can't.'

'What?'

'I can't do it to, Helen.'

'You're not doing it to her. I am.'

Afterwards he turned to her. 'D'you know something? That was so good I wanted to shout "Celtic!" afterwards.'

'Thank you,' Rorie smiled and pulled the sheet round her. 'It's just what I needed too.'

Too much.

49

It was the kind of Sunday that should have been lazy. But Helen turned up at her door at noon. 'Hi, here are some bagels and croissants. Euan took the kids and Bea for the day. He stayed in Surbiton. What do you think the chances are they slept together?'

'Well, put it like this, high.'

'I thought you'd say that. Why d'you have to be so honest all the time? You're ruthless.'

'Well, Helen darling, what were the chances of you jumping George if I hadn't turned up and he'd actually wanted to?'

'One hundred per cent.'

'There you go.'

'I've been a fool, Dette.'

'Well, let's start the Fool's Club instead as a branch of the Virgo. I've been just as big a one. Listen, you're still going to the Dawn Principles workshop on the tenth, aren't you? That's a week Monday.'

'Well...'

'Listen, I've got to go because I've got to write about the damned thing. Please come with me. Otherwise her publicist will be all over me like a rash. I won't be able to stand it if you don't come.'

'You're asking me to be in the same room as my best friend. Who is now, most likely, my husband's lover.'

'Yes, like I'm asking you to be in the same room as Cat, whose husband you asked to be your lover. And anyway, they mightn't come, being so successful and all.'

'Implying we're not.'

'Implying we're jobless, Helen.' Dette stuffed a croissant into her mouth. 'What else will we be doing with our Monday morning exactly?'

'I suppose you're right. I'll come.'

'Thanks, even though I had to drag it out of you. Now, what about some therapy?'

'I've been thinking the same thing – but they don't work Sundays. I need to sort—'

'I wasn't talking that therapy. I was talking retail therapy. Let's go to the King's Road and check out the Conran shop. I want to see what I can't afford for my new home in Ireland.'

The Conran Shop Café on King's Road provided Dette with the perfect venue to do more serious eating. They were tucking into criminally expensive ciabatta with roast vegetables and piping hot, perfectly frothed cappuccino, Dette's was decaf. For women who were supposed to be miserable they were giving a healthy impression of having a great time. Then Dette had to spoil it all by being vulnerable. 'You went through what I'm going through,

Helen. How did you cope?

'Badly.' Helen popped a chargrilled aubergine in her mouth. The lemon seasoning was sharp enough to make her wince, but then the sweet flesh of the aubergine kicked in. When she was busy she never tasted food, really. Now she could relish it. 'But it was eighteen years ago. This time eighteen years ago I was the mother of a month-old baby and bricking it. You're twenty-two years older than I was.'

'Seventeen,' Dette contradicted out of habit.

'And I didn't have your strength,' Helen continued talking as if she hadn't heard.

'Get out of it!' Dette exclaimed.

'No, I mean it. I know you're going to be able to show this child how much you love it. I had to behave like the adult I was too young to be, finish my training to provide the opportunities. My eldest daughter grew up believing I didn't love her.'

'She knows you love her now.'

'Yeah, but I'll never get back those years.'

'Oh, yes you will, sooner than you think.'

'Why? What do you know?'

'I know you have to talk to her pretty soon. She needs you, more than you realise – isn't that John Edwards in the sofa section?' Dette pointed through the glass. 'Bad smells always come back.'

Helen turned, then immediately turned back.

'What's Trotsky doing buying top-of-the-range furniture, I wonder?' Dette had a bird's-eye view of him. He was signing for something. 'You know he's looking for half of Rorie's flat? He's sent a few solicitor's letters and they're getting nasty.'

'Let's follow him,' Helen suggested.

'No.' Dette's eyes narrowed. 'I've got a better idea than that.'

Number 175 Taylor's Road, SW6, was a charming mid-terrace house in one of the most sought-after roads in Chelsea. Five minutes' walk from the harbour and three minutes' walk from the King's Road.

The Conran delivery van pulled up at eleven a.m. on Tuesday. Conran deliveries were never late.

'Don't you just love socialists who live in Chelsea? They've such great taste,' Helen said as they watched the cream sofas being taken off the van and brought to the open door. The door opened by John Edwards, dressed in a black polo neck and cream chinos – not a trace of tweed.

'Helen,' Dette smiled, 'you made a little joke there. Shall we?'

They crossed the road and nipped into the house between sofas. Fully restored stained-glass window on the return of the stairs, rush carpets, dark-stained floorboards and beige walls, original works of art.

'And this is just the hallway,' Dette whispered.

The deliverymen and John were in the living room. Helen and Dette slipped down the hallway and found themselves in a state-of-the-art kitchen.

'If he said he'd had this imported from outer space I'd believe him.' Helen picked up an Alessi lemon squeezer.

'Not just any lemon squeezer. It has to be Alessi,' Dette stared around her. 'This kitchen cost at least fifty grand to kit out.'

'About as much as he owes Rorie in rent.' Helen popped it into her handbag, then slipped in a miniature oil painting too.

'Hang on a minute, what're you doing?'

'Stealing.'

'Stop it now, Helen,' Dette was riffling through a kitchen drawer. 'You know the plan.' She pulled out proof of address and then a bonus item – which she had a quick look at then whistled. 'Now, let's get ourselves comfortable.'

John Edwards shut the door on his deliverymen, who he'd not tipped, with a satisfied sigh. He went into his living room to check out the new corner sofas, which added just the right note of comfort and splendour. Time for an espresso. Arabic brand – specially imported. The Gaggia would have warmed up nicely by now. It had been a major outlay to buy an industrial coffee machine but well worth it.

It took him more than one second and less than ten to realise Helen and Dette were joining him.

'So happy we made it.' Helen smiled sweetly. 'And more than happy you did.' She gestured around her. 'Now, before you go all defensive on us, let us tell you exactly how this is going to be. And exactly why.'

Fifteen minutes after John had left the shop, they'd gone to the assistant who'd done his paperwork.

'I'm sorry, I'm looking for my husband, John Edwards,' Dette rubbed her belly. 'He just came in here to sort out our order and I was supposed to meet him.'

'He just left a few minutes ago, madam, would you like to phone him?'

'Oh, Johnny never carries a mobile. He's gone ahead and ordered, hasn't he? I hate it when he does that. What did he choose?'

The assistant shifted uncomfortably, 'The *écru* madam.'

'The *écru*! I wanted the cerise! Let me see that order now!'

The assistant winced, 'I'm afraid I can't do that, without some proof of identification.'

'Is this proof enough for you?' Helen pointed to Dette's belly and the wedding ring she'd lent. 'This woman will end up in labour if you don't show her the order. I mean to say – the *écru*! He knew you wanted the cerise!'

'I see. Just a moment.' The assistant handed it over.

'Oh, but this is for our Chelsea house, not the one in Rye. I see. You're sure it's for Chelsea? I see the postcode here. It's not just our billing address, for the fifteen thousand pounds?'

'No, madam. Number 175 Taylor's Road as I recall.'

'Oh, my word, the relief! I shan't divorce him after all. And did he pick up the turquoise vase?'

'No, madam. He made no such purchase.'

'But I wanted it. It was my birthday present.'

'You could always put it on his charge account, madam, and take it with you now.'

'Oh, could I? Sweetie.'

When the assistant finished wrapping Dette signed for the purchase – M. Mouse.

'When will the sofas arrive?'

'Tuesday morning, madam. We have them in our warehouse.'

Dette gave Helen back her wedding ring, wished, for a split second she'd one of her own. 'Never mind,' Helen read her thoughts, 'this one might be going spare soon.'

Now, Helen and Dette were enjoying this, watching John scurry about making coffee on his wanky machine.

'And biccies. We want biccies, don't we, Helen?'

'We certainly do, Dette, and we want to know why you made such a monkey about Rorie buying her Conran chair that time when you were kitting out your little weekend palace from the same shop.'

'Now, ladies. We won't be hasty about this. I don't live here all the time.'

'No,' Dette took out her notebook, 'According to my friend Ducky, who edits the magazine I used to work on and lives round the corner, he says he's seen you a number of times. The electoral register puts you down as being here for at least twenty years. That's even before Rorie's time. But not before Janet's. And she'd certainly be interested to learn how you kept this place out of your divorce proceedings. And my friend Ducky, who is donating lots of posh second-hand baby stuff to me, suggests that he's seen a number of important-looking business types come and go, and a famous name or two. So I checked with some top-flight rental agencies and what do I discover? When you're dossing in Rorie's you're renting this place out on short-term business lets for about one thousand pounds a half week. Cheaper than a hotel and so much homier, don't you think, John?'

He said nothing, just sipped his coffee.

'So, John, what we want to know,' Helen smiled, 'is what you think we want you to do.'

'I'm not going to be blackmailed.'

'We're not going to do that. We're going to get Janet and Rorie to sue you if you don't come up with a reasonable solution to all of this. This is – I phoned an estate agent to find out – worth two million at current market levels. With this interior and the delightful glass and wood extension you've put on, we estimate at least another quarter of a million on top of that.'

'You've no proof I lived with her!' He jabbed a finger at Dette.

'No proof but for three other corroborating witnesses, all Virgos, known for their honesty, their pernickety natures, their vengeful streak. Then there's the students you laid and left over the years...I'm sure.'

'OK, OK. What do you want?'

'Your lovely money,' Dette nodded. 'We'd like some of it, please.'

'I don't have any cash. It's all tied up in assets.'

'Oh, John,' Dette sighed, 'but you do.' And she held up the bank statements she'd found in the drawer.

'What we'll do, John, is take the fifty thousand in this savings account and split it two ways between Janet and Rorie. That way you get to keep your Chelsea hovel and we get to give them back a bit of the cash you stole from them. And I suggest you write the cheques now, or expect to have us all get together to put our favourite, nasty solicitor on to you.'

'How do I know if I write the cheques you won't be at me again?'

'Because unlike you, John, we're not desperate and we

won't die alone surrounded by fancy things. We don't value them as much as people.' Well not anymore.

In Helen's car, Dette kissed the cheques.

'Did we let him off too lightly?' Helen wondered.

'We got what we could afford to get. The other way would have cost an arm and a leg.'

Rorie turned up at Dette's place as soon as she could get there. Helen went home. It was too early for her to face Rorie, she left the lemon squeezer and the miniature with a note. 'Hope you like them.'

'I can't believe you lived with the swine for fifteen years. Was it really worth twenty-five grand?' Dette handed over the money.

'No, it wasn't, but I'm still going straight to the bank after this to lodge it in case he changes his mind.'

'What're you going to spend the money on?' Dette asked.

'I know just the thing. Can I use your phone? Hello? Is that Janet?…Janet, it's Rorie. I have a wonderful surprise for you. I have a cheque made out to you from your ex-husband for a lot of money.'

Back home, Helen called Diane Henderson.

'I need to see you, please.'

'I have a vacant slot tomorrow morning. Will Euan be coming?'

'No, just me.'

The next day, Helen wanted to leave as soon as she arrived at the door. But she forced herself to turn up.

'Tell me,' she asked, before she had even sat down, 'what do you think of my husband?'

Diane shook her head. 'Helen, I can't answer that as a counsellor. I have to remain impartial.'

'Then take off your counsellor hat and pretend we're in a café. Pretend we're friends and you're advising me. What can I do to get past this?'

Diane shook her head again.

'Counsellor, answer my question or hold yourself responsible in part for the break-up of my marriage and the loss of a father to three girls.'

'OK. I won't be led as you wish to lead me. I will say this. Your husband is a fine man. You, in my impression and only in that, are someone who has decided to blame him for everything. He's safe to be angry with. He's always held that anger for you. You need to think about directing that anger to the people to whom it belongs. I will comment no further than this. Good morning.'

'Good morning to you too, Diane Henderson.' Helen left quickly.

50

Monday morning, 10 October. Twenty nervous women crowded into a hotel in Watford's tiny conference room. The stripy wallpaper was doing Dette Morgan's brain in.

'Relax,' Catriona nudged her.

'And if you can't relax, shut up,' Rorie nudged her other side.

'Where's Helen? She'd promised she'd be here,' Dette sighed.

'If she promised then she will be.' Rorie said what everyone else knew.

Dawn Nolan, the deviser and teacher of the Dawn Principles, walked in on the dot of the designated time. She was much smaller than Catriona had imagined, which made her wonder what she'd seen in her all those weeks ago.

Her height made Dette smile – no tall-woman lectures, then. Rorie, also on the short side, felt the same relief. Already it didn't feel like school. Tall women often acted like teachers in these environments, which was why she'd been reluctant to come. But Dette said, 'I just want to have us all together for one day. To sort things out. Life's getting in the way of us being together and it'll be the last we see of each other if we're not careful. We never make Angelo's any more. Please.'

She hadn't had to work half as hard on Catriona. 'You know me, I'm Mrs Workshop. Anyway, I want to meet this woman in person and tell her what an effect she had on my life. I know I was delusional and desperate at the time. But it worked.'

'Let's begin,' Dawn said, 'with me saying that I am not an ego-driven creature. This workshop is called Dawn not just after me but because it represents what all of you want. A new beginning. To get that you need to sort out your past. Think of a long-overdue wardrobe clearout and you get the picture.'

'I'm getting it already,' Dette whispered.

At that point Helen arrived and, for the second time in a week, wanted to leave again immediately.

The course ran clearly and cleanly enough. Lots of affirmation, lots of visualisation, lots of nice, jangly music and incense, scented candles and essential oils. Lunch was light and so was the conversation. Of course, the four of them clubbed together and it might have been Angelo's, except the food was dire and the central heating too high and skin-drying. They longed for wine. But Dawn had said that was the one rule: 'None at lunchtime, please. We have work to do afterwards, serious work.'

*****

The Honesty Sessions called on individuals to declare to the group what they most wanted to say and then leave behind. Yolanda, a housewife from Surrey, got up and said she felt she wanted to leave her husband.

'Can you tell us why?' Dawn prompted.

'Because he doesn't love me any more.'

'I see. You've asked him?'

'No, I just know.'

Twenty minutes of gentle prompting elicited from Yolanda that, no, she did not really know that her husband hated her, but she felt a bit like that about herself.

'Can anyone in the group identify with this?'

Catriona stood, spoke, cried and sat down. Dette stood, spoke, cried and sat down. Helen stood, spoke, cried and sat down. Rorie just cried.

'You see, Yolanda? It's a common enough emotion for us all to feel it. The question is what you are going to do about it.'

They all looked at Dawn, who laughed. 'Oh, no, don't put the guru badge on me. I only know what to do with my life and even then I'm never quite sure. But what I can do is advise you all now to take out the Principles and read through them with the task ahead in mind. Then let's make suggestions to Yolanda. After that we'll move on to the next person and they can disclose what they need to disclose, until we've done all we can to help each other, without offering to run someone's life.'

'If I can make just one small suggestion, Dawn?' Helen stood up. 'As you know, four of us here are very closely connected, and a few months ago we undertook something that has made it difficult for us to stay that way. We really need to sort this out on our own. Would it be OK if we went off together to do that, rather than making it a spectator sport?'

'Oh, I see – well…'

'Yes.' Rorie stood up with Dette and Catriona. 'We'll read the Principles again before we start and stick to your format. But we need to speak to each other. And it will inhibit us if other people who don't know us are there too.'

Dawn folded her hands. 'That's fine with me. Come back here afterwards so that I can see you're OK with each other.'

They got hotel staff to send in sandwiches, coffee and water. Then they locked the door. They faced one another as if they never had before.

'OK,' Helen breathed. 'Who wants to go first?'

No one did.

'Right, I will.'

'No,' Dette interrupted. 'Read the Principles aloud first.'

As the whole day had been, there wasn't much to take in and what there was was clear and concise:

Do make things honest.
Attempt to keep it simple.
When you make mistakes, you learn.
Now ask your fear to help you to be honest.
Please begin all disclosures with 'I declare'. It solemnises and makes you consider what you are saying.

Catriona cleared her throat. 'This all started with something I did, so that's why I'm going to start this. I declare that I once tried to make Helen's husband, Euan Clarke, fall in love with me. On New Year's Eve I was all over him and gave him a lift home and seduced him in my Volvo. He was drunk and miserable and I took advantage. We stopped because he stopped. I wanted to go all the way. But something put him off.'

'It was you? Not Rorie? Why? Where was I?' Helen couldn't remember, the shock, the shock of this.

'You were working.'

Of course. I was always working.

'I tried to get him to see me again,' Catriona continued. 'He wouldn't. When you told me that day he'd been having an affair with someone else, I was just as hurt as you – Helen, why are you laughing? This isn't funny. I'm telling you the truth. It isn't a joke.'

'Oh, no, it's not a joke. I'm fully aware of that. The joke is this: I declare that for the past few months I've been dancing with your husband and I've been desperate to get into his pants. I declare that at the competition I threw myself at him and he rejected me. He said he fancied me but he would never do that to you. I wouldn't take no for an answer until he made me realise I had to take no for answer. So I guess, Catriona, that makes us quits.'

Catriona nodded. 'I guessed as much.'

Rorie stared at the ground.

'So,' Helen looked at Rorie, 'I need to do some apologising.'

Dette put an arm round Rorie. Rorie shoved it away. 'No. You've no reason to apologise. I declare that I am in love with your husband and he's not with me. I don' think so anyway. You've always kind of known that but I declare that I took him to bed on the night of the opening. I declare it was the best sex I ever had and I declare it was pretty good for him. But he will never, I declare, love anyone like he loves his wife. And I'm not wasting another fifteen years of my life on a man who is elsewhere. I declare that I am full of remorse because my best friend since childhood and her husband will never get back together probably. That's because of me.' All three of the others protested, but Rorie raised her hand and voice. 'And I could have been honest with her when I saw Cat and Euan in the back of the Volvo on New Year's Eve, but I wasn't because I couldn't be. I didn't want their kids to suffer. I wanted everything to stay as it was. So I played God, or avoidance, depending on which way you look at it.'

Rorie sat down again.

Dette stood. 'I declare that I am in love with a twenty-five-year old man and pregnant by him. I declare I am sad because he's going to New York soon to live in a penthouse with the trophy girlfriend. I declare I am the only one, despite my chequered past, who did not shag or attempt to shag Euan Clarke or George Morehampton or even John Edwards. I am feeling, I declare, a little smug about this because a few weeks ago I would have been voted the person most likely to try it on. But I wouldn't do that to any of you. I love you. You can blame pregnancy on me coming out with this emotional garbage. Don't expect to hear it again. I know I am moving away, but I want the Virgo Club to stay together so that I have something to visit that reminds me of the one thing that worked for me when I was living in London.'

At the end of the declarations Helen whispered, 'Can

we find the results of the fidelity test now, while we're still alone? I'd like to know. I'll start. George Morehampton. Faithful.'

Dette stood. 'John Edwards. Unfaithful.'

Catriona stood. 'Martin Hardiman. Faithful until pushed into the arms of Miss America.'

Rorie stood. 'Euan Clarke. Faithful until he got confused.'

'Virgos are bad at forgiveness,' Helen said softly. 'I suggest we don't try to patch things up right now. We're asking for trouble. Let's give it a while, then meet again and see where we all are with that.'

The others nodded. There was nothing left to say. They trooped out of the room, leaving behind uneaten sandwiches and undrunk coffee.

In the main conference room there was a lot of jollity and excited chatter. The Virgos didn't contribute.

Dawn watched them, but said nothing. 'OK, everyone, great work. Let's wrap up with some reminders of what today's been about and how you can apply it to tomorrow. If you start to live in a way that tackles past mistakes and present fears, you're going to feel a bit confused, dizzy, disoriented. Keep in touch with me. I reply to all emails and phone calls. Let me know how you're doing. Soon, if you keep working, the clouds will clear and you can feel a bit happier about the results of your work.'

The Virgos left first, Dawn watching them.

51

On the way home Helen glanced at the Principles, which they'd been given in the form of a fridge magnet. A few weeks ago she'd have snorted and stuck it in the bin. Now she looked at the first: 'Do make things honest.'

She got home and picked up the phone to make three calls. The first was to Euan's mobile. No answer. She bit the bullet and tried Rorie's flat. He answered on the first ring, 'Rorie? Where are you? We need to talk. You can't keep avoiding—' She could hear their children playing in the background, asking Daddy to put down the phone and come back to them, please.

'It's me, Euan.'

'Helen, sorry, I'm just—'

'I know about Catriona and I know about Rorie. What I need you to do, though, is come home. Please come home.'

'Sorry, Helen, I can't.'

'I don't mean for good. Just for a few days.'

She dialled Ireland. A voice she hadn't heard in nineteen years answered.

'Howya, Eunice.'

Eunice knew exactly who it was. 'Howya, Helen. You left it as long as possible.'

Bea came in as Helen came off her third and final call. 'I'm going to Ireland.'

Bea flicked a glance at the calendar.

'I'm coming with you.'

Helen held her arms out to her eldest and beloved daughter. 'I thought you'd say that. I booked two seats. Can you pack in an hour? My mother is seriously unwell.'

As Helen held Bea, she realised what Dette, and most likely Bea, had been trying to tell her for a while. She also realised where the condom came from.

Dublin Airport was almost empty. They'd shared the flight with a handful of wretched-looking businessmen, who'd been over and back in a day, and a hen party. The noise of irritated paper-rustling and high-pitched female shrieks made them smile. They held hands. When the plane had landed Helen had looked out the window – Bea had forced her to take the window seat. She saw the Ballymun Towers and the new motorway. The towers had been there when she'd left, but the motorway had been a single-carriageway road. Her mother and father had moved from the North Dublin suburb of Artane to Finglas a few miles away, so at least she wasn't going back to the house where she'd grown up. She didn't think she could have stood that. The walk from the terminal to the arrivals hall was the longest she'd ever made in her life. All the times she should have done it and never had. Nothing could be done about that now. Life was for liv-

ing and her mother was dying, and if she was to recon-
cile with her she needed to show remorse but also gratitude. Her mother had done her best. It hadn't been good,
but then, she herself hadn't done any better with Bea,
who was doing a brilliant job in forgiving her. Bea was
going to have a child in February. She would be six
months younger than Helen had been when she'd given
birth to Bea.

'A doctor who failed to realise her own daughter is
pregnant. Thank you, world, for showing me what I am
before it's too late,' she whispered to herself, as she
moved towards the customs checkpoint. There were double doors and when she walked through them Eunice and
her brother Paul would be there.

'Mum?' Helen felt her hand being held. 'Are you
ready?'

Yes.

Eunice took two seconds to spot in a stranger what
Helen had not seen in her own daughter. 'Jaysus, I'm
going to be a great-auntie! I can't believe you have such
a lovely girl, Helen! She's the cut of you.'

For the first time mother and daughter looked at each
other and were glad of it.

'Come on, I'm parked on the bleedin' set-down.
They've called me back to me car once already,' Paul,
who'd only nodded when they'd come through the barrier,
said. He'd only been twelve when Helen left. Eunice had
been sixteen.

Outside they got into a kit car, complete with flashing
lights and spoilers.

'Monstrosity, isn't it?' Eunice raised her eyes to heaven.
'He races it at weekends, like the young lad he's not.'

'It's gorgeous,' Helen insisted, and Paul smiled at her. 'Why're we going into town?'

'There's no time to go to the house, Helen. Ma's bad.'

It was an environment that was so familiar to her, but she had never felt such dread on going into a hospital. It had been different for Euan's dad. She'd looked after everyone then and dealt with the staff. The lift cranked up to Intensive Care.

What she saw in the bed in the private room – where the dying were taken for privacy, with most of the equipment removed – was not her mother. This was a wasted sixty-year-old woman with cancer, like many Helen had tried to help.

She stopped outside the door. 'I'm sorry,' her voice was breaking. 'I just can't go in.'

Then she heard the voice, thin but unmistakable. 'Is that Helen? Did Helen come?'

Helen felt two hands at her back. Eunice and Bea nudged her into the room.

'Yes, Ma.'

The others left, but the way they left told Helen and Bea that they didn't want to be gone long. She took her mother's hand and buried her face in it. 'I'm sorry, Ma. I'm sorry I never came back.'

'Sure, love. We didn't go over. I couldn't get round your father.'

'You never got an invitation, not from me anyway. I was the one should've been inviting you, Ma.'

'You were busy.'

Helen shook her head. 'I should never have been that busy.'

'Is that my grandchild?'

'It is.' Helen pulled Bea closer.

'She's the cut of you. And you're still the cut of your da.'

'I didn't know he wasn't well.'

'I did what I always did there, Helen, what he asked, and I regret it now. I was a bad mother.'

'No!'

'Yes, but I was brought up to the man being right. I'm sorry for that.'

They sat in silence for a few moments. Helen could see the effort it took for her mother to talk. 'You don't say anything now, Ma. Let me tell you a bit of news. Bea's going to make you a great-granny soon.'

Phyllis smiled, whispered, 'There's nothing more precious than children.'

She died a few hours later. In the company of her family. Her eldest child held her hand all the way.

The nurses came in only when the family were ready. The consultant came and spoke to Eunice, who pointed to Helen. 'We've heard such a lot about you from your mother. I understand you're A and E?'

Helen nodded.

'The hardest job of all, done by the best people.'

Back in the house Helen learned that all the hospital staff knew what a great doctor she was. The whole street that the Larkins had moved to knew. All her nieces and nephews, the man and woman in the corner shop, the publican, the bingo caller, the supermarket checkout operator and the chip-shop man.

'She never shut up about her flipping fantastic doctor daughter,' Eunice laughed. 'Sure you took all the brains from the rest of us, Helen.'

'I'm not a doctor any more.'

'Jaysus, I'm glad she didn't find that out! And you'd better not tell anyone else,' Eunice giggled.

Paul was on the phone getting the death notice to the paper. Mary and Joan – the two sisters who came after Helen and Eunice, with Paul in between – were making sandwiches with Bea in the kitchen. Liam, Helen's youngest brother, was out telling the neighbours.

'Why did you never come back, Helen?' Eunice had started to cry now.

Helen knew it was the first wave of grief, the one that came immediately afterwards. It would disappear when the funeral arrangements took over and reappear at the graveside, then go again until the last of the guests were gone and the Larkin children realised they were orphans. She'd been to a lot of funerals. She'd never been afraid of death and couldn't understand anyone who was. But then, she'd never known the regret she was experiencing now. All the things that would now have to be left unsaid.

'Helen?' Eunice jogged her.

'I didn't think I was wanted.'

'Ah, that was only Da. You always let him get to you. The rest of us knew he was only an oul' bollix. You might have got the brains but you didn't get a thick skin, did you?'

'No.' Helen laughed. 'So I put on a doctor's coat. That's why I'm taking it off again. I need to know what the real world is like.'

'Ah, you're making a mistake there. The real world's a make-believe one anywhere you go,' Eunice said. 'But what would I know? I'm only a housewife.'

'I'll tell you right now, Eunice Larkin. You know a lot more than me.'

'Helen, how's your friend, the lovely one you always palled round with?' Eunice asked. 'She was always good to me. She never got annoyed me being around you.'

'And I did?' Helen enquired, because she'd forgotten.

'Yes, you sure did. You used to beat me over the head with a rolled-up *Jackie* and kick me out of me own room.'

'Oh, I remember that, I'm ashamed to say. I haven't changed, still beating people off with a stick. Rorie hasn't changed either. She's the friend she always was.'

Helen and Bea stayed for the week. Euan flew over with Kelly and Joyce after the funeral so that the Larkins could meet and be distracted by them, which Helen knew they'd need. She had never seen her kids eat as many E-numbers – they were high as kites and played with their new-found cousins as if they'd known them all their lives. Euan went out car racing with Paul and Liam took Bea into town to meet his friends, who all agreed she was gorgeous and didn't care that she was having a kid. They'd take her on any day.

One night Bea had taken Euan and Helen aside to tell them what had happened. He was older, he was married and he didn't want to know. 'I'm sorry. About a lot of things. We used your bed too. I feel terrible about that. I'm sorry my baby won't know his daddy any better than I did.'

Helen held her and looked at Euan, who didn't look at her. The condom in the toilet. They'd never thought of Bea.

'I want you to know, Bea, whatever you need from me you'll get.' Euan's voice cracked. 'Even if Helen and I aren't together. I'm the grandfather. Forever.' His eyes were full of tears.

'And you have a home too, for as long as you and the baby need or want it,' Helen added.

Euan and Helen had been given a double room and each night they went to bed in it and held each other. It was the natural thing to do. But there was no question of sex. For a start, Kelly and Joyce were on a mattress on the floor.

Helen promised to bring the kids back at Christmas for a few days. She hadn't invited the Larkins to her home yet because of the way things were. The way things were was that as soon as they got back to London, as soon as the kids were unpacked and settled into bed for the night, Euan left to go back to Rorie's.

'Do you love her?' Helen wanted to know.

'Yes,' he said, in the quiet way that there was no arguing with.

52

Catriona looked at her fridge magnet. She was going to Brighton for the next run of *Fiasco* and George was going to drive her down. As good an opportunity as any. It wasn't fair that he was the only one who didn't know. She wanted to keep their marriage as it was now. Without lovers.

It would be hard, she imagined, for him to give up Audrey Hepburn. But not as hard as it would have been had he still got a disappointed ice-cream-addict wife on his hands. And Magda was gone. Catriona almost felt sorry for her. All that wasted planning. On the way they were calling over to Jude and Angelo's to see the picture – Angelo was moving into Spitalfields, leaving his flat for the restaurant staff.

In Jude's conservatory George stared and didn't say a word.

'I'm going to hang it in my salon,' Jude clapped his

hands, 'especially now you're famous and everything. The tabloids will be begging me for a snap of it.'

Catriona had even attracted tabloid attention after the Surbiton first night: 'Has-Been Eclipses Hazlet'.

'And you won't give it to them because Catriona is our friend.' Angelo put his arm around Jude firmly. 'George, what you think?'

'I think,' George brought his hands together under his nose in the prayer position, 'I think it's the most beautiful woman I've ever seen and therefore the most beautiful painting. But I also know it's got to be mine. I don't want this ending up in a gallery when Catriona's a household name. I want it in our bedroom, where it belongs. Now, how much is that going to cost me, Jude?'

It cost him five thousand pounds. Jude was estimating future value. Angelo tried to persuade him to part with it for nothing.

'It goes against everything my old mother taught me.' Jude waved it and the couple goodbye. 'Course I won't cash the cheque, but it'll do her good to see what he was prepared to pay for it.'

Angelo kissed the top of Jude's head, shut the door with his foot and carried him upstairs.

Afterwards Jude admitted, 'Well worth letting five grand go, that was.'

'Thank you, darling.' Catriona leaned back in the passenger seat as they sped towards Brighton. His side profile was so handsome. Let's face it – his *every* profile was handsome.

'That's fine. I had to pay five thousand for a naked

picture of my wife and it's in the boot of our car, but it's fine.' George smiled. 'Next time you're being painted keep your clothes on. It'll cost me a lot less.'

'Yes, darling. Now, can you stay and see the show tonight?'

'Naturally, and I'll run you home after it. Helen's got the kids at her house and she says she'll take them to school tomorrow. So I'm staying tonight, as are you, at the Grand.'

'That,' Catriona murmured, 'is grand.'

It wasn't grand when they'd been in their hotel suite an hour after the curtain had dropped. It wasn't grand because Catriona had come clean and found George was not going to be so obliging. He was still in a daze about Euan. 'I can't believe he'd do that to me. I've always held him in such high standing.'

'I'm sorry.' Catriona sat on the bed and stared at the carpet, counting tufts. Something to do to steady her mind. She'd seen a confessional scene, mutual tears, forgiveness and falling into bed. She'd forgotten life was not a bloody play. Real dramas lasted a lot longer than ninety minutes.

'I wanted you to know. You haven't been a saint either, George. That's all I'll say.'

'What do you mean?'

'You've been unfaithful too.'

'Unfaithful? What makes you think I've been unfaithful?'

'Well, come on, George, there are women crawling all over you. And I know about Audrey.'

'Audrey who?'

'Sorry. The woman who looks like Audrey Hepburn.'

'Who the bloody hell is Audrey Hepburn?'

'The actress, *Breakfast at Tiffany's*.'

'Yes, but I don't know anyone who looks like her.'

'Oh, George, please – yes you do. You know you do. I'm not trying to accuse you. I'm trying to say I've been foolish as well. I think we can both learn from this and move on and be more honest with each other.'

'Well, Catriona,' she noticed he didn't call her Kate, 'let me be honest with you now. I've never been unfaithful, since the day I met you.'

'George…'

'No. Just at this moment, just when I was so happy. I need to…I need to…' He put his head in his hands. 'I don't know what I need. I think I'll just go for a walk.'

'George, please, let me come with you. I was trying to make things better between us.'

'Well, Catriona, I'm sure I'll be grateful for that. Eventually. Right now, I just want to be on my own.'

He called Reception an hour later to tell Mrs More-hampton he was going back to London.

53

When Catriona came home the next day there was a message that George was 'staying at a friend's'. Helen supplied the information.

Catriona phoned Dette immediately. Her 'hello' wasn't very responsive.

'Dette? Are you OK?'

'Sorry, Cat. I've developed a varicose vein and the reality of having this child on my own is starting to hit me. Mammy wants me to call it Kitty if it's a girl and Martin if it's a boy. I'm heading for an Irish benefit office with a buggy and my mother is going to have control of my life again.'

'Oh, poor Dette.'

'Ah, forget that. How are you, Mistress of the Entire World?'

'OK, except my husband just left me.'

'This is getting to be a habit with all of us.'

*****

Helen, who'd called to drop off the kids, and Dette sat with a weeping Catriona.

'He says Audrey Hepburn doesn't exist!'

Helen and Dette looked at each other. 'We know for a fact that she does.'

'What?'

'She's our dancing instructor,' Helen filled her in.

'Why did you not tell me at the Dawn Principles day?'

'Because we're only supposed to declare for ourselves. You know what I'm like about following rules.'

'I bloody do. That's why you took the fidelity test as far as you did.'

'Steady on there, Catriona,' Dette raised her hand. 'Remember what Helen's just been through.'

'Sorry, sorry. I shouldn't be up in a heap about you, Helen. I'll go round and punch Audrey—'

'Madeleina.'

'Where does she live?'

'I don't think that's such a good idea, Catriona.'

'Think what you like. I'll do the driving while you're thinking.'

They arrived in South Sheen after a quick drive through lunchtime traffic. George's BMW was parked outside but there was no answer to their knock.

'Well,' Dette said brightly, 'they must both be at work.'

'Yes,' Catriona said through clenched teeth, peering through the letterbox, 'they must.'

'I think I'll go home now,' Helen whispered. 'Can I go home now?'

'No, you'll bloody well stay here and help me. If it takes all day I'm going to find out what's going on.'

It didn't take all day. Madeleina came down the path with a small bag of groceries and an uncertain smile. 'Helen, how lovely to see you! And Dette, good to see you again, and your other friend? The one who is staring through my letterbox?'

Catriona made herself close it and look at Madeleina.

'Oh, my goodness. Catriona.'

'Don't Catriona me! Where's my husband?'

'I'm sorry, but he's at work. Would you like to come in and wait for him? He'll be another five hours, but you're welcome.'

They crowded into her bedsit and she made tea. No one spoke. She was wearing black Capri pants and a white blouse with a black neckerchief. Who manages to look so elegant on a Tuesday afternoon? She asked who wanted milk and sugar, then sat with them on the edge of a fold-up chair, her limbs folded so neatly Catriona couldn't get over it.

'So, this is lovely, but I think we'd better do some talking, don't you, Catriona darling? About George?'

'Sure. How long has your affair been going? Decades by the sound of things.'

'Now, because you ask that, I can tell you don't have the full story and for that there is a very good reason. I need to phone George now, if you don't mind. And I need to do it in private.'

'You need to phone my husband without me being present?'

'Yes. That's right.'

'I won't agree to that.'

There was silence. Dette and Helen shifted on the bed that was as narrow as Madeleina.

'Fine. Then be present. But I think it would be fairer

to George if you would let me talk to him alone. But I can see it's not a viable proposition.'

She stood and dialled. Obviously she knew the number by heart. 'George? I'm fine, really I'm fine. Catriona is here, with Helen and Dette. She is very upset, George, and would like some answers. Shall I give them to her?' There was a pause. Madeleina looked at Catriona. 'I'm afraid he doesn't think you're entitled to them just yet.'

Catriona stood up in a rage, grabbed the phone and took it out into the hall. There was a lot of shouting. Madeleina smiled at Helen. 'You were really rather good at the competition, darling. I hope you come back to class. We all miss you.'

Catriona came back in. 'He wants to speak to you again.' She thrust the phone at Madeleina.

'Hello, George…Yes…Yes, I see…OK, fine then. I'll start off talking, shall I?…And you're on your way?'

Catriona felt all the anger go out of her. 'It's funny,' she whispered to Helen and Dette. 'I have a feeling that I've already lost.'

'I first met George when I was eight and he was a week old,' Madeleina said. 'I was lucky enough to be home from boarding school on holiday. Our mother, Lydia, was not one for children around the house.'

'You're his sister! But she lives in Italy.' Catriona gaped. 'They haven't spoken for years. He would have told me!'

'Yes. There's a good reason why we haven't told you, a very good one. We were great friends when we met during the holidays, but for the most part we were in separate childhoods in separate schools. So we weren't grea allies, you see. Then I met Ricardo. He was my dance teacher, and that was it. I was seventeen when I left. George was only nine. I wrote to him, but they instructed the school not to pass on letters to him. I'm afraid I was rather selfish. I took my own chance of happiness, and left my little brother with no one. I understand from George that you are not Lydia's favourite, Catriona.'

Catriona nodded. She was thinking, 'I have been absolutely no help to my husband.'

Helen was shaking her head. She felt so ashamed. All the scheming to be second mistress.

Dette was thinking, Is anyone going to eat those digestives or do I have to start, as usual?

Madeleina went on. 'I've lived in Italy for years, but when Ricardo died we had nothing so I had to come back here. The thing is, and this is why we've kept our relationship a secret, George was made to sign a clause on accepting Georges Avenue and his inheritance that he would never try to contact me and never share his inheritance with me. If he does he loses everything. I am so afraid for him, being in contact with me. But he won't give it up. That's why I've refused to see you all. I came to the birthday party because he told me Lydia wouldn't be there, and then I saw her. I have no doubt she would get a solicitor to begin proceedings immediately. She hasn't softened with age.'

'She was an unasked guest,' Catriona said apologetically. 'And she was fuming because I'd spilt wine over her.'

'I saw you there. I saw he'd given you the necklace like the one Ricardo had given me. He'd asked for the jeweller specially. From what I hear, and he doesn't say much, you're getting on much better. I'm glad of that because

I'm going to leave soon, to go back to Italy where Ricardo's buried. It was a mistake to come to England.'

'No, it wasn't,' Catriona said firmly. 'This is where your living family are. This is where you belong.'

'I should warn you, he's trying to get me to take half of all his assets. I won't hear of it. That's another reason I should go.'

'But he's right!' Dette and Helen were overjoyed to hear Catriona say it. 'You're his sister.'

'If I take it there is always a chance that Lydia will find out. I'm not prepared to put your family at risk, Catriona. Really. I've been through this and thank you for your kindness, but I've decided it's best I go. George has been kind enough to risk setting me up with a stipend there.'

'A stipend? But what he has is half yours!' Catriona said.

'How did you find him again?' Dette interrupted.

'He saw my advertisement for dance classes and called me. My English name is Madeleine, so it was close enough for him to know. He'd knew I'd married Ricardo Conti – we met, all three of us, only the once for lunch. That was the last time, but for the time you came to Italy on holiday. Remember, George?' He had just walked through the door.

'George, you went *abroad*?' All the Virgos said it.

He shrugged. 'Didn't like it, very hot. Lydia found my ticket, and that was when we knew for sure there was no chance for reconciliation. She even checked my phone bills for calls to Italy for five years. That was before I met Kate.'

Kate, he called me Kate.

'I agreed to meet him for lunch,' Madeleina broke in

'I shouldn't have but I wanted to see him so badly, and then he turned up here for classes, with his delightful partner Helen, and he's been pursuing me ever since, in a brotherly way, of course. I'm afraid being only recently bereaved I haven't left as quickly as I should.'

'I'm sorry I never said anything. I'm sorry I didn't realise she looks like Audrey Hepburn.' He was beside his sister. Now Helen saw how alike they were – how stupid she had been not to spot that their similarities were genetic. Another reason not to go back to medicine. 'To my mind she's got piglets and spots—'

'Not piglets, George, pigtails,' Madeleina smiled.

'Yes, those.'

'I have to go now,' Catriona stood up. 'Rorie will be wondering where the hell I am. And I've got to keep stage management going as well as starring in the thing. To-night, as soon as the show's over, I'll come back to London and we can talk. Come to our house – your house, Madeleina.'

'But what about Lydia?' Madeleina stared at George. 'She only lives round the corner.'

'To hell with her.' Catriona pointed a finger at George. 'And you, sir, no dancing tonight with Helen Larkin. Get home and mind our beautiful children and don't even think of divorcing or leaving me. In fact, I want a word with you now.'

In the hall a slow smile spread across his face, 'Now why didn't I think of that? You clever girl.'

'Because you're a man. Men don't think of telling their wives everything. From now on, no secrets. You'd have saved us all heartache, Madeleina included, if you'd come clean.'

Helen stayed on for the dance class, and Edith Webber danced a treat with her. Dette went home to soak her swollen feet and steal everyone's lives for a novel she was thinking of writing.

54

Dette looked at her fridge magnet. Rorie was beside her. She'd called in for a cup of tea before heading off to the theatre and ended up egging Dette on to tell Junior's dad she might like to try again with him.

'If you humiliate yourself at least you're never going to see him or her again. You'll be in Ireland. He'd have to get Interpol to track you down and unless there's a good reason they won't oblige. Go on, Dette! Be the fighter you always were.'

Dette didn't need to be asked twice. She'd seen Catriona set up, and Helen had sorted herself out too – she was going back to work at weekends, no pressure, except trying to save lives under pressure while Euan minded the kids. It was a good arrangement, except that Euan was living with Rorie.

Rorie was still refusing to be drawn on the subject, except to say, 'Look, he needs time and space and he's got it at my place. We're not sleeping together. We're not even seeing each other. I'm with the play all week, now I've the money to stay away. He's at their house at the weekends when I'm home. I've barely seen him,' and I want it that way. Until I know what I need to say, and how to say it.

'Fair enough,' Dette nodded. 'Now can we get back to my favourite subject of me, please? He's not going to leave her, you know.'

'Maybe not, but your baby will be glad to know Martin's there as a dad – and Martin, whatever you think of him and I wouldn't blame you if it wasn't much – will be a very good dad. He's got values around that. Phone.'

'OK.'

It was a short conversation, with Rosemary.

'He just left. This morning. Six months living in New York, a trial to see how it works out. Sorry, Junior,' she rubbed her belly. 'I tried.'

'You can always phone him there,' Rorie persisted.

'And take away his big chance? No. Now I want to go to bed and have a good cry, please and I'm still queasy about doing that in front of other people.'

NOVEMBER

55

Rorie and Helen were on their own for the first time in months. It was a neutral venue and it was a Tuesday afternoon in late November. For the past month none of them had met at Angelo's. Even though relations were less strained they were still more complicated than they had ever been.

Rorie's run had ended and she and Catriona were back in London. Helen was working weekends and loving it. Rorie was still avoiding Euan, who was avoiding Helen, who'd been avoiding them both. Then Helen had asked to see Rorie alone. Rorie went because she knew she needed to see Helen alone too.

'He loves you,' Helen said, not one to waste time on small-talk.

'He doesn't.'

'He does. He told me.'

'He doesn't know his own mind, Helen.'

'Euan has always known his own mind. Do you love him?'

'Yes.'

'Then I'm the one in the way. I'm going to divorce him.'

'Helen Larkin, if you do that,' Rorie rose to her full five feet two inches, 'you are not the fighter I know you are.' Funny. She'd had this conversation with Dette, and now she was having it with Helen. Fight for the man I love and take him away from me. French film – more and more each day.

'One of the things I've realised is that friends make plenty of room for each other's faults,' Helen said slowly, 'and for life to change. I've been bad at life changes and allowances. Diane, my counsellor, has shown me that. You're the ones who ought to be together. You have more in common. You support Celtic. You drink stewed tea. I want you to have my husband. Please.'

'I can't believe you're saying this. You cannot want it, Helen.'

'I know. I'm not saying I'm all the way there yet, but I'm going to try. I think it's going to be harder to forgive myself for what I've done to my family and friends. The ones in Ireland too. I just cut them out like they were cancerous when I wasn't getting my own way.'

'You'd reason to at one time, Helen. They were holding you back, especially your dad.'

'Because I never let them find out who I was. I just shoved my intelligence in their faces. I was the oldest, I should have helped my sisters and brothers. Instead I was the great girl studying and they could never be quite as good as me. Look at my own kids, I do the same to them. Have done, rather. You can never be as good as me if you don't work as hard as me. I pushed Bea so far away that she's pregnant at the same age I was. A great example I've been, Rorie. A great example to all.'

'Helen, I never met a person who tried as hard as you. I saw what you had to do to keep Bea. Remember that. Remember that you didn't give her up when you easily could have. Remember she knows that. That's why she never gave up on you entirely.

'Now, here are my keys, go to my flat and get your husband. Drive him home and get into bed and make it work like it used to. If and when you think of him having sex with me, remember he didn't enjoy it as much as I did. And it was only the once. Look at your old photos and see that you didn't make a complete mess of it. It just got completely messy. You did the best you could. You're doing it now. Don't try as hard, that's all.'

Helen was out the door then turned round and came back. 'Will you come?'

'No.' Not yet. Some time in the future I'll do that. When I don't look at him and feel the empty space beside me.

Rorie watched the woman she loved get into her car and drive off to take back the man she loved. He wouldn't leave if he wasn't forced, because he was the kind of man who stayed. He knew Rorie wanted him to stay and she knew he had to go. That was why, after all the weeks of avoidance, she'd told him, last night, 'You'll always regret this, Euan.'

'No, Rorie, I won't. I love you. I even love your snoring that I can hear so loudly in the next room. I want it to be even louder. I want it to be right in my ear.'

She burst out laughing. He always did it to her, even at the saddest of times. They would always be friends because of this laughter, because of these remembered times when it flowed between them. Laughter and Celtic, and love for Helen.

'Euan, I think that's just about the nicest thing anyone ever said to me. But I'm afraid for myself and you that it will never work.'

'Why? Helen's given us her blessing.'

'Helen's still a bit mad. And she's not French. Only the French could be happy with an arrangement like this. We're not as far up the evolutionary scale, Euan. We're emotional amoebae.'

'Stop that. You're finding excuses to drive me away.'

'Exactly. I'm remembering for you, Euan Clarke, the way you loved my friend when you first met her. And all the things you went through together. As long as I live, as long as I have you, I will never get you to look at me like that.'

'I'm older now, Rorie, we're all older. It's not as simple as it was.'

'It will be if you go back to your wife.'

'No.'

'Yes, Euan. When you see her again, remember the donkey jacket and Scafell.'

That was when Euan cried. He was still refusing to go when they went to bed that night. He even tried to come with her to hers. But she sent him away and held on to her pillow for the rest of the night so as not to undo the nobility. In the morning he'd given her credit for it. 'If you feel for me half what I feel for you, that was a bloody hard thing. I'm angry, too, that you won't let me stay.'

She took the coffee he'd made for her, and felt a sharp stabbing pain. This will be the last of these he makes for me, she thought. Euan was not happy – she could see it in his clenched jaw, hear it in the way his voice got quieter, as it always did when he was angry. Even after a short time she had some intimacies, which she knew Helen knew off by heart.

'You have responsibilities to live up to, Euan – you have girls to raise and a marriage to save.'

His voice was tight when he spoke again. 'Last night I didn't agree with you there at all. This morning I'm beginning to realise you're right, Rorie.'

That was why Rorie knew Helen only had to turn up to take Euan back. She hadn't even felt a glimpse of this pain with John. He had been a habit to break. Euan's leaving broke a heart. She put her head in her hands and wept for the whole coffee shop to see. It got her a free cappuccino and a bun. Life was not all bad.

56

Catriona Morehampton sat in the solicitor's office with George Morehampton and Madeleina Conti.

'If you sign here, Mrs Morehampton.'

She signed there.

'That completes it all.'

Catriona smiled. She looked at the solicitor, at George and his sister. 'Does this mean I'm now worth millions in property and shares?'

'It does.' There was a warning note in George's voice. He was nervous because Catriona had always been crap with money.

'What a lovely feeling. Can I just enjoy it for a minute?' They all nodded and she sat back and waited for exactly sixty seconds. 'Now, are these the papers I sign to put the house up for sale?'

They all nodded. She signed immediately. And then she signed some others to confirm that she was splitting her stocks and shares equally between George and Madeleina, and would do the same when the house was sold.

*****

Bea and Dette were watching morning telly together at Dette's place. Bea was helping her pack a few boxes, but they'd both got a fit of pregnancy and sat down.

'Look at you, Madonna with child,' Dette hand's swept over Bea's designer bump. She was doing a bit of pregnancy modelling and the magazines were already screaming for more of her. 'I'm Madonna with mumps.'

The doorbell rang. Bea answered it because she was only six months pregnant and younger.

'It's for you, naturally.'

Martin came in.

Dette shook her head. 'Excuse me, aren't you supposed to be living in New York?'

'Nah. Billericay me.'

Victoria and Martin had taken off.

'Marty,' Victoria squeezed his hand, 'my friends are gonna love you.'

'Why?' He smiled because he always smiled.

'You're cute, you're authentic, a real East End guy. They never met one of those before. I might just fly over some of those yucky eels for our first party. We can wear matching pearly outfits.'

Five minutes into the London–New York flight Martin Hardiman knew he was going straight home on the next one. When he got back, he went to his mum's house.

'So I'm here.'

'So you are.'

'So, what're we going to do about that?'

'I don't know, Marty.'

'Don't call me that and do let me tell you this. I'd like to marry you.'

'Oh, well, in that case, you'd better sit down.'

Bea smiled at Martin and left the room. Martin stared at her bump. 'What? How?'

'Never mind, it wasn't you.'

'I'm relieved to hear that.'

'So, I'm being proposed to, am I?' Dette brought him back to the business in hand.

'Looks like it.' Martin sounded defensive.

'I take it I'm not to share you in a loving arrangement with Corned Beef?'

'Vicky? No, trust me, there's no loving arrangement there. Safe to say I won't get a Broadway break in the near future.'

'Ah, trust. Now that's the key word here, Martin Hardiman. I'm saying no to you, after such a romantic proposal of marriage. I am saying no because I'm keen on trust. What I've got to do, Martin, is have this little baby, who is going to be huge by the look of me, and stop putting all the effort into destroying myself that I've put over the years with unsuitable untrustworthy blokes – like you.'

'I was only untrustworthy once, Dette.'

'I'm sorry, Martin, no hard feelings, but there's no other way to say it.' Dette rubbed her aching back. 'That's experience. My age tells me what you're going to get up to in the next fifteen years. That's the age gap incidentally. I'm forty. You'll be forty before you're ready to settle, if at all.'

'How do you know that?'

'Because I was my age before I did.'

Martin stood up and made himself at home in her kitchen. 'You still drinking weed tea?'

'Yes, with a bit of honey.'

'Martin,' she started off gently, 'my dad died and that made me tough. Long before Joe, my husband, I was looking out for myself.'

'How? Writing cop-out beauty articles? Drinking like a fish?'

'You've got a cheek, Martin.'

'And you've got one, deciding you know how my life's going to turn out for me. I read your fridge magnet, Dette. I think you ought to start off being honest with yourself instead of putting it all on me.'

'I never said you'd definitely turn out like that. I'm talking about likely outcomes here, and you're not likely to make Husband of the Year, are you?'

'Why not? My dad is! He's been with my mum solid ever since they met twenty-six bloody years ago and he's ten bloody years younger than her!'

'You never told me that.'

'I should have thought it was obvious from meeting her!'

'I don't want to be that honest, Martin. I like Rosemary.'

'So do I, and Dad loves her bones. I never told you about them because you never bloody asked. They got married because of me coming along, which is as good a reason as any.' He eyed her bump. 'You've never asked anything about me, Dette, and that's the problem. You only know the bad stuff.'

'Martin, you dumped me.'

'Yeah, before you could do it and after you told me

the baby mightn't be mine. Remember?'

'You'd never have stayed anyway, Martin. And stop shouting – babies can hear in utero.'

'Well let him hear this, because his mother better. She's making a right bloody mess of things.'

'And you're going to tell me how to clear it up?'

'Yes. Marry me, let me bring up my own kid and give me a chance to make my own decisions.'

'It'll never work, Martin.'

'It works for lots of people. It's worked for Dad and Mum. Come on, Dette. No one's got a single guarantee about anything. We can only try it. If it don't work we'll sort something out.'

'But I'm going to Ireland now.'

'You still want to?'

'Yes. I don't want my kid brought up here.'

'Our kid, and you're right. We can always hang on to this place. I can commute. It'll be fine.'

'You'll be living with your mother-in-law – you've never even met her.'

'Brilliant.' He started to smile. 'I'm great with mothers-in-law.'

'Martin, what do you mean about hanging on to this place? I just sold it.'

'Yeah. I bought it for ten grand more than it was worth.'

'Oh, good,' Dette started to smile. 'I won't have to pack.'

'Is that a yes?'

'That's a yes, Martin. I'm keen to add to my collection of disastrous husbands.'

DECEMBER

57

I'm sitting in Angelo's with Angelo, drinking the last of my *grappa*. It's the first Tuesday and when I phoned round everyone was going to try to make it. But it's such a busy time of year. Isn't it?

Catriona's busy househunting.

Helen's busy looking after her children, working at the hospital and on Euan. They're doing well in counselling. They've come a long way and it'll take a while longer. But they'll get there.

Dette's busy making Martin redecorate her place for renting out. He's sorry he ever said he'd marry her, but he'd only back out of it if he died. When she's had the baby she plans to breastfeed. 'The best post-pregnancy weight-loss plan in the business.'

Then there's going to be an outdoor summer wedding in Ireland. Dette's never lived in Ireland, she doesn't realise she's organising a pool party. It never stops raining.

Me? I'm a vegetarian seeing a bit of an Irish butcher.

It's nice. He's not Euan. But it's nice. My mother dragged me home by the hair, fed me up with comfort food and forced me to meet him in the local pub where he was playing darts.

We walked into the pub. I'd warned Ma to pull no stunts, but she went straight up to him and practically yelled, 'This is me daughter. What d'you think?'

I expected to be horrified. Instead I was surprised. He is soft-spoken, his name is Michael, he has a passion for hill walking and he cuts up meat.

'I think she's lovely.'

Something tells me he won't give up easily. He kept on at me until I let him come over for the long weekend. We had a grand time and when he was going I was sorry. But I was still glad he was going. I'm not ready. He wrote to me last week, a long, lovely, poetic letter and said, 'No one's ever ready unless they try. Please try.'

I'm going to see him again at Christmas when I'm home. He wants to take me out walking in the hills. I don't take the lift any more to my flat, I take the stairs, so I think this means I must be willing to go with him.

I'm capable of not looking at the clock for the millionth time, which will say two p.m., which means everyone is an hour late and not likely to show. I'm capable of moving on like the others and accept the Virgo Club's demise.

'Where's Jude?' I ask Angelo, because these days Jude's never far away. 'Is he going to come along?'

'No, I said I'd call him. He wants you all to have some time.' Then Angelo says, 'You wait. They will come.'

Almost as if they heard him, Dette and Catriona arrive together, with Madeleina.

'Sorry, Dette had to stop every fecking ten seconds to go to the loo.'

'Well, so would you if you had two stone of pressure bearing down on your bladder! How quickly we forget our pregnancies! When I was forced to listen to you rabbiting on about piles and stretch marks—'

'OK, OK,' Catriona throws her hands into the air. She puts an arm around Madeleina, who is looking nervous and quite retiring. 'Angelo, I'd like you to meet my sister-in-law – she's been living in Bologna for almost thirty years and...' Catriona looks at me, '...is it OK if she joins us? She's not a Virgo, but I didn't want to send her home without any lunch. Not after the morning we've just had.'

'What?' I ask.

Catriona sits down, Madeleina beside her. We'll need another chair for Helen. She hands over a business plan.

Kate Conti School of Dance and Drama
Learn how the profession really works. Find real work. Leave fantasy behind until you get paid to produce it.

Proprietor: M. Conti
Directors: C. Morehampton, R. Marks

What do you think? This is what Madeleina wants to do with the money from the house. I'm afraid I spent all of ours on the place in Maida Vale. So nice to get away from Lydia and her rants. She's still insisting that solicitors will come after us and take everything we have.'

'I think it's fantastic, but what's my name doing on it?' I ask.

'It's your Christmas present. Loads more work, no thanks and a chance to train young minds properly in the business.'

'That's OK, I prefer being a background person.' I smile. It's getting warmer. Maybe it's the *grappa*. Maybe it's the friendship.

'You know what?' Catriona says seriously. 'I do too. I'm not that gone on being a leading lady forever.'

Madeleina and I share a secret smile. Catriona will die on stage at the age of eighty-eight. Already she's drifting back to the other side of the curtain.

Jude bounces in – Angelo phoned him on the sly to say the coast was clear. It's a party.

It's a party without Helen.

She does come, with Bea, and she's breathless, and sorry and wondering if we can all forgive her for being two hours late. Bea's had her scan – it's healthy and it's a girl. Bea wanted to know.

'Bloody NHS! You'd think I'd have a bit of clout,' Helen grumbles.

There's no room at our usual table for two more. For the first time in fifteen years we have to move.

'The table in the middle – it's bigger.' Angelo says.

It's not as nice, but it's nicer that there are more of us. As we move Helen sits beside me and silently, under the table, picks up my hand and squeezes it. Later Bea will tell me softly that she made her mother come. Helen still worries she might not be wanted. One day we won't feel the discomfort.

The Virgo Club is not the same as it was on the first Tuesday of August. We're losing Dette and I know won't always have the courage to make it. Sometimes I g in and lie on the futon. It's horribly uncomfortable, but it's where he slept and I feel such a longing for him.

Later he turns up to collect Helen and Bea. We'll smile and share the Celtic result. But it's never going to be the same.

Martin and George come to collect what's left of us and run us home.

Before I leave with Dette and Martin, I go up to Angelo, hold him and whisper in his ear, 'They all came.'

'I knew this.' He is still arrogant.

First thing next morning Martin bangs down my door.

'I just put down this rug. My scheme is ruined.'

'Shut up and push,' Martin hugs her. 'I'll buy you ten rugs if you get this child out.'

'You should fuck off and die. I'm about to.'

'Dette,' the district nurse – the only medical staff available – says, 'concentrate.'

'Concentrate yourself. I'm forty fucking years old. I'm supposed to take another forty to deliver a baby. Not five minutes. I want to be in hospital – where are the drugs? Get them for me, Martin, MARTIN!'

Toby Hardiman, all nine pounds of him, is born. His grannies will be disgusted with the name, but Dette and Martin like it.

Martin goes out to make tea. I sit with my friend tucked up in her bed with her child. She keeps saying hello to him. 'Look.' Dette holds his shell-pink hand – everything is about wonder. One day I want this feeling, but there's a great chance I won't get it, so I share it with my friend, which is the next best thing. 'Look, Rorie. Love works – we're all in a job.'

ACKNOWLEDGEMENTS

If you want to get something done, get a Virgo to motivate you. That's what Marie Kelly did. She provided the inspiration for Rorie by herself being a director at heart. Marian Keyes, also Virgo, also fantastic, championed in a way only she can, by being honest and fuelling with unmitigated support. Ailish Connolly told me what to do with characteristic Virgoan clarity. And Philippa O'Neill another of my September friends, thanks too for everything.

As for the rest of the zodiac. David Godwin, a rea star, and all his associates – Katie, Michael, Sarah, Rowan and all the others.

Sue Townsend, whose advice clears ground and makes headway. Joseph O'Connor, who did likewise, i the manner of a kind man. Marianne Gunn O'Conno thanks for encouragement. Ciara Considine, who pursued from the start and didn't let go, and Breda Purdu thanks for such enthusiasm. For her painstaking wor something tells me Claire Rourke is a Virgo. Haz

Orme, for magnificent attention to detail in copy-editing, take a Virgoan bow, likewise Kristin Jensen. The same applies to Heidi Murphy and Ruth Shern, the rest of the Hodder team.

My sister Amanda, as always, as ever. Gai and Morag, the other members of the steering committee. The rest of my family and friends, especially Jimmy and Marina, my parents.

Albie, always there and the only one I ever want to be.